THE KREMLIN'S VOTE

A Jayne Robinson Thriller, Book 1

ANDREW TURPIN

D1501996

The Write
Direction
Publishing

First published in the U.K. in 2021 by The Write Direction Publishing, St. Albans, U.K.

Copyright © 2021 Andrew Turpin
All rights reserved.
Print edition — The Kremlin's Vote
ISBN: 978-1-78875-016-5

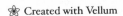 Created with Vellum

WELCOME TO THE JAYNE ROBINSON SERIES!

Thank you for purchasing *The Kremlin's Vote* — I hope you enjoy it!

This is the first in the series of thrillers I am writing that feature **Jayne Robinson**, a former British Secret Intelligence Service (MI6) officer and now an independent investigator. She has strong contacts at both the CIA and MI6 and finds herself conducting deniable operations on behalf of both services.

It is my second series. The other series, in which Jayne also appears regularly, features **Joe Johnson**, a former CIA officer and war crimes investigator. The Joe Johnson books comprise:

Prequel: *The Afghan*
1. *The Last Nazi*
2. *The Old Bridge*
3. *Bandit Country*
4. *Stalin's Final Sting*
5. *The Nazi's Son*
6. *The Black Sea*

If you enjoy this book, I would like to keep in touch. This is not always easy, as I usually only publish a couple of books a year and there are many authors and books out there. So the best way is for you to be on my Readers Group email list. I can then send you updates on the next book, plus occasional special offers.

If you would like to join my Readers Group and receive the email updates, I will send you, **FREE** of charge, the ebook version of *The Afghan*. It forms a prequel to this series and to the Joe Johnson series, and normally sells at $4.99/£3.99 (paperback $11.99/£9.99).

The Afghan is set in 1988 when Jayne was still with MI6 and Joe Johnson was still a CIA officer. Most of the action takes place in Pakistan, Afghanistan and Washington, DC.

To sign up for the Readers Group and get your free copy of *The Afghan*, go to the following web page:

https://bookhip.com/RJGFPAW

If you only like paperbacks, you can still just sign up for the email list at the above link to get news of my books and forthcoming new releases. A paperback version of *The Afghan* and all my books is for sale at my website, where you will find large discounts on bundles of my books. I can currently ship to the US and UK:

https://www.andrewturpin.com/shop/

Or if you live outside the US and UK you can buy them at Amazon.

Andrew Turpin, St. Albans, UK.

DEDICATION

This book is dedicated to my father, Gerald Turpin, who sadly passed away suddenly at the age of 95 in September 2020, just four months after my mother, Jean. He read all my previous books with great enthusiasm, but unfortunately this one was still being written when he left us.

"Whatever the laws may provide, however lofty may be their sentiments, a man without a vote is a man without protection."

President Lyndon B. Johnson

PROLOGUE

Monday, March 30, 2015
Pevensey, United Kingdom

The sharp creak of the wooden stair underfoot sounded like a rifle shot in the darkness, causing Neil Knapp to jump slightly. He instinctively moved his foot sideways on the step and stopped still, then listened for any movement on the upper story of the old building, even though he was virtually certain nobody was there.

Nothing. No sounds. He knew there was no danger of the alarm sounding, because he had skillfully disabled it on his way into the property through a rear window. He was also sure it would not have been switched on if anybody was there.

He stood for a moment, ran a hand through his mop of iron-gray hair, and tugged at the thin rubber gloves he had put on before entering. Then he continued up the stairs, now planting his feet wide at the edges of the steps where they were less worn and hopefully less likely to creak. Even if nobody was there, he still wanted to avoid making a noise.

The building, a 650-year-old former mint house that had been converted into a high-end antiques dealership, was among the oldest in the historic village of Pevensey. It stood just a few yards across High Street from Pevensey Castle, the remains of a fort originally built by the Romans in AD 290 and massively expanded by the Normans following their invasion of England in 1066.

Knapp reached the top of the stairs and paused again. He coughed heavily and then felt a sneeze coming. He tried to stifle it but failed to get his handkerchief out of his pocket quickly enough. The noise echoed around the building, and he cursed inwardly as he blew his nose. He always seemed to come down with some kind of heavy cold as winter turned into spring.

He knew from a previous reconnaissance visit to the dealership exactly where he needed to go. The business owner had installed a wall safe in the large office on the southwestern corner, and inside it were the four objects he had been commissioned to steal.

He had done a slight double take when the request came to him. Never before had he been asked to steal wooden ducks.

But these were no ordinary wooden ducks. They were finely carved decoys that were destined for sale at Sotheby's auction house the following Friday, each with an estimated valuation in excess of £200,000.

They all dated back to between 1915 and 1920 and were produced by Elmer Crowell, a master carver from East Harwich, Massachusetts. Their current owner, a friend of the dealer whose property Knapp was now in, was sending them to auction with the aim of taking a big profit on his original investment. However, Knapp's client, based in Amsterdam, had heard on the grapevine about the imminent sale a few days earlier and had called him. It wasn't the first such request from that particular client.

Within a couple of minutes, Knapp had used his set of picks and rakes to open the locked door to the office and had begun work on the safe door, which was hidden behind a hinged wooden panel. There was just enough illumination coming in through the window from a streetlight near the Royal Oak and Castle pub across the road, thus allowing Knapp to avoid using his flashlight.

He coughed or sneezed occasionally as he worked, swearing out loud in his native Liverpudlian accent every time he did so. It took him twenty minutes of head-scratching work before the door of the safe finally swung open.

Knapp saw the decoys immediately, all in thick protective plastic packaging. He removed them and placed them carefully in his backpack. There were other items in the safe, including a small plastic bag containing what looked like old coins. Knapp hesitated for a moment, glancing up at a clock on the wall, which read twenty minutes past one in the morning. Then he picked up the coins and pushed them into his backpack and zipped it shut. He was no antiques expert himself, but he figured the coins were almost certainly worth something if they were locked away. Then he closed the safe and refastened the wooden panel.

He was about to head out of the antiques dealership when from outside he heard the muffled sound of raised voices. Alarmed, he stepped over to the leaded glass window and peered around the side of the curtain.

In the parking lot next to the Royal Oak were two cars, one dark, one white, parked near to a bus shelter. They hadn't been there when he had entered the building. Next to the vehicles stood two men who appeared to be engaged in an argument.

One man, a sturdily built, military-looking type, pushed the other in the chest, causing him to stagger backward. As he regained his balance, the first man raised his right hand. Knapp could now see he was holding a pistol with a silencer attached.

There were two muffled thwacks, only just audible through the window, as the man fired twice. Knapp saw the victim, who was wearing a suit but no tie, fall backward to the asphalt surface of the parking lot, raising both arms involuntarily as he did so. His head smashed hard into the ground as he fell, and he lay still.

The gunman shoved his weapon into his jacket, moved quickly to his victim, and went through his pockets, removing what looked like a phone and a wallet. Then he turned and walked with a slight limp to a dark Volkswagen Passat station wagon. He opened the door, got in, and drove off.

"Shit," Knapp muttered. He scratched his head, feeling slightly bemused at what he was witnessing. The Volkswagen turned to pull out of the lot, which gave him a brief view of the license plate. He swore out loud again. This wasn't good.

The man's body was spread-eagled on the ground, clearly visible in the glow of the streetlight to anyone driving past the pub in either direction. It seemed inevitable that within minutes, someone would call the police, officers would be on the scene, and the entire area would be locked down and searched. He needed to get out, quickly.

Knapp headed out of the office without bothering to shut the door. He moved quickly down the stairs and out of the building the way he had come in, through the rear window he had left open.

A slight drizzle had begun to fall. Knapp made his way through the yard and over a low fence, then returned to the street, where he crossed to the other side and walked briskly through the Royal Oak's parking lot. He glanced briefly at the man's body as he passed ten yards away. He was very obviously dead.

With the towering and crumbling castle walls forming a dark silhouette to his right and the pub's walled garden to his left, Knapp walked to the bottom of the parking lot and through a narrow gate into what seemed to be an overflow parking area with a rough unmade surface. Once there, out of sight of anyone on the street, he broke into a run and continued along a path that led through some trees at the far end of the lot to a cricket ground.

Knapp, still fit despite being in his midfifties, ran across the grass at a full sprint for about a hundred and fifty yards. He almost fell in the darkness as his right foot slipped and skidded on a wet, muddy patch of earth. Now coughing intermittently, he arrived at his car, a black Toyota sedan, which was parked in a lot next to the cricket clubhouse. He unlocked the car, took off the backpack, and put it and its near-million-pound contents carefully in the footwell on the passenger side.

He was about to take off his rubber gloves but then thought better of it. He started the engine, accelerated out of the parking lot, turned left, and headed on the A259 toward Hastings.

Knapp had a nagging sense of unease as he drove. He might be a criminal, and indeed he had done a couple of short stints in prison several years earlier after making mistakes during jobs. But burglary and theft, usually to order—and occasionally punching the odd person's lights out or tying them up if necessary as part of such jobs—was as far as it went.

In his mind, anyone who took another's life was on the dark side and deserved all they got. Two of his closest friends, both minor-league burglars, had been shot dead several years earlier after inadvertently crossing a London Mafia boss, and he had found it a heavy burden to bear.

As he drove into the seaside town of Hastings along the beachfront, Knapp glanced at the digital clock on the dashboard, which read 2:14 a.m. By now, the drizzle had turned into steady rainfall. He spotted a public phone booth on the sidewalk, pulled onto the side of the road, and scrutinized the area for any sign of CCTV cameras. The silver steel structure was well away from any buildings, and there appeared to be no surveillance. Nevertheless, he pulled a woolen hat down tight over his head before jumping out of the car and walking into the booth.

Still wearing his rubber gloves, he picked up the black handset, took a handkerchief from his pocket, and screwed it into a ball and held it against the mouthpiece. He then dialed 999 and asked to be put through to the police. A male operator answered after just one ring.

"Listen to me, mate, because I'm only going to say this once," Knapp said. "I saw a murder twenty minutes ago at the car park of the Royal Oak and Castle pub in Pevensey, next to the castle."

He sneezed twice, then continued. "A man shot another bloke with a pistol. I think he had a silencer on it. They were arguing. Then he drove off in a car. A Volkswagen Passat estate car. Black or dark gray."

"Okay," the operator said. "I'm only just hearing you. Your voice sounds very muffled. Where is the body, and are you—"

"Shut up. No questions. The man is lying dead in the car park."

"I understand. But can you tell me your name and your location?"

"I said no questions."

"Right," the operator said. "Did you see—"

Feeling irritated and anxious at the handler, Knapp slammed the handset back into its cradle and ended the call.

It was only on the way back to his car that he realized he hadn't given the part of the Volkswagen's license plate number that he had noted.

PART ONE

CHAPTER ONE

Monday, March 30, 2015
London

The apartment still smelled somewhat musty to Jayne Robinson, despite having left her windows open for much of the day with a lavender-scented candle burning on her dining table.

Hardly surprising, she thought. She had only been there a handful of times in the previous eleven months, and most of those had been fleeting visits for a night or two. Otherwise the place had remained shuttered and locked.

Most of her time since the previous spring had been spent across the Atlantic in Portland, Maine, where she had moved to be with her colleague on a number of war crimes investigations and espionage operations, Joe Johnson. The previous year, they had rekindled an affair that originally took place in the 1980s in Islamabad.

But it felt good to be back in the place she had bought in

2005 after returning to London from the Balkans and still thought of as home. It was the only place she actually owned, where she could truly do as she pleased. That hadn't been possible in Joe's house, where his two teenagers, pleasant as they were, had proved a little more difficult to adapt to than she had envisaged.

She took two sets of cutlery from a drawer in her kitchen and laid them on place mats on the dining table, where she had already put wine glasses and an ice bucket. Then she turned on the oven and placed the vegetable stew she had cooked earlier on the middle shelf to reheat.

Jayne went out onto her small second-floor balcony, placed her hands on the rail, and stood staring down the street at the outlines of Tower Bridge and the Tower of London, the lights of which were visible no more than a third of a mile to the south. The location, which was very personal to her, and the view had been the selling points.

The adrenaline rush that had kept her going since her arrival at Heathrow Airport that morning was fading, and she could feel fatigue setting in. Sleeping on planes had always been difficult.

But she needed to keep going for a while longer. The man who had been her boss in 2012 when she left Britain's Secret Intelligence Service, Mark Nicklin-Donovan, was due to visit for supper on his way home. It was the only time he could fit her in, and she felt she should make the effort, as he might channel work her way at any point.

Despite the unseasonably warm March sunshine that had cast a glow over London during the day, the evening had turned chilly, and after another five minutes of silent contemplation, Jayne retreated back into her living room and closed the balcony door behind her. The aroma from her stew had begun to permeate the apartment, and the mustiness was finally receding.

The security buzzer chimed, and Jayne made her way into the hallway. The video screen showed a slightly fuzzy image at the ground-floor entrance, but it was unmistakably Nicklin-Donovan, his graying hair, as ever, combed neatly forward into a schoolboy-style fringe.

Jayne pressed the button to allow him in, and he turned and made a signal to someone, presumably his driver.

She hurriedly tidied up the entrance area, putting her running shoes into a cubbyhole and her gym bag into the cupboard. She had always been a runner, but over the past few months she had really stepped it up, with a view to doing a few half marathons and maybe the London or New York marathon. Then she opened the front door and stood waiting in the corridor.

A couple of minutes later, Nicklin-Donovan emerged at the top of the stairwell. He had been to her apartment a few times before and had never used the elevator.

"Jayne, good to see passport control let you back in," he said, slightly out of breath and with a faint grin, as he made his way toward her. "Did my people turn up this afternoon?"

"Yes, they came, don't worry."

Maintaining his friendship had its advantages: it meant she knew her apartment was definitely free of monitoring devices. Nicklin-Donovan had sent a member of his technical team earlier that afternoon to sweep it in advance of his visit. They had found nothing.

He pecked her on both cheeks, as usual, and followed her into the living room, where he placed his battered leather briefcase behind the sofa and removed his coat. He had put on a few pounds, mainly around the belly, since she had last seen him, although he was still relatively trim compared to many other men of his age.

Since 2012, when she had left the SIS, otherwise known as MI6, Nicklin-Donovan had clambered another couple of rungs up the greasy pole to become director of operations. Astonishingly to Jayne, this meant he was now the deputy to Richard Durman, the overall chief of the SIS, who was universally known simply as C—the tag given to whoever held the position.

But despite his meteoric rise, Nicklin-Donovan had remained very supportive of Jayne in her new role as a free-lance investigator. She knew why.

"How are things going?" Jayne asked.

"Bloody awful day. I'll tell you later." He stood still and looked her up and down. "You're looking trim. Have you just had your hair done?"

Jayne reflexively ran a hand through her short, dark hair. "Yes, this morning. And I've been doing a lot of running. Getting back into it."

"New England life's obviously suiting you, then?"

"It's more relaxed than here. Maybe too relaxed, although I've been getting myself fit, yes. I need to get back into work mode."

"From what I heard, you and Joe needed a break after that last episode in Russia."

"You can only recuperate for so long."

Jayne and Joe had taken a six-month break after their previous joint investigation in Russia's Black Sea region, searching for the Russian perpetrators who destroyed a Malaysia Airlines passenger jet over Ukraine. It had culminated in a life-or-death battle in an oil refinery with the oligarch and former KGB officer Yuri Severinov, who had died in an explosion triggered by Jayne.

"I've told you before, I could send you back into Russia," Nicklin-Donovan said as he sat at the dining table. "We've still got problems there."

He hadn't wasted any time. That was the second occasion

in twelve months he had suggested in general terms that she might consider working for him in Russia. MI6 had lost a number of key people on its Russia desk in London, and she knew he might find it useful to have her available as an option to use on certain deniable operations. So far, she had done no more than indicate she would bear his offer in mind, preferring to work with Joe on projects that had often involved *his* former employer, the CIA. But she had guessed that Nicklin-Donovan might revisit the subject. Indeed, that had been one reason for seeing him.

Jayne pursed her lips. "As you know, I like working with you. Let's keep talking, and if there's anything you'd like me to look at, we can discuss it."

Nicklin-Donovan was silent for a few seconds. "There's a lot going on, but nothing I can go into any detail with you about right now."

"Of course." She hadn't expected him to mention anything unless he had a concrete proposal.

"But if you're open to the idea, I will bear that in mind."

"Yes, that's fine. Are you hungry?"

Nicklin-Donovan nodded, and she turned, put on a pair of over mitts, and removed the stew from the oven.

"I think both you and the Agency have issues in Russia," Jayne said as she ladled the stew onto two plates. "You're not alone."

Both the British and the Americans had lost a number of assets in recent years within Russia's foreign intelligence service, the SVR, and its domestic equivalent, the FSB, the federal intelligence service. This was thanks in part to Russian infiltrations of Western intelligence and the recruitment of high-level spies in London and Washington, DC, including the CIA's London station chief Bernice Franklin, whom Jayne had helped trap the previous year. The result had been a sharp fall in intelligence emanating from the Russian capital and a corresponding rise in the triumphalist tone of the Russian president on the international stage. A rebuilding phase was beginning, with the main objective being to recruit more sources, and the task was proving far from easy.

"But you're doing your best to put things right," Nicklin-Donovan said. "At least, across the Atlantic, that is."

Jayne looked up sharply as she placed a plate in front of Nicklin-Donovan. "Are you trying to say I shouldn't do any work for the Agency, Mark?"

"On the contrary, our interests often coincide, although of course I would prefer you to work for us. I was actually referring to your new friend in Yasenevo."

"I don't know who you're talking about."

"Yes, you do. I'm talking about VULTURE."

Jayne had assumed, but wasn't certain, that as a key player in the Secret Intelligence Service, the CIA's closest intelligence partner globally, Nicklin-Donovan would have been briefed about Anastasia Shevchenko. She was the newly promoted deputy director in charge of Directorate KR, the SVR's external counterintelligence arm, based at the agency's Yasenevo headquarters south of Moscow.

The previous year, Jayne and Joe had trapped Shevchenko in Washington after an SVR operation that had gone badly wrong. Faced with the likelihood of being dispatched to prison or a penal colony for her failure in the US capital—a second such major failure in the space of a few months—she had then immediately offered to spy for the Agency if they agreed to help her cover up what had happened.

If Shevchenko delivered on her promises, she was now the CIA's biggest asset in Moscow, and she had stipulated that Jayne and Joe should be involved in handling her.

The Agency had code-named her VULTURE.

"I don't know if she's going to help us yet or not," Jayne said. "We haven't put her to the test."

"Time will tell with her," Nicklin-Donovan said as he picked up his knife and fork. "Let's hope it works out. Anyway, this food is looking good."

"Thank you," Jayne said. She filled their wine glasses from a bottle of Bordeaux and picked up hers. "Here's to future operations."

"Indeed. To future operations."

Nicklin-Donovan smiled as he gently clinked her glass with his own.

The conversation turned to somewhat inconsequential updates on Nicklin-Donovan's grown-up children, his wife's attempts to learn tennis in her midfifties, and Jayne's description of her efforts to settle into the neighborhood around Joe's home in Portland.

She liked her former boss. They had always gotten on very well professionally because they had a similarly flexible approach to finding solutions to seemingly intractable problems. She occasionally had the feeling that he might be attracted to her. It was just the way he sometimes looked at her and his tone of voice. She might be wrong, but either way, she definitely didn't feel that way about him. Thankfully, he had never given any sign of trying to make a move on her.

After a pause in conversation as they finished their food, Jayne rewound to his opening remark. "So, you said that today was bloody awful. What happened?"

Nicklin-Donovan swallowed, placed his knife and fork neatly on his plate, and leaned back in his chair, twiddling his wine glass in his right hand.

"A few things. First, I had to act as a punchbag for C. He came back in a foul mood after a meeting with the new foreign secretary."

Jayne nodded sympathetically. C's boss, the British foreign

secretary, Tim Pontefract, was known to be a demanding character.

"That's the problem when you mix with politicians," Jayne said. "Anything else?"

"Yes. I spent most of my time chasing business I shouldn't really have to get involved in," he said. "It was a murder, down in Sussex. The victim was from your new home territory, you might be interested to know—he was the secretary of state for New Hampshire, which is why I was roped into it. Shot dead in a pub car park. God knows what he was doing there. Happened in the early hours of this morning, about two o'clock."

A shock ran right through Jayne, and she found herself feeling light-headed. "Did you say the secretary of state for New Hampshire?"

"Yes. Bloody irritating. Right at a time when I've got a million other things to do and—"

"Curtis Steyn?"

Nicklin-Donovan paused. "Yes, that was his name. Why?"

Jayne shut her eyes momentarily.

Surely not. Poor Simone.

"I know his wife, Simone," she said, looking at Nicklin-Donovan. "Very well, actually. She was my best friend from home. I only saw her only three months ago—we met for coffee. I know Curtis too. Met him a few times over the years. She emigrated to the States to marry him."

Nicklin-Donovan put his wine glass down. "My God. I'm sorry to hear that, Jayne."

She shook her head. "What happened?"

"I only got the outline of it. The local police are all over it, of course, and they called in MI5 once they worked out who he was. And then I got a call midmorning. I've been dealing with the US embassy and the Foreign Office, and

Langley has asked to be kept updated, although as far as I know there's nothing in it that would involve them."

"What was he doing in the UK?" Jayne asked.

"He was at a conference in London, apparently."

"So why did he travel to Sussex at night?"

Nicklin-Donovan shrugged. "Nobody knows."

It immediately sounded odd to Jayne. Simone's now aged parents lived in Nottingham, still in the same house near to Jayne's old family home. Jayne and Simone had gone through junior and senior schools together and had then both won places at Cambridge University, albeit studying different subjects and at different colleges.

She remembered Simone telling her that when Curtis occasionally visited London on business, he didn't stray out of the capital. But maybe he had some secret mistress or business arrangement she didn't know about. Jayne had occasionally thought to herself that he seemed the type—a man with a large ego that he liked people to stroke and yet who kept his cards close to his chest. He was someone who needed to feel important, to hold information, to know things that others didn't.

"Do you know if the family has been informed?" Jayne asked.

"I believe so."

"Any media coverage?"

"Not yet."

Jayne knew that it could potentially turn into a big story on both sides of the Atlantic. Newspaper and TV coverage was inevitable, although how much was difficult to say. It seemed highly likely that Simone was going to be inundated with calls.

"I'll give Simone a call and see if there is anything I can do," Jayne said. "She'll need support and someone she knows who can help over here. I can perhaps coordinate between her and the police and MI5."

"Good idea. I can help you with the key contacts there," Nicklin-Donovan said. He paused and finished his wine. "It sounds like you and Simone have been quite close over the years?"

Jayne nodded. "Yes, we have."

CHAPTER TWO

Monday, March 30, 2015
London

Jayne sat for half an hour after Nicklin-Donovan had gone, undecided over whether to call Simone and, if she did, what to say. Her tiredness had gone, replaced by the old operational wave of adrenaline that had seen her through many sleepless nights over the years.

Nights spent waiting in safe houses, dark city streets, and deserted forests for sources and agents from countries hostile to the United Kingdom who were risking their lives and their freedom to provide information and documents to her. Men and women from places like Russia, Iran, Iraq, Lebanon, and Syria, often with principles that compelled them to betray their own countries and leaders.

It was that adrenaline that had propelled her through three decades of exhausting, draining work as an intelligence officer, often fighting stressful internal battles within MI6, as well as external ones.

Maybe she should wait until the next day, until Simone had had a chance to absorb the shock and discuss it with her two adult children?

But what would I want in the same set of circumstances? Jayne asked herself.

She remembered how she felt after her father had been murdered years ago, and she decided that more than anything, she would want to feel that her oldest, closest friends were there in a time of need and were responding quickly to what must be a massive shock, doing what they could to help. Simone must need a shoulder to lean on, to cry on, even if it was over the phone.

In the end, she scrolled through the contacts on her cell phone and found Simone's details. Jayne normally kept her own number blocked, but she decided to unblock it so her friend knew who it was.

"Hello, Simone's phone," an unfamiliar voice said when it was answered.

"Ah, I was hoping to speak to Simone. It's Jayne Robinson. Is she there?"

There was a muffled conversation as the person who had answered asked Simone if she wanted to take the call. A few seconds later she came on the line.

"Hello, Jayne. Sorry—the house is full of people and my phone's been going crazy. A friend has been filtering my calls." Her voice cracked and sounded strained.

"That's okay," Jayne said. "I'm in the UK and heard what happened to Curtis. I'm so sorry."

There was a pause that lasted a couple of seconds. "Thanks for calling, Jayne. I'm just trying to take it in. I only heard myself a few hours ago."

"I couldn't believe it when I heard. I was talking to an old colleague who had been briefed on what happened, and he told me." She didn't need to explain to Simone why she couldn't be more precise about where the information had come from; her friend knew Jayne operated in intelligence agency environments with strict obligations not to discuss her work externally.

There was a sob at the other end of the line. "I still can't believe it."

"I can only imagine. It's so terrible." Jayne paused, wondering how she might be able to help with the logistical problems Simone must be facing in getting information from across the Atlantic. "Who contacted you—was it the Bureau of Consular Affairs?"

Jayne knew that the bureau, part of the Department of State, was normally the channel through which next of kin were informed if a relative who was a US citizen died while overseas. She had dealt with them a few times when working at MI6.

"Yes, someone from there called me. I don't know what to do next, though. I'd like to speak to the police or someone who's investigating. I want to know what the hell happened. The bureau isn't saying much. I don't think they know much." Simone sobbed again.

"Listen, Simone, I've got contacts here in police and security services. I can speak to them and try to help, if you'd like me to. You might need someone you know to act as a go-between. I'm happy to do that."

Simone hesitated for a second. "Yes, please. That would be helpful."

Jayne felt suddenly self-conscious. It seemed a little intrusive at this stage to start asking for details about what Curtis might have been doing in an English pub parking lot in the middle of the night, but she felt she needed to try and get at least some of the background to what might have happened.

"Can I just ask, have you any idea why Curtis might have

been in a Sussex village at that time, so late? Did he say who he was meeting or anything like that?"

"Nothing. I have no idea. I was completely taken by surprise when the bureau told me where it happened. He never said anything about going there. He was staying in London, so God knows what he was doing that far away. Pevensey is at least a two-hour car journey from where he was staying. It doesn't make any sense."

"He drove there?"

"That's what the bureau said. They said police had told them he rented a car."

"What was he doing in the UK?"

"It was a work trip. He was at a conference on public administration in London. He went with another secretary of state. He'd been to the same conference the past three years."

Jayne guessed that it was standard practice for those in Curtis's type of role to attend international conferences to benchmark against and learn from similar government administration offices in other countries. She knew that the vast majority of US states had a secretary of state whose job it was to manage the local government administrative machine in their territory. Their role usually included everything from registering businesses to keeping state records and administering state and federal elections, and they worked closely with the state governor, who had overall responsibility.

Like most states, the secretary's position in New Hampshire was a political one, and he or she was elected. Curtis was a few months into his second two-year term of office.

"Who was the other secretary of state he was with?" Jayne asked. Clearly whoever it was hadn't been involved in the nocturnal parking lot meeting in Sussex.

"The Wisconsin secretary of state, Gareth Weber. He's a friend of Curtis's from way back."

"Did the bureau say anything about him?"

"No, nothing. I didn't think to ask. I was so shocked at that call." Simone paused, audibly struggling to get the words out. Then she continued, her voice shaky. "Jayne, can't you find out what happened for me? I just want someone I trust to be doing it, not some faceless policeman."

Jayne hesitated. She was tempted just to say yes and drop everything, but if the police investigative machine had already swung into action, that might not help.

"I would really like to do that," Jayne said. "But I'm thinking this will really be a matter for police to investigate. I don't think I should poke my nose into their business. I'd only end up confusing matters. I'm happy to help if I can and act as go-between, to make sure you know what's going on and vice versa, but I'm not sure it would be a good idea to go beyond that."

There came a long sigh from Simone. "Anything you can do to help would be good."

Jayne thought quickly about what practical steps she could take. "Perhaps I should try and contact Gareth, to see if he's got any information. Do you know where they were staying? Or do you have a number?"

"I don't have a number for him. But I do know they rented a two-bedroom apartment online for the four days they were in London. I'll give you the address. Just wait a minute."

There was a clunk as Simone put the phone down and then a rustling noise as she presumably went through some papers. A few moments later, her voice now somewhat less faltering than it had been, she read out the address of an apartment in the Barbican area, which Jayne realized was only around a mile from her own property.

"Thank you," Jayne said. "I'll try and reach him and see what he knows." She paused, hesitant to ask the question she had in mind, but then decided to go ahead. "I'm reluctant to ask this, Simone, but it may be important. Was Curtis in any kind of trouble, or can you think of any possible reason why someone would want to do this to him? Did he have any known enemies?"

The answer came back without hesitation. "I've been trying to think of anything in these past few hours, and there's nothing. He never mentioned a thing. And he didn't seem worried, or distracted, or anxious. He was just behaving normally, like he always had done. No different at all. Of course, he's a political man, and he had opponents, people who disagreed with him, but that's it, as far as I know."

"Thanks Simone. I had to ask."

"I know."

"Listen, I'll do all I can to help, although it'll be the police here and the security services who are going to be carrying out the investigation. I'll call or message you later. I just hope you'll be all right there. It sounds like you've got plenty of help right now, which is good." She pictured her friend at her house in Concord, the New Hampshire capital, and felt reassured that she had plenty of support on hand.

"I'll be okay. I've got our daughter and friends here at home, and our son is driving up from Manhattan as we speak. He should be here soon." Both of Simone's children were in their early twenties.

"Good. Talk later." Jayne ended the call.

It was now past ten thirty at night in London, and she decided to wait and visit the Barbican apartment in person in the morning rather than make a call in advance to someone she didn't know. She assumed that the police had already made contact.

Jayne poured the remains of the Bordeaux into her glass and sank into her sofa. This was definitely not what she had expected when she had boarded her flight from JFK the previous evening. The trip had been intended purely as a ten-day visit to check over her apartment, to catch up with Nicklin-Donovan and maintain contact with a view to possible future work for MI6, and to meet a few old buddies for drinks.

Instead, she was now thrown into dealing with the mysterious murder of the husband of her best old friend, whose family had just been shattered. She felt sorry for Simone and for their children. They were only a few years younger than Jayne had been when her father had died in 1994, and she found herself suddenly identifying strongly with them.

The entire situation was heartbreaking. She stifled a sob for Simone, the girl who had once saved her life.

CHAPTER THREE

Tuesday, March 31, 2015
London

The enormous gray concrete structure of the Lauderdale Tower soared more than forty stories above Jayne as she stood on the forecourt at its base. She had occasionally attended classical music concerts at the nearby Barbican Hall during her many years in London, as well as Shakespeare plays at the Barbican Theatre. But despite walking past on many occasions, she had never previously had a reason to visit these buildings that comprised the Barbican Estate. With its brutalist architecture and maze of apartments—all of them built on a site that had been heavily bombed during the Second World War—the estate had never particularly appealed to her.

Jayne had woken early that morning and had spent half an hour in bed, enjoying the sense of peace and solitude that was rarely possible when living with other people. It gave her a chance to think deeply about her friend Simone's situation. It was the time of day when her thoughts always seemed clearest.

By the time she got up, she had a fresh determination to do what she could to help Simone, and it seemed clear to her that speaking to Gareth Weber was definitely the best starting point. She decided to set off for his rented apartment immediately after eating breakfast.

The Lauderdale was one of three residential towers, all the same height. To Jayne's untrained eye, they looked very Stalinist and reminded her of the Soviet-era towers she had seen all over Moscow. She knew she would never have chosen to live there, although the estate remained very popular, and the exorbitant prices of the apartments reflected that.

Two police cars were parked outside the building, and a police officer stood next to them, speaking into his radio handset. Another officer was removing what looked like a black toolbox from one car. Perhaps there had been some kind of incident nearby. She wondered if officers were there to talk to Weber about Curtis. It seemed quite likely.

Jayne made her way through the entrance doors on the ground floor, past the reception desk with pink plastic flowers in a pot. The security guard had his back to her, talking to another police officer who stood next to his desk.

Keen to ensure she wasn't stopped and questioned, Jayne ignored them and headed through a swing door to the elevators.

The elevator car took her to the fourth floor without a problem, but as soon as the twin doors slid open, she guessed instantly what had happened.

There were two more policemen standing on the landing near the elevators. Both of them spun around as soon they heard the elevator doors opening. A third officer stood a few yards to the right, unwinding a reel of yellow tape imprinted

30   ANDREW TURPIN

at intervals with black lettering that read Crime Scene. One end of the tape was attached to a wall.

As Jayne stepped out of the car, an officer near the door moved quickly toward her, his hands on his hips, his face forbidding. "I'm sorry, but you can't come in here, madam. Can I help you?" he said.

"I'm looking for Gareth Weber," Jayne said. "He's in number three on this floor." On the far side of the landing the door to an apartment was open. She couldn't see the number on the door but somehow guessed that was the one she needed.

But the man, wearing a yellow reflective vest marked Metropolitan Police, shook his head and firmly folded his arms, his feet planted some distance apart. "I'm sorry, we're closing this floor. You can't come in. We have an incident ongoing."

Jayne stiffened. "An incident?"

"I can't comment on what has happened, madam. Can I ask who you are?"

Jayne briefly explained she was a friend of the wife of one of the occupiers of the apartment, who had been shot dead the previous day. She asked to speak to the officer in charge.

Before the policeman could reply, there came the sound of a minor commotion inside the apartment, and two paramedics appeared through the door, one at each end of a wheeled stretcher. A white sheet covered the stretcher, and beneath it was the unmistakable outline of a body. Although it was at least a dozen yards away, Jayne could see there were two large bloodstains seeping through the sheet, one that appeared to be in the center of the chest, the other in the head.

The sheet didn't quite cover the body, and a few locks of gray hair were poking out from beneath it at the end nearest to Jayne. It looked to her as if the hair was matted in blood.

"My God," Jayne muttered.

Close behind the stretcher were two other men, both wearing dark suits, who Jayne assumed must be detectives.

The men with the stretcher stopped just outside the door, but one of the men in suits continued toward Jayne.

"I'm detective chief superintendent Watson. How can I help you?" he said, in a slightly abrasive tone.

She stepped forward, introduced herself, and briefly explained why she was there. This time she added in a lower voice, so she wouldn't be overheard by the other officers, the extra detail of her connections to the Secret Intelligence Service.

But the detective, clearly preoccupied and looking somewhat stressed, stood squarely in front of her.

"As you might have noticed, we're in the middle of a major incident here," he said. "I would have thought that being ex-MI6, you would know better. Please leave." He then somewhat brusquely instructed another officer to deal with her.

The man she had originally spoken to took her gently by the elbow and steered her away to one side near the stairwell. "You heard the boss. You can't stay here, but we may need to talk to you further," he said. He asked for her contact details and address, which Jayne gave.

By that stage, the stretcher had been taken down in the elevator, and the detective chief superintendent had gone with it. The officer who was unwinding the yellow crime scene tape had completed his task, effectively fencing off the landing outside the apartment where Steyn and Weber had been staying.

Jayne, feeling more than a little stunned by the turn of events, could see that, hardly surprisingly, she was going to make no progress with the police officers there. So she turned, went through the door to the stairwell, and made her way down to the ground floor, where she watched as the stretcher was loaded into the waiting ambulance.

After it had gone, followed by a police car, Jayne found a nearby bench. She decided to call Nicklin-Donovan to update him on events.

After she had dialed him using the encrypted service they both used when communicating with each other, she explained what had happened. He listened carefully, asking the occasional question.

"One thing is for certain, Mark: these killings have nothing to do with a London public administration conference." Jayne drummed the fingers of her right hand on the wooden bench, her left clamping her cell phone to her ear.

"That's obvious. What did the police say?"

"Nothing. The detective chief superintendent wouldn't talk to me. I explained the connection and why I was there, and he just got one of his guys to take my details. They said they might want to interview me as the investigation goes on. I feel like I want to interview them."

Nicklin-Donovan sighed. "Police process. Let them get on with it. It's not our business."

"I'd like to be able to report something back to Simone. I owe her that."

"Can't you leave it to the US embassy to coordinate with Simone?" Nicklin-Donovan asked.

"She's been speaking to the Bureau of Consular Affairs, part of the State Department. But they don't seem to know much, and so she's had very little information."

There was a pause at the other end of the line. "You don't change, Jayne, do you?"

Jayne resisted the temptation to give him a sharp reply. It was true she had always been persistent, probably sometimes to the point of being annoying. It was also true that she should let the police get on with it. But she hated giving up on any task.

"Listen," Nicklin-Donovan continued. "I do know an assistant chief constable in Sussex, Rod Bunting. I heard he just got promoted. He was the detective chief superintendent —headed the whole criminal investigation department. A homicide specialist. I'm guessing he'll be all over the Curtis Steyn case, and given what's happened to Weber, he'll probably be coordinating with his Met police counterpart too— probably the detective chief you've just spoken to."

Nicklin-Donovan explained that he had gotten to know Bunting when MI6 resettled a Russian spy who had defected to the UK a few years earlier. Bunting had provided confidential advice on locations for a safe house within Sussex for the Russian, who was given a new identity.

"Can we call this Bunting?" Jayne asked.

"I can try."

"Great. Give it a go."

CHAPTER FOUR

Tuesday, March 31, 2015
London

The plush third floor of the Secret Intelligence Service building at Vauxhall Cross on the south bank of the River Thames stood in contrast to the other ten above ground, Jayne couldn't help thinking, and certainly to the six below ground.

During her time in the service she had only occasionally visited the third floor, which was occupied by C and his senior team of executives. Despite its futuristic appearance from outside, the remainder of the building's interior was largely bland, with a maze of plain walls, open-plan offices, unmarked corridors, and a few laboratories and technical rooms.

Now, though, she found herself sitting in a leather armchair outside Nicklin-Donovan's office, near to his secretary and just two doors away from Durman's office. Her feet sank into a sky-blue deep pile carpet.

She had forgotten how quiet it was on that floor, with only the occasional distant murmur of voices. Indeed, she could distinctly hear the ticking of the grandfather clock that stood right outside C's mahogany door.

Jayne knew the legend of the clock, which had been personally designed and built by Captain Sir Mansfield Smith-Cumming, who headed the service from 1909 until 1923 and was the first C of all. The timepiece had remained one of MI6's office heirlooms ever since, and she was glad to see Durman was keeping it in a prominent position.

After a few minutes, Nicklin-Donovan emerged from behind his closed office door. "Apologies for the delay, Jayne. Come in. I've got Rod in here—he was a little early."

After receiving Jayne's call that morning, Nicklin-Donovan had located Bunting, who was in London for meetings with Metropolitan Police chiefs at New Scotland Yard. He had agreed to make a detour to see Nicklin-Donovan and Jayne on his way back to Sussex Police headquarters in the town of Lewes.

Jayne stood and walked into the office. When she had worked for Nicklin-Donovan, they had both been located on the fifth floor, her home since MI6 moved to Vauxhall Cross in 1995. He had previously occupied a much smaller office at the rear of the building. This one on the executive floor was several times the size, and its expansive windows, triple-glazed with security glass like the rest of the building, offered a magnificent view of the River Thames outside.

She had seen the array of modern art on the walls of Durman's office, including an enormous piece by abstract expressionist Patrick Heron, and equally modern minimal-istic furniture to match. However, Nicklin-Donovan had gone down the traditional route, with four large oil paintings in gold-leaf frames, an expansive mahogany desk, and a matching coffee table that stood between two padded sofas in striped fabric.

Sitting on one of the sofas was a tall, angular man with gray hair cut in a trendy, layered style that complemented his tanned face, a long nose, and a dark suit rather than a police uniform. He stood as Jayne walked over to him and held out a hand.

"Rod Bunting," he said. "Good to meet you. Mark's just been telling me about you and a little about the issue with our case down in Pevensey."

"Good to meet you too," Jayne said. "Yes, it's an interest, not an issue, but only because it's personal."

"Your friend's husband?"

"Correct. I grew up with Simone, and we went to university together. She moved to New Hampshire after meeting Curtis."

Nicklin-Donovan stepped forward and offered them both coffee, which they accepted, and then picked up his desk phone and repeated the order to someone.

"Sit down," Nicklin-Donovan said. "The coffee will be here in a couple of minutes."

Bunting returned to his place on the sofa, and Jayne and Nicklin-Donovan sat on the one opposite.

"Mark briefly told me about your track record here, Jayne," Bunting said. "I guess you know all about difficult investigations."

"It often feels like that," Jayne said.

"This will be in that bracket," Bunting said. "I've just come from a meeting with the detective chief superintendent in the Met who's handling the Barbican shooting. We'll be cooperating because of the links—it seems likely to be the same gunman, almost certainly. I've had the background to the two victims, both secretaries of state in the US. The Pevensey shooting was about two in the morning, the Barbican one about quarter past five, we think. But early indications from my officer in charge in Pevensey show a lack of obvious forensics, which wasn't helped by the rain that night. There's no CCTV footage, and the one witness in the Pevensey case can't be located."

"The *witness?*" Jayne asked, leaning forward. "There *is* one?" She leaned forward, her forehead creased.

"A man phoned in anonymously to report it. Saw it happen in the pub car park."

"What do you mean, anonymously?"

"He made an emergency call at about twenty minutes past two in the morning from a public phone booth in Hastings, about eleven miles away. He spoke for maybe fifteen seconds, then put the phone down. He told the call handler he saw the shooting."

"That doesn't make sense. He saw it, drove away, phoned, then vanished?"

Bunting shrugged. "Yes. It doesn't make sense, but he obviously had a reason."

"Is it possible he could have been the gunman?"

"I would say highly unlikely, but it's possible. Criminals just don't do that as a rule."

Nicklin-Donovan's secretary appeared, carrying a tray with three coffees that she placed on the table between them, then withdrew silently.

Jayne leaned back and folded her arms. "We just need to know what the hell Curtis was doing there. His wife hasn't got a clue. Did you find his phone?"

"It was gone. So was his wallet. We're assuming the gunman took them. We're getting the phone records—the call log and messages."

"Do you have a recording of the phone booth call from the witness, or a transcript?"

Bunting nodded and took his phone from his pocket. "The officer in charge sent it to me. Listen."

He tapped on the screen a couple of times, and a slightly distorted recording began to play.

Jayne concentrated carefully.

"Listen to me, mate, because I'm only going to say this once. I saw a murder twenty minutes ago at the car park of the Royal Oak and Castle pub in Pevensey, next to the castle."

The voice sounded quite faint and indistinct, although Jayne could make out what was being said. There were two loud sneezes, then the voice continued.

"A man shot another bloke with a pistol. I think he had a silencer on it. They were arguing. Then he drove off in a car. A Volkswagen Passat estate car. Black or dark gray."
"Okay. I'm only just hearing you. Your voice sounds very muffled. Where is the body and are you—"
"Shut up. No questions. The man is lying dead in the car park."
"I understand. But can you tell me your name and your location?"
"I said no questions."
"Right," the call handler said. "Did you see—"

At that point, there was a click and the call ended.

Bunting glanced at Jayne. "Not much to go on. Our call handler might have pushed him a little too much for his details. Possibly put him off. Difficult to say. We are sure he was trying to disguise his voice, maybe speaking through a cloth, a handkerchief, or something like that."

"Best just to let him talk, I'd have thought," Jayne said.

"Anyway, I could hear enough to make out that's a Liverpool accent, or at least he's from that area."

"Yes."

"And he's seen the type of car, the Volkswagen. Can you play it again?"

Bunting nodded and tapped his phone screen. The recording played again.

Jayne sat back, thinking hard, then asked Bunting to play the recording for a third time, keen to make sure she hadn't missed anything.

But there was nothing else in the brief exchange that struck her as being useful.

Bunting stood and buttoned his jacket. "I need to go, unfortunately," he said. "I have a meeting with the chief constable in Lewes at five o'clock. I can't afford to miss it."

Jayne nodded. "My guess is that the FBI might want to take an interest in this. To have one secretary of state murdered overseas might seem unfortunate. Two looks like something quite different. There's something going on. I've got decent contacts with the Feebs, and I'm also well plugged in to Langley, so I can help smooth the path. They might be able to help."

She instinctively downplayed the role she might take, but increasingly, Jayne felt she wanted to get as involved as she usefully could in the rapidly escalating investigation. Her gut reaction was that she needed closure for Simone and justice for Curtis and Gareth. It was the same instinct that had driven her for the whole of her career. She found it very difficult to just back off and let others do it.

"Yes, you're right. Let's keep in touch." Bunting gave Jayne a business card and offered his hand, which she shook.

"Give me a call if you think of anything that might help or if you have questions," Bunting said. "I am certain the officer in charge will need to talk to your friend very soon, and probably in some detail. I'll send you a message with his details if you can give me your phone number and email."

"Thanks," Jayne said. She removed her own business card from her purse and gave it to Bunting. "Likewise, if there's anything I can do to help, let me know. If you need someone to coordinate with Simone, I can do that."

Nicklin-Donovan called his secretary and asked her to summon a security guard to escort Bunting out of the building.

Once they had gone, Nicklin-Donovan began gathering his papers together. "I need to get to a meeting with C," he said. "Contingency planning for Brexit—if the Tories win the election in May there'll be a referendum. And I think Britain will leave Europe."

"Really?"

"Yes. There's a high risk, in my view. There's a big debate to be had about whether a referendum would be a mistake. Should they put these highly complicated decisions in the hands of the general public who don't properly understand the issues or the consequences? I think not."

"You might be right," Jayne said.

"Anyway, back to matters at hand," Nicklin-Donovan said. "You need to know that I've had a call from Langley about these two secretaries of state."

"I'd be surprised if you hadn't," Jayne said.

"Yes. They're in a state of mild panic. Your friend and mine, Vic Walter, wants a conference call later tonight."

"You've spoken to him?"

"No. Not yet. It was one of his team."

Vic Walter, a gnarled CIA veteran who thrived in the shadows, was director of the Agency's National Clandestine Service, generally known as the Directorate of Operations. Jayne knew him well, having first come across him as long ago as 1988 when she was working for MI6 in Islamabad and Vic and Joe were both CIA operatives in the same city.

"Give him my regards," Jayne said. She and Joe had worked on several freelance operations and investigations in recent years for the benefit of the United States and the United Kingdom. Vic had ended up playing a significant role in many of them and had benefited from some of them.

Most recently she and Joe had unmasked none other than the president's national security advisor, Francis Wade, who had been channeling top-secret military and political information to the Russians and, on being discovered, had committed suicide. His handler had been Anastasia Shevchenko, and their activities had come to light as part of the Malaysia Airlines and Severinov investigations. It had been a complex web of intrigue and betrayal that had taken Joe, Jayne, and Vic a long time to unravel.

"I will give him your best wishes," Nicklin-Donovan said. He fixed Jayne with a look. "I'm surprised he hasn't called you already. You and he get on well, don't you?"

Jayne shrugged, not wanting to give anything away. But Nicklin-Donovan was correct—she did get on well with Vic, who had also made clear he might want her to do some work on a deniable basis for the Agency. "He's a decent guy," Jayne said.

"Just keep me ahead of him in the pecking order when you're deciding on your work priorities," Nicklin-Donovan said with a faint smile on his face.

Vic and Nicklin-Donovan were long-term sparring partners who had worked together and cooperated on many joint CIA-MI6 operations over the years, some of which had involved Jayne and Joe. Yet there remained between them a hot vein of competition, a desire to come out on top, to be *primus inter pares*, "first among equals," that reflected the exact same competition between the respective intelligence services they worked for. It made her situation tricky at times.

Jayne said nothing in reply.

Nicklin-Donovan stood. "All right, I need to get moving. Keep in touch."

He ushered Jayne out of the office and indicated toward the two security guards who were standing watchfully near to the carpeted walkway that ran behind his secretary's open-plan desk. "One of them will see you out. Thanks for coming in."

Nicklin-Donovan began to move toward C's office, a few yards to his left. Then he stopped, turned, and gave Jayne an oblique glance. "Oh, one other thing. Helping the investigation into these two secretaries' deaths is one thing. But don't go too far—I know what you're like. Police can be a bit territorial, as you well know. Contribute, yes, and keep me updated. But I don't want complaints from them that you're interfering."

Jayne nodded. "Sure."

Nicklin-Donovan turned again and headed off toward his boss's office.

Her old boss was ever the bureaucrat, Jayne thought to herself. Whereas she had always leaned too far the other way, often not going by the book. That was probably why he was now sitting in a large third-floor office on a fat salary, while she was a freelancer.

I know what you're like. Ha! He did, for sure.

A few minutes later, as Jayne stood in the elevator heading to the ground floor, she felt a slight wave of unease about the double murders. Her gut instinct still told her there was something significant going on.

But what?

There seemed no obvious answer to that.

* * *

Tuesday, March 31, 2015
London

It was only much later that evening, when Jayne was about to start eating a simple supper of omelet and salad in her Whitechapel apartment, that it struck her. She had been mulling over the brief recording of the call that had come from the witness in Pevensey, wondering if there was something obvious she was missing.

As she sat down at her dining table with a glass of sauvignon blanc to accompany the food, she realized: the caller had sneezed twice during the call, very loudly.

If he had been in a phone booth, did that mean there might be phlegm or spittle, possibly enough to obtain a DNA sample, somewhere in the booth? If there was, it seemed unlikely that it would last there for long.

She hesitated for a few minutes, thinking to herself that surely the forensics team in Bunting's force would have picked up such evidence. In any case, the investigation wasn't her business—she told herself not to interfere, as Nicklin-Donovan had instructed. More than once in her career she had been informed that one of her character flaws was a tendency to be a control freak.

But after a few sips of the wine, a voice in the back of her head kept nagging away, telling her what she knew from years of experience in espionage: it's often the obvious that gets overlooked.

Knowing she might regret not speaking up if it later emerged that her thinking was correct, she picked up her phone and dialed Bunting's number.

The police chief seemed surprised to hear from her and

was initially somewhat monosyllabic in his response. But he listened as she briefly explained her thoughts.

He paused for a few seconds before answering. "Neither the officer in charge nor forensics have mentioned the sneezes and the possibility of phlegm to me. It doesn't mean they haven't taken care of it, of course. They did say they were lifting fingerprints from the booth, though. I will get them to chase it—the overnight team will do it."

"Thank you," Jayne said. "I don't like to interfere. It's your investigation, and I'm certain it is likely all in hand, but you never know."

"I can tell you, confidentially, we've had a significant development in terms of the witness. We think we know how he saw the killing. A property overlooking the car park was burgled overnight at the same time. It's an upmarket antiques dealership, only occupied during business hours. Some very valuable items were taken from a safe. It only came to light this afternoon when the owner returned. Turns out the alarm system had been disabled by the burglar, who then got into the safe. Definitely not an amateur job. It was possibly our mystery caller who did it. It would explain why he was so nervous and keen to get off the phone."

"That sounds promising. Yes, it would explain his state of mind. But would a burglar stick his head above the parapet and make the phone call in the first place? That seems a little odd. And is there anything for forensics in the antiques dealership? If he was sneezing in the phone booth, maybe he was doing the same in there too."

"No prints or other forensics so far. He was careful. But your point is valid. I will ask the team to check."

"Thank you for that."

Jayne hesitated, unsure whether to make her next request or not, but then decided to just go for it. "I am sure your officer in charge and his team are completely on top of everything, but I was wondering if I might come down to Pevensey, to the murder scene, just to see if there's any perspective I can offer."

Bunting remained silent for a couple of seconds. "Yes, I am sure that can be arranged," he said, slightly stiffly. "Let me know when you'd like to come."

"I could come tomorrow?"

"Actually, I am planning to go to the scene myself at eleven o'clock to meet the officer in charge and forensics for a briefing." Another pause. "We will need to talk to the wife, Simone. Perhaps you could join us then and make yourself useful by helping us set up that call at the same time?"

Jayne could see that Bunting didn't particularly like her involvement, which was fair enough, but he was tolerating her because of her connections to Nicklin-Donovan and to Simone. She wasn't going to back off, though; she felt a deep need to do all she could to help Simone.

"Yes, I can get there by eleven," Jayne said. "And I will speak to Simone and arrange a call with her for you."

"Good. We've also had ballistics reports back from our lab and from the Met for the Barbican incident. It was definitely the same weapon responsible for both shootings."

"What gun?"

"Ruger Mark Two. No doubt about it. There were two rounds in each victim. Chest and head shots. Bulls-eyes."

"Hmm. A pro." Jayne knew the MKII was a powerful, accurate weapon and though since superseded by newer variants, it had been in demand by various armed forces, including US Navy SEALs. She had fired the gun herself on MI6 ranges during training exercises and had been impressed, although not sufficiently to abandon her favorite Walther PPK, ideally the .32 variant, as her weapon of choice when on operations.

"Yes, definitely a pro," Bunting said. "Bloody dangerous."

Jayne narrowed her eyes. "Sounds like a contract killer. They were almost Mafia-style hits, gangland murders."

"I would agree with that assessment. Two clean kills. But for what reason? I'm certain it wasn't just to grab a phone and a wallet. Were these two victims involved in some kind of illegal business dealing that went wrong? Was their visit to London actually linked to that rather than to the conference they were supposedly at?"

"True, government administration conference attendees wouldn't normally be out meeting people in the middle of the night," Jayne said. "However, I've no idea about Weber, but Curtis has no history of Mafia or any other criminal involvement, as far as I'm aware."

"Indeed. As far as you're aware." A pause. "I'll see you tomorrow morning."

CHAPTER FIVE

Tuesday, March 31, 2015
    Washington, DC

"There's a couple of cables just come in from London," Vic Walter's secretary told him as he returned to his desk to prepare for his regular update meeting with the director of the CIA, Arthur Veltman.

"Thanks, Helen. I'll take a look," he said in a gravelly voice.

"There's a coffee on your desk."

"I'll need a drip feed for this meeting, not a cup." He pushed his metal-rimmed glasses up his nose.

"I'll get the medics to come and set it up."

Vic Walter gave Helen a lopsided grin. He still liked the fact that everyone at the Agency still referred to the communications received from far-flung stations around the world as "cables." It took him back to the time when he was applying for a training position at Langley in the early 1980s and was reading all the books and articles he could find about the CIA, many of which referenced diplomatic cables.

The mystical "cable" in those days was a telegraph, a dispatch sent using the network of underwater communications cables that ran along the seabeds of the world. Always encrypted, they tended to be short and to the point.

It was the means by which he had informed Langley of some of his greatest early triumphs. The downing of Russian Mil Mi-24 attack helicopters—the dreaded Hinds—in Afghanistan during the late 1980s, using Stinger missiles covertly provided to the Afghan mujahideen by the CIA as part of Operation Cyclone. That had been possibly the biggest covert operation in the Agency's history and had paved the way for the mujahideen to push the Soviet Union out of Afghanistan altogether, a decade after its invasion of 1979.

Then came the recruitment of several Cold War spies from behind the Iron Curtain and the lethal games of chess with successive Soviet leaders and their KGB lackeys, followed by the battles against Saddam Hussein and al-Qaeda.

Now that electronic communications had evolved, cables were more complex and often longer, more akin to secure emails, but had still retained the same tag.

Vic walked back to his desk and picked up the Starbucks latte that Helen had left there for him. Somehow she always timed it perfectly, taking the long trek down from the seventh floor in the original headquarters building at Langley to the Starbucks cafeteria and back, just in time for his arrival at his desk from some meeting or other, or for when he was preparing for one.

Usually Helen instinctively knew when he needed a shot of caffeine without him having to ask. It was definitely a prerequisite for the daily and sometimes torturous meetings with Veltman, whose office was next door to his own, albeit larger and more fancy.

Helen Lake had been at the CIA since the early 1980s, and she was far more capable than her title suggested. Vic had snapped her up and taken her with him to the seventh floor after her previous boss, former Near East Division chief Robert Watson, left the Agency in disgrace.

Vic maneuvered his lean frame onto his swivel chair, logged back on to his computer, and clicked through to the in-box where new cables arrived. He filtered the list so only the ones from London were visible.

For the past day, Veltman had been somewhat sidetracked by the issue of the two secretaries of state, from New Hampshire and Wisconsin, who had been shot dead while attending a conference in London. The first murder, that of New Hampshire secretary of state Curtis Steyn, had in itself immediately generated some mentions in the media, particularly among online news outlets.

But the confirmation a few hours later of a second murder, this time of Wisconsin secretary of state Gareth Weber, had sent journalists into something of a tailspin and had propelled the story into the number one slot on many evening prime-time news programs on Monday.

It hit the front pages of several newspapers on Tuesday, including *The Washington Post* and *The Wall Street Journal*, and there were many follow-ups on the morning shows that day. There had been a lot of speculation about the causes and much scrutiny of both men's business and personal lives, but nothing of substance had emerged.

The only reason Veltman had engaged with it was because the White House, stirred up by the Department of State, was asking if Langley had picked up any information on the likely motives for the killings. President Ferguson had asked his aide, Charles Deacon, to make inquiries. He wanted clarity—

not least because the issue had already been raised by the overwhelming favorite for the Republican nomination in the following year's presidential election, the governor of Maryland, Nicholas McAllister.

McAllister was already proving a real thorn in Ferguson's side. He was particularly adept at digging in the knife and asking awkward questions when he knew the president didn't have answers.

Normally Vic would have shrugged it off onto the FBI, which he was certain would be coordinating with British police investigative teams in any case. It definitely sounded like a law enforcement matter. But given the chain of interest, he had sent a short missive to the CIA's London station asking if they had picked anything up. The initial answer had been a firm no.

But now a further cable, headed TOP SECRET Eyes Only 31X3 and with the subject line Secretaries of State: Contract Killing Suspected, was sitting in his file.

It came from the CIA's new London chief of station, Bob Ager, and stated that information received from British police forensic and ballistic tests indicated the murders had been carried out with the same weapon, a Ruger MK II, equipped with a silencer, and had occurred within three or four hours of each other in the early hours of Monday morning.

The cable continued, "These were almost certainly professional contract killings, carried out to order by the same assassin, in a clinical manner, according to police. It raises substantial concerns, given that the two victims were in the UK ostensibly to attend a local government administration conference. Further investigation at FBI and/or CIA level urgently required, in addition to ongoing UK police operations. If CIA, then more resources will be required than we currently have here."

"Shit," Vic swore out loud. He cupped his hands behind his head and rocked back in his chair, trying to think. He knew that Ager was still trying to get his sea legs following his appointment as chief of station a few weeks earlier. His entire London team was swamped with work, including preparations for the forthcoming general election in the UK, rising Euroscepticism among the British population, and the likelihood of a referendum on Britain's membership in the European Union. A vote to leave the EU was a distinct possibility, and that would cause a massive realignment of Britain's relationship with both Europe and the US. There was also the continuing threat of a resurgent Russia on Europe's eastern doorstep, where it had already annexed the Crimea from Ukraine, and it was threatening further potential incursions into that country.

With that workload, as Ager was indicating, it would be difficult to allocate London resources to a double murder investigation that had nothing obvious to do with the CIA, that was for sure.

Vic glanced at his watch. It was time to go and join Veltman. He scribbled a couple of additional points in his notebook relating to the London cable, picked up his coffee cup, which was now half empty, and made his way out the door and along to Veltman's office.

The daily meetings usually took a fairly predictable course. Veltman would sit Vic down at the conference table in his office and talk for ten or fifteen minutes on what he saw as the current list of priorities. Mostly these were updates on ongoing situations, based on inputs received from the White House, Capitol Hill, the Defense Department, and elsewhere. Occasionally Vic would ask a question, but usually he let his boss just talk. The two men would then have a discussion about what progress was being made and how to approach new issues that were upcoming.

Today, however, Veltman started off in a slightly different vein.

"I was thinking, we're not getting much so far from VULTURE. Any thoughts?"

Vic sipped his coffee. "We agreed we'd give her time to gain trust internally in that new job. The finger of suspicion has been pointed at her, and counterintelligence will have been watching her like a hawk. But yes, I agree time is marching on."

Anastasia Shevchenko's recruitment had not been carried out in the manner that Vic would have liked. Rather than being a willing, voluntary recruit, the Russian had effectively been backed into a corner. Her SVR career had been threatened with destruction after she was captured in Washington. If Langley had sent her back to Moscow in disgrace the previous August, after Jayne Robinson and Joe Johnson uncovered her handling a high-level US spy, she would have been finished.

But in an initiative born of self-preservation, she had offered to work for the CIA in exchange for a cover-up, and Vic and Veltman had agreed, given that their other key assets in Russia had been blown over the previous two years.

But Shevchenko's recruitment had been seven months ago, and pressure on the CIA was mounting.

It was, in truth, a desperate time, not least because President Ferguson wanted to keep the thumbscrews on Russia over its persistent policy of keeping military forces in eastern Ukraine—effectively an invasion—despite international pressure on Russia to withdraw. Obtaining high-quality intelligence out of Moscow was critical to that, and Ferguson was pushing Veltman hard.

"It's time VULTURE started earning her keep, Vic," Veltman said. "We've had more from SOYUZ than we've had from her, and he's not given us much after that promising start."

SOYUZ was the only other asset of any significance the CIA currently had within the SVR, a man named Pavel Vasilenko who was a little lower down the chain of command at Yasenevo than Shevchenko but was nevertheless number two on the Americas desk. He had been recruited the previous year not long before Shevchenko, and it was actually his information that led the Agency to Shevchenko in the first place.

Shevchenko knew Vasilenko was also an agent for the CIA, because Vic had used her as a conduit to funnel some information requests to him. But she didn't know Vasilenko's part in leading the Agency to her, and hopefully never would.

"I'll get things moving," Vic said. "Ed Grewall's got a channel open to VULTURE. She'll be okay." Grewall, known to all as Sunny, was the Moscow chief of station. He had exchanged a few very short text messages with Shevchenko using a burner phone she kept for the purpose.

"I thought she asked for either Johnson or the Brit, Jayne, to do the handling."

"She did. She insisted on it. I think she saw them as some sort of kindred spirits. But Ed's made a start," Vic said. "It's just to keep communication open. We'll put something more permanent in place and get her fixed up with an SRAC as soon as we can. It's no good relying on burner phones for anything other than occasional very short messages, and satellite burst transmitters can be intercepted. She needs to get settled in that new role."

An SRAC, or short-range agent communication device, would allow Shevchenko to transmit substantially sized encrypted electronic documents and messages wirelessly to a hidden receiver buried somewhere secure in Moscow. They operated using transmissions of three or four seconds over short distances. Unlike phones, which could be triangulated, or satellite burst transmitters, which could in theory be intercepted, SRAC transmissions were not possible to intercept without knowledge of where the base receivers were located in order to get close to them.

"I would keep her happy these first few months. Give her what she asked for. Send Johnson or Jayne to see her, then get Ed involved a little further down the line once everything is running smoothly and VULTURE is comfortable."

"We can't be sure we can trust her yet."

"No. But act like we do trust her," Veltman said. "We'll soon find out."

Vic nodded. "Johnson won't get involved right now, though. I spoke to him only a couple of days ago. He's taking some time out with his kids after the last operation, and in any case, he much prefers to have a war crime to chew on. It will have to be Jayne."

"All right, send Jayne over to see VULTURE, then. Isn't she living over here now, with Johnson?"

"Yes. But she's in the UK at the moment. Visiting friends, as I understand from Johnson."

Veltman folded his arms. "Friends? Not our friends from Vauxhall Cross, I hope?"

Vic shrugged. "No idea."

"That's the issue with using external people."

"She's done some good work for us."

"Maybe she'd like to solve this riddle of the secretaries of state, if she's in London right now. The White House is getting worked up about it. They want to know what the hell those two were doing. I mean, running a local government department isn't usually going to get you gunned down in the street. Have you heard any more?"

Vic drained his coffee and put it down on the oak table. "I had a cable from London just now," he said. He briefly ran through the content of what he had received from Ager and summarized the media coverage he had seen.

"Ager needs to get his people onto this," Veltman said. "I'm sure British law enforcement are good, but there has to be more to it. One man down could just be coincidence, bad luck, whatever. Two in the space of a few hours definitely isn't."

"I agree with you. But Ager tells me all his good people are snowed under."

Veltman shook his head. "That's bullshit. He's got an army there in London."

The CIA station in London, which employed more than a hundred people, was buried within the US embassy in Grosvenor Square, in the exclusive Mayfair district. Plans were well advanced to move the embassy to another location three miles away south of the River Thames, at Nine Elms.

"He says the army's not big enough."

Veltman shook his head. "It's nonsense. But get Jayne to do that job as well then, if she's in London anyway. She must know people across the police and MI5, who I assume have gotten involved. All we're looking for is to keep on top of what's happening in the investigation—not to carry out the damn investigation."

Vic paused before replying. That was not a bad idea, although the whole idea of using people from outside the Agency always left him feeling a little anxious, not least because of the hostile opposition to such practices from the CIA's deputy director of counterintelligence, Ricardo Miller, who was paranoid about the risks of classified information being leaked.

But he didn't have to tell Miller, who was less senior, albeit a powerful and important presence in his own right at Langley. Jayne would be very capable of delivering what they needed, and his boss was correct—she would have very good contacts across the full spectrum of security services inside the UK, including police.

"All right. I agree we could try and get her to do it. I'll put a call in when we've finished here."

Veltman checked his watch. "I think we *have* finished here. I've got a videoconference with Tel Aviv in five minutes. I'll need to psych myself up for that one. We've got the Iranian nuclear program on the agenda. Could be a long one. Wish me luck."

Vic took his cue and stood. "Thanks, boss, I'll keep you informed." He headed for the door.

"Oh, Vic."

Vic stopped and turned around.

"If you're going to get Jayne involved with these two secretaries of state, just make sure you keep it below the radar of our friend Nicklin-Donovan, or anyone else at Vauxhall Cross, for that matter. He might think we're interfering on his turf."

Vic nodded. "Will do."

CHAPTER SIX

Wednesday, April 1, 2015
    Pevensey

Jayne steered her rented BMW, a dark green sedan, down a narrow lane next to the Royal Oak and Castle and reversed into a parking spot between the pub and the castle wall. She had sold her own car the previous year after deciding to live in Portland with Joe. It was difficult and expensive to find a safe storage space in her area of London for a long period, and she was reluctant to leave the vehicle on the street when she couldn't keep an eye on it.

But there was an independent car rental place near Aldgate station, only a few minutes' walk from her apartment, where she knew the manager and could easily get a vehicle at short notice if she needed one.

There was a white-and-blue tent that covered a small area behind a bus shelter at the end of the parking lot nearest to the street. That must have been the spot where the body lay, Jayne surmised. A gray van, marked Scientific Support

Branch, was parked next to the tent. Clearly the forensic team was hard at work.

The top half of the lot, including the tent, was cordoned off by yellow crime scenes tape. Inside the area was a small white Ford with a rental company sticker on the rear window.

Sitting at a small table outside the pub door was Bunting, wearing his uniform, together with another man who wore a suit but no tie. Two empty coffee cups stood on the table.

Jayne approached and Bunting stood and shook hands, then introduced the other man, the senior investigating officer in the case, detective chief inspector Aidan Foster, an unsmiling man who slowly shook hands as he scrutinized Jayne up and down, then gave her his card.

"Has there been any progress overnight?" Jayne asked.

"Forensics are still at work, so nothing to report immediately. They've been combing the antiques dealer's building across there." Bunting pointed toward an ancient-looking redbrick building across the street from the pub, with a massive chimney at one end.

Jayne could see it was the only property from which it was possible to get a good view of the pub parking lot. There was a single-story building housing tearooms next door to the antiques dealer, but a fence blocked the view from its windows toward the lot.

"What about the phone booth where the call came in from?" Jayne said, feeling a little impatient now but trying not to show it. Having raised the possibility of phlegm in the booth, she hoped that Bunting had addressed it.

"The phone booth as well, yes," Bunting said. "They found some material, which went off to the labs during the night for testing, but how significant it is, I just don't know yet."

Despite feeling slightly disappointed that the tests hadn't been completed, Jayne told herself not to push Bunting.

"We're going to go into the antiques building now. You want to come in?" he asked.

"Sure." Jayne pointed at the white Ford. "I presume that was the car that Curtis rented to get here from London?"

"Correct."

Bunting led the way across the parking lot, over the street, and up to the enormous aged oak front door of the property, which was being guarded by two other officers.

He handed Jayne a set of blue plastic shoe covers and thin rubber gloves from a pack outside the door, which she put on, as did Bunting himself and Foster. Inside, all three of them had to duck to avoid the low-hanging beams, and their feet echoed across the heavily worn red quarry tiled floor. Foster took them up the staircase, their footsteps creaking loudly in the silence.

"This place is supposed to be haunted," Foster said as he glanced back at Jayne. "A double murder in the 1580s. A merchant killed his mistress and her lover."

At the top of the stairs, an officer wearing technician's overalls was placing what looked to Jayne like clear plastic evidence bags into a box. Another man was tapping on a laptop. Bunting nodded at them as he approached.

"How is progress?" Foster asked the man who was handling the evidence bags.

"We've found plenty of material—human hairs mainly," he said. "We'll get it all processed as quickly as we can."

"Good," Foster said. "Have you finished in the office? Can we go in?"

The man nodded. "Yes, it's all yours. Finished in there." He held out his hand to Jayne, and she shook it.

"Dave, from forensics," he said by way of introduction. "And you are?"

"Jayne Robinson," Jayne said. "Just accompanying Rod."

"She's ex-MI6," Foster said shortly, without offering any further explanation.

Foster led the way into an office, where a wall safe was exposed, the hinged wooden panel that hid it hanging open.

"That's where the antiques were stolen from," Foster said, pointing at the safe. "Old decoy wooden ducks. Four of them, worth the best part of a million pounds. And some ancient coins."

Jayne whistled softly. She had no idea that wooden ducks could be worth anything like that amount. She looked around, then walked to the window. "If the witness was our burglar, he might have seen the killing from here, then," she said.

"Quite possibly," Foster said.

Jayne stared out at the parking lot and the pub. A handful of tourists were circumnavigating the cordoned-off area and walking through the ancient stone archway into the castle.

She tried to imagine the scene that the burglar might have witnessed. Then she turned to Bunting. "If the burglar is our witness, then he might have had a good view of the killer."

The assistant chief constable inclined his head. "Yes, I guess so, although the lighting is not good outside that pub."

"Maybe enough to give some kind of description."

"Let's hope so."

Foster, slightly overweight and muscular, ran his hand across his close-cropped scalp and scrutinized Jayne. "If you want a job in my department, let me know."

Jayne wasn't sure if he was having a joke or a dig at her. She decided to give him the benefit of the doubt and gave a brief, thin smile. "Will do."

She felt her phone vibrating in her pocket and pulled it out. It was Vic Walter. She checked the time on the screen. It was just before twelve, so seven in the morning at Langley.

What was this about? She tapped the green button and put the handset to her ear.

"Vic, hello. What are you calling about so early in the day?"

"I understand you're in the UK right now. Can you talk?"

"I'm here to check out my apartment, see some friends. I've left Joe to his own devices for ten days." She didn't want to say she was also meeting Nicklin-Donovan but knew there was a chance that Joe had told Vic. The two men had been close for years.

"I need to have a chat about some potential work. What do you know about secretaries of state? Specifically the New Hampshire one."

Jayne raised an eyebrow. Out of the corner of her eye, she could see that Foster had also just answered a call on his phone and was busy, but Bunting was gazing at her.

"Strangely enough, quite a lot," Jayne said. "I can read the newspapers, you know. Look, I'll need to call you back. I'm a little tied up right now."

There was a pause at the other end of the line. "Okay," Vic said. "That's fine. Talk later."

Jayne pushed her phone back into the pocket of her jacket and stood quietly while Foster continued his conversation a few yards away. He was pacing up and down and appeared to be becoming increasingly animated. Eventually he ended the call and glanced first at Bunting, then at Jayne.

"Any good news?" Bunting asked.

"There is, actually," Foster said. He turned toward Jayne. "Rod mentioned to me your thought about the possibility of phlegm in the telephone booth where the witness's call came from."

Jayne nodded. "It was just something that occurred to me."

"Well, it proved to be spot-on. Forensics have pulled a

DNA match from some they found on the booth window. These phone booths are rarely used these days, so there was virtually nothing in there. There was only the one sample. It's almost certainly from our caller."

"Excellent. Did they get a crossmatch?" Jayne knew the DNA profile would be run through the national database of samples taken from offenders and suspects.

"Yes, it's a guy convicted twice a few years ago of burglary. Name of Neil Knapp."

Jayne felt a surge of adrenaline kick through her. "So it *was* the burglar. Do you know where he lives, where he is?"

"We're going through the database, trying to trace the guy now. Hopefully we'll get an address soon. We're looking."

Jayne pressed her lips together. "And if we find him, let's hope he's got a good memory and is willing to use it."

What are the chances of him being able to describe the guy, even if he got a good look at him? she wondered.

Then another thought crossed Jayne's mind. "Is there any matching DNA in the antiques dealership?" she asked.

"Forensics are still going over it. No luck so far."

"No prints, nothing?"

Foster shook his head. "A few marks on dusty surfaces, but no actual prints, not even on the window he entered through. He was almost certainly wearing gloves and was bloody careful."

Jayne realized the implications immediately.

Without proof the suspect had raided the antiques dealership, police would be lacking leverage to persuade him to give evidence against the gunman.

"Prints or DNA are going to be important," Jayne said. "He's not exactly going to admit to breaking in here otherwise."

Foster nodded. "And therefore not going to admit having witnessed the shooting. Evidence of illegal entry and that he stole the ducks could enable us to do a deal, maybe get a plea bargain, negotiate him a reduced sentence or something in return for a testimony."

"Let's hope he slipped up somewhere in this place, then," Jayne said.

Now that progress was evidently being made, she felt less anxious and decided to call Vic back. She excused herself, took a few paces away from the two men, searched for Vic's number, and called him using a secure connection.

"That was quick," Vic said, when he answered.

"I'm always quick."

"Right. Well, I'll get straight to the point. There's a couple of things I'd like you to do. Important things. So hopefully you can help me out. I'm not going to say too much on the phone, but as I indicated earlier, the first relates to the secretaries of state. As you probably saw, they were both shot dead and—"

"I know. I'm right where the first one was shot. In Pevensey, Sussex. I'm with the police officers investigating the case."

There was a short pause. "What the hell?"

"This one's personal for me, Vic. The guy was my oldest friend's husband. I grew up with her and went to university with her." Jayne briefly explained the background to her friendship with Simone and what she had discovered so far, without mentioning her dealings with Nicklin-Donovan.

There was a silence. "You never fail to astonish me, Jayne. The case is causing some concern at the White House, so Veltman is getting very worked up about it. We'd like you to help us out. And I also want to talk to you about possibly going to Moscow to start things moving with VULTURE. Time is passing, and she's had time to settle in now."

Jayne glanced over her shoulder to make sure that Bunting wasn't eavesdropping, but he was busy in conversation with

Foster, who was tapping away at his phone screen. Nevertheless, she took several more paces so she was farther away
from them before speaking again.

"I agree with that, yes," she said, lowering her voice and
not wanting to mention code names out loud. "She does need
to start producing for us, and I'm happy to travel and set
things up."

"Good. I'll keep you updated on our thinking. But be
ready when the time comes," Vic said. He paused, then
continued, "Are you investigating this killing in Sussex, then?"

"No, I wouldn't say investigating."

"It sounds like you are to me."

"Not as such," Jayne said.

"What *are* you doing, then?"

It was a damn good question, Jayne thought. What *was*
she doing? The biggest factor was Simone, but even without
her friend's connection to this case, she seemed to have some
kind of built-in compulsion to pursue justice, even when it
was truthfully none of her business. This was a police matter.

"I'm just following my nose. And that's only because
Simone asked me to. But the farther I go, the smellier this is
getting."

"Hmm. So it appears. You haven't mentioned any of this
to your friends at Vauxhall Cross, have you?"

Oh God. Now I'm going to upset Vic.

"Actually, I have. That was how I first found out about it.
I had dinner with Mark, and he mentioned it. I realized then
it was Simone's husband who was murdered. Mark introduced
me to the senior police officer I'm with now."

She glanced over her shoulder again, but Bunting and
Foster were still busy and weren't trying to eavesdrop.

"All right," Vic said. "I was just concerned that Mark
might not like us getting involved in something in his territory, but too late now. Given that you're already there, all I'd

like you to do is keep us informed of what's happening. If we can help, let us know."

"I don't think Mark will be too upset, Vic. It's not his investigation. It's police and MI5. I wish I could tell you why two US secretaries of state have been gunned down thousands of miles from home. There obviously is a reason, and as soon as I get any more on that, I'll let you know."

Jayne became aware of slightly raised voices behind her and turned her head to check, just in time to see Bunting look across and make eye contact.

"We've got it," he called out.

She nodded and again spoke to Vic. "I think we've just got an address for the witness who saw the Steyn shooting. I've got to go. Will be in touch."

Jayne ended the call, realizing as she did so that Simone had not replied to a text message she had sent the previous evening, asking her if a call could be arranged with Bunting to discuss her husband's murder. She made a mental note to give her another try.

CHAPTER SEVEN

Wednesday, April 1, 2015
  Hastings

The bungalow was somewhat run-down and stood on a narrow winding lane on the hillside on the eastern side of Hastings. Positioned at the top of a steep set of steps that led up from the lane, it overlooked the sea, which was about a quarter of a mile away beyond a stretch of gorse bushes.

The grass on the small lawn at the front of the property was at least a couple of inches long, and weeds were growing profusely in the flower beds.

Jayne sat quietly in a wicker chair in a cluttered conservatory that formed the entrance to the property. In the kitchen next door, she could hear the sound of voices as Foster and one of his detective colleagues continued to talk to the man they believed had burgled the antiques business and witnessed the killing outside, Neil Knapp.

Bunting had decided not to accompany them to Hastings

and had instead driven back to police headquarters for a series of management meetings.

Knapp, a lithe, gray-haired man in his fifties, had instantly gone on the defensive when he answered the door to find two police officers on the doorstep. He had first demanded to see a search warrant, but after Foster pointed out he was doing himself no favors, he backed down and eventually allowed the officers inside.

Rather than arrest Knapp immediately and take him to the police station for formal questioning, Foster had decided to offer him the alternative of a voluntary interview at home. This was a more informal approach that he hoped might give a quick indication of whether he and his officers were on the correct track.

After a short and robust exchange of views, Knapp reluctantly agreed to the voluntary approach rather than the police station.

But then he pointed aggressively to Jayne.

"Who the hell is she?" Knapp shouted, his face reddening. "She doesn't look like a cop. If she's not a cop, get that bitch out of here."

Foster had appeared more than a little irritated and curtly instructed Jayne to wait in the conservatory while he and his colleague spoke to Knapp. Jayne was left feeling that his irritation was more because he didn't want her there in the first place than because of Knapp's attitude.

But now, half an hour later, as the conversation in the kitchen continued, Jayne could tell the officers were making little headway.

Judging by his occasional sneezes and coughs, Knapp was suffering from a cold, which would explain the phlegm in the phone booth and account for the sneezes on the recording of the call made to police.

He was being very monosyllabic in his responses to the

questions being put to him, and Foster's voice was rising steadily in tone. The policeman sounded frustrated and stressed.

Jayne looked around the conservatory, which consisted of a three-foot brick wall topped with glass panes in a white PVC frame. Apart from the closed door that led into the kitchen, there was also a toilet and a utility room leading off it.

On the floor lay a clutter of empty beer bottles, plastic supermarket bags, and a box of wrenches and screwdrivers. A plastic bucket and mop stood in one corner. Beneath the chair on which Jayne was seated were two pairs of running shoes, one of which was muddy and slightly damp and of the same brand that Jayne used, Asics.

The door to the kitchen opened and Foster appeared. He closed the door behind him and stood, arms folded, shaking his head.

"Any luck?" Jayne asked.

"No. He's not going to play ball," Foster said. "He's denying everything. He admitted he was in the phone booth after we told him about the DNA evidence but says he didn't actually make any calls. He says it was at half past nine the previous evening when he was in there, not twenty past two in the morning. He claims his phone was out of charge and says he went into the booth to phone his wife to ask if she wanted a takeaway pizza but changed his mind at the last moment and didn't call."

"I'm assuming he's denying the burglary too."

Foster nodded. "Of course he bloody is. Says he's never heard of an antiques dealership in Pevensey. We'll have to take him into the station and question him properly."

Jayne pressed her lips together. This was what she had been expecting.

"Can't you search his house for the ducks?" she asked.

"We're getting a search warrant right now."

She nodded. The procedure took time.

"Hopefully some of the DNA collected from the antiques place will match his," Jayne said.

"Let's hope so. We'll get those tests done as quickly as possible."

"Can I come into the station with you? Perhaps I can contribute," Jayne asked, although she guessed from Foster's attitude toward her and his body language what the answer was likely to be.

Foster shook his head firmly. "No, definitely not. You'll need to leave it to us from now on. I shouldn't have brought you here. I think it's best if you head back home and leave us to it. I'll keep you informed, of course."

There was a distinct edge to his voice. He had made his mind up, Jayne could see. That was fair enough. It was his inquiry.

"Okay, I'll go now," Jayne said.

"Yes. There's nothing helpful you can do here."

Jayne stood, shook Foster's hand, and thanked him for the unofficial help he had given her so far, which was not part of his job. She opened the door and made her way down the steps through the overgrown garden to the street, where she had parked her rental car.

She started the engine and slowly headed back along the lane toward the Old London Road, which was her route back to London. Beyond the green fields to her left the sun was glinting off the sea.

She was some way off her usual beaten track, getting involved in a police investigation in the south of England. Foster had been diplomatic, but he was correct: this was something for his team to deal with.

Her mind flitted to her conversation with Vic and the need he had mentioned for her to get to Moscow and

reestablish contact with their recently recruited mole in the
SVR, Anastasia Shevchenko. That was more in line with what
she felt she should be doing.

But then there was Simone, the woman who had rescued
her from being held at knifepoint that time in Cambridge
when, as a twenty-year-old student, Jayne's had gone out to
celebrate the end of exams, and a drunken evening had
turned into a nightmare.

The thought made her realize that Simone had still not
replied to the message Jayne had sent requesting that she
have a call with Bunting to discuss Curtis's murder. Jayne
glanced at the dashboard clock. It was well into the morning
in New Hampshire now. That seemed odd. She really needed
to give Simone a call if she wasn't responding to the texts.

As Jayne reached a junction, she braked to a halt and
paused for several moments. Her way home lay to the right,
which would take her to the A21, the main artery that led
through Sussex to London.

As she sat there, a van pulled up behind her, and the
driver honked his horn twice, a clear message to her to get
moving.

On a whim, almost without thinking much about it, Jayne
let out the clutch and, instead of turning right, took a left
turn, on the route that led through Hastings back toward
Pevensey.

CHAPTER EIGHT

Wednesday, April 1, 2015
   Pevensey

The police forensics van and tent were still in the parking lot when Jayne arrived back at the Royal Oak and Castle pub, so she decided to leave her car farther down the village street and walk back. She didn't particularly want to draw the attention of the officers working there, given that she had agreed with Foster not to involve herself further in his investigation.

Before leaving her car, she pulled on a blue cap she used for running and a pair of sports sunglasses and switched her blue jacket for a gray one. The items changed her appearance just enough, she figured. There were also a number of tourists wandering around, thankfully, so Jayne did not feel as conspicuous as she otherwise might have.

She walked past the old antiques dealership and crossed the street in front of the Royal Oak, then stood still next to the coffee tables, thinking about what to do next. As she did so, she noticed a forensics officer standing next to his van. It was the same man who had been working inside the antiques business when she went in with Bunting.

He looked directly at her for a second or two, then turned away. There was no sign of recognition.

Clearly her light disguise was enough, but it made her think a little about what she was doing. Why was she back here in Pevensey?

She knew. Just as Nicklin-Donovan, Joe, Vic, and everyone else she had worked with knew. She was something of a control freak and had always found it difficult to trust someone else to do a job as well or as thoroughly as she thought she could do it herself.

That was why she hadn't risen to the higher levels of management within the Secret Intelligence Service and had always remained in a more hands-on type of role in which she could get personally involved in operations.

But Jayne put those thoughts to one side. She needed to focus on the task in hand and to logically think through Knapp's likely actions.

If he had been in the antiques dealership and had seen Simone's husband gunned down outside, he would undoubtedly have wanted to get out of there as quickly as possible, Jayne figured, given the high likelihood that police and other emergency services would be on the scene soon.

Where would he have parked? She guessed that he would not have wanted to leave his car within sight of the property he was entering, nor where anyone could easily see it. She knew what English villages were like, and any strange car parked at night would likely have been noted by a nosy resident.

The streets near to the pub and the antiques dealership were all within sight of multiple houses, so it seemed probable that Knapp would have parked some distance away and walked there. Her bet was that he would have put his car on the fringe of the village out of sight of any homes. She also assumed that he would have wanted to minimize the likelihood of being seen walking through the village on foot, where he might have been picked up by CCTV cameras.

She took out her phone, opened her satellite maps app, and studied the layout of the village from above. High Street ran east to west through it like a ribbon. He wouldn't have walked along the High Street going east from the pub, and there seemed nowhere obvious where he could have parked that led off it. Similarly, in the area west of the pub, around the castle wall and along the street, there seemed to be no secluded parking options.

Jayne frowned. What would she have done in the same circumstances? It was tricky to work out.

Then, on the satellite map, she spotted a cricket ground. The Pevensey Recreation Ground was located at the southeast corner of the village and had a large parking lot adjoining the A259, the highway that skirted the eastern side of the village and led to Hastings.

She looked up from her phone screen and down the pub parking lot to an additional parking area beyond, its surface rough and paved with old bricks. Behind the trees at the bottom end lay what looked like a pathway to the cricket ground.

Jayne decided to take a look. She strolled through the gate of the second parking area and down past the ruined ramparts of the castle on her right to a narrow path that led through the trees onto the sports field.

While she was on the path, her phone pinged as a message arrived. She scrutinized the screen. It was Vic.

Any progress? W House called Veltman again this morning.

Jayne emerged onto the sports field. She decided to ignore the message. She would reply later.

The large expanse of grass had been mown recently, and

there were loose clippings on top of the turf. She stood on the edge of the mown area for a few moments, then strolled slowly in a straight line toward the cricket club parking lot, next to a pavilion. The ground was still quite damp underfoot from rain, and her feet occasionally squelched beneath her. Preparation work for the forthcoming cricket season was clearly underway, and the rectangular pitch area in the center of the field, bounded by ropes on poles to keep passersby off it, had been mown short in neat stripes.

After about a hundred yards, as she drew near to the pavilion, Jayne noticed a line of dark footprints to her left, spaced well apart, where the shoes of someone who had been running had thudded into the soggy turf, leaving indentations that in some places were a quarter-inch deep. She continued a little farther, then saw a large patch of mud, several feet across, where new grass seed had been sown.

The runner's footprints went straight across the mud, disturbing the new seed, and in one place there was a large skid mark, almost two feet long, where it appeared the person's foot had slid on impact.

Jayne stopped still and stared at the footprints in the mud and the skid mark. The first thing she noticed was the mold and shape of the prints: they had been made by someone who used the same brand of running shoes as she did, Asics. The lines and curves of the tread marks were very distinctive, and the foot size was significantly larger than her own. It was likely to have been a man who had made them.

The second thing that flashed into her mind was the image of the pair of muddy running shoes that she had seen under the chair in Neil Knapp's conservatory earlier that morning.

She was certain of it: these were Knapp's footprints, made as he fled the burglary scene.

Jayne sank to her haunches next to the mud patch, took

out her phone, and carefully photographed the footprints, some of them close up so that the fine detail of the Asics sole molds could be clearly seen. She also photographed the long skid mark where the runner's right foot had slipped on impact.

She knew that Bunting and especially Foster wouldn't like her doing this on her own initiative, but it seemed obvious that the police forensics team had not yet spread their net this far from the antiques dealership. They were, understandably, focused primarily at this stage on safeguarding and collecting the forensics surrounding the actual killing, not those concerning a potential witness.

She glanced up at the sky, her mind now working in overdrive.

Dark clouds were scudding inland from the direction of the sea, which lay less than a mile to the south, and the wind was increasing. Time was of the essence: one more heavy rain shower and the prints would probably be destroyed.

Jayne couldn't let that happen.

She knew it was crucial that she didn't compromise any legal case against Knapp for the burglary by doing something that might corrupt evidence. Otherwise Bunting and Foster would be down on her like a ton of bricks. She had to make sure police properly recorded the footprints.

On the other hand, she realized she couldn't hang around here. She urgently needed to get information from Knapp about the killing he had seen before he was arrested and charged with burglary, and the likely lengthy legal process around the case got underway.

Otherwise, it would probably be too late. Once charges had been made, Knapp and his lawyers would almost certainly give away nothing of value before the case came to court, and Jayne's chance of finding out what he had witnessed would be gone.

She made a decision.

Bunting had seemed more approachable than the prickly Foster. She quickly looked up Bunting's number in her contacts list and pressed the call button.

It would be foolish not to pass the information about the footprints at Pevensey Recreation Ground to him and his team.

But Jayne figured she could perhaps use it in other ways first.

Five minutes later, she had briefed Bunting on her findings, and he had promised to get the forensics team to the cricket ground as quickly as possible to preserve the evidence. He also informed Jayne that a search had been made of Knapp's property a couple of hours earlier and there had been no trace of the stolen wooden ducks. With no reasonable grounds to arrest Knapp, they had left him at home.

As Bunting ended the call in order to contact his forensics team leader, Jayne stood and began striding swiftly back to her car. While she walked, she quickly tapped out a short follow-up text to Simone and pressed send.

Bunting and his crew would now hopefully be focused on the cricket ground for a while.

But Jayne had another objective in mind.

CHAPTER NINE

Wednesday, April 1, 2015
  Hastings

All the curtains were drawn at Neil Knapp's bungalow as Jayne edged her way up the steps from the street, scanning the property as she did so. There was no sign of movement, and it crossed her mind that the burglary suspect might well have fled.

Her thought was that if she could somehow persuade Knapp to give up some detail that might lead her and the police to whoever had killed Curtis Steyn, perhaps a good description of the perpetrator, it would be worth the risk she was now taking.

She made her way along the cracked cement path to the door of the conservatory. She eyed the doorbell button for several moments, then pushed it firmly.

There came the sound of an electronic jingle from somewhere inside the house as the bell rang.

Jayne waited for what seemed like an interminably long time but in reality was no more than a minute. There was no response, so she repeated her push on the doorbell.

Again, nothing.

Jayne eyed the conservatory through the glass. Nothing seemed to have changed since her visit earlier in the day. The doors leading off the conservatory to the utility room and the toilet were slightly ajar, and the one to the kitchen was closed. To her surprise, the muddy running shoes still rested beneath the wicker chair.

She placed a hand on the door handle and slowly pressed down. To her astonishment, the door immediately clicked an inch open, and Jayne instinctively and quickly tightened her grip to prevent it from swinging farther inward.

Then she stood there, holding it, feeling somewhat unsure about what to do next.

It seemed odd that Knapp hadn't answered the door if he was at home, which she assumed was the case given the unlocked door. Unless, that is, he had left in such a hurry that he had forgotten to lock up. Or maybe he had left the conservatory unlocked but had secured the kitchen door, which she noticed also had a lock.

Should she go in and call for Knapp? It felt as though time was of the essence. If she was to speak to him alone, she needed to do so before Foster's officers got there and arrested him. After that, he would without a doubt say absolutely nothing. She knew that from previous experience of dealing with suspected criminals.

Jayne had no option. She made her decision, pushed the door farther open, and stepped through it.

She was about to knock on the closed door that led into the kitchen and call for Knapp when she had a second thought. To her mind, the key evidence that she and the forensics unit would need to nail Knapp for the burglary were the muddy running shoes, which would pin Knapp to the Pevensey location. Perhaps forensics would be able to link them to footmarks in the antiques dealership too.

Jayne took a couple of steps over to the wicker chair and bent down to pick up the shoes. She turned them upside down and examined the soles. Sure enough, several grass seeds were embedded in the mud that was stuck there. That seemed very careless for a burglar. Perhaps he had simply forgotten about them.

Well, it was for Foster's team to take the shoes, not her. She replaced them on the floor and was just about to stand up when from the toilet door behind her came a slight noise.

Jayne hadn't even had time to turn her head when she was shoved hard in her back, knocking her off balance and propelling her into the wall of the conservatory next to the kitchen door. She instinctively jerked her head back to avoid having her face and skull crushed, but her chest slammed into the plaster, winding her sharply.

A knee crashed into her buttocks, pinning her against the wall, and both of her hands were simultaneously grabbed in an industrial-strength grip and pulled hard behind her back. The move wrenched her right shoulder joint, causing a sharp stab of pain to run down her arm.

A man's menacing voice, unmistakably that of Knapp, hissed in her ear. "What the hell are you doing in here?"

"I need to talk to you," Jayne croaked, her voice high and reedy. She felt another sharp stab of pain at the base of her spine as Knapp dug his knee harder into the top of her buttocks.

"You stupid bitch," Knapp snarled. "You're the non-cop from earlier, aren't you? Who are you—some sort of undercover detective or something? Your boss had this place searched top to bottom an hour ago. Why are you back here? You have no right to be coming in here."

Jayne cursed herself for not following her initial instinct and calling out to Knapp before picking up his shoes. She could have handled this much better—had him less on edge and perhaps more likely to listen. Now she had her work cut out for her.

"I'm not a cop and I'm not interested in what you've done. It's what you might have seen," she said, her voice rasping from the pain. "I'm trying to find the killer of my best friend's husband. You might have seen it happen."

There was another pull on her strained right shoulder as Knapp yanked her hands lower and even tighter.

"I've seen nothing," Knapp said. "I told your boss. He's made a big mistake."

"He's not my boss. I said that. My best friend has lost her husband. Gunned down in Pevensey. I'm trying to help her. I know you called in to report it. I just want to know what you saw."

"Nothing." Now Knapp's hiss in her right ear was loud and threatening.

"All I want is a description. What the killer looked like. Accomplices. Anything. We're desperate. I don't care what you were doing there. I won't even tell the cops what you—"

"Bullshit. You think I'm a bloody idiot?"

Knapp pushed harder on Jayne's wrists, bending her hand back to almost ninety degrees. She could feel the tendons and joints in her wrist straining and stretching.

God please don't break them.

She realized she had a chance of kicking backward into his groin area or at least his shins and briefly considered doing so. That was what she had been trained to do, and it would give her a chance of getting out the door. But that would also destroy any chance she had of getting him to talk.

"Look, there's no witnesses here. You can tell me. Nobody will know," Jayne said.

Knapp again pushed her hard in the back, ramming her chin up against the wall and forcing her head back so far she could only stare at the ceiling.

"You're wired, aren't you?" Knapp growled.

"No. I'm not wired. I'm not recording anything. I told you. I've got nothing to do with the police."

"Prove it."

"I can't prove it—not with you holding me like this."

"Where's your phone?"

"In my pocket."

There was a shift in Knapp's position behind Jayne. The pressure from his knee on her buttocks reduced, and he let go of her left wrist momentarily. There was a rustling, and Jayne felt Knapp removing her phone from her trouser pocket.

"I'm turning this off," he said. A few seconds later he placed it on the wicker chair.

The next thing she knew, he was lashing her wrists together with a length of rope. He yanked the cord so tight it dug deep into her tendons, and then he tied it. Jayne tried to move her wrists to test it but couldn't shift them.

"I'm going to check you for a wire," Knapp hissed.

She felt his hands running up and down her torso, under her armpits and down over her belly, then finally around and under her breasts. The sensation made her feel like retching.

Knapp's hands slipped lower, circling around her buttocks, up and down her thighs, and then to her horror, between her legs, where he let his right hand rest a couple of beats longer than necessary.

This time she snapped. "Get your bloody hands off me, you bastard."

Somehow, Jayne restrained herself from what was becoming an overwhelming temptation to try and hurt Knapp. Her gut told her that he wouldn't be bothering to frisk her for a recording device if he was planning to just throw her out the door without saying anything.

Knapp spun her around so she was facing him, her hands with their rope ties now against the wall. He shoved her in the center of the chest hard against the wall at full stretch, and then he stood sideways to her so that if she attempted a kick she couldn't get to his private parts.

"I saw on the news who that man was," he said. Now his eyes, so dark they were almost black, were boring into hers. "Why was he hit?"

Jayne quickly summarized who Curtis Steyn was and how she knew his wife. "She saved my life once, and I owe her. I have no idea why he was shot. That's what I need to find out."

Jayne wanted to keep it personal and appeal to Knapp's emotions. She had ruled out any mention of the CIA or the White House's interest in what had happened. Given his obsession with not falling into a police trap, that was only likely to scare Knapp into silence.

"Where did you know this friend of yours from?" asked Knapp.

"Nottingham, where we grew up."

"What's her name?"

"Simone Steyn."

"That's her married name?"

"Yes," Jayne replied.

"Her maiden name?"

"Harrison."

"Her middle name?" Knapp rapped out.

"Teresa."

Jayne could see what he was doing. Asking for personal details, looking for any hesitation, any sign she might be lying. She would probably have done the same.

"What school did you both go to? And I'm going to check." He almost spat out the words.

"Nottingham Girls' High School."

"Were you in the same year as her?"

"Yes."

"What year did you finish?"

"1979."

"Did you go to university? Did she?"

"Yes, both of us."

"Which one?"

"We both went to Cambridge. I studied international politics. She studied history."

"What's her current address?"

"She lives in Concord, New Hampshire. I can't remember the street name, but it's in my phone. I have it."

There was silence for a few seconds. Was Knapp satisfied with her answers? Surely he wasn't really going to go and check her school and university?

What could she do to change the momentum here? She decided to ask him a question.

"Tell me one thing. Why did you report the shooting? There was no advantage to you. It was a risk."

It was a question that had continued to float around inside Jayne's mind, and she knew there must be a reason he had made the call.

Knapp eyeballed her again, glancing occasionally out the window of his conservatory down the steps toward the street. He was clearly on edge.

"I'm not saying whether I made any call or not."

"All right, but—"

"But I will say this. I lost two very close friends once. My best mates. Also to a gunman. Shot up close in cold blood. It was bloody terrible. Bastards. Took me a long time to recover."

"I'm sorry to hear that."

Knapp nodded. Jayne found an odd disconnect in his eyes, which looked hard and calculating, and his voice, which was full of emotion.

"They were like brothers to me," Knapp said. "Made me angry." Now Knapp's Liverpool accent was becoming deeper and stronger.

He paused and stared into Jayne's face, his focus visibly flitting from her left eye to her right and back. "I tell you what—I'm going to help you out. Now listen. You get one bite of this cherry, then you go, and you don't come back, and you tell nobody. Especially not the police."

"Yes."

"MF12," Knapp said. "That's the first part of the gunman's number plate. Got it?"

Jayne felt her scalp tighten. This was it.

"MF12," she repeated, trying to gather her thoughts. "What about the rest of the number?"

"That's all I know. I got a quick look at the car. A dark VW Passat estate."

"Okay." She frantically committed the number to memory. "Which way did the car go from the car park?"

"West. Eastbourne direction. Now go." Knapp grabbed Jayne by the shoulders, turned her, and opened the conservatory door. Then he swiftly untied the knot binding her wrists and shoved her hard out the door so she stumbled on the first step, almost losing her balance.

"Bugger off. If you come back or if you tell the cops, I'll kill you," Knapp said. He sounded as though he meant what he said. He probably did.

"And here's your phone," he said, reaching behind him. He picked up the phone from the chair and threw it at her.

Jayne tried to catch it but her wrists felt numb and her hands somehow wouldn't go where she told them to. She ended up dropping the phone and picked it up, thankfully unbroken, from a patch of weeds. As Knapp shut the door she made her way a little unsteadily down the steps toward the street.

She turned at the bottom to see Knapp standing behind the door, watching her through the glass.

CHAPTER TEN

Wednesday, April 1, 2015
Pevensey

Jayne sat in her car, trying to process the information she had just received, her head filled with conflicting thoughts. Her first and strongest instinct was to find a way to trace the partial car license plate number that Knapp had given her. That was the next logical step.

But at the same time, she found herself slightly confused by another thought. Was Knapp laying some kind of trap for her?

Probably not. He had produced an explanation for giving her the plate number and for why he had made the call to the police after the killing. And although it was the type of emotive reasoning she would not have expected from a hardened burglar, it nevertheless kind of rang true.

Still, she had difficulty quelling a somewhat cynical feeling about it. Was there another, darker reason for what he had done? Or was she overanalyzing it?

Jayne shook herself out of her thinking pattern. She needed to get away from Knapp's house before Foster's officers returned, which she guessed could happen any minute.

She started the engine and drove back to the main road, then headed through Hastings in the direction of Pevensey once more.

This time she did not drive to the parking lot at the Royal Oak and Castle but instead diverted past the Pevensey Recreation Ground, where she saw to her satisfaction that a police forensics van was parked and a white tent had been erected above the patch of mud where she had found the footprints and skid mark.

Jayne continued past the pub and antiques dealership and pulled over to the side of the street to think through her next step.

She still had a strong, almost unstoppable desire to get to the bottom of who had killed Curtis Steyn—she recognized it was a personal desire because of Simone and it was a professional one, because of Vic's request.

In an ideal world, she would now go to Foster with the partial license plate number she had and ask him to take it from there. But she figured he was likely to be so angry with her for revisiting Knapp that he might refuse. It seemed risky. There might be some kind of dramatic showdown, and she could do without that.

Rather, if she could just get the full license plate number, then she could call Bunting instead and ask him to trace the owner. He seemed far more likely to be helpful.

But how could she get the full number? The obvious way would be to obtain some CCTV images. Now that she knew most of the plate number and the car model, video footage should yield the rest. But where from?

There were no obvious CCTV cameras outside the Royal

Oak, but perhaps the killer had driven past other premises that did have cameras installed.

Jayne took out her phone and started up her maps app in satellite mode once again. She studied the route heading west out of Pevensey in the direction of the town of Eastbourne, which lay about three or four miles away.

Her immediate thought was to look for pubs, restaurants, or petrol stations along the route, as they were the most likely types of establishment to have CCTV. Sure enough, there was a pub only a few hundred yards west of the castle, the Heron, and another one slightly farther away.

It also seemed obvious to Jayne that if the gunman had driven from Pevensey directly to London in order to kill Gareth Weber, he would not have been on local roads for long. He would have headed straight for the capital on the fastest route—one of the A-roads that ran through Sussex northward.

Both the pubs she had spotted were on the route she guessed the killer might have followed, taking him to the A27 and A22 arteries that headed toward London. She decided to try the Heron first.

She put the rented green BMW into gear and navigated the half mile or so to the pub, where she pulled into the parking lot that ran down the left side of the historic-looking building. The pub was painted mainly cream with blue details and had flower tubs filled with spring daffodils standing outside.

Jayne cast an eye over the gabled frontage and arched windows. There was an advertising sticker for Harvey's Sussex Best Bitter in the door window, which reminded Jayne of a night out she had had in Eastbourne many years earlier when she had enjoyed a few glasses of that particular beer. Then she spotted what she was looking for: two CCTV cameras pointing toward the quaint-looking street, which was mainly lined with ancient Tudor and redbrick cottages.

She was about to climb out of the car and go find the pub landlord when her phone rang. It was Foster.

"Hello, Aidan."

"We've nailed Knapp for the burglary," Foster said without preamble, his voice low and level. "Now we'll grill him and find out exactly what he saw outside as well."

Jayne remained silent for a second. Surely the footprints hadn't brought a result that quickly. "What do you mean you've nailed him?"

"It was a bunch of hairs our techs found on the floor of the antiques office. He must have scratched his head or something. The DNA cross-matched with our database. Got the results through just twenty minutes ago."

"That's great news," Jayne said, thinking furiously. Should she now disclose that she too had had a success with Knapp, albeit of a very different kind than Foster? If she did, Foster would likely give her a telling off in no uncertain terms.

"Yes. We're arresting him right now. He was still at home. We've also got the forensics from the footprints in the mud you told us about, although they're somewhat superfluous now. We found some muddy running shoes in his house, and we're cross-matching the prints."

Jayne decided she had better come clean now, while the detective chief inspector was still in a good mood following his triumph with the DNA match. Knapp now seemed certain to be convicted of the antiques burglary, for which he deserved a long prison sentence.

"I have a confession to make," Jayne said. "I went to Knapp's house and got some information."

"You did *what*?"

"Yes, sorry. I managed to get a car plate number off him. The one for the killer's car in the pub car park."

"What did you do that for? Are you trying to screw up the whole thing? I gave you instructions not to get involved any further in this investigation. I said leave it to us. We're all over this, as you can see."

"I know, I know. I apologize. I can see you're all over it." She paused for a second. "But I did get some vital information."

Jayne briefly described what she had learned from Knapp, her pride causing her to omit the detail of how she had been ambushed and pinned to the wall as she entered the conservatory. That had been amateurish, to say the least, and she wasn't going to admit it, especially to an arrogant cop like Foster.

"How the hell did you persuade him to give up that detail?"

"I'll tell you when I see you. The important point is I'm at a pub in Westham, the Heron, that might have CCTV footage of the killer's car as it drove past. We know part of the plate number, so video can give us the rest. I was about to go and see the pub landlord and—"

"Well, don't go and see the bloody landlord. Wait until we get there. We'll get the footage, if he's got any. That's our job, not yours."

"I know it's your job. I—"

"I'm not interested in excuses. You spooks are all the same. You obviously think you can operate the same way around here as you do in Moscow or Kabul or somewhere. It's not Moscow rules around here—it's Sussex police rules. I might come myself, actually. Just sit in your car and don't bloody move. You got that?"

Jayne exhaled. This guy liked to be in control—a bit like her. She had to concede he was correct in terms of pure police process. But would Knapp have given up the information she had secured if he had been arrested first? Almost certainly not.

"All right, I'm sitting tight," Jayne said.

"We'll see you in about twenty minutes."

Sure enough, almost on the dot, Foster arrived at the pub twenty minutes later in an unmarked black police Volvo.

He climbed out, tieless and with white shirt sleeves rolled up, along with a colleague wearing a dark suit, and walked over to Jayne's car. She wound down the window.

"We can talk about police process later," Foster said, his face grim. "You wait here, and we'll go and see if we can get the footage."

He beckoned his colleague, and they disappeared into the side door of the pub.

Jayne settled back in her seat, anticipating another long wait. It was bound to take some considerable time to go through recordings that were a couple of days old, assuming that the device the pub used kept old footage. She knew that some of the older security recording equipment only kept recordings for about twenty-four hours. She would have to hope the Heron's was better than that.

While she was waiting, Jayne sent a message to Nicklin-Donovan, updating him on what had happened and, mindful of his instruction not to interfere with the police investigation, downplaying the degree to which she had done exactly that. She expressed cautious optimism that progress was being made in terms of tracing the killer of Curtis and Gareth.

To her relief, a short reply from Nicklin-Donovan came back almost immediately.

Good work. Let me know further progress.

There was still no reply from Simone. But it was to be expected. She must have been devastated by what had happened as well as inundated with calls and messages.

Then Jayne exchanged a series of text messages with Joe in Portland, using the secure link the pair of them always used when communicating. She started by telling him what had happened and expressing some frustration with the process-driven nature of police work.

Foster reminds me of the pen pushers at Vauxhall Cross, she wrote.

Joe replied swiftly. *Media coverage of the deaths widespread here. President under increasing pressure and political oppo vultures circling. Stories in WaPo and Monitor suggesting a recent big fight between Steyn and NH state governor over some major financial matter—defense contract procurement or something.*

That gave Jayne pause. She had seen much of the news coverage online but guessed that in the pressure cooker environment at the White House, the situation would be extremely tense. The stories in *The Washington Post* and the *Concord Monitor* sounded potentially significant, so she made a mental note to read them online later.

But with each successive exchange of messages, the tone of the conversation changed and became increasingly flirty. Jayne's mood lightened considerably as they took turns at describing how and precisely why, in physical terms, they were missing each other and what they would do to each other once they were reunited in the king-size bed in Joe's two-story Cape Cod—style house on Parsons Road.

A grin crossed her face as she pictured Joe tapping away on his phone while sitting in his favorite chair on his porch in the garden, no more than a long stone's throw from Back Cove, an inlet that led off Casco Bay on the Atlantic coast. His teenage kids, Carrie and Peter, whom she had grown to love, would be at school, and Joe was likely by himself at home.

It actually felt a bit strange to be engaged in an investigation without Joe. The past few had all been in tandem with him and had been initiated by him, and she had thoroughly enjoyed the sheer adrenaline rush that had come from working alongside him and gradually falling back in love with him at the same time.

But if Jayne was to be honest with herself, the work she was doing now was also somewhat liberating. She was, after all, something of an introvert, a loner, who drew energy from time spent by herself and by working on her own initiative. Maybe acting as a sole operator would suit her on occasion. The challenge would lie in delivery. Could she succeed by herself?

Jayne's concentration on the messages was such that she failed to notice Foster had emerged from the pub until he knocked on her car window.

She jumped in slight surprise, put her phone down and got out of the car.

"How did you get on?" she asked, trying to be polite.

"We've got it," Foster said, his face still somewhat stony. "Thankfully he's got a decent CCTV system." He nodded at Jayne. "Job done."

"Excellent," Jayne said. "That's great. So quick too." It was not a bad idea to flatter him a little, given the look on his face.

She looked him in the eye. "Listen, I apologize for jumping into your investigation when I shouldn't have. It wasn't correct procedure."

Foster inclined his head to one side. "It damn well wasn't, no."

"I didn't mean any disrespect."

"Apology accepted. We got a result but let's not see a repeat performance. Understood?"

Time to swallow humble pie, Jayne thought. "Yes, completely."

"Good."

It seemed as though they had a truce. It was time to change the topic.

"Are you able to run the plate through your system?" She didn't dare ask what the full plate number was.

"Done it already," Foster said. "It's a rented car. Came from Heathrow."

A jolt went through Jayne.

That figured.

Her thoughts all along had been that the killings of Curtis Steyn and Gareth Weber had the hallmarks of some professional hitman, probably an international operator, stamped all over them.

"I assume it was one of the big rental companies."

"Yes. Thrifty. We're heading to the airport now to see them," Foster said, placing his hands on his hips.

Jayne hesitated for a second. "I don't want to intrude further, but if you don't mind, I'd like to come along with you to Heathrow. I'd just like to be around when you finish this one off."

Foster exhaled and said nothing for a second or two. Then he shrugged and threw up his hands. "You can't come in the car, no. We've got some confidential calls we need to make." He hesitated, then continued. "But I suppose you can follow us if you want to."

That suited Jayne. She couldn't take a couple of hours of Foster's high-handed patter in any case. And anyway, she needed to get her car back to London.

"That's fine. I'll tag along behind you. Thanks."

* * *

Wednesday, April 1, 2015
    Heathrow Airport

. . .

The car rental company office and parking lot, located on an industrial stretch less than half a mile south of Heathrow's Terminal Four, was typical of the type found all over the world: a single-story, prefabricated building in the center of an expanse of tarmac that was crammed with cars, vans, and 4x4s.

Foster pulled up outside the office and strode in with his colleague without waiting for Jayne, who parked and then hurried in after him. He had already located the manager, a skinny guy in his early thirties who nervously scrutinized Foster's police warrant card that showed his official ID.

"We need to check this vehicle," Foster said, pushing a piece of paper that bore the Passat's license plate number across the desk to the manager.

The manager moved to his computer terminal. "I will check that registration number for you, sir. Hang on."

He scrolled through a few screens of details and then hunched over the terminal, both hands cupping his chin and elbows propped on the desk.

"Yes, I have the vehicle here. It's out with another customer at the moment, unfortunately. They took it first thing this morning. It was returned on Monday morning."

Jayne swore inwardly, although it was too much to hope that the killer still had possession of it and might show up behind the wheel. Monday morning would have been a few hours after the killer had gunned down Gareth Weber in his Barbican apartment.

"Well, can you tell us who was renting it on Sunday and Monday?" Foster's colleague asked.

The manager clicked over to another screen and again scrutinized the contents. "Yes, it was a guy who came in here on Sunday afternoon. I didn't see him. My weekend duty manager dealt with him. A Canadian passport holder. Rudy Kurnow."

Jayne stepped forward. "Do you have video cameras operating in here?" She pointed to a camera mounted to the ceiling just above the manager's desk. Foster flashed her an irritated look.

"Yes, we record everything. Just in case," the manager said.

"Could you possibly get the footage of when this Mr. Kurnow came in, please?" Jayne asked, ignoring Foster's continued look. "It would be useful to see."

The manager stared at Jayne for a couple of seconds. "You'll have to wait. It may take a little time. I suggest you all take a seat." He indicated toward a row of seats next to the office window.

The manager turned his back and disappeared into a room at the rear of the office.

It was certain that the Passat had been rented under a false identity, so Jayne knew that video footage of the driver's face would need to be run through intelligence agency facial recognition systems. She had in mind the Tundra Freeze database, operated by the National Security Agency at Fort Meade, Maryland, and the British equivalent, run by Government Communications Headquarters—GCHQ—in Cheltenham. It was likely that Foster would also want to run it through the police national database too.

There was a chance that the gunman's face could have been recorded somewhere along with his true identity.

Jayne sent two short messages—the first to Vic, the second to Nicklin-Donovan—both with an update about the video, asking them to put the NSA and GCHQ on standby. There were definitely advantages in such situations to having contacts in both camps.

Vic replied immediately. *Not a problem, will contact them now.*

A minute later a second message arrived from Vic.

FYI president increasingly focused on this. Potential for blowback in his direction with opposition becoming hostile. Anything you can get will be helpful. Might be more requests to follow. Also might need you to return here for discussions on next steps.

Jayne mentally shrugged. She wasn't surprised to read about the political fallout. In the febrile environment of Washington politics, any sign of trouble or weakness on the part of President Ferguson was inevitably targeted for political gain by his enemies, of whom there were many, especially with preparations for the following year's presidential election already beginning. In particular, any issues occurring overseas for which the president did not have immediate answers or solutions were the subject of close focus. The cold-blooded murders of two reasonably high-profile state officials fell very much into that category.

She replied briefly.

Political blowback predictable. Hope to have update very soon.

After about twenty-five minutes, the manager reappeared and beckoned the three of them into the rear office. On a monitor screen was the frozen image of a man walking through the front door of the office.

"Watch this," the manager said. "See if this is what you need."

He pressed the space bar on his computer keyboard, and the video began to roll.

The man, stockily built with unkempt, long blond hair that was receding on both sides of his temples, moved awkwardly through the door and walked with something of a limp to the counter. There was no sound, so Jayne had only the image to work with.

The footage showed the man, who also had a large, equally unkempt mustache, producing his passport, driver's license, and credit card. None of them seemed to provoke any reaction from the manager as he scanned the documents and processed the transaction. Clearly they had all appeared in order and had triggered no alerts.

The blond man signed the documents and then waited while the manager disappeared, presumably to fetch the keys for the Passat.

It was at that point that the man glanced around the office, first to his left, then to his right, and then finally upward, straight at the camera.

Jayne leaned forward and peered at the monitor. "Stop the video there," she said.

The manager obediently tapped the space bar on his keyboard, and the video stopped.

Jayne scrutinized the image of the customer's face.

"You recognize him or something?" Foster's colleague asked.

"I don't know. I don't think so, but I'm not sure." The face somehow rang a bell at the back of Jayne's mind, but she couldn't work out why, or who it might be.

Foster turned to the manager. "Can we get a copy of this video, please? On a flash drive or memory card if possible."

"And copies of his ID documents and the rental agreement with his signature too, please," Jayne added.

The man nodded. "Sure. I'll get you all that." He turned back to his keyboard and tapped away for several minutes, then inserted a small SD memory card into his computer. After a few moments, he withdrew the card and handed it to Foster.

"It's on there."

"Thanks." Foster looked at Jayne, who had also stood. "We'd better run this through the database as fast as possible. I'm assuming your spook colleagues will need this immediately too."

Jayne's view of Foster softened a little. He was doing the right things and saw the urgency in the situation.

"Yes, definitely. I've warned them it's coming."

"I can send it from my laptop in the car."

Jayne nodded. "Thank you. You can send it to me. I will forward it."

The three of them shook the manager's hand, took his business card, and made their way to the parking lot, where Foster and Jayne climbed into the front seats of the Volvo, the other officer into the back.

Foster loaded the contents of the SD card onto his police laptop, dispatched it to a colleague who would run it through the police national database, and then also sent it to Jayne using a secure connection.

"Now we wait. Let's see which of the two organizations works the fastest," Foster said. "I assume it's going to GCHQ?"

"Yes, correct, via Vauxhall Cross," Jayne said.

Foster glanced at Jayne in the passenger seat. "I think I've broken a number of rules by working with you in this way, but never mind. We somehow appear to be getting the job done. Thanks for your inputs." He gave a faint smile.

Jayne nodded. "No problem."

She then sent the video and documents to Nicklin-Donovan. She didn't dare to tell Foster it had gone to a third organization—at Langley—and that a fourth, the NSA, would also be analyzing them. Her guess was that that number of rule breakages would without a doubt ignite another explosion from the detective chief inspector.

She gratefully accepted Foster's suggestion that while they were waiting, they drive to a nearby Starbucks for a much-needed coffee. She decided to take her car so she didn't need to return and collect it later.

It was an hour and a quarter later, while they were each on their second latte, that Jayne's phone rang. It was Vic, calling on his secure line. It seemed that the Americans had won the race.

Jayne typed in her key in order to accept the call. "Hang on, give me a minute," she said to Vic.

She excused herself to Foster and his colleague, not wanting to conduct a conversation with the CIA within the policemen's earshot, and made her way outside to the coffee shop parking lot.

"All right, Vic, what have you got?" she asked.

"Are you sitting down?"

"Unfortunately not."

Vic hesitated. "I've just had a call from Fort Meade. Your man is not Rudy Kurnow from Toronto."

"I was assuming that, Vic." Jayne tried to keep the sarcasm out of her voice, but knew she had failed. "Tell me something I don't know."

"He's Russian."

A chill ran down Jayne's back.

"*Russian?* Are they certain?"

"Yes, it's certain. And more than that, it's someone whose name you might recognize."

Jayne pressed her lips together. "Go on."

"It's Georgi Tkachev."

Jayne now felt as though she did indeed want to sit down. "The Kremlin's assassin," she murmured. "My God."

Something immediately struck her about the video she had seen. "What about the long scar on his cheek?" Jayne asked. There had been no sign in the video of the old wound that Tkachev carried on the left side of his face.

"They think makeup was used. The video enhancement tool picked that up," Vic said.

The last time she had seen Tkachev had been eight months earlier, when he was lying with heavily bleeding and seemingly fatal leg injuries on the concrete floor of an enormous empty petrol tank at a refinery at Tuapse, on Russia's Black Sea coast. He had been a victim of an enormous explosion that Jayne had triggered in order to rescue Joe from a likely grim fate at the hands of the Russians.

At the time, she and Joe had had pistols in hand and the opportunity to dispatch Tkachev for good. But being of a mind not to take someone's life in cold blood and not unless their own was threatened, they had instead chosen to leave him, confident he was bleeding out and was on the way to meet his Maker in any case.

Except the former GRU Spetsnaz special forces operative apparently was not dead.

PART TWO

PART TWO

CHAPTER ELEVEN

Thursday, April 2, 2015
Moscow

There had been nothing concrete. No official memo or briefing or report. There had been no scheduled meeting to discuss its implications, as far as Major General Anastasia Shevchenko could determine. But at the beginning of that week, rumors trickled slowly through the sprawling main office complex at Yasenevo, south of Moscow, which housed the headquarters of Russia's foreign intelligence service, the SVR.

As far as Shevchenko could determine, based on a snatched conversation overheard outside Director Maksim Kruglov's office, an operation in the UK, using one of the Kremlin's small but deadly team of freelance former Spetsnaz operatives, had resulted in the demise of two American nationals.

Indeed, by Monday afternoon, the news of their killings

had hit the media, and there was a rash of stories running on all the US- and UK-based satellite news channels. None of the news organizations nor security services or police, in either the UK or US, had been able to determine a motivation for the murders.

It appeared to be yet another bloody secret to add to the hundreds, thousands, that the SVR's walls had kept tight over the decades.

Though not surprised, Shevchenko, promoted the previous September to deputy director in charge of Directorate KR, the foreign counterintelligence department, wanted to know why. Information at the SVR was strictly compartmentalized on a need-to-know basis. But she intended to find out. It was a detail that she knew would be invaluable to her new unofficial paymasters at the CIA.

So she had gotten to work. Like anyone with access to online news websites, she knew that the victims were the secretaries of state for New Hampshire and Wisconsin. But more information was harder to come by. It seemed odd that two relatively obscure regional bureaucrats should be the target of such a clinical assassination operation. There had to be a good reason for it.

Now, three days later, Shevchenko had still not been able to determine the reason for the strikes. One murder had apparently been carried out in a parking lot within a few meters of a castle she had once visited as a tourist eighteen months ago during her ill-fated stint in the SVR's London *rezidentura*.

Shevchenko had spent the morning thinking the issue over in her private second-floor office. It was located at the end of the northeastern wing of the Y-shaped original office building that, together with an adjoining twenty-one-story block, formed the heart of the Yasenevo complex, known to all as Moscow Center.

Since taking up her new role, Shevchenko had done very little to channel intelligence to the Americans to whom she had offered her services that fateful day in Washington, DC, at the end of July the previous year.

There were very good reasons for this. The new role, running foreign counterintelligence for the SVR, effectively spying on Russia's spies and—ironically—looking for moles in the organization, was highly complex and very demanding.

For example, a case she was currently engaged with, involving a senior SVR officer working undercover in the Paris *rezidentura* as an industrial attaché, had taken up much of her time recently. He was suspected of being in the pay of the French intelligence service, the Direction Générale de la Sécurité Extérieure, the DGSE. However, she was still searching for proof, and it was proving a difficult task.

As a result, she hardly had time to breathe, let alone think about setting up lines of communication with the Americans, dead drops, and methods of securely copying documents. Instead she had spent her time working fourteen and sometimes sixteen hours a day at Yasenevo, punctuated with trips to foreign capitals to carry out interviews and investigations into certain SVR officials who, like the officer in Paris, were suspected of leaking Russia's secrets to foreign governments.

Furthermore, Shevchenko knew that following her return from Washington seven months earlier, she was under considerable scrutiny and suspicion in certain quarters within the organization.

While in Washington, Shevchenko's main source in the US government, the president's national security advisor, Francis Wade, had committed suicide just after a covert meeting with her had been discovered and blown by the CIA. She had been caught at the same time and had offered to spy for the Americans in exchange for a cover-up of her failure. To ensure the plan worked, the CIA and the White House had portrayed the suicide as purely linked to the security advisor's affair and failing marriage and had suppressed the fact that he was a traitor.

Her inability to keep the meeting and her source secure and covert was, in truth, a serious professional failure on her part and the second similar disaster within a few months, the previous one being in London. Without the cover-up and alliance with the CIA, the alternative would without doubt have been a summary ejection from the United States for espionage, followed by a consequential dismissal in disgrace from the SVR and exile to some modern-day gulag—a penal colony or remote prison where death would probably seem an attractive option.

It was obviously impossible that her failure in Washington was known to the SVR, otherwise the promotion would not have been confirmed.

Based on her outstanding previous track record over a long period, apart from the operation that had gone wrong in London, the overall SVR director, Maksim Kruglov, had championed her appointment. Another who had pushed her for promotion had been none other than Igor Ivanov, special advisor to the president and a master of the dark arts of manipulation. These were powerful men indeed.

But there were definitely those who viewed her with suspicion, including her former boss Yevgeny Kutsik, whose role she had taken over following his promotion to head of Directorate PR, political intelligence, and confirmation as first deputy director of the SVR, or number two to Kruglov.

She was good at picking up on the unconscious signals given by others, and she could see the unspoken doubts in Kutsik's shrewd eyes and shifts in his body language when he had conversations with her.

To Kutsik, a naturally cynical character who had been well suited to counterintelligence, the American national security advisor's suicide had seemed too coincidental and the explanation from the White House too glib and well-rehearsed. To him, the long gap between Shevchenko's covert meeting with Wade and her next contact with Moscow Center was suspicious.

It had not been a surprise, therefore, when she had been subjected to four countersurveillance interviews during her first two months in her new role. Shevchenko knew that Kutsik and others had probably whispered in Director Kruglov's ear.

Because Shevchenko headed up the counterintelligence directorate, the interviews were carried out by Gennady Sidorenko, a paunchy man with somewhat protruding blue eyes, who was chief of the specialist small counterintelligence team located within Kruglov's office, quite separate from her own department.

The counterintelligence team spying on counterintelligence. Dog hunting dog.

The director's counterintelligence team, known internally as DX, consisted of only eight people. Sidorenko, previously head of Directorate KR and therefore a former occupant of Shevchenko's current office, was given the role of running it after proving himself to be unsuited to managing the sprawling and huge main counterintelligence operation. He was known as a notorious sadist who liked nothing better than the opportunity to interrogate victims in a soundproof basement suite at Lefortovo or Butyrka prisons.

Like Kruglov, Sidorenko was known to be close to Ivanov, the black-eyed former GRU officer who was now in charge of special operations at the Kremlin—effectively Putin's right-hand man. Ivanov used Sidorenko almost like his own personal interrogator when required.

All of the interviews Sidorenko subjected Shevchenko to were quite general in tone, asking about her contacts both inside the SVR and externally, her methods of working, her interests outside work, her friends, and her extracurricular activities.

He behaved himself. There was no physical contact. But all the interviews touched on the operation in Washington and the subsequent death of Wade, as well as her previous failure in London. She had kept her nerve and stuck to her story, but she was clearly on a list of those to watch that had been drawn up by someone.

Therefore, Shevchenko had kept her head down in an effort to rebuild trust. She took no risks during those first few months, and the only communications she had with Langley were carried out via the Agency's Moscow chief of station, Ed Grewall, using very occasional short and bland text messages from a burner phone that she stored in a cavity behind a maintenance hatch in the emergency rear stairwell of the apartment block in which she lived.

The precaution proved a sound one. Indeed, when Shevchenko carried out a sweep of her home, a two-bedroom apartment on Ulitsa Seregina street, northwest of Moscow's city center, she found evidence that Sidorenko's team had been at work. There were two tiny microphones, one concealed in a ceiling rose in her living room and another in an air-conditioning unit in her bedroom. She had left them in place, not wanting to alert the counterintelligence team that she was aware of being under surveillance, and instead made all phone calls and worked on her laptop from her spare bedroom, which was clear of bugs.

They had undoubtedly searched her apartment but had been too professional to leave any noticeable traces.

It was a concern, though not a shock, that SVR technicians had been to access her fifth-floor apartment so easily. It overlooked Petrovsky Park and was less than a kilometer from the home ground of her beloved Dynamo Moscow soccer team, which was currently in the middle of being rebuilt after the old stadium had been closed for demolition in 2008.

Despite the obvious surveillance on her, she had felt obliged to use the burner phone to send a slightly longer missive on Tuesday evening, two days ago.

Strong internal rumor circulating re Russian role in UK killings. Trying to get more information. Will report back soon as possible.

Shevchenko leaned back in her huge black leather swivel office chair and placed her hands behind her head, as she often did when she needed to think. She might need to think laterally in this situation. How could she find out more about the assassinations in the UK without making it obvious? After all, she had no real reason for doing so.

There was one other person within the SVR who she knew was a mole for Western intelligence, and that was Pavel Vasilenko, second in command of the American department, which was located on the third floor, one story up from her own office.

She only knew about Vasilenko because the CIA had asked her to smuggle a few requests for information to him a few months earlier. It was seen as a priority for Vasilenko—an obvious recruitment target for Langley, given his American desk role—to have the minimum amount of direct contact with anyone at the Agency, to reduce the chances of discovery. So they had asked Shevchenko to pass on the messages instead.

Perhaps she should now use him to carry out the subtle inquiry that would be needed to discover the background to the shootings. As a senior American department leader, it would be more natural for him to ask the questions. It would certainly be less problematic than trying to do it herself.

In her counterintelligence role, she would naturally have Vasilenko on her watch list of SVR officials on whom she would need to keep a close eye, given his access to a large amount of top-secret US-related material. Therefore she could quite plausibly spend some time with him on the pretext of carrying out a routine interview without raising any red flags with suspicious onlookers. It would hopefully be seen as just another of the face-to-face meetings with senior officials that she needed to carry out in the normal course of her counterintelligence duties.

Shevchenko rose from her seat and went to the window, where she stared out over the large expanse of pavement that formed the parking lot outside the building. Unlike Kutsik, who had habitually kept the blinds closed and worked in semidarkness when occupying this office, Shevchenko liked to gaze into the distance for her inspiration and ideas.

She had watched the headquarters more than double in size since 2007 with the addition of several more buildings around the originals. To her regret, a huge number of trees had been hacked down to make space for the new offices and the accompanying parking spaces for vehicles. Everyone drove to Yasenevo and she guessed there were at least a couple thousand cars standing outside.

Shevchenko ran a hand through her dark hair flecked with gray. Yes, she would go and make an appointment for an interview with Vasilenko. That was the solution.

She made her way out of the department and up the stairs to the third floor, taking the steps two at a time. Her slim, wiry physique was very well toned, especially considering her fifty-nine years, and she was well aware that most men in the SVR in her age bracket did not fail to notice that. It was something she occasionally used to her advantage.

Vasilenko's modest office was located beyond that of his boss, the American department head and third deputy director, Fyodor Unkovsky. It was at the end of a corridor that housed portraits of the first three SVR directors following the split in 1991 of the old KGB into the SVR, which took over responsibility for foreign intelligence, and the FSB, domestic intelligence. There was also a large photograph of the White House in Washington, DC, in the same corridor.

As she turned a corner near to Vasilenko's office, to her dismay she almost bumped into Kutsik, who was heading in the opposite direction. She swiftly sidestepped to avoid a collision and nodded politely. She hadn't seen him for at least a couple of weeks, and he stopped and eyeballed her, his face unsmiling.

"Hello, Anastasia. How are you progressing?"

"I am working my way down a very long list of tasks and actions that need tackling." She shrugged. "I am getting there."

"Where are you heading now?"

She hesitated. There seemed no point in lying. "I am going to see Pavel Vasilenko." She tried to assume an air of bored indifference and added, "The usual checks. Routine."

"Good. Do call in to my office sometime soon. It would be useful to catch up with you." Kutsik held Shevchenko's gaze as he nodded again and then, to her relief, went on his way.

Shevchenko continued until she reached Vasilenko's office door, which was open a fraction. She paused and smiled when she caught the eye of his secretary, Ekaterina, who years earlier had been Shevchenko's own secretary and was among the few people she still trusted at Moscow Center. They were the same age and had grown up within a few hundred meters of each other in spacious, high-ceilinged apartments in Tsarist-era mansion buildings in central Moscow.

"Is he in there?" Shevchenko asked, pointing at the office door.

Ekaterina nodded. "Yes, and he is free."

Shevchenko thanked her and knocked firmly.

"*Da*. Come in."

Shevchenko pushed the door open to find Vasilenko sitting at his desk in front of her, the light glinting from his polished head, which was shaved all over in an attempt to deal with his rapidly receding hair.

Although the two of them were aware of each other's status on the CIA's payroll and that both were in touch with Ed Grewall, she still felt there was a risk attached to what she was about to do. Vasilenko had been keen on the Directorate KR role she had been given, and his feelings toward her might not be entirely benevolent. However, she had no choice, and in any case, both of them were in a position to literally have the other vaporized by the Kremlin—a kind of mutually assured destruction. Given that, she thought it unlikely that Vasilenko would do anything to harm her.

Five minutes later she left his office after a conversation during which neither made any verbal reference to the CIA, with an agreement to meet the following Monday morning at eleven o'clock for a standard countersurveillance interview. The agreed location was a safe house near the Botanical Gardens in central Moscow.

However, during their verbal conversation, the two of them also took turns to scribble short and cryptic notes in tiny writing on a small piece of paper that Shevchenko had brought with her.

Recent events UK? Shevchenko wrote in Russian.

I know a little. No detail, Vasilenko replied.

I need detail. Who and why.

Will discover more before Monday.

At that point, Shevchenko carefully ripped the piece of paper into tiny fragments. She then leaned over and fed them into the high-specification shredder next to Vasilenko's desk, which immediately chewed them into even smaller unreadable pieces.

Shevchenko left Vasilenko's office feeling as if she had made some progress. He seemed confident he could find out more. Hopefully, the conversation the pair of them would have on Monday would yield her far more than the usual type of counterintelligence interview.

CHAPTER TWELVE

Friday, April 3, 2015
Washington, DC

It had not been a surprise to Jayne to find herself summoned immediately back to Washington to brief Vic and Veltman in the wake of the discovery that one of the Kremlin's top-level undercover and deniable hitmen had been responsible for the killings of Curtis Steyn and Gareth Weber.

But within an hour and a half of waking up, she was somewhat stunned to find herself whisked by a CIA car from her hotel in downtown Washington not to Langley but to the White House instead.

Vic had called her before seven in the morning, when she was still half asleep and jet-lagged, to say that President Ferguson's aide, Charles Deacon, was asking for an urgent update meeting on the UK killings at nine o'clock. He needed to write a brief on current running foreign issues by noon for the president, who had a scheduled meeting early that afternoon with his secretary of state Paul Farrar.

Deacon wanted to include a mention of the killings in his brief because Farrar, in turn, was due to have a videoconference later that day with his new UK counterpart, foreign secretary Tim Pontefract, to discuss their strategy toward Europe and other issues. The likelihood was that the shootings would come up during that call.

The president also had a personal call due the following week with the Russian president, Vladimir Putin, to discuss Ukraine and put more pressure on him to withdraw his forces, Vic told Jayne. The call had been arranged because Ferguson wanted to underline the determination of the United States and the wider G7 to continue with sanctions against Russia. The president might include on the agenda for his call a protest at the UK killings, Vic said, adding that Deacon wanted to ensure that the UK was on board before making such a move so that communications could be coordinated.

Thus, at just before nine, Jayne found herself with the two Agency chiefs waiting in the White House Situation Room. It was her second visit there. The first had been the previous August following the recruitment of Shevchenko, when the president had requested a briefing from Veltman and Vic, which both she and Joe had attended.

Jayne, Vic, and Veltman were sitting along one side of a long, gleaming wooden table in the main conference room within the Situation Room. On the walls were a number of video screens, all of which were switched off apart from one, which showed CNN's rolling news channel.

Before her first visit, Jayne had envisaged the Situation Room as just one adrenaline- and testosterone-filled chamber, but she discovered that actually, it comprised an entire suite of rooms buried deep in the basement of the West Wing. It included a number of conference rooms, smaller meeting rooms, and another area from which watch officers monitored banks of screens and communications tools that received inputs from all over the world.

She had also expected the Situation Room to be a highly organized, formal place, but instead it appeared to her to be in a permanent state of disorganized hyperactivity. Four watch officers were going back and forth carrying a large number of heavy-looking cardboard boxes from a meeting room into the reception area.

Jayne and the others had been told to leave their cell phones in a lead-lined security box in reception. She found it slightly worrisome that this left her feeling somewhat anxious and antsy, a feeling not dissimilar to the one she'd heard ex-smokers describe in relation to giving up cigarettes. Smartphones were definitely addictive.

After a few minutes, Deacon walked through the door. He had acquired a salt-and-pepper beard since Jayne had last seen him, and his hair seemed less well-groomed, although his pair of black-rimmed glasses looked unchanged. He was tieless and carrying a plastic folder stuffed full of papers under his arm.

He sank into a chair on the opposite side of the table from his three visitors and gave an exaggerated sigh, accompanied by a grin. "I sometimes hate this job," he said. "Anyway, thanks for coming in. The boss has noted the UK killings, as you can probably imagine."

Deacon looked at Jayne. "I remember you from last year. I gather it was you who discovered the Russian connection?"

"Yes, it was," Jayne said. "It came as a shock too, given I thought the individual involved had departed this world last year."

"Indeed." Deacon shook his head slowly. "Anyway, that's good work. But the job's not finished because we don't have a clue about why these hits took place, which I guess is the crucial question. They were certainly well planned. Are you picking up anything at Langley?" He looked first at Veltman, then at Vic, and raised his eyebrows.

"We're cooperating closely with the Feebs on this," Vic said. "Iain Shepard's team is working on it."

Shepard was the FBI's executive assistant director in charge of the counterintelligence division, known internally as CD. Jayne had met him the previous year as part of the investigation into Shevchenko and Francis Wade.

"Any leads so far?" Deacon asked.

"Not much. There are a couple of—"

But Vic was interrupted by a slight commotion at the door, which swung open without a knock to reveal two men in dark suits standing outside. Then the door frame was filled by an imposing figure in a charcoal-gray suit. It was President Ferguson.

"Charles, I need to interrupt you for a second," the president said. "I've just had a conference call with London. I'm going to need that briefing from you at eleven, not twelve." The president drew himself up to his full six feet two inches and eyeballed Deacon. "Plans are changing."

From his vantage point in the doorway he glanced around the room and took in the identities of the visitors. "Ah, Mr. Veltman and Mr. Walter. What brings you here this morning?"

"The secretary of state killings, Mr. President," Veltman said. "We're briefing Charles, sir."

"Yes, I noted that. Worrisome. I'd like to know a little more, given the Russian involvement. I may raise it with Putin on my call next week."

"I'm getting a download from these two," Deacon said. "I'll include it in your briefing, sir."

"Good," Ferguson said. His gaze came to rest on Jayne. He then glanced momentarily over his shoulder, seemingly checking that his Secret Service agents were out of earshot.

"And I think I recognize you," he said as he turned back to her. "You helped bring in the SVR woman last year. I apologize, I've forgotten your name. Wait, is it Jayne?"

"Yes, Mr. President, Jayne Robinson. We had a briefing here after we recruited the person you're referring to."

"Thought so. Are you working on this UK issue now too?"

Vic leaned forward. "She is. It was Jayne who discovered the Russian connection to these shootings, sir."

Ferguson pursed his lips and nodded. "Very good. Important work. Keep me briefed. We need to get to the bottom of this."

The president glanced at Veltman. "I'm hoping to get some results from your SVR friend before long—I need to know Putin's thinking on Ukraine. I'd like confirmation that he knows he's fighting a losing battle there. Intel is critical. But I gather she's been running silent and deep so far?"

The president was known for his frequent use of submarine terminology during meetings, a throwback to his time working on subs in the US Navy during the Cold War.

"She has," Veltman said. "But that is by design, sir. We haven't wanted her to surface too early. There are some in her service who don't entirely trust her. However, we have had a couple of short communications from her indicating rumors at Yasenevo of Kremlin involvement in the UK killings. We expect her to send further details."

The president's eyes narrowed a little, and he ran a hand across his neatly coiffured gray hair. "Interesting. She is in a very good position to get what we need, I would guess. Did that come via your Moscow station?"

"Yes. Via Ed Grewall, sir. And we plan to connect her with Jayne here too. I'll make sure Charles gets what few details we have for his brief."

"Good. I would like some concrete evidence of why they've done this, and I can't afford to let it drag on for a long time." His eyes flicked back to Jayne. "Just make damned sure you don't lose Shevchenko overboard in the process."

Ferguson glanced at his watch. "I need to go. I'll look forward to reading the brief later, Charles."

With that, he was gone.

There was a pause. Veltman turned toward Jayne. "I think you've got a foot in the door with him." He inclined his head toward the door where Ferguson had just been standing.

She looked at him quizzically. "What do you mean?"

"He remembered your name. He usually doesn't remember mine. And you heard what he said. Just make damned sure you don't lose our Russian friend overboard."

Deacon grinned at the joke.

Vic leaned forward and caught Jayne's eye. "I think that first, though, you need to go see your friend Simone and see what she's got to say for herself. She's been running silent too, it seems to me."

CHAPTER THIRTEEN

Saturday, April 4, 2015
   Concord, New Hampshire

Jayne leaned over from the front passenger seat and kissed Joe, who had turned off the engine of his blue Ford Explorer and was smiling at her.

"Thanks," she said, winking as she dropped a hand down onto the top of his thigh and squeezed it. "I'll find a way to repay you. I do appreciate you bringing me down here. I'll call you when I'm finished."

Joe had driven her southwest from their home in Portland to the New Hampshire state capital, Concord, a journey of an hour and three-quarters, for her meeting with Simone. While they talked, he would take a walk around the city center and explore a little.

"No problem, though I'll still look forward to the repayment," he replied with a smile, caressing the back of her neck. "Besides, it was nice to have some time to chat. I sometimes wish I was on this investigation too."

"You can be if you like."

But Joe shook his head. "I need a break, and it's not my type of project. It's your show this time."

Jayne smiled and climbed out of the car. She knew Joe preferred his investigations to have a war crimes angle of some type.

They had parked only a stone's throw from the imposing gray granite walls and portico of the state capitol building. A sign proclaimed it to be the oldest state house in the country where the legislature was still in its original chambers. An American flag fluttered from a post positioned high up in front of the building's central tower, which had a golden dome.

She walked southward down North Main Street and turned right onto Pleasant Street, where she found, just as her friend Simone had described, the café White Mountain Gourmet Coffee in an elegant redbrick building across the street.

Jayne pushed open the café door and looked around. It was a narrow space with high ceilings, spotlights, and a long counter with a vast array of different coffee beans stored in jars along the left side.

She still felt slightly put out that Simone had proposed meeting here rather than inviting her to her smart home near the Merrimack River, where she had been a couple of times before.

But she accepted Simone's explanation that she needed to get out of the house and escape the endless stream of phone calls and visitors following her husband's demise. It was anything but a normal death, and the consequent media and political attention the case had received must have seemed overwhelming. Jayne didn't envy her friend.

Jayne eventually spotted her, sitting at a circular table toward the rear of the café, slightly apart from the other tables. She was tapping on her phone screen, and a full glass of orange juice stood in front of her.

Simone looked up as Jayne approached. Her face was definitely grayer and more lined than it had been when Jayne had last seen her, and she hadn't bothered to put on any makeup, which was unusual. She was wearing tortoiseshell glasses instead of her usual contact lenses, and her long hair, usually thick and lustrous despite the inevitable heavy gray streaks amid the original auburn, looked somewhat dank and unkempt.

She stood and gave Jayne a hug, but it seemed mechanical and different than Simone's usual enthusiastic, emotional greeting.

"How are you doing, Simone?" Jayne asked. "I've been worried about you."

They sat down on opposite sides of the table, facing each other.

"It's been bizarre. I can't get my head around it," Simone said. "One minute he was there, the next he's gone. Since then, things have been utterly chaotic. I've had the FBI on the phone or visiting just about every day, asking question after question. Most of them I just can't answer. I've had relatives, friends, my attorney, Curtis's work colleagues, all descending on me. It's been extremely stressful. That's why I needed to get out of the house for a change to meet you here."

Although her travels and years living in the US had softened Simone's original Nottingham accent significantly, making it much lighter than Jayne's, it was still there, particularly in the way she pronounced her vowels.

"I'm sure it's been chaotic," Jayne said. "And it's more than bizarre."

Simone looked down at her glass. "I feel like I've hit rock-bottom, to be honest. It's one thing to lose your husband—

these things happen to people—but it's the circumstances that have completely knocked me sideways. I feel like I've been hit by a truck or something."

She shut her eyes momentarily and pressed her lips together. The pain was obvious.

"Yes, I know. I keep trying to put myself in your position," Jayne said. "But I can't even begin to imagine it."

Simone opened her eyes and shook her head. "Are you having something to drink?" she asked

Jayne looked around. "This looks like the kind of place where the coffee is going to be very good. I think a cappuccino. Would you like one too? I'll buy—I insist. I think you need one."

"Oh, thank you. And yes, please. A latte for me."

Jayne got up, walked to the counter, and placed her order. It was hard to know what to say to comfort her friend. Words and phrases came to mind, but they all seemed too trite and inconsequential. Maybe she should try and focus the conversation on the practicalities and do her best to get any information from Simone that might help the investigation. That was probably the most useful thing she could do.

When she returned with the steaming cups of coffee, the two of them spent the next few minutes discussing everything that had happened, including Jayne's recent findings in the UK. Thankfully, it turned out that the FBI had kept Simone up to date with most of it.

"So, the Russian involvement. What do you think?" Jayne asked.

Simone looked down. "I don't know what to think. But the FBI agents who came to see me yesterday asked me about Curtis's shareholding in US Defense Systems, which was quite significant, similar to Gareth Weber's. They both still have a lot of shares in the company."

"What's the significance of that?"

"Well, USDS sells a lot of military hardware to Ukraine. Curtis invested many years ago when it was a small business, and it grew massively."

"Ah, I see." Jayne knew only too well that any country or company selling military equipment to Ukraine was not going to be in favor with the Kremlin, given the conflict between the two countries that had been ongoing since Russia annexed the Crimean Peninsula from Ukraine in early 2014. But the more she considered the idea, the more it didn't seem to add up given the amount of time that had elapsed since their initial investment.

Jayne sipped her cappuccino gently.

"Since Curtis invested in USDS years ago, and he was later a government administrator, it doesn't seem to make sense that he's being targeted, even if he is still an investor in that company," Jayne said.

Simone twisted the ends of her hair in her right hand and swept it back over her shoulder. "I would agree, but I don't know. I'm just telling you what the FBI said."

"Not unless there was more to it than just being an investor," Jayne said.

Simone shrugged and sipped her juice. "I've no idea. To me, it seemed simply a sound investment, and I'm certain that Curtis just viewed it that way too. He occasionally updated me on how the shares were performing or what the company was doing. I don't think there was any more to it than that."

"That makes sense. An investment that came good. I could do with a few of those," Jayne said.

Simone nodded. "Listen, Jayne. Thank you for looking into all this over in Sussex. It means a lot. I know it took up a lot of time up and you were there for a break, not work." She wiped the back of her hand across both eyes.

"It's fine. It's the least I could do. After Cambridge '81, I still owe you. I'll never forget that."

It was true. Almost daily she still felt a deep gratitude toward Simone for the way in which she had sprinted down a dark alley, screaming at a man who was pushing a very drunken Jayne at knifepoint toward a waiting car. The man had turned and fired a stream of obscenities in Simone's direction. But when Simone had then bravely picked up a length of rusty steel from below a hedge and frenziedly whacked the man on the arm and shoulders with it, he had shoved Jayne into the hedge and run off.

She had been rescued from what would certainly have been a very messy fate, in which she would likely have been raped and killed. Although she had been in many hair-raising situations since during her professional life in the SIS and as a freelancer, the Cambridge episode had taken on a much greater significance, probably because she was younger and more vulnerable and impressionable.

Remarkably, Simone had then run after the man and memorized his car license plate number as he drove off, with the result that he was subsequently arrested and imprisoned for that and a number of other offenses.

"I acted on instinct," Simone said, now looking down at the floor again. "You'd have done the same for me."

Jayne liked to think she would have too, but thinking back to her twenty-year-old self, without any training in self-defense and against a man wielding a knife, she was unsure.

"Anyway, I think there's more to these shootings than is obvious," Jayne said. She hesitated, then decided she needed to revisit a question she had asked Simone earlier on the phone but that continued to trouble her. Circumstances had changed, and it needed asking again. "Do you think it's possible Curtis was involved in something dark that he never confided in you about?"

Simone looked up sharply. "What, you mean an affair?"

"I don't necessarily mean an affair. Anything. Maybe something business related. I don't know . . ." Her voice trailed off.

Simone shook her head. "Do we ever know everything about our spouses? I think not."

Jayne didn't feel particularly qualified to answer, given that she had never been married, although she had had a couple of long-term relationships in the past, prior to getting back together with Joe. But Simone had a point, and maybe she was trying to convey a message too.

"I don't want to pry, but what about your finances? Were you in a good position?" Jayne asked.

"You've seen our house. Mortgage paid off. Curtis had that big slab of USDS shares. He had a well-paid job. Get the picture?"

"I guess so."

They chatted for some time about how Simone was struggling to cope with the deluge of media interest and about how her two adult children were handling it.

Then Simone glanced at her watch, fished out a ten dollar bill from her purse, and put it on the table. "That's for my latte," she said. Then she stood.

"No, Simone. I said I'd buy the coffee. It's way too much, anyway."

"Sorry, Jayne. I must apologize, but I need to go. I don't want to appear rude, and you've come a long way. I really appreciate it. But I've got so much to do and I'm feeling overwhelmed, to be honest. I promised I would meet another friend outside in a minute. Everyone's been so kind, calling me and asking if they can meet up. I'm trying to fit everyone in, but it's difficult, and I'm feeling pressured about it all."

A little surprised, as she had made a hundred-mile journey and they had only been talking for half an hour, but at the same time understanding what Simone was saying, Jayne also rose. "Okay, I can see how difficult it is. It's good to have friends who care. Let's keep in touch. I'll let you know how things are going. I need to travel on business very soon, but I'll be on email, if not phone. Who are you meeting?"

"An old friend. Anna."

Jayne wished she could tell Simone she was probably heading to Russia, but that had to remain confidential given that the purpose of her visit wasn't entirely connected to Curtis's murder.

Simone gave Jayne a long, tight hug that was more in line with the warm, affectionate person she had always been, then stood back.

"Jayne. Just be careful," Simone said. She reached out and touched Jayne's elbow. "I appreciate all the work you're doing, and I really want to find out what happened—none of it seems to make any sense. But we've both seen what happened to Curtis. I don't want you to be hurt too."

Jayne nodded. "I will. Don't worry about me. You take care too."

Simone squeezed Jayne's arm, turned, and walked out.

Jayne paid the check and wandered outside. About thirty yards down the street she saw Simone deep in conversation with a slightly overweight woman with blond curly hair. After a few moments they both walked off together in the opposite direction.

CHAPTER FOURTEEN

Monday, April 6, 2015
Moscow

Shevchenko felt that there was no logical need to do a long surveillance detection route prior to her meeting with Vasilenko. After all, the planned meeting was ostensibly a standard counterintelligence interview of the type that she conducted quite widely with senior people across the SVR organization.

But she decided to do an SDR anyway, purely because she was interested to see whether she was under surveillance from someone in Sidorenko's team and, if so, how many observers were involved. That would give a clue as to how heavy an approach they were taking.

The route from her apartment on Ulitsa Seregina to the safe house—actually an apartment—in Protopopovskiy Pereulok was only about eight kilometers, and she would normally expect to drive it in about twenty-five minutes, possibly less, depending on the traffic. The usual route took her past the Dynamo Moscow soccer stadium site—currently a huge construction site—and onto the city's Third Ring Road heading east as far as Rizhsky railway station, then south along Prospekt Mira.

But today she took a much more circuitous route, south through Begovoy district, onto the Garden Ring, keeping a watch all the time in her mirrors for repeating vehicles. She slowed and she accelerated, checking her mirrors continuously for other vehicles doing likewise behind her. A stairstep route took her into the Arbat district, then westward over the Moskva River using Kutuzovsky Prospekt.

There was no sign of a tail, so eventually she doubled back on herself, driving along the river just south of the Kremlin and Red Square, heading north again, past the embassies and Moscow State University's botanical gardens until she reached her destination, not far from Prospekt Mira station, about an hour after leaving home.

The safe house was on the second floor of a modern four-story apartment building that was occupied by a mixture of young families, professional people, and retired folk. Shevchenko parked a couple hundred meters farther down the street and paused for ten minutes, watching carefully for surveillance. When she was confident there was none, she approached on foot, still seeing no sign of a tail.

It seemed that Sidorenko either did not know the meeting was taking place or had decided to leave his henchmen at home today.

Vasilenko had sent her a very short secure message the previous evening. *I have some of what you need. Details tomorrow.*

That was probably as close as Vasilenko could get to a positive message about what he had obtained, and it had put Shevchenko in a good frame of mind. In turn, she had sent a short message from her burner phone to Ed Grewall.

Meeting SOYUZ tomorrow. Useful details expected. Will communicate later tomorrow.

That upbeat feeling had remained with her as she made her way beneath the covered porch and through the double electric doors at the entrance, then headed for the stairs rather than the elevators.

The corridor in which the apartment was located was deserted. The heavy-duty carpeting muffled Shevchenko's footsteps as she walked, and she paused for a few seconds outside the door, listening. Silence.

She used her key to let herself in. It was five minutes before eleven, and Vasilenko hadn't arrived yet, so she shrugged off her jacket, poured herself a glass of cold water from a jug in the fridge, and settled in one of the functional SVR standard-issue safe house armchairs to wait for him.

The apartment was typical of safe houses all over the world and several that the SVR owned in Moscow. The walls were painted plain white. It was furnished with secondhand chairs, tables, and a sofa and equipped with an old kettle, chipped mugs, and a humming fridge. The curtains were a drab, faded shade of green. The property was there purely for short meetings, a rendezvous away from the headquarters office when required, and for someone to stay overnight in an emergency.

Shevchenko walked to the window and looked out over the street. A couple of kids were riding their bikes, and an old man carried a shopping bag, bent almost double. It was quarter past eleven, and Vasilenko still hadn't showed up.

She sat down again and checked her messages. There was nothing.

Then came a soft double knock at the door. At last. Shevchenko jumped up and walked softly to the entrance. She released the latch and turned the knob.

There was a bang, and the door burst inward with huge

force, swinging back and narrowly missing Shevchenko's face. It smashed into the hallway wall to her right and she involuntarily took a step backward.

Standing outside were three men, one of whom had clearly just applied a heavily muscled shoulder to the door as she turned the knob. All were dressed in black suits.

"*Dermo*. Shit," Shevchenko said, again involuntarily. Behind the three men, a fourth stepped into view. It was Sidorenko, the whiteness of his frog-like eyes standing out in the gloom of the corridor.

Shevchenko fought to stop the rising red tide of fury that she could feel inside her.

"What the hell are you doing?" she said, her gaze fixed on Sidorenko and her voice tense, although she tried to maintain an appearance of normality. "I have a meeting here with Pavel Vasilenko."

"I know," Sidorenko said, the traces of a grin on his lips. "And I apologize for the forceful entrance, but we are just carrying out routine checks. Mr. Vasilenko will not be able to come here today, and we would like to carry out an interview with you too."

They know. She had told nobody else about the meeting with Vasilenko. What else had they learned?

"*Another* interview?" Shevchenko asked, battling to remain calm inside. "Here?"

"No, not here. I would like you to come with us."

"Now?"

"Yes. Now."

Shevchenko knew there was no choice. She also knew what this meant. It was different from the previous interviews, which had all been at SVR headquarters and held in a comfortable office. Her gut feeling was that this was going to be tough. They already had Vasilenko, that was clear, so she had to hope he held out just as she planned to do. He was known as a tough nut. But what if he didn't hold out? And what if she also couldn't take it and cracked? What if they had gone through her apartment building and found her burner phone?

She picked up her jacket and put it on, and they escorted her down the stairs, one black-suited man holding each of her arms.

Outside was a gray BMW sedan parked in front of a dark blue van, both with blacked-out windows, and neither of which had been there when she arrived.

They opened a sliding side door of the van and put her into the back seat with one black suit placed on either side of her. She saw Sidorenko climbing into the BMW just before one of the men wrapped a blindfold around her head.

The van set off with a jerk of the clutch. Now she had only her sense of direction to tell her where they were going.

Shevchenko concentrated on each turn, her well-honed internal compass logging the movement and speed of the vehicle and the type of road they were on. As the van accelerated hard, she soon realized they were back on the Third Ring Road, going clockwise and heading east.

Lefortovo prison, then. It had to be. Butyrka prison lay in the other direction from the safe house, counterclockwise on the ring road, to the northwest.

* * *

Monday, April 6, 2015
    Moscow

The dark blue smock, of the one-size-fits-all variety, hung loose over Shevchenko's trim body as she stood in the center of the cell, which was no more than four meters long and two meters wide. A steel toilet stood near the door, and there was no heating. The room was freezing cold. The dirty walls had a number of smeared dark red stains and spray marks.

She didn't know what time it was, as all her belongings, including her clothes, phone, and watch, had been removed from her as soon as she had arrived. Her best guess was that it was probably about ten o'clock in the evening. The circular fluorescent light in the high ceiling remained constantly on.

Since her arrival, nobody had spoken a word to Shevchenko. She had not been told where she was, although she knew from the distinctive metal-on-metal squeal of the gates—which she recalled were blue—as the van entered. There was the echoing sound that she recalled from previous visits of the van's engine and exhaust as it entered the underground parking area. Then, after they removed her blindfold inside the building, she also remembered the decor.

It was indeed Lefortovo, one of Russia's most notorious political prisons, often the destination of those who spy against the regime or are suspected of doing so.

Shevchenko had been there a handful of times before when the boot was on the other foot and she had come to interview prisoners. She knew the brown-and-beige carpets in the corridors and the silence, quite different from the raucous noise in most prisons she had visited.

And she knew the gruesome history and high-profile victims of this K-shaped four-story building, which dated back to 1881. Since then it had been run for the most part by the country's security and intelligence services or the Ministry of Justice, which was currently managing it.

She sat on the bed, the frame made from metal with a thin mattress on top, and tried to think.

It was not a surprise that this was happening. In fact, she had expected it much earlier, given she had arrived back in Moscow from Washington more than seven months ago.

Since then she had done nothing that could have aroused suspicions, unless, that is, they had found the burner, and that was highly unlikely. So she could only conclude that something deeply sensitive was going on and that this was a warning not to poke her nose in, a shot across her bow.

There was a metallic clanking at the door, then a click, and it swung open to reveal two men in dark jackets and peaked caps. One of them beckoned Shevchenko to come out of the cell.

She did as instructed. As they had on her way to the cell, while the guards were escorting her, they sometimes made a metallic click-clack sound using handheld silver steel devices. On two occasions, after making double clicks, they pushed her into one of many stinking closets, like broom cupboards, spaced at intervals along the corridors. From the darkness within, the air thick with the smell of stale urine and vomit, she could hear footsteps outside.

This was normal practice at Lefortovo, she knew, to prevent prisoners from seeing each other. After the footsteps receded, the guards let her out again, and the silent journey continued along another series of cream-painted anonymous corridors.

Eventually, after descending two flights of stairs, they ushered her into a small office equipped with a table in the center with, bizarrely, a vase of flowers on it. There were two chairs on either side of the table and two other chairs against the wall beneath a barred window with frosted glass.

On the far side of the table sat Gennady Sidorenko with another man whom Shevchenko had never seen before.

The door clanked shut behind her as the guards exited.

"Please, take a seat," Sidorenko said, indicating with his hand toward the chairs opposite him.

Shevchenko paused.

Stay strong, keep your secrets tight within, locked away in a box where you and they cannot reach them. Keep to your story no matter what.

It was the mantra she had stuck to in the previous lighter interviews they had carried out, and now that the stakes were higher and the scenario grimmer, she was determined not to surrender anything.

On the table in front of Sidorenko were two plastic folders lying open. One of them contained a document that Shevchenko recognized as the detailed forty-page report she had written for Director Kruglov on her return from Washington the previous August.

She slowly moved to the table, took a seat, and fixed Sidorenko with her gaze. "I do not know why you are going through this charade," she said. "I have nothing to hide, and I have reported everything in great detail. You know where my loyalty lies—to my country."

"That is what we need to be clear on," Sidorenko said, his eyes seemingly bulging even more than usual. Then he stuck the knife straight in. "Are you working for the Americans?"

"No. Of course not. And you do realize that while you are unnecessarily holding me here, there are men and women out there, Russians, who *are* spying for the Americans and who are going undetected. Why the hell do you think I am working eighteen hours a day holding interviews with senior people across this organization? It will be your fault entirely if some of them go undetected, and I want that on the record. I know you are filming this." She looked around the room in a show of searching for the hidden cameras and microphones that she knew would be there, whirring away.

Sidorenko didn't blink. "We need to go through everything again. I am sure you understand our need to be thorough."

There was a glass of water standing on the table next to

the vase of flowers, which Shevchenko assumed contained a hidden microphone. She picked up the glass and took a sip.

And so it began. A slow, methodical series of questions relating to every tiny detail of the period Shevchenko had spent in Washington, DC, the previous year. Sidorenko frequently referred to both of the folders in front of him. It became obvious that the second one was a detailed note of answers that she had given in previous interviews.

Shevchenko knew what going on. The search for inconsistencies, changes, variations. The constant probing, starting now at nighttime to heighten the likelihood of her losing concentration and making mistakes as she became more and more tired under the barrage.

How did she arrange to meet Wade, the national security advisor? Where was the meeting location? What information was passed? What did he say and do?

Then Sidorenko moved on to Wade's suicide. What frame of mind was he in? Did she suspect he might take his own life? If not, why not?

"He committed suicide because the CIA found out he was betraying American secrets to you, did he not?" Sidorenko demanded. "It was not because his marriage was finished and because of his affair. Tell me the truth."

"No." Shevchenko shook her head. "They did not know he was spying for us. I know that for certain."

"And they said nothing publicly about Wade's espionage in order to cover up the fact that they had recruited you."

Svoloch. You bastard. Shevchenko forced herself to continue leaning forward, keeping her body language positive. "Absolutely not true."

And then came the long overnight gap between the Wade meeting and the suicide and the next communication between Shevchenko and Moscow Center.

"Why did you delay in getting in touch?"

"I have told you. I could not risk communicating. I needed to remain invisible. I had been taking secrets from a man who was suddenly at the top of the news agenda after committing suicide. Security and surveillance in Washington at that time were off the scale. I had to be certain I could communicate securely."

"What happened during the twenty-four hours after his suicide? Where were you?"

"At my apartment."

The truth was that Shevchenko had spent the night at FBI headquarters, the J. Edgar Hoover Building, as the CIA, the FBI, and the White House discussed her offer to work for the Americans.

All the time, the second man sitting next to Sidorenko took notes, although Shevchenko knew the interview was being recorded. Occasionally he chipped in with a question, pushing for more clarity on something that his colleague had asked.

Her biggest fear now was that the interview, so far conducted in a hands-off manner, would switch to the physical.

The beatings, the electrical nodes on her nipples or the conductive metal peg inserted into her personal cavities, the water treatment, the drugs. She knew what might happen, and they knew that she knew. But that was what they were playing on, her fears.

Sidorenko leaned across the table and cupped his chin in his right hand, elbow on the table. Now his face was only half a meter from hers. His expression said he didn't believe her.

"How well do you know the American investigator Joseph Johnson or the British woman Jayne Robinson?" he asked.

A sharp tremor ran through Shevchenko's guts at the mention of the two people who had trapped her in Washington and who had thus effectively forced her into the CIA's arms. Afterward, seeing kindred spirits in them both, she had requested the CIA to use them as her principal handlers. She fought to keep the emotion away from her face, but she was good at that.

"Only from the problems we had in London last year," she said. "As you know, I had to return here in a hurry after they uncovered our operation."

"So they have leverage against you?"

"Nothing that you are unaware of. I have reported everything."

They don't know, surely? They're fishing, clutching at straws. Stay firm.

"Tell me about Pavel Vasilenko," Sidorenko asked, changing his angle of attack. "Why were you meeting him today?"

"I told you, I'm just doing my job. It was a routine counterintelligence interview. Of course I am going to put him under scrutiny. He is deputy in the Americas department, and I am suspicious of everyone in that department. I am seeing everyone from there, being very thorough."

There were many more probing questions about Vasilenko. What did she know about him? Did she have any suspicions? How many times had she met him before? But eventually, they moved to other topics.

And so it continued. On and on. Shevchenko felt the adrenaline that had initially pumped through her fade away, her energy sap, and exhaustion slowly overtake her.

She badly wanted to ask where Vasilenko was but knew she must not. She needed to divert attention away from him, not toward him. He was likely in another cell there at Lefortovo or maybe some other prison.

The light of dawn was appearing inky blue through the frosted window. It must now have been about half past five in the morning, Shevchenko calculated.

This could go on for a few days. She willed herself not to make a mistake.

Then Sidorenko closed the folders in front of him and leaned back in his chair.

Has he finished? Is it over?

"I have taken this interview as far as I can," Sidorenko said. "It is time to hand you over to another team. They are specialists. They will take you to a different place."

CHAPTER FIFTEEN

Wednesday, April 8, 2015
Washington, DC

The laptop screen shone bright in Vic's somewhat gloomy office when Jayne walked in. Hunched over it were Vic and Veltman, and there on screen was a ghostly image, though nonetheless an identifiable one.

It was the Moscow chief of station, Ed Grewall. Although he was half Indian, his face nevertheless looked white and overexposed against a dark backdrop, and he was speaking in low tones.

On the other side of Vic's desk, away from the laptop screen and with his hands placed behind his receding mop of curly ginger hair, a dark look on his face, was Ricardo Miller, the CIA's counterintelligence deputy director.

Jayne immediately, and subconsciously, fingered the green contractor's identity badge that hung around her neck, different from the blue ones worn by permanent CIA staff. She knew that

Miller wasn't keen on the use of contractors, especially foreign nationals, as he viewed them as a security risk. The process to obtain the badge had been tortuous, involving lengthy background relationship and financial checks, as well as a polygraph.

Vic turned round as Jayne entered. She read the look on his face.

"We've got a problem," Vic said, his voice gravelly and tense. "Come and sit down. Sunny's just started to explain."

Jayne had traveled back to Langley from Portland after being summoned that morning by Vic. It had cut short her plans to spend a few days with Joe following her meeting with Simone. Vic hadn't been specific about why she needed to return urgently, but he made clear it was connected to the Russian assassinations in the UK.

Grewall had stopped speaking when Jayne came into view of the camera and he realized who the newcomer was.

"Hi, Sunny," Jayne greeted him.

"Hello Jayne, good to see you," he said. "I can start again. I'm afraid it's not good news."

Grewall and Jayne had met the previous year during an operation that had taken Jayne and Joe to Russia's Black Sea coast to rescue Joe's children, who had been kidnapped by a long-standing ex-KGB officer turned oil oligarch Yuri Severinov.

"Good to see you too. Yes, please do start again, if it's not too much trouble," Jayne said. She sat on a chair that Vic pulled up next to the laptop. "What's gone wrong?"

"It's about VULTURE. She's disappeared."

Jayne felt as if someone had hit her in the stomach. "Disappeared?"

"Yes, it seems so. I had a short message from her on Sunday night, promising to get in touch the next day with an update following a meeting she had scheduled with SOYUZ, who was going to give her some useful information on the UK killings."

"So she's obviously not got in touch?"

"Correct."

"Maybe a comms screwup? Or just her being careful?"

"We thought that initially. But we have developed a backup source in her apartment building, a caretaker. She doesn't know about him, of course, and the caretaker thinks our contact man is from the local electric utility. He says she's not been seen since Monday morning. That was when she was meant to have been meeting SOYUZ. She hasn't been back home after that."

"Shit."

"It gets worse, though." Now Grewall's voice had dropped another couple of tones. "It's not just VULTURE. It seems SOYUZ has also vanished and is off radar. We can't get any response from him either."

There was a loud snort from Miller on the other side of the desk as he pushed his black-rimmed glasses back up his nose. "Someone's tipped off Moscow Center."

Veltman ignored his counterintelligence chief but pursed his lips. "What chance is there of tracking them down?"

"FSB surveillance has gone red hot these past three days," Grewall said. "They're all over us like a chickenpox rash. Not sure what's going on or whether it's connected to VULTURE and SOYUZ. Difficult to know. However, it makes it damn hard for us to get out on the street without being tailed. I had two cars on me on my way into the office this morning. They picked me up as soon as I left the house. One of them followed me into the shop when I stopped for cigarettes and a newspaper. Very blatant. Most of my people at the station here have had the same thing. Heaviest coverage we've had for quite some time. It's unreal."

Veltman screwed up his face. His slightly puffy, rough-edged visage and barrel chest always reminded Jayne of a laborer, not a top US intelligence chief. He tried to offset the look with a pair of professorish wire-rimmed glasses.

"They've got some ongoing operation they're trying to protect," Veltman said. "It's going to make meeting VULTURE or SOYUZ very difficult."

"Impossible," Grewall said. "Given current FSB surveillance, none of us here can meet them. Far too much risk. They'd be sent to Lefortovo or killed. I don't want that kind of blood on my hands."

Vic tapped his fingers on the desk next to the laptop. "Well, we need to speak to both of them urgently, given that they seem to be picking up info on the UK killings—and that's more than the Feebs are doing at this end."

He briefly outlined his most recent phone conversation with Iain Shepard, the FBI's counterintelligence chief. Despite pursuing various angles within the US, including interviews with Simone Steyn and her late husband's boss, the New Hampshire state governor, as well as Gareth Weber's wife and others, the FBI had turned up no useful leads.

Vic turned back to the laptop screen. "Got any suggestions, Sunny?"

"My best suggestion is we get someone in here who is off the FSB's radar to track down VULTURE and SOYUZ," Grewall said. "And if Jayne's meant to be a prime handler for VULTURE, then I'd suggest getting her over here. Get her a decent new ID and cover story."

Vic glanced sideways at Jayne, then a little nervously at Miller, who was imperceptibly shaking his head.

Vic turned back to the laptop. "We've discussed sending Jayne already, Sunny. It's possibly the way forward and—"

"I'd like to discuss it more," Miller interrupted. "You know my views."

"Yes, we know your views," Vic said. "And I've been listening. But it's my operation and my source in Moscow Center, and it's going to be my decision, providing Arthur is on board with it."

Veltman nodded and eyeballed Miller. "I think we're running out of options, Rick. What's the alternative? The FSB is all over Sunny's team. Jayne seems like the sensible option. We can deny everything if she's caught."

Throw me to the wolves, you mean, Jayne thought. She kept silent, however.

Miller still had his hands stuck defiantly behind his head. "It's entirely your responsibility, then. Don't say I didn't warn you. She's a foreign national and shouldn't be working for us anyway."

Vic exhaled loudly. "That's the whole point, Ricky. She's a foreign national. So nobody will think she's working for us. That's why we've quietly fixed her up with an indefinite US visa and that badge around her neck." He turned to Jayne. "Are you happy to go?"

"*Happy* isn't the word I'd use. What are your terms?"

"Is that a yes?"

Jayne shrugged and raised an eyebrow. He hadn't answered her question.

"We can talk terms," Vic said. "But don't worry, they'll be A-grade. Generous expenses too. Very generous—more than your friends at Vauxhall Cross, I can assure you. We'll also get moving on your new legend."

"Don't worry, I've already got three good legends," Jayne said. She did indeed have three false identities that she had used at various times. Her usual and most-used was that of Carolina Blanco. However, that was off the table because she had used the passport to enter Russia on her previous foray last year but had not officially exited.

"We'd better thoroughly check out the one you have in mind," Vic said.

Jayne nodded. "It's clean."

"Good. We'll need to move fast now. I'm going to connect you with the techs, because you'll need to get better comms gear to VULTURE and SOYUZ, assuming we can find them. You'll also need to spend time with Rick's countersurveillance team." He cast a glance at Miller, who didn't respond. "They'll get you up to speed with how to counter the latest FSB techniques. And finally, you'll meet with our head of disguise. You'll need it."

Miller stood, removed his glasses, and waved them in the air as he walked toward the door. "I tell you what, Jayne. I'll fix you an appointment with Gypsy Rose," he said. "She'll find you a good luck charm, a rabbit's foot or something. You'll need that too."

With that, he walked out.

CHAPTER SIXTEEN

Thursday, April 9, 2015
Konstantinovsky Palace, Strelna

Igor Ivanov watched the president's laser-blue eyes as they carefully and systematically worked their way around the small group of men sitting at the ornate circular conference table that had been specially installed in the Marble Hall. Ivanov averted his gaze just before the president's eyes reached his. It was better to appear submissive, he knew.

The click-clack of the drinks attendant's heels on the mustard-colored marble floor receded as he walked to the far end of the hall, passed beneath a multitiered golden chandelier, and exited through the door at the far end.

As the door shut, Ivanov refocused his attention on his boss, Putin, as he spoke for the first time.

"Thank you for attending this week, gentlemen," the president said. "We have a difficult few days ahead. Tough talks will be had and hard decisions made. But it is critical we set our strategic course regarding our main rival, and these discussions will be an important part of that. Important steps have already been taken down the road that we are on, but we need to be 100 percent focused on our end destination and 100 percent committed to achieving it. Do I make myself understood?"

There were nods around the table and grunts of assent.

Ivanov felt a sudden surge of pride as he surveyed the gathering. It was *his* conference, *his* idea to locate it here at the historic Konstantinovsky Palace, thirty kilometers west of St. Petersburg, and he intended that the outcome would be part of *his* legacy to the Rodina, the Motherland.

The conference table at which the attendees were seated formed an outer ring, a little like a doughnut. An inner ring consisted of another smaller circular table beneath which were positioned large flat-screen TV monitors, tilted at a slight angle so the men could view them easily from their seats.

The somewhat high-tech arrangement contrasted with the dignified, elegant backdrop of the hall itself, with its ornate golden marble pillars, arched windows, and decorative ceiling. It was the same room where the G8 leaders had met at their summit in 2006—Bush, Blair, Merkel, Chirac, and the rest. They had all paid homage to Putin at the place that had become the president's official summer residence, Ivanov reflected.

"I would like to sum up my view of our stance and my thinking as we get closer to the next US presidential election," the president continued. "There is no doubt that the continued development and success of shale oil and gas in the United States under President Ferguson's regime is very negative for our oil and gas industry. It is interesting that the opposition candidate Nicholas McAllister is less pro-shale. He cites the environmental impacts. There is also Ferguson's stance regarding eastern Ukraine. As you know, Ferguson has been very opposed to our growing influence there. But it is becoming clear that McAllister is more likely to favor a separate Russian-influenced region in that area of Ukraine. I believe that McAllister is also more likely to pull Russia into a US orbit rather than push us into a Chinese one because he is a realist—he knows, as we all do, that a Russia-China alliance is unlikely."

The president paused and picked up a red leather-bound folder from the gleaming mahogany desk in front of him. He held it up in front of him. "You all have copies of this, which details what we intend to do about the situation as we near the US election. You have doubtless all read through it, and I have no intention of repeating what you have already digested."

Putin turned to his left, where the director of the SVR, Maksim Kruglov, was sitting with his first deputy director, Yevgeny Kutsik. Next to them were Nikolai Sheymov, the director of the Federal Security Service, the FSB, and his deputy.

"Maksim, you have sessions planned for the next few days that will allow discussions about this plan," the president said, waving his red folder. "Can you briefly tell us what they will consist of?"

This was interesting, Ivanov thought. The president was turning first to the head of his foreign intelligence service rather than the prime minister, Dmitry Medvedev.

Kruglov cleared his throat. "Yes, Mr. President. I will be leading the discussion about our plans, and I will be joined by two of the key members of my team at Yasenevo who are responsible for devising it, my third deputy director and the head of the American department, Fyodor Unkovsky, who most of you know, as well as his number two, Pavel Vasilenko, who you may not know so well. They have both been diverted from their normal duties and were brought here on Monday."

At this point Kruglov eyed his audience and gave a short laugh. "I can disclose that neither of them were particularly happy at this diversion, as we gave them no notice. Since then, they have been locked away in my office here working on plans that must remain top secret—so secret that we cannot discuss everything here, and I apologize for that. However, we will be able to have a good discussion about the broad outline of our plans and strategy, if not the fine details. I hope you all understand."

Ivanov wasn't surprised at the disclosure about giving Unkovsky and Vasilenko no notice. He would have done the same himself. And he knew exactly what Kruglov meant about the need for security: it would be far too risky to discuss the fine details of their plans, which Ivanov himself had been instrumental in devising.

Ivanov had made clear in no uncertain terms to both the SVR and FSB chiefs that they must crack down hard on the slightest sign of any weakness in security. There must be no leaks. Anything suspicious must be investigated ruthlessly, and anyone who gave the slightest sign of potential treachery against the regime must be eliminated.

Already, he knew, the recently appointed SVR deputy director in charge of counterintelligence, Anastasia Shevchenko, was being grilled at Lefortovo to ensure she was clean. He felt confident she would prove herself to be so— indeed, he had championed her appointment the previous year, so he hoped that was the case. But it was reassuring that Kruglov was taking a tough approach to make certain.

Ivanov sat back and listened as Sheymov described to the group the initiatives he had taken within the FSB to step up surveillance of known or suspected Western intelligence officers among the diplomats based at embassies in Moscow, particularly the American and British.

A few, such as the CIA's chief of station, Ed Grewall and

his British counterpart, Oliver Kirton, were declared intelligence officers. However, the majority of them were employed under false cover roles, such as industrial and business liaison experts, cultural attachés, or environmental advisors, all with diplomatic immunity. The FSB was highly skilled in detecting which diplomats had genuine roles and which were actually spies.

When Sheymov had finished, Ivanov leaned forward. "Can you tell me who is leading this surveillance initiative in Moscow?" he asked.

Sheymov turned to him. "I have assigned it to Colonel Leonid Pugachov."

Putin had been sitting silently as Sheymov went through his presentation. Now the president put down a glass of water from which he had been sipping. "Make sure that Pugachov locks up Moscow tighter than a prison cell," he said. "I want the city watertight. If any of those we think are CIA or MI6 go out, we need to be all over them. I want records and photographs of where they go and who they meet, either Russians or Westerners."

Ivanov leaned back, pleased to see that Sheymov was taking notes of what the president had said and was nodding in agreement. As a former KGB intelligence officer, the president always had security at the forefront of his mind, and sensibly, the FSB chief was taking his comments extremely seriously, as he should. He knew Pugachov, a high-class operator who had begun his career in the KGB's foreign intelligence service during the 1980s. He had switched to the domestic FSB after the breakup of the Soviet Union in 1991 and was currently a hands-on head of counterintelligence.

Among the key attributes that Ivanov had developed was to relentlessly forge contacts across the spectrum of political, intelligence, law-enforcement, military, and industrial organizations within Russia. As a former GRU officer,

Ivanov had a hard-won reputation for ruthlessness and manipulation, and having senior people he could phone at all hours to do his bidding was critical to the slightly informal way in which he operated. Both Sheymov's and Pugachov's office and private numbers had long been logged in his cell phone.

Ivanov had at one time become deputy prime minister but was now running special operations on behalf of the president and his small group of senior executives. Among the triumphs he had chalked up since assuming the role was the organization of black operations to generate hostility against the Ukrainian government in the Crimea and in eastern Ukraine, thus allowing Russia a foothold and greater influence.

The latest triumph, which Ivanov had engineered using one of his old GRU Spetsnaz contacts, Georgi Tkachev, had gone completely to plan. Tkachev, who had made a remarkable recovery from a bad leg injury sustained in an oil refinery explosion the previous year, had operated with surgical precision in assassinating two US citizens on British soil. And he had done so without being identified, as far as Ivanov was aware. Certainly, all the intelligence reports he was receiving from Sheymov and Kruglov indicated that there were no obvious signals that Tkachev had been detected. He hadn't lost his touch while going through a lengthy and tough physical rehabilitation program following his injury, that much was clear.

Most people in and around the Kremlin referred to Ivanov as the Black Bishop, sometimes to his face. He rarely reacted, never smiling, never frowning, but secretly he loved the moniker. He was proud of his skills in the dark arts.

For the remainder of the short introductory session, the president invited the attendees to outline briefly what their respective sessions would comprise. They included Medvedev, as well as his foreign affairs minister, his deputy prime minister for industry and energy, and the defense minister.

After the session concluded and the attendees broke away for tea and coffee, Ivanov went for a stroll outside Konstantinovsky Palace, originally built in 1807 but restored at massive cost by Putin in 2001, complete with drawbridges, fountains, and canals. He stood overlooking the shore of the Gulf of Finland, which lay only 750 meters away across an uninterrupted stretch of landscaped grounds to the north. Finland itself was just 150 kilometers to the northwest, across the gulf.

Ivanov turned and gazed back at the magnificent white stone frontage of the palace building behind him. Through the triple central arches that ran through the center of the building, a statue of Peter the Great mounted on a horse was visible in the plaza beyond.

It was this kind of trophy asset property that Ivanov coveted. A dacha a tenth the size of this would do.

Who knows, he thought, *if this operation against the main enemy goes to plan, it is going to be huge, and the rewards could be correspondingly huge.*

He checked his secure email inbox. There it was, the confirmation he had been waiting for. The next step of the operation would be carried out in the morning in Washington.

Excellent.

CHAPTER SEVENTEEN

Friday, April 10, 2015
Washington, DC

The news alert from *The Washington Post* app pinged on Jayne's phone just as she was climbing the stairs to Vic's office on the seventh floor at the CIA's original headquarters building.

Jayne paused on the landing of the third floor, grateful for an excuse to stop. Normally she took the stairs rather than the elevator at every opportunity, but sometimes she wondered why she bothered. After all, given the amount of running she was now doing, she was as fit as she'd ever been.

She put down the latte she had bought from the Starbucks outlet on the ground floor and tapped on the screen of the phone, a new secure device that Vic had arranged for her.

Secretaries of State Killed in UK Were Investors in Ukraine Defense Equipment Supplier, the headline ran. A subheading questioned whether it meant there was a Russian connection.

Tell me something I don't know.

That information was exactly what Jayne had been told by Simone several days earlier. Good to see the *Post* was quick off the mark with its news coverage.

Jayne scrolled down the story. It was more or less in line with what Simone had said.

The company the two secretaries were shareholders in, US Defense Systems, supplied night-vision goggles, anti-tank missiles, rocket-propelled grenades, and a variety of ammunition for different weaponry to the Kiev government, the story said.

The article added that the company had also supplied equipment to the US military in Afghanistan during the 1980s, when the United States was supporting the mujahideen against occupying Russian forces.

There were quotes from a company spokesman confirming that the two men were indeed investors. However, the spokesman had declined to confirm the Ukraine order, citing customer confidentiality. Well, that was often normal practice in the defense industry.

The story went into some detail about the shootings in the UK, but although it quoted defense industry sources suggesting that the perpetrator was possibly Russian, this was speculation because of the Ukraine arms supply link, not because the journalist had any hard information.

Jayne was about to close the *Post*'s app and resume her climb up the stairs when her attention was caught by the final paragraph of the story.

The two secretaries of state were long-standing friends, dating back to their time serving together in the US Army, including postings in Afghanistan and Iraq. Both graduated from West Point US Military Academy in 1986. Sources said that it was during their time in the military that the men became aware of the potential of US Defense Systems, which was a supplier of equipment to the army at that time.

Well, that was interesting, Jayne thought, and it was something that Simone had not mentioned. She made a mental note to check whether the two men's long history together in the military, prior to becoming secretaries of state, might be relevant to what had happened to them.

Then she checked her Twitter feed. Sure enough, the story was being widely tweeted and retweeted by a large number of users.

Jayne slipped her phone back into her pocket and continued up to the seventh floor toward Vic's office. Later that morning she was due to meet the Agency's deputy chief of disguise, Joanne Menary, followed by another meeting with the officer delegated by Vic to do a thorough check on Jayne's chosen false identity for her trip into Russia, that of British history teacher Siobhan Delks.

Vic had also already arranged for two items of secure and highly sensitive communications equipment, currently at Langley, to be transported by the Department of State to the US embassy in Moscow in a diplomatic pouch.

The pouches, secured with locks and tamperproof seals, were technically for the transport of sensitive official documents or other items from the Department of State to any US embassy premises worldwide and had diplomatic immunity against search or confiscation by customs. But occasionally, the Agency took advantage of this and slipped their equipment through as well.

The equipment comprised an SRAC transmitter and receiver, each compact with a brushed-steel case. Once they had been delivered by the diplomatic courier, who had immunity from arrest, Jayne would collect them from Ed Grewall and devise a plan to bury the receiver somewhere appropriate

in Moscow, where it could be remotely accessed wirelessly by
Shevchenko and someone from the CIA station. The transmitter would need to be handed over to Shevchenko so she
could send data securely to the receiver.

The high level of surveillance of CIA officers in Moscow
meant it would be highly risky for one of them to attempt to
bury the receiver themselves.

Jayne had also been given details of two exfiltration routes
out of Russia that she could use in emergencies, both for
herself but also for an agent if required in extreme circumstances. They were Route Green One, via the Black Sea, and
Route Green Two, via the Gulf of Finland. One of Ricardo
Miller's counterintelligence team, who was responsible for
intricate exfil arrangements, had explained the logistics
involved and also arranged for the necessary small piece of
communications equipment Jayne would need to be sent to
Grewall's office in the diplomatic bag along with the other
items.

When Jayne arrived at Vic's office, she discovered that the
FBI's Iain Shepard was there with Vic, who already had the
Post story open on his computer screen.

After greeting the two men, Jayne pointed to the story.
"What do you make of that?" she asked. "I just read it."

"It all seems so vague," Vic said. "Interesting, yes, that
they're both involved in the company supplying weapons to
forces who are against the Russians, but it's a bit tenuous."

"I'm more interested in the long-standing military history
the two of them shared," Jayne said. "They've had very similar
careers, as far as I can see. And they're friends. Now they've
both been killed by a Russian assassin." She spread her hands
wide in a questioning manner.

Shepard, who had been perched on the edge of Vic's desk,
eased himself off and stood with arms folded, bouncing a
little on his heels. He was about three inches shorter than Vic

and slimmer, with cropped gray hair. He looked like an athlete.

"I also saw that. Interesting," Shepard said. "I'm not sure of the relevance, but I'm going to get our team to have a look at it. The *Post* has done their research."

"Or maybe they've been spoon-fed by someone," Jayne said.

"Possibly that's true," Shepard said.

"Anyway," Jayne said, "I see the story has been tweeted a lot. Reminds me of the Russian Twitter offensive last year."

She was referring to the barrage of tweets from a Russian troll factory, aimed at blaming the US, the CIA, and Ukraine for the downing of a Malaysian passenger jet over Ukraine the previous year. She had helped Joe to expose the activity.

"Maybe the Russians are trying to send a message again," Vic said.

"They've definitely sent a message," Jayne said. "Two dead bodies in the south of England is a message in big capitals."

"Yes," Vic said. "The issue is, we don't know what the message means."

He placed his hands on his hips and looked at Jayne. "We're relying on you to find out when you get to Moscow. No pressure."

* * *

Friday, April 10, 2015
Moscow

Shevchenko's back was still aching from the electric shock treatment that had sent it into an uncontrollable spasm, and her anus felt as though it were on fire from where—as she had feared—a conductive peg had been inserted and connected to a powerful vehicle battery.

Her bones were, surprisingly, intact, but only because of the expertise of the Lefortovo torture team to whom she had been handed over by Sidorenko. They had managed to leave her black and blue without causing any fractures. They had been good, she had to admit; they knew exactly how to find the nerve endings with their probing fingers.

She felt dehydrated and dizzy and knew she had lost several kilograms in weight because the food she had been given had been both minimal and inedible.

Always their focus had been on that meeting in Washington and the circumstances of Francis Wade's suicide, and the delay before she had contacted Moscow Center again. As pain coursed through her body, the questions were relentlessly focused on that twenty-four hours or so.

What happened during that time? Where was she? Why did she go silent?

She knew they were as suspicious as hell but could prove nothing.

Poshël ty. They could all piss off. She had resolved to never surrender, to bury her secrets deep inside and lock them away.

And that, to her great pride, was exactly what she had done. She had not surrendered.

Through the red haze of agony, she could almost see their point.

It *had* been a mistake not to get back in touch earlier, and she cursed herself for that. She even apologized repeatedly to her interrogators. Several times, she used a phrase she had learned while in London: it was a case of cock-up, not conspiracy, she told them. They appeared to reluctantly believe her—eventually.

Ublyudoks, bastards, she muttered to herself as she hauled herself into the elevator of her apartment building.

Just imagine this happening at Langley or at Vauxhall Cross. Pah.

She pressed the button for the fifth floor and used the rail that ran around the elevator car at waist height to prevent herself from falling over.

The anonymous car from the Lefortovo fleet had dropped her outside her apartment building five minutes earlier, and she had taken that long to walk the twenty meters into the downstairs lobby.

Shevchenko felt the slightly metallic taste of old blood from the cut inside her mouth, where they had slapped her repeatedly. She spat on the floor of the elevator as the doors opened.

So this was the way of things in Novorossiya—Putin's new Russia. Well, if she needed any justification for her actions in changing her allegiance in Washington all those months ago, she now had it.

We just need to be completely certain, the interrogator had said. *You have a critical role. Please don't take it personally.*

She wouldn't. It had happened to too many people whom she knew. The truth was that most people in the service who were carrying out any kind of role that involved interaction with rivals would probably face an investigation at some point.

And no doubt they expected her to go back to her desk at Yasenevo the next morning and carry on her duties as if nothing had happened. That was the way they operated. *Pigs.*

Shevchenko limped to the door of her apartment, let herself in, and made her way straight to the freezer. She took out a bottle of vodka, poured a large measure into a tumbler, and collapsed with it into an armchair.

Is this a case of karma, of reaping what I've sowed?

Her mind flashed back to the times she herself had taken a ruthless approach when dealing with sources and agents she didn't completely trust.

Then she shrugged inwardly. As always, she'd done what she had to do. Everybody in the organization did it.

She sipped the icy liquid—like everyone, she drank vodka that way. It was how her father had taught her. And she gasped slightly, as she always did, when it hit the back of her throat.

It was a celebration of sorts. She had come through four days of hell. She had been cleared. They had not gotten their confession, and they had no evidence.

Shevchenko looked around the apartment. There was little doubt they would have searched it again while she was locked up in Lefortovo. She got up and checked the two traps she always left: the first was one of her hairs that she attached between the kitchen door and the door frame with a tiny piece of gum; the second was a similar device on her bedroom door. Sure enough, both had been disturbed. No matter. They wouldn't have found anything useful.

She would have to wait a little while before going to check on the burner phone she used to communicate with Ed Grewall. She needed to let him know what had happened, but the last thing she wanted was for one of Sidorenko's goons to come and disturb her while she had the phone in her hand.

In spite of the alcohol, or perhaps because of it, the fog in Shevchenko's mind had begun to dissipate and she mentally ran through her list of priorities now.

The first was to determine what had happened to Vasilenko. She had an idea about how she could do that, and the obvious route was to speak to his secretary, Ekaterina, whom she trusted. She would need to be very careful in her approach, however.

Once she had achieved that, the second was to obtain the

information that Vasilenko apparently held about the killings in the United Kingdom, which they should have exchanged at the abortive safe house meeting four days earlier.

How she was going to get that from him, she had no idea as of yet.

Third, her instinct for self-preservation told her she needed a counterintelligence coup, a scalp, to restore her credibility at Moscow Center and to see off her enemies, the doubters like Kutsik and Sidorenko, in order to put herself back on firm ground. She needed to prove her supporters like Kruglov and Ivanov right and her persecutors wrong.

She didn't yet know how she was going to deliver that, either, but she would have to find a way.

CHAPTER EIGHTEEN

Friday, April 10, 2015
   Gorelovo Air Base, St. Petersburg

A flock of squawking seagulls spiraled into the air as the report from the VSS Vintorez rifle shot echoed across the expanse of scrubby wasteland.

Georgi Tkachev kept his head still and his right eye glued to the powerful PSO-1M2-1 telescopic sight mounted on top of the weapon, trying to see whether he had hit his target, a wooden post with a piece of white paper pinned to it. His gut feeling was that his shot had struck home, like the last one, but it was difficult to be certain from a distance of more than 850 meters.

The stretch of land, just south of Gorelovo Air Base, a former military airfield twenty-three kilometers southeast of St. Petersburg, was one he had used frequently as a makeshift rifle range during his time stationed in the city while in the GRU. He hadn't been there for several years but now took advantage of a few spare hours to get some practice before his meeting at four o'clock.

Very little had changed since his last visit ten years earlier, except that the original military airfield had been converted for civilian use during the 1990s and now had many more light aircraft standing on its aprons. Clearly business was booming in St. Petersburg, and it wasn't just the oligarchs who had money to spend.

Tkachev glanced at his watch. It was time to go. He didn't want to be late for his meeting with Igor Ivanov and Maksim Kruglov.

He hauled himself to his feet, wincing a little as he did so from the pain in his lower right leg, and methodically packed the rifle and sight away in a soft black carry case. When he had done so, he made his way across the stretch of ground, partly covered with grass and bushes, until he reached his Subaru 4x4 pickup.

His limp, very pronounced until as recently as a month ago, was gradually decreasing, although he suspected he would always have it.

In many ways, Tkachev viewed it as something of a miracle that he could still walk. His lower right leg had been badly mashed the previous year by an explosion at an oil refinery at Tuapse.

He had been found unconscious and bleeding heavily by his friend Leonid Pugachov, a colonel in the FSB with whom he had worked on operations previously, and was probably lucky to still be alive.

It had taken three operations by a skilled surgeon to repair the damage to his tibia and calf and associated ligaments, and since then, he had gone through an intensive rehabilitation program lasting several months to restore his mobility. The task still wasn't finished, and his military physiotherapist estimated it would take another three months of

work to get him back to 80 percent of his previous functionality. But it was more than enough for him to resume work,
which he needed to do in order to support his wife and two
teenage sons at their apartment in Moscow.

Remarkably, he could even run when needed, although
not for long distances. His recovery bore testament to his
extremely high level of fitness and muscle strength prior to
the accident, the surgeon had told him. For that, he had his
old Spetsnaz special forces unit to thank—they had drummed
into him a level and culture of fitness that was second to none
anywhere in the world.

The explosion had been caused, he was certain, by a
British woman, a former MI6 officer named Jayne Robinson,
who he knew had been working with ex-CIA officer Joseph
Johnson. At the time of the blast, Johnson was in his line of
sight inside an empty fuel tank, whereas Robinson was
nowhere to be seen. It had to have been her who triggered it,
and he sometimes dreamed about the revenge he would
wreak if he got the chance.

Tkachev slung the rifle case into the Subaru, climbed into
the driver's seat, and set off.

Fifteen minutes later, after showing his security clearance
and thus avoiding the usual lengthy check and vehicle search
at the main gate, he pulled into the parking lot at Konstantinovsky Palace in Strelna. In the distance, the blue-black
waters of the Gulf of Finland glinted in the afternoon
sunshine.

It was Tkachev's third visit to the palace, so he knew
where he was going. He made his way into a reception area
that led off the triple arches beneath the center of the building, checked in with security, and sat in an armchair to wait.

Tkachev fingered the scar that ran up from the left corner
of his mouth toward his ear, a souvenir from a knife fight in
Afghanistan many years earlier, and glanced at his watch. As

usual, the wait was longer than should have been necessary, but that was the way the likes of Ivanov operated. They were always late for appointments, seemingly deliberately so.

Eventually, an aide beckoned him through a set of double oak doors, then along a corridor, through another heavy wooden door, and into the meeting room, which was in fact a private dining room. Tkachev had been here before and had admired the ancient brick fireplace and intricate pattern of marble floor tiles.

Sitting in high leather-covered chairs at the ornate mahogany dining table were Ivanov and Kruglov. Both men got up and shook his hand, but neither smiled.

"Thank you for coming here, Colonel, and congratulations on the job in the UK," Ivanov said. "Very admirable, although I expected nothing different."

"Thank you," Tkachev said. Although he was now a freelancer working almost exclusively for the Kremlin, he liked the fact that Ivanov had used his old rank from his time as a former senior commander in the Spetsnaz, or special forces, of Russia's GRU foreign military intelligence organization. These men knew how to flatter when required.

"Yes, you delivered perfectly," Kruglov said. "How is your leg now?"

"It is continuing to improve slowly," Tkachev said. "Sometimes it is still a little sore and stiff, but it will not affect my work, thankfully."

"That is good to hear," Ivanov said. "Please, take a seat."

Tkachev sat opposite the two men. Ivanov picked up a slim plastic folder that lay on the table and pushed it across to him.

"This is your next assignment," Ivanov said. "It is going to require some preparation and forward planning, but I know you can deliver. Read through it, then destroy it. This is what I would like you to do."

Tkachev took the folder, opened it, and glanced at the first page, which comprised a summary of the task that Ivanov was proposing.

His eyebrows rose momentarily as he read, and he looked up. "In via Cuba and Mexico. Are you serious? This is ambitious."

The Black Bishop of the Kremlin nodded. "Yes, we are. I agree, it will not be easy. However, we think you are the person most capable of delivering success, and I am very pleased that you have overcome the injuries you sustained last year. Now, let me explain," he said as he began to run through details of the task that he had in mind.

When he had finished about ten minutes later, Tkachev pursed his lips. "Can I ask, why do you want this done?"

Ivanov frowned, tapping lightly on the table with his fingers. "Listen to me. I can tell you what I want you to do and I can tell you we need to move quickly. But I cannot tell you why—it is classified."

Tkachev nodded, unsurprised at the response. That was often the way of things. Best as always to get on with the job and not ask too many questions.

CHAPTER NINETEEN

Thursday, April 16, 2015
Moscow

Getting into Russia had proved to be the easy bit, as it turned out. Jayne's route in, via flights to London and then the thriving Lithuanian capital Vilnius, where she switched to her false identity of Siobhan Delks, had worked well.

With her hair now blond instead of its usual dark color, she had gone straight through customs at Moscow's Sheremetyevo International Airport two days earlier, on Tuesday afternoon. There had been only one cursory question about the purpose of her visit, which she told the border guards officer was to research a school visit by her history students that was planned for the following year.

But once installed at Moscow's Hotel Metropol, a historic art nouveau building positioned among the other tourist hotels and a few minutes' walk north of Red Square and its hundreds of sightseers, the extent of the challenge she faced did not take long to become clear.

The issue was not so much with her but with the man she needed to meet, Ed Grewall.

Before Jayne left Langley, the technical team—the directorate of science and technology—had equipped her with a so-called covcom device. It was an online, encrypted digital covert communications channel accessible via her phone.

The smartphone she used for this purpose, also supplied by Langley, was separate from a cheap old phone into which she had inserted a SIM card for a local phone operator, Mega-Fon, bought at the airport using her Delks passport. Jayne mostly kept this phone turned off and the SIM removed so it could not be tracked.

To use her covcom device, Jayne needed to dig deep into the bowels of her smartphone using what appeared to be a standard social media app but was anything but that. A distinct series of keystrokes and taps on buttons unlocked the hidden message functionality that was buried inside. She was able to use it to communicate with those who had a similar app, including Vic and Grewall, and it was undetectable to a nosy police or customs officer if they happened to inspect her phone.

But even with the device, there remained a risk of surveillance inside Moscow hotel rooms, so she usually tried to go elsewhere to make calls or send messages if she could.

On arrival in Moscow, she had exchanged a couple of encrypted and heavily codified messages with Grewall and was told that her "birthday present," namely the SRAC equipment, had arrived in the parcel—the diplomatic pouch.

However, handing it over would clearly be difficult.

There's a deep freeze over my department and it is difficult to move because of the ice, Grewall said in his message.

He wasn't referring to the sudden drop in Moscow's spring temperatures that had occurred immediately after Jayne's arrival. There had been a sharp freeze and an unseasonal overnight snowstorm that had left piles of frozen slush on the roads and ice on the sidewalks of Moscow.

Rather, Jayne knew he was talking about the high level of FSB surveillance that he and his colleagues were currently experiencing.

She replied saying that they would need to find a way to rapidly defrost the situation and that this needed to happen urgently.

It wasn't until Thursday that a way forward emerged.

Jayne received a message that morning from Grewall, sent using the covcom phone device, instructing her to walk to his usual gym, CityFitness Dobryninskiy, which was about four kilometers south of her hotel. She should arrive at about five o'clock that afternoon, request a visitor's day pass on arrival together with a blue gym towel and a locker key, and he would look out for her in the workout areas.

The gym was popular with tourists and business visitors to Moscow, and it was normal for casual nonmembers to turn up for one-off workouts and simply buy a day pass, Grewall said.

The message continued with a series of instructions that Jayne read carefully. They seemed simple and relatively straightforward.

Although Grewall was very often tailed by the FSB, they had never followed him into the gym, he said. They always waited outside, so the chances of surveillance making a connection between them was very slim.

The time required for Jayne to walk to the gym from her hotel would also function as a surveillance detection route, allowing her to check for any tail, although it seemed unlikely she would be targeted by the FSB.

Meanwhile, Grewall was planning to follow his usual late afternoon practice of driving to the gym from the CIA station at the US embassy, about four kilometers away near the Moskva River, in the Arbat district.

Grewall would then park outside and enter on foot, as normal. He used the gym about four times a week, so this activity should arouse no suspicions with an FSB onlooker.

With that reassurance, Jayne put on a heavy jacket and slung a small backpack containing her gym gear over her shoulder and set off from the Hotel Metropol at about half past three. She figured that would allow her enough time for a fairly circuitous route and a stop for coffee along the way.

She rigorously followed her usual streetcraft routine, doubling back on herself once, visiting two shops, and taking one short journey on a bus and another on the metro, just for one stop. The freezing temperature meant she was glad of the occasional break indoors.

Jayne had identified that the gym was near the Dobrynin-skaya and Oktyabrskaya metro stations, which gave her options for both arrival and departure, but she decided that walking was her best choice.

The route heading south toward the Moskva River took her past St. Basil's Cathedral, where she stopped and took tourist-style photographs of its towering and colorful domes, and she cut across Red Square, with the Kremlin on her right. Occasionally she also took imaginary calls on her cell phone, using the photos and conversations as an excuse to quite naturally look around her. For the same reason, she stopped and smoked a cigarette on Bolshoy Moskvoretsky Bridge as she crossed the river.

There was no sign of any coverage. Nobody ducking between parked cars or suddenly window shopping. Nobody walking behind her while speaking on a cell phone, loitering in the shadows, or looking around anxiously for a taxi.

At about ten minutes to five, Jayne arrived at the gym, which was in the Yakimanka district a couple of kilometers south of the river. It was located on the ground floor of a fifteen-story granite-fronted office building that also housed banks, a corporate headquarters, a couple of fashion boutiques, and a fitness shop.

There was a line of parking spaces outside the building, only half of which were occupied. Jayne assumed that Grewall would park there.

She made her way to the gym's reception desk, staffed by a young blond woman whose name badge read Natasha, and used her Siobhan Delks passport to obtain a one-day pass at a cost of a thousand rubles, just under fifteen dollars. Natasha glanced through the passport, but to Jayne's relief didn't appear to note the details.

Jayne also requested one of the blue gym towels from a rack behind the desk, and a locker key for the changing room. Natasha enthusiastically obliged, gave her directions to the changing room, and began to deal with the next customer.

A few minutes later, Jayne had changed, stored her clothes and backpack in a locker, and begun to work out on the weights machines, which were lined up against a wall. There were only two other people in the gym, neither of whom were Grewall. Her position gave her a good view of the entire gym, including the door that led from the women's and men's changing rooms and the row of six treadmills.

After a short time, three trim middle-aged women came in, all obviously friends judging by their constant chat, followed by an elderly man.

A couple of minutes later, another man entered the gym, who was in his late thirties, dark-haired, and fit-looking, with a large pair of headphones clamped to his ears. He didn't look at Jayne as he went past her to the leg press machine, where he fiddled with his phone for a while and then began to pump away.

Then, finally, there was the unmistakable figure of Grewall, his darker skin standing out against a white T-shirt, and a rolled-up blue towel and bottle of water in his hands.

He glanced quickly around the gym for a moment but showed no sign that he had recognized Jayne as he strode toward the treadmills, three of which were occupied by the middle-aged women. He headed for the treadmill nearest the window and placed the towel on the floor between it and the neighboring machine, which was occupied. He then put his water in the bottle holder and began fiddling with the speed settings.

Jayne continued her workout, using a selection of lower and upper body machines and glancing only occasionally at Grewall. After about fifteen minutes, the woman using the treadmill next to him finished her workout, and Jayne decided it was time to join him, as instructed. The CIA man was still pounding away, sweating heavily, his feet thumping on the rubber surface and his breathing heavy.

Jayne placed her towel on the floor right next to his, as instructed, set her treadmill to a somewhat slower pace than his, and settled into a steady, rhythmic run. They both continued in parallel for no more than another two minutes, at which point Grewall pushed the stop button on his treadmill, and the machine slowly ground to a halt.

Jayne kept an eye on the other gym users, but they all seemed entirely focused on their own workouts rather than on the other visitors. The three women were helping each other with stretching exercises, while the man with the headphones was still on the weights machines and facing toward her, now doing hamstring curls, interspersed with spells of fiddling with his phone.

Grewall got off his treadmill, took a swig from his bottle of water, picked up Jayne's towel, and walked to a gym mat at the right of the room, still in her line of sight. He did a few cursory stretches and then headed out the door toward the changing rooms.

Jayne gave him a couple of minutes, then stopped her machine and casually picked up his rolled-up towel from the floor. She could tell from the weight that the SRAC equipment, compact but nevertheless weighing maybe a pound, was inside it.

A glance around told her that nobody else was looking in her direction, so she had some water from the drinking fountain near the door and also headed for the changing rooms, the towel held unobtrusively at her side.

By the time Jayne had showered, dressed, and emerged from the changing room, Grewall and the others who had been in the gym during her workout had gone.

She made her way out of the building, the rolled-up towel now tucked safely into her backpack, and headed toward Oktyabrskaya metro station. From there she had a straightforward journey, involving one change of train, that got her back to the Hotel Metropol in about half an hour.

Again, Jayne took extra precautions to check for any sign of surveillance. There was none. Nevertheless, her normal process in such situations was to move hotels frequently. She made a mental note to speak to Grewall about moving from the Metropol to a safe house, if he could offer that option, or if not, then to another hotel.

When she arrived back in her room, she finally opened up the towel. As intended, the SRAC transmitter and receiver, both of which were small rectangular steel devices no bigger than cigarette packs, were neatly packed inside. There was also a map and grid reference with precise instructions to bury the receiver among bushes in Petrovsky Park, across the street from the apartment where Shevchenko lived.

Jayne dispatched a short message to Grewall.

Have unwrapped birthday gift. All looks great. Thanks. Will now deliver Aunt's present. Also need new place to stay ASAP before meeting her for the party. Please advise.

CHAPTER TWENTY

Thursday, April 16, 2015
Moscow

Less than half a kilometer east of the Hotel Metropol, Colonel Leonid Pugachov took a final drag from his ninth LD cigarette of the day. He walked to the desk of his sixth-floor office in the forbidding gray and yellow granite Lubyanka building, and crushed the stub into a large glass ashtray.

Decades of smoking had yellowed his white mustache and stained his teeth. But without the cigarettes—almost always his favorite LD brand—he struggled to think clearly enough. And so, despite the advice of his doctor, he continued to light up. If he kept his intake to below fifteen cigarettes a day, he considered it a small triumph, but that rarely happened.

Pugachov picked up his spiral-bound notebook and glanced around his office, with its heavily chipped veneered desk and bookcase. He knew he hadn't left any sensitive papers on display, but force of habit ensured he always made one final check before leaving. He knew the consequences of not locking them in his steel filing cabinet—more than one colleague had disappeared, never to be seen again, after failing to follow the rules.

Then he left the room and locked the door behind him. The corridor, with its interlocking parquet wooden floor and pale green walls, had no paintings or decoration, and stank of antiseptic floor cleaner. In fact, apart from the occasional lick of paint, it hadn't changed ever since he first walked into the building to begin his career with the KGB in 1980.

These days, the name of his employer was the FSB, the Federal Security Service, responsible for internal security within Russia. However, his job, as head of counterintelligence, was not dramatically different. The aim was still to root out traitors to the Motherland, those who betrayed Russia's secrets to foreign governments. Many Russians still referred to the FSB as the secret police, originally named the Cheka.

Pugachov made his way down the bare concrete staircase, with its eerie echo, to the fourth floor, where he headed for a meeting room that was directly above the old third-floor office where the KGB's and now FSB's director had always had their quarters. The current occupant, his boss Nikolai Sheymov, had been preceded over the years by some of the darkest characters in Russian history, legendary men like Yuri Andropov and Lavrenty Beria.

Pugachov's mind went back to the telephone briefing he had had from Sheymov the previous week telling him that the president had issued direct orders to further ratchet up the already heavy surveillance of foreign intelligence officers, especially the Americans and British.

Sheymov had reported back the words of the president, which, typically of him, he had apparently written down. *Make sure Pugachov locks up Moscow . . . I want the city watertight . . . If CIA or MI6 go out, we need to be all over them . . . records and photographs of where they go and who they meet . . . Russians or Westerners.*

Pugachov pushed open the door to find two of his subordinates sitting in front of a video monitor screen that was mounted on the wall.

"What have you got?" Pugachov asked without preamble.

The man nearest to him, Roman Gurko, turned his head. "We have had eyes and cameras on six of them today, including the CIA station chief."

"Good. Anything worth following up?"

"Possibly. You want to look at some of the video?"

Pugachov nodded his head and sat down next to them.

After Sheymov had confirmed Pugachov as head of counterintelligence a few months earlier, elevating him from a previous spell as roving troubleshooter, Pugachov's first act had been to move Gurko, one of his most trusted lieutenants, from the St. Petersburg office back to Moscow.

Gurko was an FSB surveillance expert, and in line with the orders from Putin, Pugachov had detailed him to increase monitoring of the known CIA operatives inside the US embassy at Bolshoy Deviatinsky Pereulok, west of the city center, and their MI6 counterparts at the British embassy next to the river, a short walk from the US building.

Pugachov's best estimate was that of the 1,200 or so people employed at the US embassy, about 300 were Americans and the rest locally employed people—for example, drivers, accountants, electricians, and guards. Of the 300 Americans, about 25 were CIA, he thought, give or take a few. Numbers at the British embassy were slightly less, he estimated.

The FSB held detailed files on all of the suspected spies. Gurko and his men had their work cut out to monitor all of them and so tended to rotate coverage in a fairly random way so that their targets would never know if they were being followed or not.

"Take a look at this," Gurko said, pressing a button on a remote control unit he was holding. "This is the Marriott hotel. Target is Michael Warner, supposedly employed as an archivist at the US embassy, except he is not just an archivist."

On the screen, a video appeared of a man walking down a corridor. As he reached a doorway, he bent down, pushed an envelope beneath a door, and then continued onward.

"Warner has just pushed that envelope under the door of a room booked by a mid-ranking manager in the defense ministry from Odessa, who's staying here for a conference."

Pugachov pursed his lips. "Get the Odessa guy in."

"Now?"

"Yes, tonight," Pugachov said. "We will let him stew overnight, and you will have to grill him in the morning, as I am in meetings all day. Anything else?"

"Yes, there is this one," Gurko said, pressing the remote control again. "This is the CIA's station chief, Ed Grewall, again. Third day this week watching him. This time we got into his gym."

A video began to play showing somewhat jerky footage of a gym full of treadmills and weights machines.

"How did you film this?" Pugachov asked.

Gurko tapped his left ear. "Headphones. Big ones. Built-in camera. It's controllable from a cell phone, which records the footage. Our surveillance tech got a day pass for the gym. Got there a few minutes ahead of Grewall—we knew where he was going."

Pugachov nodded and focused on the screen. As the video rolled, he immediately spotted Grewall, who walked to the treadmill nearest the window, carrying a towel and water bottle. He began running on the machine, next to a young woman on the neighboring treadmill.

"You think he's using the gym as a meeting place?" Pugachov asked.

Gurko shrugged. "I do not know. It is among the few places outside his home and office we have not had access to previously, so he has been in there many times unobserved. We decided to change that this week, given your instructions to step things up."

"Good thinking." Pugachov watched as Grewall pounded away. "Does he actually have contact with anybody on this visit? It does not look like he is having anything to do with that woman next to him."

Gurko shook his head. "No, no sign of any communication. Not with that woman nor with another one who used that machine later. Look at this." He pressed the fast-forward button on the remote control, and the video whizzed onward until the point when the second woman appeared on the treadmill next to him, at which point Gurko slowed the film down to normal speed again.

There was definitely no evident interaction between Grewall and the woman, blonde and middle-aged, whom Pugachov also scrutinized closely. He creased his forehead a little. There was something about the woman that looked vaguely familiar, although he couldn't place her or think why he was getting that feeling.

"Are you seeing anything?" Gurko asked. "You are frowning."

"No, I am not seeing anything. I thought I might have seen the woman before, but perhaps not."

Gurko shrugged. "I do not recognize her at all." He paused. "Do you want me to forward to the next relevant part, where he leaves?"

There was a grunt of asset from Pugachov.

Gurko fast-forwarded to the point where Grewall stopped his machine, picked up his towel, and walked away.

The video had been running at normal speed again for only a second or two when there came a sharp double knock at the door of the meeting room, which then squeaked loudly as it opened. Pugachov and Gurko turned their heads.

It was Sheymov's investigations directorate chief, Sofia Maninova, a fearsome high-flier who Pugachov thought had a particularly appropriate surname.

Maninova, who sported a military-style gray crew cut, stood in the doorway, hands on her hips, and stared at Pugachov. "Ah, there you are. I've been looking everywhere for you. The boss wants you to join a conference call in half an hour. In my office."

Pugachov, who had always disliked Maninova, frowned. "What is it about?"

"He wants to discuss a corruption investigation I have got running. We think there might be a counterintelligence angle to it, so he wants you on the call."

Pugachov exhaled. "All right. I will be there. Half an hour."

Maninova nodded and exited the room, closing the door behind her with another sharp squeak.

Pugachov turned back to the screen, where the video of Grewall had finished running.

"Stupid woman. I cannot stand her," Pugachov said.

"I know," Gurko replied. "Arrogant, aggressive, rude."

Pugachov nodded. "Sums her up." He pointed toward the screen. "Have we seen all of that one now?"

"Yes."

"And you noticed nothing? No interaction on his leaving?" Pugachov asked.

"No. Nothing."

"All right. Next film."

The men watched videos of four other CIA operatives out and about in the city, all of whom had been filmed covertly with cameras hidden in bags or caps. But apart from Warner at the Marriott, none of them appeared to be doing anything that warranted further investigation.

CHAPTER TWENTY-ONE

Friday, April 17, 2015
Moscow

Shevchenko knew that she had to pick her moment carefully. She had to catch Ekaterina, Vasilenko's secretary, in a good frame of mind and to do so when there were few other people in the vicinity so she would not feel self-conscious about being seen having a conversation with a superior.

As it happened, Shevchenko was busy until after half past four on Friday, by which point most staff at Yasenevo had either gone home or were preparing to do so. She had to spend most of the day dealing with the latest drama in the saga that had been running for several months at the Paris *rezidentura*.

The senior SVR officer in Paris suspected of being in the pay of the French intelligence service, the Direction Générale de la Sécurité Extérieure, the DGSE, had fallen for a trap Shevchenko had set. She had ensured he saw false documents supposedly detailing the weapons systems to be potentially installed on later versions of the Russian Navy's Borei-class nuclear submarines.

The information would be too good not to pass on to his French paymasters, and so Shevchenko was making arrangements for the officer to be caught in the act of making the transfer. She would need to travel to Paris for his apprehension by her hard men in Line KR's enforcement team in order to carry out the subsequent interview with him at the *rezidentura*.

It was only after Shevchenko had completed the necessary discussions with her counterintelligence officer in Paris that she was able to think about Ekaterina, who she knew from personal experience was one of the most diligent and hard-working secretaries in the organization and was therefore likely to be last out the door.

Sure enough, when Shevchenko arrived on the third floor, having taken the elevator rather than the stairs due to her aching body, she found Ekaterina still tapping away at her computer keyboard. There were only three other people visible on the entire floor.

"Hi, Katya," Shevchenko said, using her former secretary's usual nickname. "How are you doing? I would like a quick chat with Pavel. Is he around this afternoon?"

Ekaterina looked at her doubtfully, then took a quick glance to her left and right. "He's not in his office at the moment."

"Is he back this evening?"

"Er, I do not think so."

Shevchenko was getting the sense that Ekterina had probably been instructed not to divulge any information about her boss's whereabouts. That was normal at Yasenevo, so she didn't read too much into it.

"Could you get a message to him, then?" Shevchenko asked. "It is urgent, actually. An operational matter concerning something that Director Kruglov asked me to do for him."

She knew that invoking the director's name was likely to get a result, and so it proved. No secretary would want to run the risk of upsetting the top man.

"I can get a message to him, yes. He is in meetings, though."

"Here? It would be best if I see him face-to-face."

Ekaterina hesitated. "That is not going to be possible. He is out of town."

Shevchenko, who had picked up on the grapevine that Kruglov was in St. Petersburg, decided to push her luck.

"Ah, he is with the director in St. Petersburg, then."

Ekaterina, now clearly thinking that Shevchenko was in the loop, visibly relaxed. "Yes, he is. He loves Strelna."

Strelna? So he was at Konstantinovsky Palace with Kruglov. That sounded major. Usually SVR officials were only summoned to the president's residence to work on a project or operation that stemmed directly from him.

Shevchenko, who had been to Strelna four times previously, decided to try her luck again.

"Yes, it is beautiful. But he will have a tough time, given the president's involvement."

Ekaterina inclined her head and raised her eyebrows. "Yes. He said it was going to be stressful. It always is."

So the president *was* there. Shevchenko's mind was now in overdrive. Was this connected to the information that Vasilenko had obtained about the deaths of the two Americans in England? she wondered.

"Can I phone him there?" Shevchenko asked.

Ekaterina shook her head slightly and again looked around. "They are completely locked down. Even I cannot phone him. Messages only. You will have to wait until he comes back."

"Okay. Monday?"

"No. Not Monday. I think he will be there all next week."

Bozhe. God. Another week. Were they plotting an invasion of California or something?

"All right. Do not worry," Shevchenko said. "I may be going to St. Petersburg myself next week. Perhaps I can see him there. Is he staying in the city or at Strelna?" She actually had no intention, or time, to go to St. Petersburg because she was almost certain to be heading for Paris instead. Rather, she was just fishing to discover where Vasilenko was quartered.

"Strelna. As I said. He's locked down. They won't let him out." She gave a slight hint of a grin, as if to say her boss was in a difficult situation.

"I understand." Shevchenko responded in kind with a slight grin. "I know what it is like. When you next send him a message, please include a request for him to call me on a secure line."

Ekaterina nodded. "I will." She leaned back in her chair and scrutinized Shevchenko. "Are you all right?" she asked in a concerned tone.

"Me? Yes, I am fine."

"You look as though you have lost weight. A little bruised around the face. Are you sure you—"

She knows. Word of her interrogation had probably spread around Yasenevo like a forest fire.

"Katya, do not ask so many questions. You should know better around here." Shevchenko gave her another brief grin. Her former secretary missed little, which was why she regretted they were no longer working in tandem.

Ekaterina looked down at her papers, then back up again. "I know what you mean. Listen, take care. I miss working with you."

"Likewise."

Shevchenko made her way back to her office. If Vasilenko was going to be at Konstantinovsky Palace for another week, it would not be easy or safe to have the conversation with him that she needed, nor to obtain the information that he apparently had.

There was one way she might get a message to him, if needed, using a security guard she had cultivated with heavy tips, flattery, and slightly flirtatious conversation during previous visits, but she didn't want to go down that route unless forced to. If it went wrong, it might be fatal, given her Lefortovo experience. Rather, she would wait and see if Ekaterina facilitated the call she had requested first.

She swore softly as she waited for the elevator to take her back down one floor. There was definitely something major going on. She could feel it in the air. That might be part of the reason for the interrogation she had endured and probably for Vasilenko's seemingly enforced incarceration in Strelna.

But how was she going to find out what it was?

Now she had two problems on her hands—Paris and Vasilenko—both needing urgent attention in tandem. She had no answer to the second of yet, but she needed to find a solution, and quickly.

CHAPTER TWENTY-TWO

Saturday, April 18, 2015
Moscow

Dusk was well advanced by the time Jayne sat on the park bench at just before eight thirty. The figures of dog walkers had turned to black silhouettes, and the group of youths gathered near the bus stop looked like some kind of backlit modern art photograph against the bright lights of the restaurant window on the other side of the street.

She sat still for some time, watching and waiting, her senses in overdrive, looking and listening for any sign of surveillance. There had been none during the previous four hours that she had spent wandering around the streets and parks of northwestern Moscow.

The cafés, shops, and bars of the Begovoy district, the areas near the new Dynamo Moscow stadium construction site, and finally Petrovsky Park, where Jayne was now sitting, had provided a good and varied set of environments. They enabled her to test for any sign of coverage.

She wasn't expecting any, given that to the best of her knowledge, the Russian security apparatus was not aware of her presence in the country. So she felt confident but not complacent; she could never be certain, not with the ever-present threat from powerful zoom lenses, CCTV, and drones. The task of getting "black," free of watching eyes, was definitely more difficult now than it had been when Jayne had begun her career in the Secret Intelligence Service in 1984.

During her four-hour sojourn, she had bought a large triangular steel cake knife from a department store. It was far less obtrusive and more easily explainable than a garden trowel and yet would serve precisely the same purpose for what she had in mind.

She pulled a pack of Winston cigarettes that she had bought at a tobacconist earlier in the day and lit one. Usually she didn't smoke, but it was good cover when required on operations, and on this occasion a quiet cigarette helped explain her presence on the bench.

As she did so, she looked through the silhouetted trees toward the apartment block seventy meters away across the other side of the street. That was where Shevchenko lived. Then she glanced over her shoulder at a clump of bushes a few feet behind her, up against a three-meter-high redbrick wall that marked the boundary between the park and an enclosure that held a group of businesses: a car wash, a children's home, and others.

It seemed that Grewall's team had chosen an ideal location, adjacent to Shevchenko's apartment, thus allowing an evening stroll to be used to transfer data to the receiver, yet hidden and unlikely to be discovered inadvertently.

It was now dark, and Jayne's black jacket and trousers ensured she melted into the background. She checked her surroundings yet again: there was nobody nearby, no loitering passersby or courting couples.

She walked a few meters to the bushes behind her and slipped the cake knife out of one pocket and the SRAC receiver out of another. The earth was damp and soft after the winter's snow and rain. Within a few seconds, she had dug a shallow hole about fifteen centimeters deep, inserted the receiver, and covered it with earth again. She tapped it flat with the sole of her shoe and swiftly returned to her bench, checking once again for any sign of observers. Again there was nothing.

Jayne casually rose and made her way out of the park, part of her task for the evening now completed.

Until the receiver had been buried and its location fixed, there had been no point in meeting Shevchenko to hand over the transmitter. But now she could start making arrangements.

She sent a one-word message to Grewall: *Done*.

That was a signal to him that she had succeeded with the receiver and was therefore in a position to press ahead with their meeting, provisionally planned for later that evening, if they could both be certain they were black.

Handing over a piece of SRAC kit was something that could be done in silence in a gym. But making secure arrangements and choreographing a sophisticated meeting with the West's highest-placed agent in the SVR, including the handover of SRAC kit, required some face-to-face discussion.

But she knew Grewall wouldn't take a risk and would only meet if he was completely certain he was clear.

She found a café, ordered a hot chocolate, and waited.

Fifty minutes later, she received a short message. *Site TIGER 23:11*.

Site TIGER was a stairwell in a multistory parking lot only a kilometer away on the other side of Petrovsky Park, and it was now half past ten. That gave her forty-one minutes. She buttoned her jacket and set off.

By nine minutes after eleven, she was waiting in a stairwell on the first basement level of an underground twenty-four-hour parking lot beneath a small shopping complex near to the half-built Dynamo Moscow soccer stadium. There were no cameras in that stairwell, Jayne noted, and her timing was spot-on, because within a couple of minutes, Grewall appeared through a set of swing doors opposite that led to the parking area beyond.

He nodded at her.

"Sure you're clear?" Jayne asked in a low murmur.

A flicker of irritation crossed Grewall's face. "Yes. Well done tonight. Let's discuss the VULTURE meeting." There was no time for pleasantries. They needed to be quick.

"Yes. It needs to be soon."

"I agree. I have a good location, a quiet street, 130 meters long, next to the metro, with trees on one side and alleyways for a quick exit if needed. We've labeled it site EAGLE. It works for VULTURE because she will stop there on her way to the airport. She has a flight to catch. It will be Monday evening, seventeen minutes after nine. It's the quietest night of the week, with fewer people on the street."

Jayne nodded, appreciating the tradecraft. It was a general rule in most intelligence services that meetings between case officers and agents should take place at an odd number of minutes past the hour to avoid predictability and to make them appear more random and coincidental.

Grewall handed Jayne a small piece of paper with a street name on it and the name of the metro station, Voykovskaya.

"That's site EAGLE. I will arrange for VULTURE to enter the street from the west, where she can park unobtrusively. You will enter from the east, near the metro station. Usual four-minute window to make the rendezvous or otherwise abort. You'll meet in the middle, on the side of the street with the trees, and will then have six minutes to walk and speak. Then you must split and continue onward."

"Good," Jayne said. That was a normal procedure. Six minutes was a short time to speak, but should be enough, and the risk of continuing for longer would be too great.

"Can you arrange for some countersurveillance at both ends of the street?" she asked. "I don't want to take risks."

Grewall frowned. "I'm not a big fan of CS for these meetings. More bodies attract more attention."

"Maybe, but on the other hand, if they are good, we can get a heads-up if they see FSB surveillance approaching." She had in mind that an abort signal could be given in such an eventuality.

Grewall remained silent for a couple of seconds. He was clearly reluctant. "All right, then. We can have one at each end. I will detail a couple of my juniors to that task, probably Yvonne and Chris. Make sure you know who they are, and we will double-check during tomorrow and Monday that secure communications between us all are working as intended. Our disguise tech is going to be busy. How about you? Did Langley set you up with a disguise?"

"Yes, two changes," Jayne said. Joanne Menary had provided her with glasses, a wig, a hat, a reversible jacket, and other props that could easily and quickly be used to change her appearance if needed.

"Make sure you check out the site tomorrow and work out where the alleyways leading off that street are in case the worst happens and you need to run."

"Thank you. Goes without saying," Jayne said. "Can you put cars with drivers in neighboring streets so I can get to them easily if things go wrong, or if I can't use the metro?"

"That is already in the plan. I will give you precise locations."

Jayne nodded. That was good.

"Right. I will get the meeting details to VULTURE," Grewall said. "You don't need to contact her unless it is extremely urgent."

He reached into his pocket and took out a small black velvet bag, then handed it to Jayne. "That's the comms kit for the exfil routes you've been briefed on by Langley. It came in the diplomatic bag. You're happy with the arrangements?"

Jayne took it. "Thanks. Yes, Green routes one and two. No problem. Hope I don't need them."

She removed a small black box, only seven centimeters long, from the bag. This was the all-important transmitter that would send a very low frequency activation signal, via satellite, including her precise GPS location, to the offshore team responsible for the exfil operation. Langley had shown her how to operate it. She pressed a test button on the side of the box, and two green LED lights flicked on.

"This seems good," Jayne said.

"Anything else?"

"Yes. I will need a weapon, ideally a Walther PPK .38. Couple of spare magazines, and a silencer too. I also need the number for VULTURE's burner in case of emergencies."

"We have Walthers at the station. I'll get one for you from the weapons locker," Grewall said. He gave her the burner number.

"Thanks. And I also need to move from my hotel. This will be my fifth night tonight. It's too long. Do you have a safe house I could use?"

Grewall pursed his lips. "I agree. I think one will be free on Monday morning, first thing. I will have a car left for you near the hotel. Someone will put the key under your hotel room door with details of where it is and the license plate number. The plates will be false, and you'll need to change them when you can find a suitable spot and you're sure there's no surveillance. Just a precaution. There will be two other sets of false plates in the trunk and a screwdriver."

They discussed a few other minor details, then Grewall checked his watch. "We need to separate now. I will be in touch sparingly." He nodded with an encouraging half smile, turned, and headed back through the double doors toward the parking area.

Jayne also exited the building the way she had come, her antenna for coverage still on alert. When she got outside into the darkness, she remembered she needed to dispose of the cake knife, which she took from her pocket and shoved into a nearby trash can.

* * *

Saturday, April 18, 2015
Moscow

The apartment that Pugachov had inherited from his parents, Feliks and Lidya, had a somewhat better view than his office. The fourth-floor home looked out over the Moskva River northeast toward the redbrick walls, towers, and palaces of the Kremlin complex, and his balcony caught the sun in the morning.

But Pugachov took a grim pride in knowing that his apartment building's history, stretching back to 1931, was just as gruesome as that of his workplace.

It was a spacious place, one of more than five hundred other apartments that were located in the House on the Embankment, the huge building that stretched across an entire block on Serafimovicha Street.

The Soviet elite—the civil servants and politicians—lived here in the 1930s. But the problem with them all being on one site was that Josef Stalin suspected them of plotting with each other, and he knew where to find them. More than a third of the occupants were killed during the purges of that decade. Everyone feared the knock on the door.

Pugachov had spent the entire previous day in FSB management and planning meetings that ran from eight in the morning until half past seven at night. It was a monthly ordeal that he had to suffer through, and he hated every minute, mainly because it took him away from the job he considered to be his priority: chasing moles.

After the meetings, the senior team had again, as usual, gone out for a dinner at a nearby restaurant that involved a large volume of alcohol and continued until two thirty in the morning. As a result, Pugachov had stayed in bed until ten that morning and then tried his usual array of hangover cures, none of which had a great deal of effect. At the age of fifty-nine, his system just didn't recover as quickly as it used to.

During the afternoon, he had headed off to see a couple of old friends from his KGB days for a long-arranged reunion. That had involved several coffees, followed by a few vodkas as afternoon turned into evening.

As a result, it was past ten o'clock by the time Pugachov arrived home, and he hadn't eaten yet. He removed a plate from the fridge containing a dinner prepared by his maid and pushed it into the microwave oven.

As he sat eating his chicken, potatoes, and vegetables, watching the lights of the Bolshoy Kamenny Bridge reflecting in the river below him, and as the effects of the vodka began to wear off, his thoughts went back to work, as they invariably did.

One of his character traits, which he recognized was sometimes positive, sometimes negative, was to be somewhat obsessive and relentless in his pursuit of any objective. It led him to seek absolute control over his environment, something reflected in the spotlessly clean countertops and orderly bookshelves in his apartment and in the paperless environ-ment of his office.

These tendencies had cost him two marriages and meant he had no children. The sprawling three-bedroom apartment, with its expansive living areas, three bathrooms, and huge kitchen, remained empty in his absence.

But when it came to work, he had quickly discovered that his attention to detail and unwillingness to leave stones unturned were a major positive. It meant he got results. When presented with a challenge, particularly by his supe-riors at the Lubyanka or, as was increasingly the case, the gods at the Kremlin, he was like a dog with a bone. He couldn't let go.

Now his thoughts focused on the need to firstly identify moles within Russia's own intelligence agencies, and secondly those individuals on the other side, at the CIA and MI6, with whom they were liaising.

In his head, he ran through the list of those who required closer scrutiny. As he did so, a picture flashed in his mind of the second woman in the gym who had been running on the treadmill next to the CIA station chief, Ed Grewall. He had occasionally thought of her the previous day, while stuck in his meetings, but hadn't had the time to really concentrate.

Who the hell was she?

She had short blond hair, like many women around Moscow, but certainly didn't look like a Russian, not SVR or FSB. But she still triggered a memory from somewhere, and he prided himself on his memory for names and faces, so he felt increasingly frustrated.

It was about half an hour later, after Pugachov had cleared up the remains of his dinner and sat on his sofa to relax with a glass of his favorite sweet dessert wine, that it came to him.

He remembered the extensive inquiry that had followed

the debacle in Tuapse the previous year, when he had gone to help his old KGB friend turned oil-and-gas oligarch, Yuri Severinov. A couple of huge fuel tanks at the refinery had been blown up, costing Severinov his life and badly injuring his ex-Spetsnaz friend Georgi Tkachev.

The FSB investigation that followed had confirmed that the explosion had been triggered as part of a successful covert operation by Western intelligence to rescue the children of a former CIA officer, Joe Johnson, who had been kidnapped by Severinov.

It also confirmed that the explosion was caused by Johnson's girlfriend, a British intelligence officer, formerly with MI6, named Jayne Robinson. She, like Johnson, had sneaked into Russia on a false passport, under a name he now couldn't recall. And she had somehow been exfiltrated afterward along with Johnson and his kids, because there was no record of her or the others departing the country via official channels.

Pugachov had spent some time last year scrutinizing photographs of her, and he now had a flash of memory that left him wondering whether it was her face that he had recognized in the video footage from the gym. He began increasingly to think that it might well be.

But hadn't she had dark hair before? He was certain she had, although he knew that would be easy enough to alter. Nevertheless, the face rang a bell. He might be able to confirm her identity by cross-checking the video footage from the gym using the FSB's new facial recognition system.

Pugachov sat up in his chair, slightly spilling his wine as he did so, feeling energized once again.

But if it was Robinson, how the hell had she gotten into Russia once again, despite a red flag over her true name and her alias?

And what was she doing training in a gym next to the United States' top intelligence officer in Moscow? He would make sure to find out. This, surely, could not be coincidence. And if they were communicating in the gym, then how?

As he drained his glass, an anomaly struck Pugachov as he continued to replay the gym video footage in his mind.

Dermo. The towel.

He realized with a start that Grewall had been carrying a towel when he walked into the gym. Had he taken it with him when he walked out? That irritating woman Maninova had walked in and interrupted them just as the video was showing Grewall leaving, and he had not checked. Then they had moved onto the next video. The more he thought about it, he had a feeling that the American might not have actually picked up the towel.

He had better go and watch the video footage once again to see. He would have worked all this out before if he hadn't been locked up in damned meetings for the entire day. Now he was going to have to resolve it tonight, otherwise he wasn't going to sleep well.

Pugachov glanced at the clock on his wall. It was just after half past eleven. He pulled on his shoes and a jacket, picked up his wallet and keys, and headed down in the elevator to the parking lot in the building's internal courtyard, where he had left his black Audi A5.

Then he drove to the Lubyanka, three and a half kilometers away. The security guards in the vehicle garage and at the office entrance didn't blink at the sight of a senior officer arriving at the office at nearly midnight on a Saturday night. It happened all the time. Often the officer was accompanied by a gray van containing someone who had been hauled in for an all-night interrogation.

Within ten minutes of arrival, Pugachov was seated once again in front of the video screen in the meeting room he had used with Gurko on Thursday. Despite being seen by some of his junior colleagues as a Lubyanka dinosaur, he had adapted easily to the many new technologies that the FSB had introduced, and he quickly found the gym footage stored on a secure server, complete with triple password protection and encryption.

Pugachov pulled out a pack of LDs from his jacket pocket and lit one as he watched the opening sequences. To his relief, he was immediately able to confirm his recollection that Grewall had indeed arrived carrying a towel and a water bottle. The video clearly showed him placing the towel on the floor between his treadmill and the one next to him. He then put the water bottle into a holder on the machine and started exercising.

Pugachov took a deep drag on his cigarette and fast-forwarded to the point in the video where the second woman arrived, also carrying a towel. Then he slowed the replay to normal speed. He hunched forward, studying the screen, with his left hand cupping his chin, his right holding his cigarette. The only illumination in the office was from a desk lamp and the video screen, which cast a somewhat eerie blue glow across his face.

Concentrate.

The video showed Grewall as he pushed the off button on the treadmill and picked up his water bottle. He then picked up his towel from the floor and walked away.

So it wasn't the towel.

"*Svoloch*. Bastard," Pugachov muttered, exhaling a stream of smoke that was highlighted by the desk lamp as it rose to the ceiling. "Then how?"

He sat there, his focus now on the blond woman. Thankfully Gurko's surveillance colleague had kept his camera running. No more than a couple of minutes after Grewall had left, she also finished her session and turned off her treadmill. Then she bent down and picked up her towel and also walked away. The video caught her taking a drink from the water fountain and then leaving the gym, at which point the film ended.

Pugachov leaned back and finished his cigarette. Now he was feeling frustrated. There had to be something.

Maybe he should watch the recording one more time.

Pugachov rewound the video, lit another cigarette, and played it again. This time he changed the setting to slow motion.

Was he missing something?

When he got to the point where Grewall turned off his treadmill, Pugachov hunched forward once more, his fore-head creased, staring at the figures on-screen that were now moving as slowly as spacemen on the moon.

And it was then, as the video ran at a snail's pace, that he suddenly realized.

Pugachov banged his fist on the arm of his chair and swore out loud.

It *was* the towel.

Before leaving, Grewall had reached over and picked up the towel nearest to the woman's treadmill.

He had taken *her* towel—not his.

That meant, then, that she had taken *his* towel.

Pugachov knew immediately he had just witnessed a gymnasium version of a brush pass, the transfer of something from one intelligence officer to another. He would bet a large amount of money that wrapped up inside Grewall's towel was something sensitive: maybe a wad of documents, some money, or some kind of electronic equipment, such as a USB flash drive.

One thing was certain: if they were carrying out that kind of transfer covertly, then there must be something afoot that they needed to hide from the Russian authorities.

And the more he stared at the woman, the more

convinced he was that it was indeed Jayne Robinson, despite her hair color.

Pugachov pulled out his phone from his pocket. The time showing on the screen was 12:46 a.m. But Pugachov didn't think twice. He tapped on Gurko's number.

"Roman, I am in the office, looking at your gym video from Thursday," he said as soon as the call was answered, not bothering to greet his colleague or apologize for calling when he was likely to be asleep. "It is about that woman on the treadmill next to Grewall. The second one, not the first."

There was a pause, and Gurko began to respond, his voice slow and croaking. "It is Saturday night. I was asleep. Why are you calling at this—"

But Pugachov didn't let him finish. "I think the woman is actually Jayne Robinson, British, former MI6," he said. "I'm 90 percent certain of it. She picked up something that Grewall left for her in the gym, wrapped in a towel. They swapped towels. How did you not spot it?"

There was a long pause. "I don't recall, sir, but it is—"

Pugachov cut his colleague off before he could make the feeble excuse he could see was coming. "Forget it," he snapped. "We need to make sure it is her—we can double-check that using facial recognition. I think she's changed her hair from dark to blond. Then we need the ID she is using now, which I assume is false and is what she used to get into Russia. And I need to know where she's staying in Moscow. You need to get into the office right now and get on it— forget your bed for tonight. Understood?"

Gurko paused for a beat, doubtless cursing his boss, before answering. "Yes, sir, sure. I'll get on it."

"And when you find out, I need a team on her immediately. I need to know what she's doing, who she's seeing, and why she's here. I don't want her to change her underwear without us knowing about it. But don't let her know we're onto her—if she's here on a fishing trip, I want to know most of all who she's trying to catch."

"Of course."

"And make sure you have someone tailing Grewall too, obviously."

"Yes, we will get someone back on him."

"Back on him? You mean you have nobody on him right now?"

Gurko hesitated again. "Not since the gym meeting, no, sir."

"Idiots."

Pugachov stabbed hard at the red button with his forefinger and ended the call.

Despite the hour, all his instincts were now on full alert. His gut, finely honed from decades of watching and participating in subterfuge, deception, late-night operations, and sophisticated mole-hunting on Moscow's darkened streets and in the shadows of its embassies, told him that on both sides of the fence there was much at stake here.

The instruction from the president, via Director Sheymov, to escalate surveillance, the summit taking place at Konstantinovsky Palace, and the encounter he had witnessed in the gym all told him he needed to be on top of his game. It was the kind of situation that could end up being career-making or career-breaking. And at his age, he couldn't afford to be thrown on the scrap heap because he knew nothing else.

CHAPTER TWENTY-THREE

Monday, April 20, 2015
  Moscow

It wasn't until just before midday on Monday that Pugachov finally got the result he wanted.

First, the video taken by the FSB's surveillance officer of the woman in the gym believed to be Jayne Robinson required some enhancement before the technical team had an image that was good enough to run through the agency's facial recognition systems. It had not been taken close up, and to get a still image from the video and enlarge it to a size that was usable proved a difficult task.

When they did run the check, it gave a 95 percent likelihood that it was indeed the person who Pugachov suspected it was, despite her hair color now being blond. The FSB and SVR had acquired a number of images of Robinson over her years as a Secret Intelligence Service officer, dating right back to her time in Islamabad in the late 1980s. The previous ones showed her with dark hair, as Pugachov had correctly recalled.

The next step, which proved a tougher challenge and explained the long delay before Pugachov got his outcome, was to identify what false name she had used to travel into Russia on this occasion.

Although the FSB's border guards, who ran immigration controls at Russian airports, were exploring facial recognition technology, the systems were still very much in the trial stages. There were as yet no automatic links to FSB or police records, and indeed, they were not expected to be implemented for several more years.

Therefore, Pugachov's team, led by Gurko, had to download tens of thousands of images of passengers arriving at Moscow's three international airports—Sheremetyevo, Domodedovo, and Vnukovo—over the previous two weeks onto hard drives and take them back to the Lubyanka for proper analysis using separate facial recognition software.

Pugachov guessed that Robinson would not have entered Russia any earlier than she had to and that her meeting with Grewall in the gym would have taken place quite quickly after arrival in the city. He therefore set two weeks as the time frame for the initial analysis, hoping it would prove sufficient.

He decided to start with the passengers at the largest airport, Sheremetyevo, twenty-eight kilometers north of the city center. The digital trawl through the virtual pile of images took a long time and threw up three possible results, which Pugachov and Gurko finally sat down to scrutinize.

The first was a woman named Tracey Furlong, holding a British passport, who had arrived directly from London on a British Airways service on Monday, April 13, and was scheduled to stay for ten days. The second, Nathalie Casartelli, was an Italian passport holder, who arrived using Aeroflot on Sunday, April 12, from Rome with a one-week stay. And the third was Siobhan Delks, another British passport holder, who had flown into Sheremetyevo on Tuesday, April 14, on an Aeroflot flight from the Lithuanian capital, Vilnius. She was scheduled to return on April 25. All three had flexible tickets, so their return dates could easily be amended.

Pugachov mentally ruled out Furlong, betting that Robinson would not have taken such an obvious option as to travel direct from London. He also guessed Casartelli was unlikely because to convincingly appear Italian would be an unnecessary complication. He therefore homed in on Delks.

He studied Delks's background, which indicated she was a history teacher researching a school trip to Moscow planned for her pupils the following year. It appeared solid enough. Yet that didn't surprise him. If the legend, with all its carefully backstopped details, had been constructed by MI6, he would expect it to be convincing. But her face was—to his mind, and according to the facial recognition software—Robinson's.

Pugachov, seated at his computer, turned to Gurko, who was standing behind him.

"This is her, Siobhan Delks, in my view," Pugachov said. "Get alerts out to all hotels in the city. We need to find her urgently and bring her in. If she is not in the hotels, we will widen the search."

"I will press the button now," Gurko said. He nodded and strode out of the office.

The FSB's process to locate individuals across Russia was a well-oiled, highly efficient machine that was utilized constantly and involved a track-and-trace methodology that swept hotel booking systems, airline and train ticketing, and credit card, internet, cell phone, and email usage.

It therefore took only an hour and forty minutes before Gurko returned to Pugachov's office, slightly out of breath from dashing up the Lubyanka's stairs and along its corridors.

"We have found where she has been. Staying at the Metropol the past six nights," Gurko said.

"Good. Get a surveillance team on her, then. I want to know who she is meeting." Now Pugachov was smelling the blood of a traitor.

"She checked out this morning at eight o'clock."

Pugachov tried not to roll his eyes. "Cell phone number?"

"Yes. She bought a MegaFon SIM when she arrived at the airport last Tuesday using the Delks passport, and she gave the number to the Metropol. But there's no phone active right now using that number. It must be switched off."

"*Dermo.*" Pugachov slapped the desk with the palm of his hand. He stared momentarily out the window across the gray expanse of Lubyanka Square, which stretched right across to shops, offices, and the white arches of the metro station entrance at the far side.

His instincts told him that something was about to happen. If Robinson had checked out, she was likely preparing for a meeting of some sort with an informant, following which she would most probably try to leave the country. Grewall had to be involved too.

"And just confirm to me that you have someone tailing Grewall?" Pugachov asked.

"Yes, as you instructed, we have been back on him since first thing yesterday morning, after you saw the gym video. But he just went straight into the embassy this morning as usual."

Pugachov leaned back in his chair, his hands placed behind his head, thinking.

Who is she going to meet?

To that question, Pugachov had no answer. He knew only one half of the equation. So his focus would have to be on Robinson and Grewall.

He turned back to Gurko. "If Robinson checked out at

eight, can you get CCTV from outside the hotel and see where she went? Get a license plate number, whatever you can see. That is our best chance."

Gurko nodded. "We will do it."

"This is difficult," Pugachov said. "But I see no other option. We will have to dramatically increase sweep searches across the city tonight. Focus on the areas we know are good meeting points. If we get anything from the cameras or other sources between now and then, we can narrow it down."

"Yes, sir. I will inform the surveillance teams."

CHAPTER TWENTY-FOUR

Monday, April 20, 2015
Moscow

The soles of her feet ached, her right knee was stiffening up, and she was feeling a little dehydrated after four hours of walking through the streets, parks, and shopping centers of northwest Moscow and riding metro trains and buses.

Jayne stepped out of the metro car and walked along the island platform of Voykovskaya station, one of the most northerly stations on the Zamoskvoretskaya line, shown as dark green on the metro map.

The north- and south-bound tracks ran symmetrically on either side of the island, both sides of which were bordered by rows of granite-clad concrete pillars that stood a few meters apart. A single giant advertising poster for a cell phone provider was mounted on the blue-tiled station wall on the far side of the tracks.

Jayne's rubber-soled shoes squeaked a little on the shiny brown granite slabs that formed the platform surface and, hyperconscious of every sound now, she tried to walk a little more deliberately to reduce the noise.

She had to admit, Moscow's metro stations were significantly more elegant and aesthetically pleasing than London's or New York's, with their murals, mosaics, candelabras, and other artistic elements.

Thankfully, there were only a handful of other people there, all making their way, heads down, toward the exit, which made it easier for her to check one final time for any sign of surveillance. There had been none all evening, of that she was certain, but she had learned from previous bitter experience that a four-hour surveillance detection route counted for nothing if she failed to spot some anomaly during the final minutes.

Jayne glanced at her watch. It was eleven minutes past nine. She had another six minutes to get upstairs to the street and get herself into position. She knew from the test run she had carried out the previous day that it was more than sufficient.

She made her way up the stairs, through one of the eight chunky steel ticket barriers, and out across the empty ticketing hall toward the exit. A lone ticket agent sat behind his glass screen at the kiosk to her right, reading a newspaper.

The chilly night air hit her in the face as she emerged onto the plaza outside the station. The temperature had dropped sharply since the sun set, and she was glad of the warmth provided by the thick jacket she was wearing, as well as the hiding place it provided for the Walther pistol, two spare magazines, and the silencer that she had pushed into its inside pocket.

Now she was looking forward to getting this meeting over with and returning to the safe house to which she had driven that morning, an apartment on Novopeschanaya Street, in the Aeroport district, ten kilometers northwest of the city center. As promised, Grewall had left a car for her near the hotel, a silver Škoda Octavia sedan, similar to thousands of others in the city.

Despite all the years of experience of meeting agents and informers in some of the darkest corners of the globe, she still felt a prickle at the back of her neck and a sharp twist in her stomach as the moment drew closer.

She knew that if she got something wrong at this stage, it would amount to far more than just a blot on her copybook. It would without any doubt lead to the death of Shevchenko at their very first meeting on Russian soil—the Russians would show her no mercy, that was for sure. For Jayne, it would likely mean a spell in some Russian prison.

Her eyes flicked across the plaza, which spanned the fifty-meter gap between the ends of two streets. The remainder of the space between the two streets was filled with a small park, comprising an expanse of neatly cut grass, dense trees, and a couple of narrow concrete pedestrian paths.

Jayne scanned the plaza and the park for anyone who looked out of place, and secondly for the countersurveillance officers that Grewall had promised.

There were no loitering commuters, nobody eating take-away food on the bench, no cars waiting outside the station with engine running and windows down. That was positive. Then, at the northern side of the plaza at the end of the street where the meeting was to happen, she saw a man in a black leather jacket, leaning against a lamppost and smoking a cigarette with a newspaper tucked under his arm. That was Chris Joint, a CS guy, as promised. Jayne ignored him.

She walked until she was off the plaza and on the sidewalk that separated the park from the street where she was to meet Shevchenko. She paused beneath some trees and checked her watch again. One minute to go. It was quiet, but the background hum of traffic provided just enough cover to help muffle their voices. That was good.

To fill the minute, Jayne pretended to make a phone call, which allowed her to turn and check once more behind her. Everything looked in order. She finished the mock call, pocketed the phone, and focused on the far end of the street, about one hundred meters to the west.

From around the corner beneath a streetlight on the left, a figure appeared on the sidewalk, moving at a steady pace. It took only a second for Jayne to know that this was Shevchenko. Despite the dark coat, she could make out the sprightly, almost athletic gait that she recalled from their previous meeting in Washington, DC, against the background of the trees to the left of the street. She was right on time, although Jayne would have expected nothing less.

This was it. Jayne felt a surge of adrenaline flow through her, and all thoughts of her aching feet and legs vanished. She also began to walk, her aim being for them to meet roughly at the halfway point of the street.

"Greetings, Jayne," Shevchenko said in a low voice as they drew level. "You are looking well."

"You too, Anastasia," Jayne said, although at first glance in the gloom she felt that Shevchenko looked thinner in the face than she recalled. Finally meeting her in person seemed strange after such a long wait. "It's been longer than I expected. Eight months. I'm glad to see you."

Shevchenko looked her up and down. "Have you had a long walk tonight?" She clearly wanted to be sure that Jayne had carried out a thorough surveillance detection route.

"Four hours. I didn't want to take any risks. Things seem difficult here right now. A lot of surveillance. And you?"

"Three hours, mostly in my car. I parked in the next street." She pointed through the trees to the far western side of the park. "I am going to the airport directly from here, then taking a flight to Paris. We have no time to waste. Let us walk." The Russian indicated that they should walk back the way she had come, to the dark end of the street, away from the metro station and the traffic.

Jayne nodded in agreement and mentally listed the items she needed to discuss. First was a date and time for the next meeting. That was always the priority in case they were interrupted.

"For our next date, can I suggest site BUZZARD, in exactly two months. June 20. Same time," Jayne said. Site BUZZARD was much nearer to the city center and the suggestion was based on the assumption that Shevchenko would not need to head to the airport afterward, as was the case tonight.

"Yes, perfect."

"Now, what do you have? I am especially interested, as you might imagine, in the case of the two Americans shot dead in the UK."

Shevchenko hesitated a fraction. "Yes. I know about that. But I have found it difficult to obtain the information I need over the past two weeks—the why, the reason for those shootings."

She turned her head to look at Jayne, and in the light from a restaurant on the other side of the street, Jayne saw for the first time a large bruise beneath Shevchenko's left eye. And now she was certain: her face was definitely thinner.

"Are you all right?" Jayne asked, tapping her own cheek. "The bruise. You look as though you have lost weight."

"That is the difficulty," Shevchenko said. "They have suspected me. Not based on any evidence, but you will remember the delay last August before I contacted Yasenevo after Wade committed suicide. It was while I was volunteering my services to you and to Langley. They have had issues with my explanation. They put me in Lefortovo last

Monday and gave me a lot of shit last week. Five days of it. I cannot tell you how bad it was."

A chill ran down Jayne's back. "I'm very sorry indeed to hear that. I can only imagine what it was like. I hope you're recovering? Are you all right?"

"Yes. But do not worry. I gave nothing away, and they had nothing. I stuck it out, with difficulty and much pain. Bastards. But it meant I have struggled to get hold of the information I wanted."

Shevchenko briefly described her ordeal, which Jayne listened to in grim silence. She felt her spirits fall a little, partly at the news of Shevchenko's physical beating and also because she had been hoping for insight into the shootings.

"That is not good to hear," Jayne said. "Do you think you are now in the clear?"

Another pause. "I do think I am cleared, yes. They really have nothing on me. I have kept my nose very clean since coming back and have done some good work. There is more work to be done tomorrow in Paris, which is why I am going there. A mole who has been leaking our military secrets to the French will be uncovered, and I will get credit for it, hopefully up to the president's level, even. I am hopeful that will restore me fully in their eyes. We will see."

"Good. So what are the prospects of obtaining the information we need sometime soon?" Jayne asked.

As she spoke, Jayne continued to scan the small park to her left, among the trees, the street ahead, and the intersection at the end. There was a woman on the corner, wearing denim and smoking a cigarette while apparently engaged on a phone call. That was Yvonne Broad, the second of Grewall's countersurveillance team.

"Well, there is good news and bad," Shevchenko said. "The good first. I do believe that our mutual friend, the one you have code-named SOYUZ, has what you need."

"You believe? You haven't spoken to Vasilenko?" She didn't need to use code names; they both knew who SOYUZ was.

"No. Messages only. And that is the bad news. He has been locked up, sequestered, you might say. He is at a special planning conference or something near St. Petersburg. At Konstantinovsky Palace, in Strelna. The president's residence."

"I see. Locked up? You mean for security reasons?"

"Precisely. I suspect that something big is being planned. But I do not know what. That is the issue. Everything is tightly contained. He was included, and also his boss Fyodor Unkovsky, who heads the American department, but because of the suspicions they had, I was not included in this particular project, this operation."

A thought crossed Jayne's mind. "Is this operation part of Operation Pandora?"

"I do not know. I am sorry. It may be."

Operation Pandora was an umbrella operation that Shevchenko had mentioned the previous August. It comprised a wide set of active measures and individual operations to infiltrate, influence, and compromise the United States at political and corporate levels over a number of years.

"So, what are you saying?" Jayne asked. "We need to speak to Vasilenko about this?"

"You are correct. Yes. I am not in a position to do so. I was due to meet him the day they took me to Lefortovo, but he did not come. At first I thought they were interrogating him too, but I have since discovered it was because they wanted him at Strelna. You need to speak to him as quickly as possible. I believe there is some urgency."

Jayne privately felt a surge of gratitude that they had been able to have a face-to-face meeting. There was no way such information could be safely exchanged via electronic messaging.

They were getting near the end of the street, and Shevchenko signaled with her hand that they should turn around and walk back the other way, toward the metro station.

The two women fell into step once again. As they did so, Jayne reached into her pocket and removed a plastic bag containing the SRAC transmitter, which she handed to Shevchenko.

"That is your covcom," Jayne said. "The receiver is in the park, seventy meters across the street from your apartment, buried up against the brick wall in the bushes. The precise location is on a piece of paper in the bag. Read it and burn it. The transmitter is standard kit. You will know how to operate it. It will connect up to twenty meters from the receiver."

"Good work. Thank you." Shevchenko slid the package into her inside coat pocket. As she did so she glanced sideways. "Are you carrying a gun?" she asked, nodding toward Jayne's midriff.

This old vixen misses nothing.

"Yes. Just in case. You?"

"No. I need to go directly to the airport from here." She dipped a hand into her own jacket pocket and then held it out toward Jayne, who took the small object, a USB flash drive.

"There is a lot of material on there. Mostly navy and air force stuff. Forward planning, some technology details. All top secret. I think your people will like it," Shevchenko said.

"Thanks." Jayne put the flash drive into her pocket and glanced at her watch. They had another minute. Best get back to the important issue at hand. "So how do I get to speak to Vasilenko if he's locked up at the palace in Strelna?"

"I have requested a call from him, via his secretary. But that may take time. I have only one other option."

"Which is what?"

"I know a friendly security manager at Strelna. He has helped me with a few discreet things I have asked him to do, information I needed, and I have rewarded him financially. His wife works at the palace too—she provides certain services to the leadership. They would now have a lot to lose if I made a complaint about them, shall we say, so they help me out. It is *kompromat* at a local level." Shevchenko gave a short laugh.

"I understand," Jayne said. She didn't ask what he had done for her but presumed he had likely given her information about guests at the palace. Time was short, and such arrangements were how Russia functioned. "His name?"

"Gavriil Nikitin. Big guy, built like a bear. I can tell you his number. I memorized it this morning, just in case."

She slowly recited a cell phone number, which Jayne repeated twice, committing it to memory.

"Do you have his address?" Jayne asked. "It might be safer to pay him a visit rather than message his phone." It seemed quite likely that if he was a security guard at the palace, his phone would be monitored.

Shevchenko nodded and gave the address of a house in Strelna, which Jayne also memorized.

"Strelna?" Jayne asked. "Near the palace?"

"Very near, yes. Though his house is anything but a palace."

Shevchenko paused, apparently thinking. "If you are going to meet Vasilenko, it will of course be high risk. Do you have an exfil arrangement in place, just in case the worst happens?"

Jayne nodded. "I have one via the Gulf of Finland, not far from Strelna, actually. Hopefully it won't be necessary."

"Good."

Jayne scanned the end of the street yet again. Through the trees, now on her right, she could see the red gleam from the large backlit letter M above the metro station entrance on the plaza.

At that moment, a car slid slowly across the intersection at the end of the street they were on, appearing from behind the trees and vanishing as it passed behind the buildings to the left. It must have driven over the plaza next to the metro station, Jayne thought.

She glanced over her shoulder just in time to see another car pass across the other intersection behind them, this time moving a little quicker.

Then, just as she turned back, a third car turned onto their street from the plaza, crawling very slowly in low gear. Its headlights were off, and it was using sidelights only.

As the car turned, there was a small, bright flash of light from the countersurveillance officer standing fifty meters away from them. He had turned his cell phone, screen brightly lit, in their direction. A prearranged signal. Not that she needed it. A sixth sense, fueled by the appearance of the cars and the slow speed at which they were traveling, had told her there was trouble here.

"Shit," Jayne said. She pushed Shevchenko in the small of her back toward the trees, but the Russian had realized what was happening and had already begun to move in that direction.

As soon as they were in the shadow of the trees, Jayne hissed at Shevchenko, "Go."

They began to run across the grass, dodging between tree trunks. Jayne hoped that the darkness and the trees would provide enough cover to prevent them from being seen.

As she ran, she heard the whine of an engine being thrashed in low gear and the squeal of tires on pavement as the car in the street accelerated.

"FSB," Shevchenko panted, unnecessarily.

As they ran straight over the footpath that ran through the park and into the trees on the other side, Jayne glanced over her right shoulder and caught a glimpse of someone running along the footpath in their direction, maybe forty meters away.

Bloody hell, who's that?

She felt certain the car hadn't stopped yet. There came the screech of brakes behind them, confirming her thought, then the slam of a car door and a loud shout in Russian. "*Stoy!* Halt!"

Jayne pulled an iron-gray wig from her side jacket pocket as she ran and pushed it down over her dyed blond locks, jammed a knitted wool hat over the wig, then grabbed a pair of brown plastic glasses from her breast pocket and put them on. Next to her, Shevchenko was also pulling on a wig, a short salt-and-pepper one, followed by a Russian fur hat with earpieces that she put on over the wig.

Ahead of them, beyond the trees, was the street on the other side of the park. Jayne knew from her reconnaissance trip that there was a narrow alleyway that bisected the apartment buildings roughly halfway along. No car would fit down there. And she recalled that the street beyond was where Shevchenko had said she parked her car.

"You take the alley," Jayne said. "Get your car. I will draw the surveillance. I'm going to the metro."

"But—"

"No. I will take them with me."

Jayne had in mind that it would be better for her to be caught than Shevchenko.

For her, capture would likely mean an awful few months, maybe even a year, behind bars, followed by ejection from the country in some sort of prisoner exchange.

For Shevchenko, however, being caught would mean certain death.

She had to give her agent the best possible chance.

There came another shout behind them. "*Stoy! Stoy!*"

"Go!" Jayne said, sensing hesitation on Shevchenko's part.

Shevchenko nodded and ran toward the street and the darkness of the alley between the apartment buildings beyond.

Meanwhile, Jayne sprinted along the street toward the metro station, keeping as close to the trees as she could. This was risky, but she had no choice. She wanted FSB surveillance to follow her, not Shevchenko. Her gamble was that if she could make it down the stairs and onto the platform, there was a chance of getting on a train before her pursuers realized what had happened. And her disguise, meager as it was, might be enough to confuse matters if she was caught on CCTV.

There came the loud revving of another high-powered car behind her, more screeching of tires, and Jayne found herself caught in headlights, her long shadow stretching out in front of her as she ran. This had to have been one of the other cars she had seen previously.

Dammit.

Jayne cut to her left nearer the trees, trying to get out of the headlights. There were more shouts behind her, followed by two gunshots in quick succession.

On hearing the shots, Jayne instinctively weaved even farther to her left, then right again as she ran.

The car behind her was getting closer. She could hear its engine whining.

"Shit," she muttered as she neared the end of the park.

Another thirty meters to the metro.

There were two more gunshots behind her as she tried to put in another burst of speed.

Seconds later came the screech of locked brakes and the squealing skid of rubber on road, followed by the loud thud of an impact.

A long, piercing woman's scream cut the night air, making Jayne's hair stand on end. A moment later came the sound of another crunching impact.

Oh God.

Jayne kept running across the plaza and down the steps beneath the red neon M sign. She slowed to a brisk walk just before she came into the line of sight of the ticket office and tugged her hat down farther over her forehead. Once through the barriers, she ran again down the stairs and onto the platform.

There was a rumble in the distance but no train in sight.

Come on.

Jayne glanced behind her, her stomach tied in knots, waiting for the clatter of pursuing boots down the stairs.

She fought the urge to run again and instead walked briskly to the end of the southbound platform, farthest from the entrance, and stood behind a concrete pillar, pushing the ill-fitting glasses back up her nose.

Quickly, please God.

Finally, in the darkness of the tunnel at the far end of the platform, appeared a row of six headlights, getting rapidly larger. There was a flash of blue-green branding and fluorescent light through the windows of the train, which came to a halt with a squeal of steel on steel.

Jayne emerged from behind the pillar and strode through the opening doors of the end car. She was the only person there apart from a white-haired lady with a plastic shopping bag and a small terrier that sat at her feet.

A minute later, the train began to move, and Jayne put her head between her knees, a feeling of nausea rising inside her.

She guessed what had happened back there.

CHAPTER TWENTY-FIVE

Tuesday, April 21, 2015
  Moscow

"Of course, it was the lying FSB. Who writes this shit?" Grewall said as he threw the newspaper across the room.

The headline over the story, buried halfway down page nine in the Russian-language paper, read Drunk Hit-And-Run Driver Kills Pedestrian. The article, only six paragraphs long, was based on a briefing given by a police spokesman and did not identify the victim, saying only that she was thought to be an American visitor.

Jayne stood, hands on hips, not knowing what to say. She felt another wave of revulsion rise up inside her and looked down at the floor. There was silence from the other three CIA officers who had gathered at the safe house where Jayne was staying.

It seemed like a quiet moment of tribute, of respect, for Yvonne Broad, who, in attempting to divert the attention of

the FSB's surveillance team that was pursuing Jayne and
Shevchenko, had been mown down by the rapidly acceler-
ating car as she emerged onto the street.

Whether the FSB driver had driven into her deliberately
or accidentally was impossible to say. The Moscow police
dealing with the incident had put up a wall of silence, doubtless under instruction from on high.

Jayne had more or less guessed what had happened, but
the scenario had been confirmed by the other CIA countersurveillance officer, Chris Joint, who had seen it unfold from
the other side of the park.

As Jayne and Shevchenko ran for cover, Broad had seemingly realized what was going on and sprinted from the street
corner where she had been posted with her cigarette and
phone across the park. She had run through the trees and
into the melee that developed as the chase heated up,
intending to distract or confuse the Russians.

But Yvonne had been hit full on by the fast-moving FSB
car, sending her spinning more than ten meters forward into
the windshield of a parked van.

Yvonne had effectively given up her life to save Jayne's,
because it was assumed the only reason the FSB had halted
their pursuit was because they immediately recognized who
Yvonne was and the need to cover up what had happened.
She would have been known to the FSB, without any doubt,
and there would be detailed files on her at the Lubyanka,
complete with multiple photographs.

The incident had allowed Jayne the time to make it onto
the train and out of the station. She had traveled two stops
south, exited the train, and then made her way on foot
through a tangle of narrow streets to the nearest bus station,
from where she had returned to the safe house.

It appeared that the FSB had simply departed the scene,

placing the mess in the hands of police. A classic cover-up of the type that they had all seen before from the Russians.

It also flew in the face of the unwritten traditional rule that intelligence services do not inflict violence on members of rival services, much less kill them.

Whether Broad's sacrifice had also saved the life of Shevchenko was not yet known. There had been no communication from the Russian since Jayne last saw her running toward the alley between the apartment buildings. It was hoped she had made it to the airport and on her late flight to Paris.

Of course, there would be a huge outcry at the death of an American, but it would be difficult to handle because Broad was not a declared intelligence officer. Rather, she had been operating under the guise of an archivist at the US embassy.

The Agency couldn't admit she was a spy, although that might well come out in time.

It was even more impossible for the CIA to admit to the operation that Broad had been a part of, given the involvement of Shevchenko, its biggest asset within Russian intelligence, and Jayne, a freelancer. Doing so would instantly sentence Shevchenko to death.

Grewall strode to the window, where the newspaper had landed, picked it up, and tore it up. Then he threw the pieces into a trash can in the corner.

"What I'd like to know is, how the hell the Lubyanka knew about the meeting in the first place," Grewall said as he turned around. "That's what worries me."

He glanced in turn at Jayne, Joint, and his deputy chief of station, Diego Cuenca, a streetwise operator and former narcotics cop from El Paso, Texas. All of them had made their way individually to the safe house in the Aeroport district to which Jayne had moved. They all took risks in doing so but knew they needed to get together to determine a way forward and to collectively pay some sort of tribute to Broad in their grief. Jayne didn't even know her, but the others had worked alongside her for the previous eighteen months since her arrival fresh from Langley.

"Jayne, I know the answer, but I have to ask. How sure are you that you were clean before the meeting?" Grewall asked.

"Completely," Jayne said. "No question about it. I was black." She glanced at Joint, who nodded in agreement.

"She's correct," Joint said. "I saw nothing."

There was a pause of several seconds before Cuenca answered. "I assumed so. Could have been just a routine patrol and we got unlucky. They've recently been increasing their sweep searches, as they call them."

"Maybe." Grewall glanced at each of his colleagues in turn. "Anyway, we don't have time for a proper inquest now. That can come later. So what are we going to do?"

"We screw them over in return," Cuenca said.

Jayne nodded. "I got my lead from VULTURE. I'm going to make damn sure we make use of it."

She had already briefed them about the intelligence she had received relating to Vasilenko and the apparent secret summit meeting going on at Konstantinovsky Palace in Strelna. The details of the potential security guard contact at Strelna, Gavriil Nikitin, and Shevchenko's ordeal at Lefortovo had also been passed on, and the contents of the flash drive obtained from Shevchenko had been downloaded, encrypted, and dispatched to Langley.

"There is something major going on," Jayne continued. "Langley and the White House are not going to forgive us if we compound the screwup over Yvonne by letting this slip."

Grewall stared at her. "You do realize you're going to be

target number one, or let's make that number two, if they put two and two together and work out that VULTURE is our source."

"Yes, I know. It's our job, my job, to make sure they don't. She's not going to give herself up—we know that. She survived being beaten up and having electricity shoved through her nipples and up her ass in Lefortovo without cracking. If she can put up with that, I'm damned sure I'm not going to make a mistake and give her away. Anyway, she told me she was about to reel in a big informer in Paris, so that might put her back in credit with the Kremlin. She's got balls of steel."

"So I see. Who's this informer?"

"One of the SVR people there is a mole for the DGSE. Naval secrets."

Grewall did a lap around the living room, his thumb stroking his chin. "All right. Maybe you're correct. You need to get to St. Petersburg and see if you can somehow use this security guy to make contact with SOYUZ. You can leave me and Vic to sort out the mess with Yvonne and get her body repatriated back to New Orleans." He briefly looked skyward. "I wouldn't like to be the one who has to inform her family. But we have another problem, don't we?"

"Several, but what specifically?" Jayne asked.

"We don't know whether the FSB has your identity, either real or your legend, do we?"

Jayne shook her head. "No, but we're not going to have time to put another legend together now and do it thoroughly. So either I head north and risk it, or we lose the lead we've got."

"True." Grewall paused. "Do you want to go through the arrangements for your exfil route again?"

"Route Green Two, Gulf of Finland. Vic's team briefed me

on it before I left Langley. I have the necessary comms kit, as you know."

Grewall picked up his laptop from the coffee table in the center of the room. "Fine. It might be best if I go through the logistics with you again, though. You'll need to memorize the detail very carefully. Just in case you actually need it."

CHAPTER TWENTY-SIX

Tuesday, April 21, 2015
Moscow

"So, one more time. How certain are you that the woman who ran off toward the metro was her?" Pugachov asked. He stabbed his forefinger on one of the four photographs of Jayne Robinson across the desk and looked up once again at the driver of the FSB surveillance car.

The man, a stocky guy with a shiny, greasy head who had been at the wheel of the car that had hit CIA officer Yvonne Broad, scrutinized the prints once more in turn. "I am fairly certain. It was dark. But slim, a bit athletic. Yes, I think so."

"You think, but you don't know," Pugachov said. It was a statement, not a question.

"I think I saw her putting on a dark wool hat when she was running through the trees," the driver said.

"Right. And what about the third person who ran off? Can you describe him or her?"

"No, I did not get a good look at all."

"Woman or man?"

The driver shrugged and shook his head.

"Go, get out. You need more observance training if you are going to do this job." Pugachov indicated with a jerk of his thumb toward the door of his Lubyanka office, and the driver rose to his feet and made his way out.

When he had gone, Pugachov leaned back in his chair, looked across the room at Gurko, and closed his thumb and forefinger together until they were nearly touching.

"We were this close. This damn close," Pugachov said. "Then that idiot hits the wrong woman, which means the other one gets away. It had to be Robinson, I am sure of it. And he does not even get eyes on the traitor, the big prize, who also escapes. Useless."

Gurko chewed his bottom lip. "He deserves a kicking."

Pugachov nodded. He felt the same. His surveillance teams, using CCTV footage, had tracked Robinson from outside the Hotel Metropol, where she had picked up a car parked a couple of streets away. She had driven alone northeast from the city along Leningradsky Prospekt, a huge divided highway with several lanes that was the main route out of Moscow in the direction of St. Petersburg.

The images from police traffic cameras showed the car, an anonymous silver Škoda sedan, traveling as far as the Aeroport district, where it turned off Leningradsky Prospekt into the suburbs, heading southwest.

But there the camera images ran dry, and they lost the car. The license plates had turned out to be false, and there were no further traces of them from cameras around the city, so Pugachov assumed Robinson had stopped and changed them somewhere unobtrusive and out of camera range.

After that, Pugachov had used his gut instinct. He assumed that Robinson was heading for a safe house somewhere in that Aeroport district, and further assumed that for geographical and practical reasons, any meeting with an agent of hers could possibly take place in that vicinity.

Aeroport district, named for an old aerodrome that once operated there, made sense. It was right at the center of a transport hub, near the point where several metro lines crossed, and where the Leningradsky Prospekt turned into the Leningradsky Highway and headed past Sheremetyevo International Airport out of the city. It was also near a cross-roads where a big artery that ran from northeast to south-west, the Ulitsa Alabyana, crossed the Leningradsky.

So Pugachov had ordered his surveillance teams to focus on the metro stations within a three-kilometer radius of the point where they had lost the CIA car, and to concentrate particularly on the vector heading toward Sheremetyevo.

His instincts had proved to be spot-on. The Voykovskaya station, where the action had taken place, was on the green metro line, the Zamoskvoretskaya, and was almost next to the Leningradsky Highway.

The FSB cars that almost trapped Robinson were system-atically trawling the area around the station looking for her when one crew spotted her and her companion, who had to be an agent. Otherwise, why would they have run the way they did?

If it hadn't been for the driver hitting the CIA woman, who he guessed was playing some kind of countersurveillance role, his feeling was that they could have caught the pair.

The CCTV images that came back from the metro station, which were not great quality, showed a figure wearing glasses and a black baseball cap over gray hair. But the walk was Robinson's—the athletic gait was the same as that seen in the video footage outside the Metropol.

Pugachov *knew* it was Robinson.

More CCTV footage had shown her getting on a train, then exiting the station two stops farther down the southbound line at Aeroport, which fit with his theory about where she might be staying. But from the metro station, she had disappeared.

His gut instinct told him that Robinson's agent had to be someone high up in either the Kremlin or the SVR, or God forbid, the FSB—someone with access to valuable secrets. She wouldn't have been wasting her time and taking such risks with an underling.

What a massive coup it would be if he could catch that individual as well as Robinson. He had a quick vision of receiving a Hero of Russia medal from the president at the Kremlin as his reward for such a monumental double strike at the main enemy.

Pugachov's phone rang. He fished it out of his pocket and glanced at the screen. It was his boss, the FSB director, Nikolai Sheymov, who was still at Konstantinovsky Palace with the president and others at the summit meeting that was continuing. He pressed the green button and tapped in his security key to accept the encrypted call.

"Hello, sir," Pugachov said.

"Leonid, listen to me. I have just come out of a meeting with the president, Ivanov, and Kruglov. We have read your short report about what happened last night. Your team messed it up badly—killing a US national in that manner is going to cause trouble at a time when we want to keep our profile in the United States as low as possible for reasons that will become clear in time."

"I'm sorry, sir, I have spoken to the driver. I believe it was an accident that occurred while we were chasing a bigger prize, and I—"

"I know what you were trying to do," Sheymov interrupted. "You do not have to explain. What we need to do is make sure we put things right. Ivanov has the knives out for me. You know what the bastard is like. My concern now is what the Americans are trying to do. We need to second-guess them."

"My worry, sir, is that Robinson's agent, whoever that is, has briefed her on the Strelna summit meeting," Pugachov said. He hesitated. "Do you have any further thoughts on the identity of that agent? Have you discussed it any more with Kruglov and Kutsik?"

There was little love lost between the FSB and the SVR. They had an intense rivalry for the affections of the president and his most influential subordinates such as Ivanov. Pugachov didn't expect his boss to have picked up anything of substance from the SVR leaders, as they would be keen to keep such intelligence to themselves and collect the glory if they did manage to unearth a mole, which he thought doubtful.

"Not much, as you would expect," Sheymov said. "They say little."

"What about Shevchenko? Do you think she is in the clear now?" Pugachov asked. He had discussed the Shevchenko case with his boss a couple of times after learning that the SVR counterintelligence chief had been hauled into Lefortovo for an intensive interrogation at the behest of Kruglov's personal counterintelligence guru, the frog-eyed Gennady Sidorenko.

Sheymov gave a short ironic laugh. "If she was not in the clear before, she is this morning."

"What do you mean?"

"Word came through from Paris earlier. Kruglov has been gloating about it. Shevchenko has personally caught a mole who was leaking our nuclear submarine secrets to the DGSE. It has been going on for the past year or so. He has done a lot of damage. I am hearing she laid a bear trap and he fell right into it—she fed him a batch of false documents about weapons systems for the Borei subs. He gave it to the French, who started subtly asking questions behind the scenes with the weapons manufacturers. So it was obvious it had come from him. Shevchenko is in Paris, overseeing it. They trapped him early this morning. He will be on the next flight back to Moscow, and then I guess next stop Lefortovo. The president has been in a good mood this morning because of that."

Pugachov grunted. "Good for her," he said, a sarcastic edge to his voice. "We could do with a catch like that."

"Over to you, my friend. You trap Robinson's mole, and he will be in an even better mood. But I am warning you, that could change in a flash. He is paranoid about the operation we are discussing here. If it leaks, you and I will be history."

Pugachov swallowed reactively. "I obviously do not know the details of your discussions, but to me, it sounds like a critical strategic meeting."

He held back from asking more. Such unnecessary inquisitiveness would do him no favors with his notoriously conservative boss. Indeed, he felt he had already possibly gone too far.

"You must never refer to this summit," Sheymov said, his voice taking on a distinctly abrasive edge. "As far as you are concerned, outside those four walls of your office, it is not happening."

"Of course, sir."

"But purely for your background information, you are correct. It is important. I need to be able to reassure Ivanov and the president that this gathering and the discussions being held here are in no danger of being infiltrated, and I need you to take steps to ensure that. You understand?"

"Yes, sir. I think you can give that reassurance."

"You fool. I have already told them that. But I need you to actually deliver it now. I will need you to travel to St. Petersburg to manage it—to make sure that the Strelna meeting stays watertight. And take with you whomever you need. Then do whatever it takes. This is possibly the most important operation of my career and certainly of this decade. Understood?"

"Got it, sir."

"Good."

The line went dead.

PART THREE

PART TWO

CHAPTER TWENTY-SEVEN

Tuesday, April 21, 2015
Atlanta, Georgia

There were two routes that Chuck Driscoll normally chose from to pick up his wife on Tuesday evenings from her job at the Carter Center. The quickest was to head a short distance up the busy Interstate 85 with its six lanes of chaos, which he hated, then cut along Freedom Parkway NE from its western end.

But as he pulled his silver Cadillac CTS sedan out of the parking lot opposite the Georgia state capitol building, where he served as secretary of state, he decided to take the slightly longer but quieter and greener route along Memorial Drive SE and north up Moreland Avenue NE.

His day, like every day in the role since he started five years earlier, had been crazily busy, with a nonstop schedule of meetings including a working lunch with his boss, Governor William Bruyn.

The Tuesday evening routine that he had gotten into

with his wife, Eve, of meeting her after work and then going for a quiet meal at their favorite seafood restaurant had become a two-hour haven from the stress that governed the rest of his working week. It was the only night when he wasn't in the office until at least eight o'clock. Sometimes it was more like ten before he left the building.

As the traffic lights turned green, he accelerated smoothly past Oakland Cemetery and tried to relax. He left his radio switched off, and the faint hum of the engine and the air-conditioning system were the only sounds inside his car.

But relaxation had been harder to come by more recently, especially after two other secretaries of state, both of whom he'd been close to, had been murdered in cold blood in England three weeks ago.

His mental state had deteriorated rapidly since then, though he'd been a little on edge ever since the National Association of Secretaries of State annual conference in Washington, DC, a couple of years earlier. That was when it had all changed, and not for the better.

I always thought I was invincible, he muttered to himself. *Idiot.*

Driscoll had come through intense experiences in the army in Afghanistan and Iraq and had always had a reputation for calm decision-making under heavy pressure. That was why his army career had flourished and why, after leaving the military, he had subsequently performed well as a management consultant for some of the international businesses operating out of Atlanta.

He had made a lot of money out of those attributes over the years, and they had been among his main selling points when campaigning for the secretary of state's role.

But now, for the first time in his career, at the age of fifty-one, he was suffering from poor sleep and a distinct lack of sharpness. Eve had become worried about it, and he found himself snapping at his two teenage children.

He knew the reason for his deteriorating state of mind.

Maybe it's time to back down, wind down, and get out.

But how?

It seemed as though he was in too deep.

Yes, he earned a salary well into six figures for his current job and had done the same while working as a management consultant. He had an army pension secured. But there was a large mortgage still outstanding on his house in Atlanta as well as on their beachfront holiday home at Tybee Island, near Savannah. He had school fees to pay and expensive holidays to cover, and there was little prospect of the financial demands easing for a few years to come.

He found himself thinking enviously of his wife and her relatively straightforward existence as a senior administrator at the Carter Center, where she worked alongside its founder Jimmy Carter, the former US president and onetime Georgia state governor. Her job, which she had held for more than ten years now, was to help promote human rights and resolve conflict globally. The organization did an incredible job, Driscoll had to admit, even if his political views did not always coincide with those of the aging Democratic former president, whom he had met several times.

If only she knew.

As Driscoll reached the intersection opposite Freedom Park, he piloted the luxury Cadillac left onto the eastern end of the single-lane Freedom Parkway NE, down through parkland and trees toward the Carter Center.

To his right, on an elevated path that ran parallel to the road on top of a grassy bank, a slim, athletic woman dressed in dark green Lycra was running hard, arms pumping.

Driscoll braked as he drew near the entrance to the Carter Center on the left and turned up the steep driveway into the parking lot, where he pulled into a space in front of the low-slung, elegantly curved structure of the building. He glanced at the clock on his dash. Eve wouldn't be out for another few minutes.

He leaned back in his seat and stretched, trying to ease some of the tension out of his body. Then he climbed out of the car, thinking that a short walk among the trees and landscaped grounds might help.

Driscoll wandered down through the parking lot for a couple hundred yards to a small traffic circle overlooking a pond, where he stood for a moment, gazing across the water, before turning and heading back again.

It was a balmy evening, the warmest of the year so far, with the temperature in the midsixties.

As he drew near to the main entrance, he saw Eve making her way out of the glass front doors of the center and down two short flights of steps between the trees to the parking lot.

She looked up, saw him, and waved, her long dark hair blowing in the breeze, a smile on her face as was invariably the case when he met her from work.

As she continued down the steps, there came the throaty roar of a powerful motorcycle as it revved up the driveway from the road outside the center. Driscoll turned his head to look at the bike.

The leather-clad biker gunned his engine as he rounded a small traffic island outside the main entrance, then drove sharply straight toward Driscoll.

The rider braked to a halt just ten yards away, turned his engine off, and still sitting astride the bike, lifted the visor on his helmet.

Driscoll stared at him.

"Charles Driscoll?" the biker asked in a heavy accent that Driscoll couldn't immediately place.

A reporter, here?

"I'm sorry, I don't take questions in this manner."

Right then, Eve came up behind her husband and put her left hand on his forearm. "Hi, Chuck, who's this?" she said, indicating with her other hand toward the biker.

"I don't know," Driscoll said.

"Are you Eve Driscoll?" the biker asked her.

"Ah, yes—"

The biker looked back at Driscoll. "Your wife."

He was starting to grow irritated. "She is, yes, but who are you and why are you asking?"

The biker unzipped a pocket in his jacket and smoothly took out a pistol that Driscoll could see had a silencer attached.

A shock wave immediately ran through Driscoll. "Hey, what the hell are you doing?" he said, his voice rising sharply in alarm. He instinctively took a step toward the biker.

But the biker raised the gun, forcing Driscoll to stop. The man flicked off the safety and pointed the barrel toward Eve, who began a piercing scream.

She was cut short almost instantly by a double thwack as the gunman fired two quick shots in rapid succession. The first hit her straight in the chest, knocking her backward, the second in her forehead.

"Eve—"

But Driscoll didn't get chance to complete his cry.

His wife's shattered body had only just hit the ground when the biker adjusted his aim and pointed the gun directly at Driscoll, who instinctively raised an arm in self-protection.

But the gunman repeated the performance, drilling two shots with unerring accuracy straight into the secretary of state's chest and forehead.

CHAPTER TWENTY-EIGHT

Wednesday, April 22, 2015
  Washington, DC

President Ferguson folded his arms and remained silent for a few seconds. It was his trademark technique, and Vic could feel the tension building around the conference table in the White House Situation Room, where he had been summoned along with Veltman, Iain Shepard, and Shepard's boss, the FBI director, Robert Bonfield.

Bonfield had just finished outlining a brief explanation of what had occurred the previous evening in Atlanta, where the Georgia secretary of state, Chuck Driscoll, and his wife, Eve, had been ruthlessly gunned down right outside the main entrance to the Carter Center.

News of the double killing had reverberated across the US overnight in a dramatic way that even outstripped coverage of the double murder of two other secretaries of state in the UK three weeks earlier. Journalists were scrambling to uncover possible linkages between the shootings.

Inevitably, there were also connections being made in some news outlets to the death two days earlier of US embassy worker Yvonne Broad in Moscow, although nobody had so far discovered she was a CIA officer.

The Atlanta killing was the front-page main story in just about every newspaper in the country and had dominated morning TV news programs. Vic had sat at home, glued to the footage of police and ambulance crews outside the Carter Center during the night and blue-and-red lights flashing, and then watched the crime scenes investigation team at work this morning behind a cordon of yellow tape.

In truth, the shooting had taken him and Veltman by surprise, although he admitted it probably shouldn't have.

"I've had Jimmy Carter on the phone this morning, wanting to know how this could have happened at his own workplace," the president said. "He was his usual diplomatic self, but he was angry and distraught. He had worked with Eve for a decade and met Chuck several times. He is taking it personally, hardly surprisingly."

Nobody spoke, and Ferguson stroked his chin with his thumb and forefinger. He seemed to have difficulty holding his emotions in check. "So the guy on the motorcycle—is there any video footage of him?" he asked eventually.

"There is, yes sir," Bonfield said. "But he was wearing a helmet, so we didn't get a view of his face. The only witness is an employee at the Carter Center who heard a scream, presumably from Eve Driscoll, and looked out a window. She saw Chuck Driscoll being shot and the biker riding off immediately afterward and had the presence of mind to note the plate number. But they turned out to be the plates for another bike registered to a man in San José, who's quite innocent. The woman who saw the bike was the one who called police and raised the alarm. But local police haven't yet been able to track where he went to. The likelihood is he stopped, changed the plates again, probably changed his clothing, maybe dumped the bike, and vanished."

The president shook his head. "That's three secretaries of state who have been torpedoed without warning."

Vic and Veltman exchanged subtle glances at yet another submarine analogy from the president, who continued without appearing to notice.

"The first two were shot by the Russians, we know that," Ferguson said. "Presumably this one was too. What's the link between them—and why the hell are they being picked off like this?"

Ferguson's voice rose steadily as he spoke, and a slight tinge of color rose up his cheeks. He drummed his fingers on the conference table and gazed in turn at his visitors from his vantage point at its head. Vic and the others were sitting down the left side of the table, while Charles Deacon sat opposite them on the right.

Vic leaned forward. "There are links, sir. Our investigators have just this morning discovered that Driscoll was in the army at around the same time as the other two, and all three served in Afghanistan and Iraq. After leaving the military, they all did different things but ended up in similar jobs as secretaries of state. It's emerged that Driscoll, also like the first two, was an investor in an arms company, US Defense Systems, which has been supplying Ukraine. That seems like a possible motive for the Russians, although we need to investigate it further."

Out of the corner of his eye, Vic caught sight of Bonfield raising an eyebrow at the new information, which caused him to smile inwardly. He glanced at Veltman, who was nodding, clearly not unhappy at his team for appearing better informed than the Feebs, especially in front of the president.

"Thank you. We will check that information," Bonfield said.

Even as he spoke, Vic thought of an idea. If these secretaries of state were connected from way back in their army days, he had a possible way of checking exactly what those links might be, quite separately from the inquiries that the Feebs would now doubtless make. He made a mental note to do so once back in the office.

"Is this another operation against the States?" Ferguson asked. "Your agent in the SVR told us about Operation Pandora last year when Wade's treachery came to light, and indicated there could be more to come. Is it part of that, or is it something else? What about your officer who was killed in Moscow? How does that fit into the picture?"

They were justifiable questions, and Vic could see a thin film of sweat developing on Veltman's forehead.

"We don't have answers to all that yet, sir," he said. "We haven't heard any intelligence that links this to Pandora. But we're still waiting for a proper download from Moscow, and until then we're keeping an open mind."

Vic was pleased that Veltman had refrained from adding that Shevchenko had told Jayne to meet with Vasilenko. That was so sensitive he didn't want to give it to the president in front of the FBI men. Nobody else had been told that. He momentarily wondered what Jayne was doing right then and whether she had begun the next stage of the operation, but he forced himself instead to concentrate on what the president was saying.

"All right," Ferguson said. "Get a move on it. I need answers. I started off thinking these assassinations were somehow political, but I don't see how they can be."

Next to him, Deacon was nodding in agreement. "All three victims were Republicans, and they're not even national politicians. They're just secretaries of state."

Exactly the same thought had been running through Vic's

mind. The president was right. It didn't make any sense. This couldn't be political.

So, what was it?

* * *

Wednesday, April 22, 2015
Strelna, St. Petersburg

When Shevchenko had given her the address of the security guard Gavriil Nikitin in Strelna, Jayne had been surprised. She somehow expected that an address in the same outer suburb of St. Petersburg as Putin's spectacular summer residence would be out of reach of a low-paid security guard.

But just one-and-a-half kilometers after passing the spectacular entrance to Konstantinovsky Palace on her right, she came to a left turn on the opposite side of the main highway, which took her southward, away from the palace, past some smart apartments, a park, and some boutique shops.

As she followed the satnav app on her phone deeper into Strelna, she crossed the railway tracks and entered a very different area of housing.

The changes were quite dramatic. While the stylish homes in the area near to the palace had shiny tiled roofs and high-end cars parked in block-paved driveways, these houses were in many cases partly unfinished, often roofed with rusty corrugated iron, and several had worn-out vehicles parked outside that looked unfit to be on the road.

In contrast to the stretch of highway that ran past the palace, the road surface here was cracked and full of potholes. Plastic bags of rubbish lay uncollected on the sidewalks, and many of the fences separating the properties from the street were rustic and tumbledown.

It was now seven o'clock in the evening, more than eleven hours after Jayne had left the safe house in Moscow. Rather than take the direct route up the M10 highway, a distance of about seven hundred kilometers and requiring less than seven hours, she had deliberately chosen a more circuitous way that involved heading much farther west, to within a hundred kilometers of the Estonia border. Her intention was to avoid the main highway with its stretches of toll roads that were bristling with traffic police and license plate recognition cameras.

It had added another 250 kilometers and an extra four hours to her journey but still hadn't eliminated the risk completely, because Jayne noted a small handful of traffic cameras, mainly near the large intersections. Nevertheless, Jayne judged that it was considerably safer than the direct route.

As she drove, a black-and-white film kept running through her mind of that final minute or so near the Voykovskaya metro station, when she caught a glimpse of a woman, who she now assumed had been Broad, running toward her and Shevchenko through the trees—running toward her death. She tried to distract herself from the image, but it kept returning to her.

After a while, in an effort to reduce her risk level further, she had stopped in a deserted farmyard about halfway through the journey, just before a major intersection where she guessed there might be cameras, and had screwed on the third set of license plates provided by Grewall.

However, the long drive, with just four stops for coffee and sandwiches, had left her struggling to keep her eyes open.

She had tried to remain vigilant for surveillance throughout the journey, deeply conscious that the FSB would have her high on their list following the tumultuous meeting with Shevchenko and the death of Yvonne Broad. But she knew she just wasn't as alert as she needed to be—not that she had a choice. Time and speed were the critical factors now. She needed to get to Nikitin, and Vasilenko, before the FSB traced her.

However she was alert enough to remember to make one further stop at a roadside store to buy a new pay-as-you-go SIM card for her burner phone, this time for the MTS network. It was possible that if the FSB had traced her in Moscow, they could have picked up details of her MegaFon SIM card. Better to be safe. She again had to show her Delks passport to buy it, but her guess was that it would take quite some time for the paperwork to find its way back to Moscow.

The satnav took Jayne down a right turn off the broad street that ran through what was almost looking like a slum area, and she headed eastward along a narrow single-track lane between houses. Kids playing soccer in the street stepped to one side to allow her past, and a cluster of chickens scattered squawking in all directions.

It was dusk now, and she swore out loud as the car hit a deceptively deep pothole, causing the chassis to strike the rutted asphalt surface with a loud scraping noise. After crossing another intersection, Jayne crawled along in first gear. Then she saw it.

Number 32 was a run-down chalet-style house with a gray corrugated metal roof and ill-matching window frames, some brown wood, others painted white. The neighboring homes were of a similar style. A steel mesh fence, painted white but heavily rusted and with some posts leaning drunkenly at an angle, ran across the front of the property.

Two cars stood in the driveway, which was heavily over-grown with weeds. The first was a dented old cream Lada, its hood up. The other one was a new and immaculate black Audi A4 that looked utterly out of place. Jayne guessed it must have been supplied by Gavriil's employer.

As Jayne drove past, she saw a woman standing in the doorway of the house, arms folded, and the figure of a man bent under the hood of the Lada, which she could see was at least twenty-five years old, judging by the license plate, which was configured in the old Soviet Union style.

Just from the glimpse that Jayne got, the man looked heavily built, but she was unable to tell how tall he was because he was bent double.

Was that Gavriil? Quite likely, Jayne thought. She didn't want to slow down to look for fear of drawing attention to herself, not something she wanted to do right now.

Even though her window was only wound down a couple of inches, the pungent smell that permeated through the car told Jayne there was a blocked sewer somewhere nearby.

Despite the urgency, Jayne quickly decided that, having acquired a lay of the land, it would be safer to come back when it was dark, perhaps in an hour, after checking into a small hotel she had found online near the main highway.

She continued on, doubling back on herself until she came to the hotel, a cheap, three-star, two-story box-shaped building with no architectural features whatsoever that was set on a paved parking lot right next to the railway line.

Jayne parked the Škoda Octavia at the rear of the hotel where it couldn't be seen from the street. She took her old burner phone, threw the old SIM into a dumpster, inserted the new SIM and the battery, and sent a short message to Shevchenko's burner. There was a slight risk in doing so, but Jayne calculated that the likelihood of the FSB picking up a second new SIM was very low.

At destination. Visiting your uncle soon. Will inform you if successful in meeting our other mutual friend. Please inform him of likely visit. Also if possible keep phone connected.

Shevchenko would know who it was from. There was no need to identify herself.

Normally, Jayne would have removed the battery and SIM again. But this time, she left the phone intact. The SIM was new, and for the short term it might be useful to have it available if she ran into trouble and needed to contact Shevchenko urgently. She had no idea whether Shevchenko would do likewise.

She sat for a moment, eyeing the hotel. The place looked well overrated at three stars.

As was often the case with Jayne in quiet moments in the midst of chaos, she found herself asking why she was doing this. Why was she putting herself on the line again here in Russia immediately after such a narrow escape in Moscow instead of immediately heading for her exfil Route Green Two?

She reminded herself that it was because she needed answers not just for her friend Simone but for Vic, and for the president, who needed to know for much greater reasons why the United States was being targeted yet again by its archenemy, Russia.

But she had to admit, the answer also lay deep inside her. She had a seemingly unquenchable need to seek justice and right wrongs and to uncover the plots and the conspiracies of those who would perpetrate death, destruction, and confusion among the countries and communities where she lived and worked.

And she knew that part of the reason for that need stemmed from her detective inspector father Ken's untimely death following a bomb attack at the Israeli embassy in London in 1994, thought to have been carried out by Hezbollah but never proven. It had happened only five miles from the apartment Jayne now owned in Whitechapel.

Ken had been fifty-nine, only a few months away from retirement from his job at the Metropolitan Police's anti-terrorist branch, SO13. He had moved to London in 1973 to work for the Met after separating from Jayne's mother, Maggie, and had then transferred to SO13 two years later to help deal with the IRA bombing campaigns that were hitting the capital hard.

The bomb went off as Ken arrived at the Israeli embassy in Kensington Palace Gardens for, ironically, a routine discussion about the Palestinian terrorist threat. He was one of eighteen people injured, but he failed to recover and died two months later to little media coverage after complications from a series of operations.

Two people were later convicted of conspiring to cause the bombing, but Jayne was never convinced by the evidence, and years later both were released after a public outcry. Her suspicion was that the real culprits were still out there walking the streets. She often wondered if they would ever be found. There had obviously been some failure of intelligence prior to the attack, because it had come out of the blue.

Her father and his conversations about security, the IRA, the Palestinian terrorists, and such issues had been a driving force behind her interest in international politics and why she had joined the Secret Intelligence Service in the first place.

On the one hand, his death left her feeling prematurely robbed of her father. She had loved spending time with him and doing things with him. He was a fit man with whom she occasionally went out running or accompanied on long walks, usually along coastal paths in Sussex and Dorset or in the mountains of the Lake District.

But the tragedy, which happened when she was only thirty-four, had also shaped her. She recognized now that it had hardened her determination to succeed, to be an achiever —to be someone her father would have been proud of. It drove her to get involved in various anti-terrorism operations against Hezbollah and other groups and to learn Farsi.

However, precisely what drove her to take such risks to do

that was something she had never been able to fathom. Was it the adrenaline rush, or perhaps the need to prove something to herself, that she could operate in what was predominantly a man's world? Or was she subconsciously trying to make up for the intelligence collection failure that caused her father's death? It seemed impossible to pinpoint, and she had often spent time thinking about it over the years without ever coming to a satisfactory answer.

Now, sitting outside a cheap motel in Strelna, she knew she never would find an answer either. She shook her head and refocused her thoughts on the immediate plan of action.

She needed to get a room, have a quick shower and something to eat, and then pay a visit to Gavriil.

CHAPTER TWENTY-NINE

Wednesday, April 22, 2015
Strelna, St. Petersburg

The career pressures that had borne down on Pugachov, as they had on most of his colleagues who had survived for any length of time in the FSB, had if anything accentuated and magnified his natural tendencies toward paranoia and obsessiveness. He was a driven operator who often pored over the tiniest details in a one-eyed determination to achieve his goals and avoid the fate of those who were more careless and less dedicated.

After the abortive operation to trace Jayne Robinson and her unknown agent near the Voykovskaya metro station, Pugachov had decided that he would have to resort to some old-fashioned methodical detective work.

First, he immediately canceled all leave for his surveillance teams and, working closely with Gurko, ordered them to go over the Aeroport district, where Robinson had been captured on CCTV leaving the metro station. Their orders were to locate either Robinson herself or the silver Škoda she had used upon leaving the Hotel Metropol, or at the very least to track down its movements on CCTV somewhere.

Pugachov's team had been keeping a close watch for activity from the MegaFon SIM card that Robinson had bought, but there had so far been nothing. He ordered them to let him know immediately if the phone came on line.

Having set the operation in motion under the control of the team leader, he and Gurko flew to St. Petersburg's Pulkovo Airport on the Wednesday morning, as instructed by his boss, and were picked up by an FSB car that whisked them on the half-hour journey to Konstantinovsky Palace. There they had a meeting to explain their concerns about infiltration with the site security director, Pyotr Timoshenko, a gruff-voiced, barrel-chested man with a mouth that turned sharply down at both corners.

Pugachov told Timoshenko that Robinson was perceived to be the main current threat, but there could be others, and that it was possible that she was simply some sort of decoy to draw the FSB's attention. The two men agreed to stay in close contact and to update each other if there were developments.

Now, as he looked out the window of the expansive office allocated to him and Gurko at the rear of the palace building toward the Gulf of Finland, Pugachov knew that time was running out.

He turned away from his laptop toward Gurko, who was also busy tapping away on his keyboard.

"Any news from the surveillance team?" Pugachov asked.

Gurko toggled back to his email app. "Nothing yet."

"She's likely working with more than one SIM card. Get some checks done."

Gurko nodded. "Will do."

All Pugachov's instincts told him that the killing of the two American secretaries of state in the UK had to be the reason that Western intelligence had sent Robinson into the country. The timing wasn't coincidental. They wanted to know what was going on.

I'd like to know as well, he thought.

As ever with Kremlin- or SVR-run foreign operations, it was being kept as tightly closed as a bear's ass in winter, to borrow a phrase frequently used by his father.

Pugachov wasn't going to ask too many questions. But the fact that the Americans had deployed Robinson, a foreign national operative who had no diplomatic immunity, at considerable risk to herself, told him that, hardly surprisingly, they considered the task of uncovering the details behind the killings to be of significant importance.

Pugachov's theory was further underlined by news that had come through that morning of the murder of another secretary of state in Atlanta the previous night, which of course the US satellite news channels had covered in massive detail.

The two men had CNN running with the sound muted on a video screen attached to the office wall.

The UK and Atlanta killings had all the hallmarks of hits by someone like Georgi Tkachev, who Pugachov knew had recovered from the leg injury sustained in the refinery explosion the previous year.

"I might be wrong, but that job in Atlanta has Georgi Tkachev's name written on it," Pugachov said. "He is indestructible."

"*Da*. The hitman on the motorbike. He did that trick once before, did he not?"

Pugachov nodded. "He did. In the Crimea. But that time his target was moving on the highway, in a car. It is a lot easier when they are standing still like the guy in Atlanta seems to have been." He laughed.

Whether Tkachev or not, it certainly appeared to be the work of one of the former Spetsnaz freelancers on the Kremlin's books.

Pugachov switched his thoughts back to Robinson.

"The question is," he said, "how much does Robinson's agent in Moscow know? Is it enough to send her on a mission here to Strelna? And if so, who would her contact person be here?"

Gurko shrugged. "Let us hope our team comes up with some answers." He turned back to his laptop, as did Pugachov.

Two hours later, they did indeed come up with an answer, or at least part of an answer. Pugachov took the call from the team leader back in Moscow, where more than twenty men had been busy for most of the day working either on their own or with police and surveillance camera operators.

Their tactic had been to identify every silver Škoda Octavia that could be spotted on CCTV in the Aeroport area and try to and eliminate those unrelated to Robinson, leaving a more manageable list of those to investigate further.

There were fewer on the original list than Pugachov had expected, at forty-three, of which five bore red diplomatic plates and were instantly eliminated. The number of those left had been quickly reduced by cross-checking the plate against the registered owners, taking the tally down to just four plates that had not been registered with the Ministry of Internal Affairs and were assumed to be fake. Of the four vehicles, two were not functional—they were scrap and appeared to have been abandoned on the street. That left just two.

A sweep of all inputs from license plate recognition

cameras across the Moscow area showed only one hit: one of the two fake plates showed up on the Leningradsky Highway heading northeast past Sheremetyevo International Airport.

Pugachov remained silent for a couple of seconds after the team leader had finished his account of the search. He knew a lot of valuable time could be wasted going down blind alleys, but on the other hand, he was going to have to make a decision if progress was to be made.

Was the car being driven by Robinson? Pugachov didn't know, but his instinct told him there was a good possibility.

"Good work," he said eventually. "Your next task is to cross-check that vehicle against every camera on the route north up the M10—all the way to St. Petersburg. Get on to the traffic police and get it organized."

"I'm sorry, sir. All of them?" the team leader said. His voice sounded strained. "There are hundreds. I do not think the traffic police will be able to provide all that data."

"Every single one," Pugachov said. He checked his watch. "And I want it done tonight. If you find a trace of the vehicle, tell me immediately, then widen the search in and around St. Petersburg. Tell your police contact this is vital and the president is waiting on the data. If the vehicle has headed that way, we are going to find it tonight."

* * *

Wednesday, April 22, 2015
Langley, Virginia

As was often the case, Vic had an idea while he was walking around the campus outside his Langley office, trying to clear his head and find some inspiration. He passed the three sections of the Berlin Wall monument, taken from Check-point Charlie in 1989, and stood staring at it for several moments. What had been the western side of the Wall was still covered with the original graffiti, while the other side that had faced east was whitewashed, just as the communists had left it.

He then walked on through the CIA's Memorial Garden, located on a hillside between the Original Headquarters Building, where Vic's office was, and the Auditorium.

It was while he was passing a pond filled with koi fish that he recalled that he still needed to follow up on his mental note from the Situation Room meeting to check on links between the secretaries of state.

That might be a way for him to get ahead of the FBI, the media, and everyone else who was likely running down the connections between the three murdered secretaries of state.

It was now known that the men had all been in the army at the same time and had all done tours of duty in Iraq and Afghanistan. That wasn't unique, of course—thousands of other soldiers had done similar tours.

But perhaps there was something more specific that linked them from that time, Vic wondered.

He knew he should really let Shepard's team at the FBI do the legwork on this part of the investigation. But instead, Vic decided to bypass them. He could always involve Shepard later if needed, he told himself.

Vic had a good contact he knew at the US Army's Crim-inal Investigation Division, the CID. Deputy Commanding Officer Dave Payne, with nineteen years on his résumé as a CID special agent, had helped Vic on four operations over the years, mostly involving discreet inquiries into army offi-cers suspected of passing information to Russian agents while based in either Afghanistan or Iraq. Two of them were ultimately found guilty as a result of the assistance Payne had given.

Now based at the CID's headquarters at Quantico, forty miles farther south down the Potomac River from Langley, Payne had remained generally accessible as he climbed inexorably up the career ladder. Perhaps he was mindful that Vic, whose career had been equally successful, could similarly be as useful to him on his end. So, the two men met up once every year or so, usually for lunch in downtown DC.

Vic turned on his heel, left the Memorial Garden, and strode back to his seventh-floor office. There he picked up the phone and explained to Payne what he was looking for. Specifically, he wanted Payne to check the CID's files for any indication of connections between the three men.

His pitch was that the men might have something in their military histories, maybe something they had done while on active service duty, that caused certain parties—whom he didn't name—to want them dead, and that this might have a bearing on national security. He was appealing to Payne's sense of patriotism as much as anything.

"I'm thinking there might be a correlation or common thread between their records," Vic said. "It might shed light on why they've been targeted."

As he had done before, Vic apologized to Payne for not giving him any more information than he absolutely needed. He couldn't say anything about the Russian involvement nor about the investigative work that was being done on other fronts in Moscow. But Payne knew the rules of the game and didn't expect it.

"It's worth a try," Payne said. "No problem, I'll get one of my team to source the documents. Leave it with me. You might have to be satisfied with an off-the-record briefing on it rather than a copy of the actual file. But that might be enough."

"Thanks, buddy," Vic said. He ended the call.

Vic had no way of knowing if his hunch was correct or not. But it usually paid to be thorough.

* * *

Wednesday, April 22, 2015
Moscow

It was quite remarkable how the wheel of fortune turned, Shevchenko thought as she read the secure email that had arrived from the office of the Black Bishop of the Kremlin, Igor Ivanov.

She had only been back in her Moscow apartment for half an hour after her flight from Paris, and already it seemed that she was back in favor with the power brokers and the dark arts specialists who had previously treated her with suspicion and doubt.

It was amazing what a difference trapping a traitor to the Motherland had made to the way the Kremlin and the president's *siloviki* perceived her.

With the Paris agent, the DGSE's puppet, safely behind bars in Lefortovo and awaiting a grisly fate at the hands of a specialist team of interrogators, Shevchenko had found that she was suddenly included once again on the circulation lists for all manner of confidential and highly sensitive material that had until two days ago been denied to her.

The email from Ivanov was summoning her to the deep state planning conference that was continuing at Konstantinovsky Palace under his supervision.

The president wants to personally congratulate you on the outstanding success you have achieved in Paris. You have brought glory on our nation, Ivanov wrote. *We would like you to participate in the remainder of the discussions here along with the SVR and FSB leadership teams.*

Shevchenko snorted as she flicked through the remainder of her outstanding emails.

She then retrieved the burner phone from the emergency rear stairwell and checked it for messages. There was only one, from Jayne Robinson, who had sent it from a different number. Presumably she had bought a new SIM card as a security precaution. That was sensible.

At destination. Visiting your uncle soon. Will inform you if successful in meeting our other mutual friend. Please inform him of likely visit. Also if possible keep phone connected.

The British woman had wasted no time; she was certainly not one to procrastinate. Very confident too. Clearly, Robinson's intention was to try and gain access to the Konstantinovsky Palace site.

That made sense, as it might well be Robinson's only method of getting what she needed from Pavel Vasilenko, but she needed to be extremely careful.

Given the nature of the summit meeting going on at the palace, it was risky to send Vasilenko any kind of message that might hint at a covert visit by anyone. Nevertheless, she couldn't ignore Robinson's request, as allowing her to arrive unannounced could prove fatal.

Perhaps it was just as well that she too was now headed for Strelna, albeit under very different circumstances. Robinson might need all the support she could get.

Shevchenko pondered the request to leave her burner phone switched on but decided not to until she got much nearer to the palace. First, it might be traced, and second, there was no point, as she wouldn't be able to do anything until she arrived in Strelna even if Robinson asked.

Shevchenko made herself a thick dark tea, sweetened with honey the way her mother used to like it, and began to consider her next move. She needed to get to Strelna, clearly, but should she fly or drive?

Eventually, she decided that a few hours of solo thinking time, coupled with some music and radio listening, might be just what she needed rather than the stress of yet another flight.

She would drive. Her instinct was that a car might be useful at Strelna.

Shevchenko wrote a short secure email to Ivanov, Kruglov, and Kutsik, informing them of her intention to drive and that she would be at Strelna by the early hours of the following morning, ready for meetings during the day. If they wanted to query her decision to drive rather than use an official car and driver from the pool at Yasenevo, she would deal with it later.

Next, she went out to her car, a Hyundai Santa Fe 4x4 that she had bought on her return to Moscow the previous year, and began a thorough check of the wheel arches, all the hidden cavities she could think of, and the engine compartment. She was well schooled in where to look. Nothing.

She then took out the small jack from the trunk and lifted the chassis until she could safely crawl underneath. It took her twenty-five minutes until she found what she had suspected might be there: a small black box no larger than a cigarette pack was attached to the chassis by a powerful magnet in a gap behind the exhaust system. It was a standard transponder unit that would allow her car to be tracked by satellite in real time back at Yasenevo. It seemed that Sidorenko's men were still not satisfied, despite her ordeal at Lefortovo and triumph in Paris.

Shevchenko unclipped the back of the transponder and replaced the nine-volt battery with an identical one from her pocket that she knew had no charge.

Then she returned to her apartment and began to place clean clothing and a few other items into her travel bag, starting with something she had not been able to take with her on the flight to Paris: a PB semiautomatic. The PB was a pistol she sometimes used that was based on her usual Makarov and accommodated a screw-in silencer. She found the silencer in a drawer, together with two spare magazines, and placed them in the bag too.

CHAPTER THIRTY

Wednesday, April 22, 2015
Strelna, St. Petersburg

The look of suspicious alarm on Gavriil Nikitin's face when
he answered the knock on his door was palpable. He clearly
wasn't used to anyone calling on him at nine thirty in the
evening, let alone a Western woman.

"I apologize. I can see I've taken you by surprise," Jayne
said in Russian, keeping her voice low. "My name is Siobhan
Delks, and I was sent by Anastasia Shevchenko."

At the mention of Shevchenko's name, Nikitin's black
eyes darted out into the street behind Jayne, then back again.
He threw the cigarette he was holding onto the concrete slab
outside his door and ground it out with his foot. "Come in,
quickly," he said.

He closed the door, locked it with a large brass key, then
led the way down a rustic wooden hallway decorated with
peeling and yellowed floral wallpaper. The doors, frames,

baseboards, and stairs were all made from a dark unpainted oak that, coupled with water-stained ceilings, lent a depressing air to the place.

The living room, at the rear of the property, stank of cigarette smoke, and there was a pile of stubs in an ashtray on a plywood table.

Nikitin, who wore a plain white T-shirt with food stains down the front, stood and faced Jayne. "How do I know you are who you say you are? What is the connection between you and Anastasia Shevchenko?"

"She said you have been very helpful to her," Jayne said.

Nikitin frowned. "It is my job to be helpful. I am a security manager."

"I know. She thought you might be able to help me too. Which is why I am here." Jayne explained that she was a freelance consultant on Russia for high-level political advisory firms in London and needed to talk in confidence to someone who was currently at Konstantinovsky Palace.

"You are a spy, then," Nikitin said without hesitation.

A jolt went through Jayne. This wasn't the reaction she had been expecting from someone recommended by Shevchenko. "No, I just need to speak to someone."

Before Jayne could explain who she needed to contact, a slim, birdlike woman with long graying hair tied with a ribbon came into the room from what Jayne could see was the kitchen. She was surprisingly smartly attired, wearing a blue designer dress, and stood hands on hips. "Who is this?" she asked.

"A friend of Anastasia's. Siobhan." He introduced the woman as his wife, Raisa.

"What does she want?" Raisa asked.

"She wants our help."

"How?"

If these two could commoditize suspicion, they'd make a fortune.

But it was completely understandable. They were clearly benefiting from some kind of arrangement that could backfire badly on them if uncovered, and they doubtless feared the wrath of Shevchenko if that happened. In short, they were in Shevchenko's pocket and couldn't get out, even if they wanted to.

Nikitin turned back to Jayne. "That is what I was about to find out." He indicated to the sofa. "Sit down. Tell me who you want to meet and why."

Jayne took a place on the sofa, while Nikitin sat on a wooden chair at the table, where he lit another cigarette. Raisa sat on the far side of the table and folded her arms.

She was going to have to trust that Shevchenko's confidence in these two was well founded. Otherwise she could be about to sign someone's death warrant. But there was little option.

"The person I need to speak to is a Russian government employee named Pavel Vasilenko," Jayne said. "He is at the palace for a conference."

A look of slight horror crossed Nikitin's face. "I know the man. I have met him a few times as part of my role. He is part of the president's group."

"He may be. Do you know where his living quarters are?"

Now Nikitin's face looked deeply uncomfortable. He glanced briefly up at the ceiling, then at Raisa.

"I do not think I can tell you that kind of information," he said eventually.

He tilted his head back and blew a stream of smoke up toward a bare lightbulb hanging from the center of the ceiling. The smoke particles, caught in the light, swirled and twisted their way upward.

Jayne hesitated. She didn't want to threaten him, but time was short, and she needed an outcome. "I had clear directions from Anastasia to get from you all the help I need. If you are not prepared to do that, I will report back to her immediately. Do you want me to call her?"

There was a pause of several seconds. "He is staying at one of the cottages."

Jayne knew from the quick bit of research she had done that in the expansive grounds of the palace, next to the shoreline, were twenty individual luxury VIP cottages, originally built to accommodate world leaders for the G8 summit that was held on the site in 2006. This sounded promising. She recalled that the cottages were set several hundred meters away from the main palace, were well spaced apart, and all were named after historic Russian towns.

"Is he living in a cottage by himself, or is he sharing?" Jayne asked. "And do you know which one?"

"By himself. The one he is using is called Vladivostok."

"Thank you."

"It is the one farthest away from the palace, in the northeast corner. He is less senior than some people here so was allocated that one."

This was even better. At least the number of eyes on that particular accommodation would definitely be fewer than if Vasilenko was quartered in the main building or somewhere more central to the site.

"Listen, you have been very helpful," Jayne said. "I will make sure you are rewarded well for this information. However there is another thing I will require assistance with and—"

"I am guessing that you want to get on the palace site. That is your next request." Nikitin leaned back in his chair, stubbed out his cigarette, and folded his arms before eyeballing Jayne. "That is something I cannot help you with."

He had guessed correctly, but having come this far, Jayne was not prepared to throw in the towel.

"That is something I am going to have to ask you to help me with. I will make it worth your while." She glanced around the house. It seemed to her that this couple could do with all the money they could get. "I think it will help you. Do you have children?"

Jayne wanted to ascertain exactly what was at stake if they got into real trouble and also how useful money might be to them in return for assistance.

"No, but we would like to." Nikitin noticed her surveying the room and must have guessed her thoughts. "My job is at risk if I do what you are asking."

"If you do what I ask, your job will be safe. If you don't, then I can't promise anything. Just tell me one thing," Jayne said. "What control do you have over who enters and leaves the site?"

Nikitin exhaled softly. "I am the security manager for the main entrance and the trade entrance, the commercial deliveries, the workmen, the contractors. I control it. I am also responsible for ensuring the security of all those staying in the cottages."

"And who do you report to? Who is your boss?" Jayne asked.

"We have a site security director. Pyotr Timoshenko. He is the security chief. I report to him. But he doesn't get involved in the detail of the operations too much."

"All right. And who goes in and out of the site most?"

"At the moment, everything is restricted because the president is on-site. So essentials only—food, drink, catering staff, security, site management."

"Any foreign organizations?"

"No. Well, no, not really."

"Not really? Some then?"

Nikitin hesitated. "The only one is the geoengineering team. They are having to do work on the foundations. The palace was built in 1807. But it fell apart, and the Germans destroyed it during the Great Patriotic War. The structure had badly deteriorated. So the president had it rebuilt, completely restructured, in 2001—made it magnificent once again. It required a massive amount of strengthening work. However, there have recently been some serious further problems, cracks and so on. The team has had to continue operating right through the president's visit. But they spend most of their time in the cellars and basements, deep underground, working on the foundations and supporting walls."

Jayne leaned forward, stroking her chin. "Where is the geoengineering team from?"

"It is a Russian team, but they use a lot of consultants. From places like Denmark, Ireland, and Canada, I believe. The UK too. I see the passports, of course."

Nikitin struck a match and lit another cigarette. He rose to his feet and paced up and down the room, clearly agitated. "I know what you are going to ask."

"How much do you earn a month?"

Nikitin took a deep drag on his cigarette. "About eighty thousand rubles, usually. Including overtime."

Jayne calculated quickly. That was about $1,100. This could go one of two ways, but she figured that the groundwork already done by Shevchenko, the *kompromat*, had likely already left Nikitin with little choice. She took her purse from her pocket and removed a hundred thousand rubles, which she handed to him.

"There, take that. A hundred thousand there. There will be much more to come if you do as I ask."

He briefly shook his head. "What do you want in return?"

"I need to be on the list of accredited geoengineering consultants, and I need to get into that complex."

Nikitin closed his eyes momentarily, visibly thinking. "I don't know. It's difficult."

"Is it possible?" Jayne asked.

"There is another option."

"What?"

"I don't know what you will think of this, but certain members of the leadership team staying here have discreet requirements, at night, which go beyond the usual catering and drinks and housekeeping. They require special visitors. Do you know what I'm saying?"

Prostitutes?

"Are you joking?" Jayne said.

"No, I am not joking. That is something considered by these men to be essential."

"How high up the leadership team does this requirement go?"

Nikitin raised his hand up above his head.

Shit.

"Well, if you're asking me if I want to provide these services, then no, I'd prefer to be on the geoengineering team," Jayne said.

"Listen to me. There are advantages to this other option. It is more discreet. The ladies who come in cannot appear on the system, for obvious reasons, but they are carefully chosen. They are escorted to the specific person's accommodation and escorted off the site again once the business has been completed, maybe a couple of hours later. Some of the men like younger girls, but others prefer older and more sophisticated but physically slim and attractive options. Proper escorts. Ladies who they can talk to as well as take to bed. Ones who know their wines."

He looked Jayne up and down.

"And you think I would fit that requirement?" Jayne asked.

"You would, yes. Your Russian is very good. A little

accented, but good. Obviously your visit would not involve any of the activities that—"

"That's a relief," Jayne said, a hard edge of sarcasm in her voice.

"Of course. We would escort you to the cottage occupied by Mr. Vasilenko. He would be your customer, if you want to use that term. Then we would escort you off the premises again. That might actually be the easiest way to achieve this."

Jayne recalled what Shevchenko had told her in Moscow. *His wife works at the palace too—she provides certain services to the leadership.*

"So, who sources these ladies for the leadership?" she asked. "Not you, surely?"

"No, not me." He indicated toward Raisa. "My wife does that for them when they are in Strelna. The ladies come from St. Petersburg. They are not what you might call ladies of the street. They are high class. My wife sources them through a network of society women in return for very handsome rewards. Some of them are the wives of highly successful businessmen, how do you say in English, trophy wives, who want to earn their own money. They would not think of themselves as hookers."

Jayne tried to avoid looking shocked. From her knowledge of the way the Kremlin operated, she wasn't actually that surprised that this kind of arrangement was in place. But she was taken aback by the idea that she might get involved in it. It had caught her off guard, and she needed time to think it through.

"I'm sure they wouldn't see themselves as hookers," Jayne said. "Has Vasilenko made use of this add-on service himself previously?"

Nikitin shook his head. "I think not."

Vasilenko immediately rose in Jayne's estimation.

"Which of them have done so?" Jayne's mind immediately

turned to the potential opportunities for leveraging such knowledge.

Nikitin shook his head vigorously. "No, I cannot tell you that."

Jayne leaned back on the sofa, trying to process the suggestion being made to her. Surely this was madness. On the face of it, it seemed risky, but Nikitin, whom Shevchenko had vouched for, seemed convinced it would work.

She could see that trying to pose as a geoengineering team member would be undoubtedly more complicated than Nikitin's idea, as it would have to be carried out during the day and would be difficult to achieve without the genuine engineering team being aware of her presence. And clearly when it came to the sexual activities and proclivities of Russia's political and security leaders, the normal rigid security arrangements in existence at the palace had some flexibility. That seemed to her to be the key advantage, and there was clear logic in the argument.

What should I do?

"It would help if Vasilenko is expecting me," Jayne said. "If he hasn't used hookers before, how will that work, and how can I inform him?"

Nikitin pursed his lips. "Part of my role is to ensure the guests in those cottages are happy with their security. I can make a visit to his cottage, give him a short message, and ensure that he does want a hooker, if you know what I mean. He knows me."

Jayne nodded. That would be better than sending a message via Shevchenko.

"I don't have the kind of makeup with me that a lady of this type might wear," Jayne said. Either at home or at work, she rarely wore any unless she was going out in the evening.

"I can provide that," Raisa said from across the table. "I have it all. I am good at makeup. I do it often. And I have different clothing. You might want that too. A dress, perhaps."

"I don't think a dress will be necessary."

Jayne paused, aware that she was procrastinating when speed was essential.

"What about security on the way in?" she asked. "You said it was less rigid than normal for these ladies, and I can understand that. But what does that mean?"

"You will have to go through an X-ray machine and show ID, but that is all. No personal searches," Nikitin said.

"X-ray and ID?" Jayne asked. "That could make things very difficult."

She didn't spell out that she would be carrying a weapon and the small exfil kit provided by Langley or that her only ID was the Siobhan Delks passport.

"Do not worry. We can put anything sensitive in a bag in the car trunk. They only give it a quick check. Nothing major. It is my car. It will be fine. And we have spare ID, several drivers' licenses. You will find one that looks like you. All the ones we have are obtained locally—from a friend in the police." He smiled.

"And on the way out?"

"Nothing. No searches. No ID needed. How long will you need? You will need to allow at least one hour to make the visit look convincing, if you know what I mean. Raisa will be permitted to drive in with you to the cottage, to drop you there, and then fetch you afterward."

"Yes, one hour is more than enough." Jayne exhaled, trying to relieve the stress she was feeling. "But what about if I need to get off the site quickly, if something happens?"

"I can help with that," Raisa said. "I will wait on-site in my car. You can call me if you need to move urgently."

"And there is another thing," Jayne said, knowing that

what she was about to say could in itself threaten a safe exfil-tration if Raisa happened to be interrogated.

"What?"

"I might need you to take me, and possibly Vasilenko, to a certain place outside the palace site once our meeting is finished. I don't mean your house. I mean somewhere else."

There was silence for several seconds as Gavriil and Raisa digested what Jayne was saying.

"Where would you need to be taken?" Raisa asked.

Jayne shook her head. "I cannot say. But it is not too far from here. We might need to get there very quickly. Can you do that, if needed?"

She nodded. "I can."

Raisa sounded convincing, but in practice, how would she perform in a tight situation? It was impossible to know. But perhaps Jayne would have to take that risk. Hopefully a sharp exit would not be required.

"All right. When is a good time to do this?" Jayne asked eventually.

Nikitin checked his watch. "I am on the night shift tonight. I will be leaving here for the palace in an hour and ten minutes. I can go directly to Vasilenko's cottage after I arrive and inform him discreetly about what is happening. You will need to be ready by then—after that I am not on the night shift for another six days."

That left no choice, then.

* * *

Wednesday, April 22, 2015
   Strelna

. . .

The FSB team wasted several hours cross-checking the data and videos of silver Škoda Octavias from the length of the M10 highway and came up with nothing before their leader instructed them to widen their search and cover the alternative, far longer routes north from Moscow to St. Petersburg.

Once they had done that, they very quickly came up with some far more promising results.

Pugachov, sitting in his office at Konstantinovsky Palace, took a call from the team leader with the news once the data had been processed.

The vehicle with fake plates last seen near Sheremetyevo International Airport was later spotted on the 58K-79 road near Velikiye Luki, about 470 kilometers west of the capital, the team leader told him. It then disappeared and was never seen again.

However, a very similar Škoda was later seen traveling northward on the M20, the Kiev to St. Petersburg highway, into which the 58K-79 fed. It had different license plates, also false.

"We think it is the same car," the team leader said. "It looks like it came northward up the 58K and onto the M20 toward St. Petersburg. The plates have been swapped for another set of false ones."

"Thanks. We will work on that assumption," Pugachov said. He ended the call, turned to Gurko, and gave him a brief summary of the conversation.

He knew they needed to get the site security director involved immediately.

"Get onto Timoshenko," Pugachov said. "Tell him what we have learned and to put his team on the highest level of alert. We will keep it under constant review with him."

Gurko frowned and checked his watch. "It is ten minutes before midnight. He will be asleep. Should we not call him first thing in the morning?"

"No. Do it now. Wake him up. We cannot afford to delay. I will inform Sheymov at the same time." He knew that his boss would be furious if he wasn't kept in the loop, especially as he was still on the site.

Gurko nodded and picked up his phone.

CHAPTER THIRTY-ONE

Wednesday, April 22, 2015
Strelna

The process of preparing Jayne for her visit to Konstantinovsky Palace was carried out swiftly and with minimal fuss.
Raisa rapidly applied makeup to Jayne's face, including foun-
dation, a little blusher, and some pale pink lipstick, but all in
an understated way. She was well practiced, and the end result
looked as good as anything Jayne had seen from a professional. People often told Jayne she looked younger than her
fifty-three years, but the makeup hid some of her wrinkles
and further blurred the estimation of her age.

Raisa then produced a blue cocktail dress, at which Jayne
drew the line. The Russian would, of course, have a good idea
of what her powerful customers inside the palace preferred,
but Jayne's agenda was somewhat different.

She decided she could still meet the necessary look
with her tight dark blue round-neck sweater, black stretch
jeans, jacket, and flat-soled shoes that she was already wear-

ing. It showed off her figure well enough while still allowing her to carry her Walther and other essential items. Her concession was to accept a chain necklace and pendant that looked far more expensive than she guessed it actually was.

The final touch provided by Raisa, which Jayne accepted, were two small silver hoop earrings. Jayne had removed her usual silver studs before leaving Portland.

At quarter to midnight, Raisa climbed behind the wheel of her Audi to take her husband to the palace to begin his night duty. She promised to be back as soon as possible to collect Jayne.

While she was gone, Jayne took out her old burner phone and typed a message.

Heading in with your uncle and aunt to see our mutual friend. Look forward to updating you later.

When she had finished writing it, she dispatched the message to Shevchenko's burner phone. Then she sat in an armchair in Raisa's living room and waited.

Often before the start of operations, Jayne felt a real nervous tension, usually in her stomach, and this was no different. However, at the same time she felt energized by the prospect of heading into the unknown, toward potential danger, on a task that she knew was of great importance. She focused her mind on the role she would have to play as a high-class escort and how she would behave and carry herself while going through the inevitable checks by palace security guards.

Her biggest concern was whether Nikitin could do as he promised and make the arrangements successfully with Vasilenko. There was not a lot of time for him to do that. But there was no alternative. She would have to trust him.

Twenty-five minutes later, the front door of the house clicked open, and Raisa returned.

"We go now," Raisa said. "My husband is at the front security desk. He can ensure everything goes without a problem."

"Before we go, I need your phone number in case I need to get off the palace site quickly."

Raisa nodded and explained that she would wait on the site near the security gate in her car and could pick Jayne up if she called. She gave a number that Jayne memorized but also tapped into a notes app on her phone, written backward and with other numbers around it to disguise it, just in case.

"How many other escorts are visiting the palace tonight?" Jayne asked.

"Just one other. She will be there all night, though. She is the most expensive of my girls, but the man who is hosting her can more than afford her no matter what the cost." She gave a low chuckle.

Jayne nodded. "The president?"

"No. Next level down. Ivanov."

Jayne wasn't surprised. She mentally checked she had what she needed tucked into the small bag that Raisa had given her. All of the items would be transferred to various pockets of her jacket after passing through security.

As they walked to the car, Jayne handed the bag to Raisa, who pushed it out of sight beneath the driver's seat.

As they drove off, Raisa explained to Jayne's relief that the entrance they would use was not the imposing main driveway that led directly up to the palace but rather a side entrance half a kilometer to the east.

The entrance was, however, fully floodlit when they arrived ten minutes later. Raisa braked to a halt in front of a set of tall gray steel gates set back from the highway, and a security guard wearing a peaked cap emerged from a green hut just beyond. Raisa climbed out of the car and showed him her identity papers, and the gates slowly swung open. She drove up to another set of gates next to a small white building, from where another guard accompanied by Gavriil Nikitin emerged.

"You will need to get out," Raisa said. "X-ray and ID check here."

Jayne did as instructed, and Nikitin, who nodded to his wife but showed no sign of recognition to Jayne, instructed them both to follow him into the building. There a guard directed them both to remove their jackets and shoes and ushered them through an airport-style X-ray scanner.

The guard looked Jayne up and down as she passed through the archway, a faint smile on his lips, his gaze lingering on her breasts. "Enjoy your evening," he said, and winked. She was undoubtedly not the first escort he had seen passing through the building.

Once cleared, they climbed back into the car, Raisa lowered the window, and Nikitin spoke to his wife in a low tone, making a show of giving her directions to the Vladivostok cottage.

Raisa drove slowly in second gear, the imposing floodlit facade of the palace building to her left, past the luxury Baltic Star Hotel reserved for conference delegates.

"My husband says he has visited the cottage and made the arrangement. It is okay," Raisa said.

"Good," Jayne said.

She continued to drive through trees and parkland along a gunbarrel-straight avenue until the so-called cottages appeared on the left, all individually floodlit. In reality, they were not cottages but small luxury two-story mansions with elegant green-tiled roofs and pale cream walls, all set in their own landscaped gardens with individual driveways and parking spaces for several cars, and situated at least seventy meters apart.

The first three cottages they passed all appeared to be empty. There were no cars parked in the driveways, and the lights were all off. The others had clear signs of occupancy, with several vehicles parked out front.

Raisa made a right turn at the end of the straight road and drove along another line of six cottages, three of which had cars parked outside. She came to a halt on the driveway of the last cottage on the left, next to the sea. A discreet sign on the wall to the left of the front door told Jayne that this was the Vladivostok cottage.

Lights were on both upstairs and downstairs. At the side of the building, an ornate wrought-iron staircase wound its way down from a balcony on the upper floor, presumably a decorative feature that doubled as a fire escape.

"This is the one," Raisa said.

She reached beneath her seat, took out the bag, and handed it to Jayne, who surreptitiously transferred the Walther, spare magazines, and other items to her jacket pockets. She didn't want the switch to be easily recorded by CCTV cameras, which she assumed were everywhere.

"I will see you here in exactly one hour," Raisa said. "But call me if you need me to come earlier. I will be nearby. I will wait in the driveway of one of those unoccupied cottages."

"Thank you," Jayne said. "One hour."

She climbed out of the car, walked to the front door, and was about to ring the bell when the door clicked open. Behind her she could hear Raisa driving away.

CHAPTER THIRTY-TWO

Thursday, April 23, 2015
Strelna

The security control center in the first basement level at Konstantinovsky Palace was normally brightly lit and busy during daytime. Now, at half past midnight, it was much more subdued, and there were only a handful of officers there, of whom two were glued to a bank of monitor screens, watching for any unusual activity, and another two were sitting at open-plan workstations nearby, tapping away at computer terminals, apparently writing reports.

Pugachov glanced at his watch. He and Gurko had been standing for the past five minutes next to the locked door of an office marked Security Director waiting for Pyotr Timoshenko.

Eventually, the heavy oak door to the control center opened and Timoshenko appeared. Judging by his heavily creased blue shirt and his zip fly, which was hanging open, the security chief had gotten out of bed and dressed in a hurry. His mouth appeared even more downturned than normal.

"I hope you are dragging me away from my bed for a good reason," Timoshenko began in a deep bass voice. "I do not think—"

"We have a very good reason," Pugachov said. "I spoke to you several hours ago about the well-justified concerns we have that this site may be being targeted by Western intelligence, the Americans or the British. They are trying to infiltrate the meeting that is going on here or at the very least seeking to source information from here. Your job and my job are on the line, so I suggest you listen."

Timoshenko frowned but became visibly more alert. "And I suggest you become less dictatorial and confrontational in your approach, but go on. Who specifically are you concerned about?"

"I spoke to you before about the British agent Jayne Robinson. Well, she—"

"What about her?"

"If you will let me finish," Pugachov said, fixing Timoshenko with a stare. "We have very strong evidence she may have driven here from Moscow in the past few hours. She is operating under a cover name: Siobhan Delks. I strongly suspect she has an agent inside our security services, either SVR or FSB, and that person may be inside this complex currently, possibly involved in the meetings that are happening."

"*Dermo*. Shit," Timoshenko said. "You did not tell me she had driven here."

"We did not know until very recently," Pugachov said. "We have been given evidence from traffic cameras that show she headed toward St. Petersburg. We believe that meeting with someone inside the complex is virtually certain to be her objective."

"I cannot believe you obtained this information so late. What are your surveillance people doing?"

"Unfortunately, she is a good operator. She evaded my people in Moscow, although we very nearly caught her."

"Well, I can assure you that this site is locked down securely. I have told you that several times before. Only essential workers are on the site, and they are tightly controlled."

Pugachov frowned. "I am sure you are correct, and I'm sure your teams are controlling and monitoring them properly. But do you have a list of the people on site? There seem to be a large number of them—it is a huge complex."

Timoshenko turned to a man sitting at the open-plan workstations a few meters from where they were standing.

"Gavriil, do you have a full list of who is on-site tonight? And how many people?"

The man, who wore an identity badge that identified him as Gavriil Nikitin, stood and walked over to them.

"Yes, I do have a list," Nikitin said. He indicated with his hand toward his computer terminal. "There are 106 people on the site overnight, sir. That includes the president's group of senior people and those working with them in the meetings. The rest are support staff, including the security team, sir. They are all accounted for. We have one more due to arrive, and that is the SVR deputy director, Anastasia Shevchenko. She has notified us that she is driving here from Moscow."

Pugachov took a step forward. "Yes, I know she is on her way. So, everyone on the site overnight is an employee of the palace or the Russian government?"

Nikitin looked Pugachov in the eye again. "Yes."

"You are certain?"

This time Nikitin glanced at his boss, who slightly raised an inquiring eyebrow. Nikitin gave an almost indiscernible nod that Pugachov nevertheless noticed.

"Well?" Pugachov asked.

"We do have a very small number of others who come on-site at night," Timoshenko said, after a pause. "But they are not an issue."

Pugachov could feel his blood pressure rising, the familiar tightness in his temples and his chest, along with a sense of anger that he fought to control.

"Who?" he demanded, his voice now several decibels louder.

"There are very senior people inside the leadership team who have requirements," Timoshenko said. "And we have to ensure they are met. There are no other options. The people who come on-site at night are there to meet those requirements."

Finally Pugachov realized what the security director was referring to. "You mean *prostitutes*? Is that what you are saying?" he exploded.

Timoshenko nodded.

"How many are there here tonight? *Bljad*. Son of a bitch. Why did you not tell me before that you let these people in?"

Timoshenko looked at Nikitin. "How many tonight?"

"Only two."

"Who has them?" Pugachov asked.

"One is Igor Ivanov, of course," Nikitin said. "He always does. The other is an SVR man, Vasilenko."

"*Why?* Why are they allowed in?"

"Mr. Ivanov sets the rules," Timoshenko said. "He has allowed this exception. I assume it is because . . ." His voice trailed off and he shrugged, then looked down at the floor, clearly embarrassed.

Pugachov remained silent for a few seconds, trying to think through the situation. It seemed highly unlikely that Robinson would be able to successfully pose as a Russian prostitute to gain access to the palace site, but not impossible. Could it be that Ivanov was a traitor to the Motherland? Surely not. Vasilenko? He had no idea.

"Can we go and check these women? Get them off site?" Pugachov asked. He also wondered to himself who the hell chose them and brought them in the first place, but those were questions for later.

Timoshenko gave a sarcastic laugh. "You are going to tell Ivanov we are taking his woman away? Good luck with that."

"What about the other one?" Pugachov asked. "The one with Vasilenko. At least we can get rid of her. Who is she?"

Timoshenko shrugged and looked at Nikitin for guidance. "Who is she? Can we remove that one?"

Nikitin looked hesitant but nodded. "Yes, I am sure we can do that. She is just a high-class hooker. I will go and do it."

"I will come with you," Timoshenko said.

"It's okay. I can handle it," Nikitin said.

"I insist. I am coming. The SVR man may need an apology, and that would best come from me," Timoshenko said.

"He will understand it is necessary," Pugachov said. "Just get the hooker off the premises so we can tell the president the site is clear if he asks—obviously apart from Ivanov's mistress. Call me if you have any problems."

CHAPTER THIRTY-THREE

Thursday, April 23, 2015
  Strelna

The door opened a foot, and the face of a lean, middle-aged man appeared in the gap, his receding hairline completely shaven. This was SOYUZ.

"Come in. I was expecting you," he said. He opened the door farther to allow Jayne in, then, as she entered, closed it behind her and put his finger to his lips, indicating unnecessarily that the place was probably bugged. Jayne had assumed that.

"You look beautiful," Vasilenko said.

Jayne hesitated for a second, unsure whether he meant the compliment or if it was part of an act for the hidden microphones. She decided it was the latter.

"*Spasibo*. Thank you." She looked around, momentarily taken aback by the sheer opulence of the decor. They were standing in an extensive oval-shaped hallway with a white marble floor. A broad stairway, also in marble and with gold banisters, curved up to a landing that ran around the entire upper floor. An enormous gold and crystal chandelier hung from the ceiling. There were mirrors and animal-skin rugs everywhere.

Jayne pointed upward. "Shall we go upstairs?" She tapped her watch to make the point. Time was short.

Vasilenko nodded. "Yes, upstairs." He led the way up the stairs.

Jayne knew his story, having been briefed by Vic in some detail. He had been recruited by Ed Grewall following a personally traumatic experience while working for the SVR in the *rezidentura* in Washington, DC. During that time, his ten-year-old son, Timofey, at home in St. Petersburg with his mother, fell ill and died. The SVR leadership had not permitted Vasilenko to return home in time to see his son before he passed away.

After that, he carried an unspoken resentment against the Russian regime. So when Grewall approached him at a HC CSKA Moscow ice hockey game, the recruitment had been very much a case of pushing at an open door.

Vasilenko led the way into the master bedroom, which was lavishly decorated with burgundy wallpaper and thick pile carpets, and made straight for the en suite bathroom, where he turned on the shower.

Jayne walked to the full-length curtains and opened them briefly. Outside was a balcony, and by the light from the bedroom, she could see the metalwork of the ornate staircase that she had noticed from the driveway. It always helped to know where the exits were. She closed the curtains again.

Vasilenko turned and beckoned Jayne to join him in the bathroom next to the flowing shower water, which would effectively mask any conversation from the microphones, providing they spoke softly.

"I was surprised at this meeting and the way it was

arranged at short notice," Vasilenko said. "But it is perhaps actually a good method."

"Yes, I was also surprised," Jayne said.

"I apologize for not being more sociable or offering drinks," he said in a low murmur. "But we have a lot to discuss and I believe not much time."

Jayne nodded. "Yes. Let's make a start."

"First, I understand you had a close encounter in Moscow with the FSB. That was unfortunate. I heard what happened to the girl, I presume a colleague of yours."

"Yes, it was sad. I am not sure how the FSB stumbled across our meeting. It had all the hallmarks of a random but systematic sweep operation in the area. Anyway, we move on. It is an occupational hazard."

"Indeed," Vasilenko said. "Now, let us get to the current business. The primary thing you need to know is there is a high-level operation underway against the United States, and this is being further developed as we speak. Plans are being drawn up here in Strelna. I am a party to those discussions."

"Yes, I gathered that. Three dead secretaries of state tell their own story, so to speak. The question is why?"

"I can give you the detail of the operation, but I do not need to tell you that I am going to sail very close to the wind in doing so. If it becomes obvious that Langley knows or the White House knows, I will be at tremendous risk. There are not many in the closed circle, and fingers will be pointed. I am highly likely to be discovered, and you know what will happen to me then. Meeting you like this puts me at great risk."

Jayne nodded. She could see where this was headed. "You want out?"

"Yes," Vasilenko inclined his head in agreement. "I need to be out of here. And I think now. Once I have told you the detail, your people will not be able to hold back. The information is too, how do you say, flammable. You have an exfil option in place?"

Now Jayne felt the level of tension had ratcheted up several notches. A major disclosure was imminent that would put SOYUZ's life at risk if he stayed put. He wasn't prepared to stay and go through that.

Hardly surprising.

"We were anticipating this. Yes, we have one. It can be activated easily and will run from near here. The difficult bit will be getting safely to the pickup location."

"All right," Vasilenko said. "That is what we will do. I have just one—"

He stopped talking because above the sound of the shower, there came a faint squealing noise.

"Car brakes," Vasilenko said, confirming Jayne's initial reaction. He turned the shower tap off and put his finger to his lips.

A few seconds later, there came the loud musical chime of the doorbell ringing, followed by a series of distant knocks.

"Shit," Jayne said involuntarily. She looked at Vasilenko.

He strode to the window, eased the curtain back a fraction, and peered out. Then he walked back over to Jayne and murmured in her ear.

"It is security," he said. "They have a marked car on the driveway. This is not usual. They never call here. Only Nikitin Gavriil comes. We will have to let them in. You stay here. I will deal with it."

Jayne didn't like the sound of this. "They will know I'm here," she said, also speaking in his ear in as low a voice as she could.

"Yes, but they think you are a hooker. Most of the leadership here use hookers. It's not out of the ordinary for them."

"I hope so. But I'll come downstairs with you and position myself to take action if needed."

Vasilenko looked undecided. Jayne knew there was no time to discuss it. If he was going to open the door, he had to do it now.

"Go, answer it," she said.

She followed Vasilenko down the stairs. As she went, Jayne removed the Walther from her jacket pocket, flicked off the safety, and quietly racked the slide.

Jayne then moved into a room next to the front door, where she hid behind a large, heavy oak cabinet but with a line of sight to the open door of the room and the hallway beyond if she peered around it.

There came another heavy knock on the front door, followed by a deep man's voice calling from outside.

"Mr. Vasilenko. It is Pyotr Timoshenko, security director."

Jayne heard Vasilenko open the door.

"What can I do for you?" Vasilenko asked. "It is very late. You have disturbed me."

"I am sorry, really I am," came Timoshenko's voice. "But there has been a change in tonight's arrangements. The lady you have in there. She must go, unfortunately. Bring her out."

Jayne's mind was now racing. She didn't know if she had been blown but had to assume she had been, and if so, then Vasilenko had been blown too. Either way, there was going to be no way of talking her way out of this. Had Nikitin betrayed her?

"No, we haven't finished," Vasilenko said, his voice rising a little. "So you can't come in here right now. You know what I'm doing with her. This is my private residence while I am here."

"I do not have time to waste. She must go."

There came the sound of footsteps moving quickly across the marble floor.

"Where is she?" It was Timoshenko again, this time with a note of anger in his voice.

Jayne eased her head fractionally forward until she could just see around the side of the cabinet. Through the open doorway she could see a stocky, barrel-chested man standing in the hall, facing slightly away from her but holding a pistol out in front of him in his right hand.

Jayne was feeling trapped. Now there was definitely no alternative.

She stepped out, and the man, perhaps on hearing the slight noise, began to turn.

But before he could do so, Jayne fired two shots straight at his right shoulder. Both hit their target, and the man gave a deep-throated scream, fell to the floor, and dropped his pistol, which clattered over the marble floor in Jayne's direction.

Immediately, there came three more pistol shots from some unseen gunman out in the hall, and the plastered wall next to the door of the room in which Jayne was standing erupted in a cloud of dust.

But they were followed almost instantaneously by another single shot, a dull grunt, and a loud thud as something heavy hit the floor.

Shit, have they shot Vasilenko?

Jayne stood completely still, trying to decide whether to move to the door or remain in her concealed position.

But her decision was made for her.

"Come here, quick," Vasilenko called, his voice loud and urgent.

Jayne moved to the doorway of the room to see a uniformed security guard lying motionless on the floor, gun still in hand, with a bloodstain spreading from the center of his chest. Vasilenko was gripping a pistol that he was pointing at a third man—who to Jayne's slight surprise was Gavriil Nikitin, holding up his hands in surrender.

Before Jayne could say anything, she became aware that the man she had shot, Timoshenko, was moving on the floor, trying to reach his pistol with his uninjured left hand. Blood was pouring from the bullet wounds in his right shoulder.

Jayne took two steps, dropped swiftly to her haunches, and grabbed the pistol from the floor.

It was time for some quick decisions.

"Get their guns and phones," she said. "I'll cover you."

Vasilenko nodded. He held out his hand to Nikitin. "Phone and gun. Walkie-talkie. Whatever else you have got. Move slowly."

Nikitin, who unsurprisingly still remained silent, lowered his right hand, reached into his pocket, and removed his gun, which he tossed onto the floor. Vasilenko picked it up, and Nikitin did the same with his phone and then finally a small walkie-talkie.

"Turn out your pockets so I can see there is nothing else there," Vasilenko said. Nikitin did as instructed.

Vasilenko then went to Timoshenko, who had now lost all signs of fight and said nothing as Vasilenko went through his pockets, removing a smartphone from one and a walkie-talkie from another. He removed the batteries from both and pocketed them.

"What shall we do with them?" Vasilenko asked urgently. "Shoot both?"

"*No*," Jayne said. She didn't want to add cold-blooded murder to the list of offenses they had already committed on Russian soil and certainly didn't want to do harm to Nikitin. Vasilenko appeared to be panicking. "Let's lock them up."

She looked around the hallway. "Are there any storage cupboards?"

Vasilenko indicated toward a door on the far side. "That is for coats and shoes. We can put them in there."

Jayne nodded. "Yes, that will do. You put them in. I will cover you. Wedge that chair under the handle so they can't get out." She pointed toward a heavy wooden chair that stood beneath a mirror.

Vasilenko walked to the cupboard door, opened it, and waggled his pistol, indicating to Nikitin to move. "Get in that cupboard. Now!"

Nikitin clearly had no choice. He obediently walked slowly to the cupboard and entered. Jayne could see it was more like a small room than a cupboard, with hooks on the walls on which two coats were hanging.

Next, Vasilenko walked to Timoshenko, who was clutching his badly shattered right shoulder with his left hand, his face distorted with pain. Vasilenko grabbed him beneath the armpits, causing him to squeal like a wounded dog, and dragged him across the floor to the cupboard, leaving a smeared trail of blood over the marble.

Then he slammed the door of the cupboard and shoved the chair up against it so the back was wedged firmly beneath the door handle.

Would that hold the door? Jayne looked around and spotted a rubber doorstop near the front door. She walked around the dead guard's body, picked it up, and pushed it firmly beneath the cupboard door. Now it should be secure enough.

Her mind was now in overdrive, trying to think of what steps they would need to take to secure an exit from the palace premises and to get to the exfil site. It was going to require a neat plan, composed at speed. Meanwhile, she was expecting reinforcements from the security team to arrive at any second, sirens blaring, headlights on full beam, flashlights and pistols in hand.

First, she took out her burner phone with the MTS SIM card and called the number she had for Raisa.

"Come quickly and pick me up," she said as soon as the call was answered. "Immediately, please. We need to leave the site."

Raisa confirmed she was on the way and ended the call.

Jayne then used the same phone to call Shevchenko's number, hoping that the Russian had not yet reached the palace complex.

The phone rang at least a dozen times before it was answered.

"What is happening?" Shevchenko said abruptly. "I'm driving."

Jayne outlined in a couple of sentences what had occurred.

"*Dermo*," Shevchenko said.

"Are you near the palace?" Jayne asked. As she spoke, Jayne opened the front door of the house and stepped outside, wanting to look out for Raisa. Out of the corner of her eye, she could see Vasilenko following.

"Ten minutes away," Shevchenko said.

"Don't come here yet. Wait until we're gone," Jayne said. "I'll get Raisa to take us to the exfil site."

There was a short pause. "What exfil craft will they send?"

"An inflatable."

"In that case I have a better plan. I will take you," Shevchenko said. "I think Raisa already knows too much."

What is she getting at?

"You can't. It's too risky—for you and us," Jayne said.

"No. I will meet you at Raisa's house and take you from there." Shevchenko's voice was insistent.

Outside, a single set of car headlights was visible heading down the road toward them at speed. Was this Raisa or security? It was impossible to tell in the dark.

And Jayne was deeply conscious that the crazy sequence of events over the past ten minutes meant she still hadn't gotten the critical information she needed from Vasilenko about the operation that had so far killed three American secretaries of state.

"I will see you at Raisa's house," Jayne said. She realized it was best to concede the argument. There was no time to do otherwise. "Hopefully in ten minutes. If we don't make it, you'll know what's happened."

She ended the call, now fully aware that her life depended on whether Shevchenko was trustworthy or not. It occurred to Jayne in that moment that the Russian could easily turn in her and Vasilenko and claim all the credit, thus doubling down on her success in Paris.

Jayne turned around and stepped back through the front door, realizing that Vasilenko had disappeared. As she did so, there came two gunshots from the direction of the cupboard. Vasilenko emerged from the open door, his lips pressed tight together, pushing his pistol back into his jacket pocket. "They saw too much and know too much," he said.

CHAPTER THIRTY-FOUR

Thursday, April 23, 2015
  Strelna

The two guards circled Raisa's Audi, peering in through the windows, pistols in hand.

But then, to Jayne's massive relief, one of them signaled toward the security building, and the gray steel gates began to slowly swing open.

Raisa slipped the car into gear and eased it out through the opening, where she swung right onto the highway.

"*Bozhe*. God. Thank you," Raisa muttered as she accelerated smartly up the road.

Jayne glanced back through the rear window. There were no pursuing vehicles, no flashing blue lights or sirens. But she knew it was likely to be just minutes before the carnage in the Vladivostok cottage was discovered by the rest of the security team, and then all manner of hell was going to break loose. It would take just one unanswered call to the men's walkie-talkies.

She was still angry that Vasilenko had decided to dispatch Nikitin and Timoshenko in the storage cupboard before leaving, and without consulting her. It had been unexpected and had confused her, and also left her slightly worried, given that she was now responsible for getting him safely out of Russia.

He had made clear it was because of what they had seen in the cottage. But anyway, she could hardly challenge Vasilenko now, in front of Nikitin's wife, who remained unaware of what had happened. She would have to question him later.

Jayne leaned back from her position in the front passenger seat and banged three times on the rear seat, a signal to Vasilenko, who was lying horizontal in the darkness of the trunk, that they were out of the palace grounds.

A second later there were three bangs in reply.

Most of the streetlights were now out, apart from a few strategically placed at the main intersections, and Strelna was largely in darkness. The moon was hidden by low-hanging clouds, for which Jayne was thankful.

Jayne worried that that meant they would be more easily traceable, and as soon as they turned off the main road, she instructed Raisa to turn off the headlights and rely on side-lights only.

The street where Raisa lived was even darker. Almost every house was in total blackness. This was a working town, and most people would be up early.

But outside Raisa's house, a car stood half on the grass shoulder, half on the road, its lights off. As they approached, Jayne saw that it was a Hyundai Santa Fe. The driver's door opened and Shevchenko stepped out.

Raisa steered to park in the driveway, but Jayne told her instead to park up behind the Santa Fe. They needed to get moving.

She jumped out and went up to Shevchenko, whose face was barely discernible in the gloom.

"Have you got the details you need from Vasilenko?" Shevchenko asked without offering a greeting.

"Not yet. It has been totally chaotic. He is in the car trunk." She glanced over her shoulder to ensure Raisa remained out of earshot and then rapidly updated Shevchenko on the fate handed out by Vasilenko to the two men in the cottage storage cupboard and the escape from the palace site.

"And I could not discuss it with Vasilenko in the car, with Raisa listening, either," Jayne said.

She lifted her phone, tapped in a code that brought up the secure maps app that had been installed by Langley, and showed it to Shevchenko. "We need to get to here."

The distance marker to the exfil site indicated a half-hour drive westward along the coastal road.

Shevchenko examined it and appeared to make an instant decision. "I know that location, more or less. A good choice. You will have to drive with Vasilenko in my car so he can debrief you on what you need to know, in case the worst happens and you get separated during the exfil. I will go with Raisa in her car."

"Two cars? Why?"

In the light from the phone screen, Jayne saw Shevchenko turn her head away.

"I have a plan," Shevchenko said.

A thought crossed Jayne's mind. "Are you sure they haven't attached a tracking beacon to your car?"

"There was one, but not anymore. I found it."

Jayne pursed her lips. She didn't like the sound of this, but there was yet again no time to debate it.

"All right. Let's go," Jayne said. She walked to the trunk of Raisa's Audi, let Vasilenko out, and explained quickly to him and Raisa what they were about to do and where they were going.

"Are you okay with that?" Jayne asked them.

Vasilenko nodded but Raisa merely shrugged, her eyes expressionless. "Not really. I do not want to go. But I will do it," she said quietly.

At that moment, Jayne felt a sharp stab of pity for Raisa, who had been nothing but helpful and still knew nothing of her husband's fate.

As Vasilenko was climbing into Shevchenko's Hyundai and Jayne was about to get into the driver's seat, there came the distant whining and clattering of a helicopter taking off.

Jayne scanned the night sky and immediately saw the lights of a chopper rising from somewhere in the vicinity of Konstantinovsky Palace. The machine climbed rapidly and then hovered below the level of the overhead clouds.

Two searchlights flicked on beneath the helicopter, marking clear white trails of light down to the ground.

A few seconds later, two more choppers also took off, also with searchlights on, and the trio hovered together before splitting up. One headed slowly eastward along the coast in the direction of St. Petersburg, another moved south, and the third began to move west.

"Shit, here we go," Jayne muttered. Instead of getting into the Hyundai, she ran to Raisa in the driver's seat of the Audi. "Drive with your lights off, if you can. They're looking."

Raisa nodded. "I know these roads. I will lead. You follow. We can swap when we're nearer the place you need." She indicated with a sharp nod of her head that Jayne should return to the Hyundai.

As soon as Jayne was back in the Hyundai, she clipped her phone with its maps app activated on a dashboard holder. Raisa pulled the Audi out and headed off, with Jayne following.

Raisa proved to be a far better driver in the dark than Jayne had expected, doubtless because of her detailed knowledge of the local streets.

Within a few minutes they were heading west on the two-lane coastal road, the 41A-007, with the Gulf of Finland barely visible in the dark despite at times being less than a hundred meters to their right.

There was more traffic now, despite the late hour, and Raisa was forced to switch on her headlights. Jayne did likewise, but here they did not look out of place amid the other vehicles.

They were now beyond the suburbs and dependent on Jayne's map app to get them to the correct point. Jayne accelerated and overtook Raisa's car to take the lead.

Jayne turned to Vasilenko, sitting in the passenger seat next to her. "Now you can tell me what this is all about," she said. "Those American officials who have been killed. What's it for? I know you've been discussing it at the palace."

But Vasilenko shook his head. "No. I will tell you when we are safely out of here on a US ship," he said. "Otherwise, what incentive have you got to take me? That information is my ticket out."

"You are joking?" Jayne said. "What happens if we get split up, if the FSB bust the exfil, or if something else goes wrong?"

"No. I have decided."

Jayne battled to contain her anger, which she could feel rising up inside her. She gripped the steering wheel so tight her knuckles hurt.

Bloody Russians. First he shoots dead two guys without consulting me, then he zips up on me.

"That is just unprofessional," Jayne said, her voice low.

"It is unprofessional of you to expect me to take unnecessary risks with my own life. I will look after my own interests. You look after yours."

Jayne didn't reply. Maybe he was right not to take his passage out of Russia for granted. She could hardly blame him for being somewhat paranoid. She would probably feel the same if the positions were reversed.

She was instead distracted by the sight of a chopper in her rearview mirrors. As she had feared, the helicopter, which had headed west from the palace, appeared to have been searching in ever-increasing circles that periodically took it nearer to their location. Its twin searchlights, scanning the roadways below, were clearly visible against the dark sky even in the mirror.

Her stomach tightened into a knot as a police car screamed toward them from the opposite direction, its siren blaring and blue roof lights flashing.

But it kept going, and Jayne exhaled in relief.

They passed through the suburbs of Peterhof, past the floodlit concrete construction site at the enormous Port Bronka deepwater shipping terminal, which was nearing completion, and on for another two kilometers until Jayne's maps app told her a right turn toward the beach was required.

She turned off her lights and steered the Hyundai a short distance down a rough track before coming to a halt behind a long row of thick, tall bushes that stood between the road and the beach. Now they were out of sight of traffic on the road. Raisa, following immediately behind them, parked next to her.

Jayne climbed out of the car, took the velvet bag from her pocket, removed the transmitter, and turned it on. As soon as the green LEDs showed, she pushed the activation button on the top. A few seconds later, the LEDs began flashing red, then went solid green again. The box had connected with the satellite and had transmitted its all-important signal.

While she was engaging the transmitter, another police car screamed past on the other side of the hedge, also with its siren blaring and lights flashing.

Jayne felt her pulse rate rising rapidly and pressure building behind her temples.

She knew there was now going to be a nerve-racking and seemingly interminable wait before the US Navy SEALs in their F470 inflatable combat boat showed up. The inflatable was quick and quiet—she knew that from previous operations during which she had traveled in one. But she calculated it could nevertheless take a good ten minutes to travel the three or four kilometers from the mother ship, the Mark V special operations high-speed patrol boat that was waiting silently out in the Gulf of Finland for her signal.

She turned to Shevchenko. "You and Raisa can go now. You don't need to wait. You need to get to the palace quickly."

But Shevchenko took her by the elbow and steered her away from Vasilenko and Raisa.

"I am going to the palace, but not quite yet," Shevchenko said. "You need to take Raisa with you."

Jayne looked at her, astonished. Was she serious? "No. I'm not going to take her with me. I'm not authorized to do so. It's not necessary."

"It is necessary. You will take her. Otherwise I am going to have to shoot her. She knows far too much about me. She could sign my death warrant."

"Bloody hell," Jayne cursed.

She exhaled in frustration but immediately realized that what Shevchenko was saying made logical sense. If Raisa was caught and interrogated, it was almost certain she would not hold out for long, and if that happened, Shevchenko would indeed be history, as would Raisa, most probably.

"But she might not want to go with me," Jayne said. "And

even if she does and I do take her, what are you going to do then?"

"I will go to the palace and tell Ivanov and Kruglov I have just arrived from Moscow," Shevchenko said. "They will be angry and tell me about Vasilenko's disappearance, and I will explode and say I suspected him all along, which was why I wanted to interview him at short notice two weeks ago when they threw me into Lefortovo and prevented me from doing so. I will blame their stupidity for what has happened and specifically that idiot Sidorenko. I stated clearly for the record—which is all on their video recordings—that Sidorenko was holding up my inquiries by detaining me. I warned that a traitor would end up going free, and now I can prove myself correct. I will mention my comments to Kruglov. With any luck, Sidorenko will be sent to the gulag, not me."

Jayne remained silent for a couple of seconds. This woman had some nerve, that was for sure. She was walking a tightrope.

Jayne hated making these decisions, but there was no choice.

"All right," she said. "I will take her—if she wants to go."

Jayne glanced at her watch. Time was rapidly running short. "I urgently need to set up the infrared for the exfil team—I can't be distracted. Can you and Vasilenko explain to her what happened to her husband? She doesn't know he's dead yet, and that will be a major factor in her decision. You'll have to say he was killed in cross fire or something. You can't possibly tell her that he did it." She jerked her thumb toward Vasilenko.

Shevchenko nodded. She took out her burner phone, removed the battery and SIM card, and handed them all to Jayne. "Throw this out to sea when you get there. I will get another. I do not want the zookeepers to find them," she said.

After speaking briefly to Vasilenko, the two of them walked over to Raisa. Meanwhile, Jayne turned her attention to the millpond-flat waters of the Gulf of Finland, dark and featureless, just a few meters from where they stood. There was no sign yet of the inflatable.

Jayne flipped up a hinged plastic arm on the side of the black transmitter box and pushed a button that activated an infrared light on the arm, invisible to the naked eye but which would act as a clear guide for SEALs using infrared nighttime goggles or scopes.

Despite her best attempts to concentrate, Jayne found herself distracted by Raisa, who was becoming predictably emotional as Vasilenko told her whatever revised version of events he'd come up with.

By the time Jayne had refocused on her surroundings and checked the sea for any sign of the inflatable, she realized the distant clattering of the helicopter was becoming louder.

She looked up to see the beams of the chopper's search-lights moving quickly toward them.

CHAPTER THIRTY-FIVE

Thursday, April 23, 2015
  Gulf of Finland

The two SEALs were both tall, menacing-looking men, clad in black wet suits and with M4 assault rifles slung across their chests. One sat at the bow and the other at the stern of the Zodiac inflatable black rubber boat.

They nosed it cautiously away from the shore through the seaweed at little more than idling speed, keeping a constant watch on the FSB helicopter that was now hovering a couple of kilometers to the east. The risk was that the tiny white bow wave being pushed out by the boat might somehow be seen from above, and they were anxious to keep it to a minimum.

Jayne sat with Vasilenko and a tearful and angry Raisa in the middle of the boat. All three of them were wet from the knees down after having to wade in icy water in order to board the craft, but Jayne knew the process could have been a lot worse had the weather not been as calm. The SEALs had given them black waterproof fleece-lined jackets and trousers for warmth and to cover their lighter-colored clothing.

It seemed like an eternity before they were fifty meters offshore, and another before fifty turned into a hundred. But at roughly five hundred meters out, the SEAL at the front of the inflatable, who was closely watching the chopper, indicated with a silent thumbs-up that he was now sure the boat hadn't been spotted.

His colleague at the stern, steering with the tiller handle of a powerful outboard motor, accelerated steadily until the inflatable was skimming across the still waters at a speed that Jayne guessed must be at least twenty kilometers per hour.

This was Route Green Two out of Russia.

Neither of the two men introduced themselves, and the entire pickup had been conducted in near silence apart from a quick request to Jayne to confirm their identities. She had initially tried to explain why there were three of them, not two, but these were clearly not men to be thrown by changes in operational plans. They merely nodded and got on with the job.

Jayne glanced at Raisa, who had realized very quickly that she had no choice but to leave her homeland. However, she had not taken the news well. She sat head in hands, visibly in shock and struggling to come to terms with what had happened to her in the past few hours.

Jayne put a hand on Raisa's shoulder. "I'm so sorry for what happened," she said. "I feel as though it was my fault for taking advantage of your willingness to help. I can't bring your husband back, but I promise I will do what I can to help you."

Raisa nodded and wiped her eyes with her sleeve but said nothing.

Jayne gazed out over the flat waters in silence. Sometimes the harsh choices and uncompromising nature of this job seemed too much. The human consequences of doing what seemed like the right thing could be quite unexpected. It seemed a bit like taking drugs to cure a serious illness: the side effects were always the worst part. She found herself missing Joe. He would have been good at dealing with this type of situation, saying the right thing to Raisa, putting a comforting arm around her shoulder.

She remembered she had to dispose of Shevchenko's burner phone and took it and the SIM and battery from her pocket and threw them into the Gulf of Finland.

Finally, out of the gloom, the hull of the mother ship, the Mark V patrol boat, loomed up at them about ten minutes later.

The SEAL at the rear of the Zodiac steered it at some speed right up an integrated landing ramp at the stern of the Mark V, where it came to a halt like a beached dolphin. Three other SEALs grabbed hold of it and pulled it a little farther up the ramp.

"Out, quickly," the SEAL at the bow of the Zodiac said, indicating urgently with his hand that Jayne and the others should disembark.

Jayne stood and stepped forward to the bow of the inflatable and then scrambled over the side onto the matte-gray deck of the patrol boat, where another inflatable boat was lashed. The others followed close behind her.

She turned and watched as the SEALs hauled the inflatable farther up the ramp and tied it down. There were two M2 heavy machine guns on mounts on both sides of the low-slung Mark V, which looked about twenty-five meters long.

"Go and sit in the cabin," a SEAL said to Jayne, pointing toward a soft waterproof gray canopy that formed an extension at the rear of the hard shell of the main cabin. "Strap yourselves in. We can't hang around. FSB patrol boats will be after us."

Jayne knew he was right. There remained a long way to safety—Russian territorial waters extended twenty-two kilometers offshore, and even then, Jayne knew that the FSB's heavily armed gunboats wouldn't hesitate to go farther if needed. They were known to open fire on other boats found in their waters without permission.

Jayne followed the SEAL's instructions and sat down on an aircraft-style seat on the port side, where she fastened her seat belt. Vasilenko sat next to her, and Raisa took a place on the starboard side, across the aisle.

Seconds later, the boat vibrated as the idling engines roared into life and it accelerated hard in a westerly direction, the sudden force pushing her back into her seat.

The SEAL who had been piloting the inflatable walked past and handed each of them a bottle of mineral water.

"You all okay there?" he asked Jayne.

She nodded. "Yes, thanks very much. You did a great job." Indeed, they had. The professionalism and precision with which the exfil operation had been executed had been exemplary.

"Next stop Upinniemi," the SEAL said in a staccato voice, referring to the Finnish naval base near Helsinki. "Providing the Russians don't send fighter planes after us."

"Is that a possibility?" Jayne asked. She could see the SEAL was serious.

The SEAL nodded. "They'll do it, no doubt, if they get a bead on us and the boats can't get to us."

"How long to Upinniemi?"

"Four hours, maybe five, even in this fast boat. You'd better settle in. It's a long run. Might make it by sunrise." He paused. "Hope it was worth it."

He walked forward to the main cabin, the controls and layout of which reminded Jayne of an aircraft cockpit, and took a seat next to one of his colleagues at the helm.

Was it worth it?

She glanced sideways at Vasilenko in the seat next to her and caught his eye. Jayne felt that now was the time to find out.

"So, what will it be? An apartment in Manhattan or a beach house near San Diego?" she asked in Russian.

He didn't smile. "Retirement will not come easily."

"You haven't retired yet. There's work still to do." Jayne lowered her voice and glanced over at Raisa, but the woman was more than two meters away and definitely wouldn't be able to hear above the noise of the boat.

"You're safely out of reach of the Lubyanka now, so tell me, what is this all about?"

"It is audacious," Vasilenko said. "They are opportunists and they are relentless. You might not believe me if I tell you."

"Try me," Jayne said. She grasped the arms of her seat and waited.

"There is an American presidential election next year, yes? Well, the Kremlin is desperate to keep the Democrats, Ferguson's lot, out of power. Our president sees them as anti-Russian, too keen on their fracking and their other energy policies that will hurt our oil and gas industry. Too eager to push Russia out of Eastern Europe, too keen to stop Russian influence in Ukraine. You understand?"

"Of course I understand. But what is the Kremlin doing about it? What is Putin's plan? Tell me what's going on."

"Ivanov, at the direction of his boss, has made big inroads into the election machine of the United States. They do not want the outcome left to chance."

"How?"

"They somehow got a grip on some of the secretaries of state, including the one in New Hampshire. Of course, you know what their responsibilities include?"

"Running elections. You mean they had them on the payroll?"

"Indeed. Because if they can control the men who control the elections in certain states, they can control the outcome."

Curtis Steyn in the Kremlin's pocket?

Jayne's first thought was that this had to be bullshit. But then, Curtis was a man who to her had always seemed to give the impression of not having all his cards on the table, perhaps a keeper of secrets. One thing was for sure, though: if Curtis had been paid off by Moscow, then he must have done it behind Simone's back.

"Sounds unlikely," Jayne said.

Vasilenko shrugged. "It is true."

"But how did they get control of these men? And why the hell are they now killing them? How many are there on the payroll?"

Now her mind was whirring at full speed, the questions coming out faster than Vasilenko could answer them. She knew she needed to slow down and get the detail, and she consciously kept her voice low so Raisa and the SEALs could not hear.

"I do not know all the answers, I am afraid," Vasilenko said. "How they got control of them is something I am not certain of. They did not tell me every little detail, and I could not ask too many questions. However, they are disposing of some of them whose work is done but who have given signs that they might be about to give away the details of the plot. They were either demanding more money or having second thoughts and hinting they would disclose everything. The Kremlin felt it better to eliminate them."

The boat, now traveling at high speed, kicked upward as it struck a wave, throwing Jayne back hard into her seat. She was grateful that she was wearing a seat belt.

"What work is done? What have they been doing?" Jayne asked as the boat came back on an even keel.

"Well, there are many ways of trying to control election outcomes. It is possible to rig postal votes, hack into electoral computer systems, steal ballot papers, and so on. But the quickest way is to remove names from the voter roll so that they cannot vote in the first place. And that is what Ivanov has done—his people have blackmailed and bribed these secretaries of state to remove voters from their rolls very aggressively."

Jayne felt her scalp tighten. "They can't just remove people from voter rolls, surely. That has to be illegal."

"That's where you are wrong. I have seen some of Ivanov's planning documents. There are many circumstances that allow secretaries of state in the US to cull their voter rolls—if people do not vote for a while for whatever reason, perhaps because of work commitments, if they change addresses, forget to return confirmation notices. All kinds of reasons. There is a lot of scope for individual secretaries to either be aggressive about the culling or not."

Jayne leaned back in her seat. She could see clearly that if the Russians were trying to favor the Republicans, whose voters traditionally tended to be wealthier, to own property, to be better educated, and to hold better jobs, then it would make absolute sense to target the other end of the spectrum. That would include people on lower incomes, ethnic minorities, perhaps disabled voters, young voters, those who didn't speak the language very well, and those who moved homes frequently. Maybe even workers paid by the hour who had difficulties in making time to vote. All of those were, on balance, more likely to be left-leaning Democratic Party voters.

"My God. So, effectively, the election in those areas is no

longer really a proper people's vote," Jayne said. "It becomes more like the Kremlin's vote."

"The Kremlin's vote," Vasilenko said. "Yes, correct. Controlled by Russia."

Jayne paused, thinking through Vasilenko's disclosures. "But surely they can't strip out enough voters to make a big enough difference to swing a presidential election?"

"Ivanov's strategy is to target the swing states, the ones where the margin of victory previously has not been great and where stripping out a swathe of Democrat voters could either firm up existing Republican candidates or alternatively cause the balance to tip from Democrat to Republican."

"But you'd need big numbers to make it work," Jayne said.

"Correct."

"Well, how many? Tens of thousands?"

"No, many more than that. These secretaries have stripped out hundreds of thousands of voters—millions. Massive numbers. Ivanov's got it all planned out. You know how many US voters were removed from rolls the past couple of years?"

Jayne shrugged. "No idea."

"About sixteen million."

"*Sixteen million?* Seriously? But surely Ivanov's not engineered all those. That is a natural process."

"Some are natural, yes. Of course, a lot of people drop off the rolls for good reasons, but that is precisely why it has been difficult to spot what Ivanov's been doing. He's used it as his smoke screen. Across the United States, four million more voters have been cut from the rolls these past two years compared with the numbers cut between 2006 and 2008. That was in Ivanov's strategy paper."

"And you're telling me that Ivanov's fixed the four million? Bullshit."

"Not all. But a good number are in the states that he's

targeted, yes. And there are going to be more to come, unless it is stopped."

"Do you know which states this has happened in?"

"That is the problem. They have kept it very tight, very secure. That is detail I haven't seen. The only ones I know about are the ones who have been in the news—the guys from New Hampshire and Wisconsin and the one from Georgia."

"How many others, do you think?"

"I think at least three others. Maybe more."

Jayne's stomach turned over in alarm as she digested the implications.

"But it's not just about rigging the elections, is it? You're telling me these other three secretaries of state could also have targets on their backs?"

"Quite possibly, yes. If they have already made the changes to their voter rolls and are demanding more money or threatening to inform the authorities or something, they will be targeted."

"And you don't know who?"

"No. Sorry."

PART FOUR

CHAPTER THIRTY-SIX

Thursday, April 23, 2015
Helsinki

The Helsinki CIA chief of station, Pieter Moss, tried to make small talk by explaining the recent refurbishment work that had been carried out at the four-story Georgian-style redbrick embassy as he led Jayne and Vasilenko up in the elevator to the top floor.

But after virtually no sleep on board the Mark V patrol boat, she was in no mood to listen to his inconsequential chat about the adjacent modernistic new innovation center, the glass entrance lobby, and the other improvements to the embassy, which had occupied the same three-acre site next to the sea since the 1930s.

There was too much of importance to communicate to Langley, and Moss, who was running one of the smallest CIA stations in Europe with just a handful of people on his team, was frankly just irritating her.

She just wanted to get the debrief over with and get to her

hotel bedroom for a shower and some rest. It was the same for Vasilenko—who was being discreetly monitored by two CIA guards—and Raisa, whom she had left waiting downstairs in a reception room.

There would be a need to negotiate a compensation settlement with Raisa for the massive upheaval she had suffered. This would typically comprise a large cash payment and a house. In return, they would need a commitment to keep her silence over everything she had learned, particularly about Shevchenko. She might also need a new identity.

Raisa had indicated that she thought she could find work in Finland and for the time being wanted to remain in Helsinki but would take some time to make final decisions. However, to Jayne, the safest option seemed to be a transfer to the US, where she could be better protected from any potential Russian revenge operation.

Thankfully, when they arrived at the secure conference room, a kind of boxlike structure within the CIA station, with its soundproof bare white walls, floors, and ceilings, Jayne found the monitor screen was already showing three familiar faces from 4,300 miles away at Langley. Vic, typically sipping from a Starbucks takeaway cup, was sitting there with Veltman and Ricardo Miller. All looked tired, but it was the early hours of the morning for them in the US.

"We have it all set up," Moss said, unnecessarily. A tall man, with a professor's air about him and a mop of unruly hair, he realized there was no sense in trying to take over proceedings and sat at the far end of the table, ceding the two chairs nearest the screen and the static camera to Jayne and Vasilenko.

She poured two cups of coffee from a French press on the table, handed one to Vasilenko, and sat down.

The three men at Langley were leaning forward toward their own camera and screen, waiting expectantly. Jayne had already had an exchange of messages earlier with Vic to update him.

"Glad to see you, Jayne," Vic said. There was genuine warmth in his voice. "Also good to see you, Pavel. We greatly appreciate the sacrifice you have made. We're a little concerned about VULTURE. Have you heard from her?"

It was typical of Vic to address the human side of the operation, the fate of his agents and his main operative, before getting on to the wider intelligence briefing.

"I haven't," Jayne said. "But I don't expect to immediately. She was heading for the palace, and security will be airtight." She didn't voice her serious concerns that Shevchenko might come under renewed heavy scrutiny and could be in real danger. That could be done in a private conversation with Vic later.

"Tell us what you both know," Veltman said, anxious as ever to get to the detail. "The White House will want a briefing immediately after this. It sounds serious."

"It is," Jayne said. "You might not believe much of it, as I didn't. But let's get through it and then we can discuss it all."

She deferred to Vasilenko, who spent the next twenty minutes recounting in as much detail as he could what he had already told Jayne. He was interrupted only by occasional expletives of disbelief from Vic and the odd request for clarification from Veltman and Miller.

"It seems remarkable to me that the Russians were able to get so many of these secretaries on the hook," Vic said. "There has to be some leverage they have, some hold over them. I'm still waiting for a reply on my query to my CID contact about their army records."

"I agree," Jayne said. "There must be some connection. We also need to find out exactly what those secretaries have done. How many voters have they stripped off the rolls, and what difference could it make when the election comes around? I still can't believe they would find it so easy to do."

"They're the ones in charge of elections in their states," Veltman said. "I'm no local government expert, but I assume their departments do what they say, providing they're not breaking any laws. And they don't have to break laws to cull rolls. It *is* that easy. The biggest worry I have is that there are other secretaries of state out there also on the Russians' payroll. How many more are there?"

"I don't know precisely," Vasilenko said. "But I think three more."

"*Three* more?" Veltman said. He leaned back in his seat and placed his hands behind his head. "Who?"

"I was unfortunately not able to find out who they are," Vasilenko said.

"Well, we *do* need to find out," Vic said.

"Yes, but they're not exactly going to be broadcasting it from the rooftops if they're on the Kremlin's payroll," Jayne asked. "I can try Simone Steyn to see if she has any clue on this."

"Yes, try her," Vic said. "I will also ask the Feebs to reach out to her again. But I'm thinking, if these secretaries are on the Russian payroll, it seems like they could be in a huge amount of danger. And they must know it, watching the others being picked off. If they can't sleep at night, it might change their thinking about breaking cover somewhat."

"Perhaps, but what's it going to achieve, killing these guys?" Veltman asked.

"Dead men can't tell tales," Vasilenko said. "If I hadn't told you why they are being killed, you wouldn't know about the voter roll manipulation. By the time you found out, it might have been too late."

There was a couple of seconds of silence as the others digested Vasilenko's logic.

Jayne glanced out through the triple-glazed window of the conference room. Easily visible less than a mile out to sea to the east was the sea fortress of Suomenlinna, which was built on a group of islands, and the waters of the Gulf of Finland beyond, back in the direction they had come earlier that morning. It suddenly seemed significant to her that the fortress had been built to protect against Russian expansionism in the 1700s. Not much had changed.

"Pavel, had this operation against the secretaries of state begun when you were based in DC, and were you involved in it if so?" Vic asked, referring to Vasilenko's spell at the *rezidentura* in Washington, which had ended three years earlier.

Vasilenko shook his head. "No."

"We need to inform the FBI," Vic said. "I'll get on the phone to Shepard after we're finished. The Feebs are going to have to grill the other secretaries to try and work out who's been doing this and therefore who's at risk."

"All the states?" Veltman asked. "There's forty odd more. Most have a secretary."

"Not all," Vic said. "Anyway, I'll get the Feebs to focus on the swing states first. Those are the ones particularly targeted, it seems."

Jayne thought she detected a note of satisfaction in Vic's voice at the thought of the FBI scrambling around the country trying to locate the traitors among those secretaries who were left, but maybe she was wrong.

"We need you and Pavel back to Langley as quickly as possible, Jayne," Vic said. "An Agency plane will be heading to Helsinki from London later today with a security team on board to escort you. And we'll need to start making arrangements with Raisa as soon as possible. Can we trust her?"

"We'll have to," Jayne said. "I'll warn her of what will happen if she thinks about letting us down. She wants to stay in Finland for now, but I think the US would be a safer option for both her and for us—and VULTURE. I feel terrible for her." She gave a sideways glance at Vasilenko.

"We'll do what we can to help her," Vic said. "I'll get the resettlement people here to work with Pieter and his people to ensure Raisa's looked after properly. You may be right. The US would be safer. Okay, then, you need to get some sleep before the security team arrives later to take you to the airport."

"Yes, sure," Jayne said. "But if you're thinking about using me to find Tkachev, I suggest you mobilize the FBI instead. And you'd better tell them to get moving, before we have more casualties."

* * *

Thursday, April 23, 2015
   Strelna

The faces around the circular conference table in the Marble Hall were solemn. *Very Soviet*, Shevchenko thought as she sat, hands folded in her lap, staring at them each in turn.

It was only a quarter past seven in the morning. She had not had time for breakfast yet, and this was going to be a meeting of the highest level to be endured and negotiated through. It would be a game of mental chess, in which it would be difficult, maybe impossible, to discern the agendas of the others around the table.

But she was good at such games, which was why she was sitting there.

It wasn't where she wanted to be, of course. Not after less than two hours of sleep, a long, exhausting drive from Moscow, and a nerve-racking mission to ensure Jayne

Robinson and Pavel Vasilenko were safely exfiltrated out of her country. However, there was no escaping it.

She had arrived back at Konstantinovsky Palace in the middle of the night to find, predictably, that all hell had broken loose. It had worked in her favor, because all focus was on the Vladivostok cottage, where there was a blood-bath, and on the security team, which was now missing two of its leaders. Few even noticed her arrival.

Shevchenko had been admitted by security after the usual rigorous but this time somewhat frenetic check of her identity and a search of her car, then had made her way past groups of security guards, cars with flashing blue lights, and two ambulances to the vacant cottage in the Consular Village that she had been allocated, named Irkutsk.

There, she had immediately seized the initiative by calling Kruglov, despite the hour, on the basis that she calculated it would look odd if she hadn't done so, and had demanded to know what was going on.

Now, Kruglov sat opposite her, his Italian designer suit and striking red silk tie immaculate as usual. He was always impossible to read—inscrutable and with a disconcerting habit of saying and doing the opposite to what might be expected.

True, he had supported her the previous year when he had promoted her into her current role, but there was no guar-antee that support would continue despite her success in Paris. After all, he had acquiesced to the humiliating interro-gation she suffered at Lefortovo that had been initiated by his private counterintelligence chief, Sidorenko.

But Kruglov wasn't her biggest concern at this table.

Four places to her right was the president, his laser ice-blue eyes watching everyone.

It was, in fact, Putin who—turning toward her—spoke first. "Thank you, Major General, for joining us all here. We have made good progress over the past few days, as you will no doubt have gathered, and I expect that your inputs going forward will be valuable. I would like to first congratulate and thank you for your recent operation in Paris to identify and detain the traitor in your service."

"Thank you, Mr. President, sir," Shevchenko said. "It was an honor to be of service in that way."

She knew as she spoke that his words would vanish like a fleeting ray of sunshine as the storm clouds rolled in.

"Yes, indeed," the president said. "It pleased me greatly. I was, however, less happy to discover that we had another traitor in our midst. Pavel Vasilenko now seems to have vanished, presumably defected to the West, taking all the secrets we have been discussing here with him. He appears to have been assisted by the wife of one of our security heads who has also gone, leaving her dead husband behind in the Consular Village. Her car was found abandoned at the beach near Port Bronka. No doubt they are all on an American submarine right now. Our helicopter surveillance crews appear to have had some kind of meltdown last night, an appalling failure. And it seems almost certain that these defections were facilitated by the British agent Jayne Robinson, who we know was in Moscow and then came to Strelna. We think she posed as a lady of a different kind to gain access to the palace complex. We will get to the bottom of exactly what happened, do not worry. An investigation is underway."

Shevchenko noted that the president threw a quick glance in the direction of Ivanov as he made the veiled reference to escort girls, but offered no criticism.

"You do not need me to tell you how much of a disaster this is for our operation, for our planning," the president continued. "What we would like to know is what your thoughts are about all this, as chief of our counterintelligence directorate."

Then he leaned back in his seat, folded his arms, and stared at Shevchenko.

This was the disadvantage of working for a president who had previously been in the KGB, she reflected. He knew too much about what everyone's role should involve within the intelligence services.

Shevchenko folded her hands on the desk and returned the president's gaze. "I have had my suspicions about Vasilenko for some time. This does not come as a great surprise. It is why I had scheduled an interview with him a couple of weeks ago, before he came here to the palace. Unfortunately my interview with him never took place, as I was incarcerated at Lefortovo for several days. By the time I was released, he had already traveled here." She shrugged. "Too late. The horse had galloped out of the stable."

"Why did you not mention your concerns about him before?"

"I warned those interrogating me several times that while they were busy subjecting me to that ordeal—a pointless exercise—traitors to the Rodina would be going undetected. In terms of Vasilenko specifically, I had no hard evidence at that stage. I did not want to accuse him before I had accumulated that. But I had my own thoughts about him, make no mistake."

Shevchenko knew this was slightly dangerous territory, to go on the semi-offensive, but she felt she had to defend herself. Too many people had until recently doubted her loyalty. Out of the corner of her eye, she saw her former boss, Yevgeny Kutsik, shifting in his seat, all neatly parted greased black hair and acne-scarred cheeks.

Here we go. He's sharpening his knife.

"Tell me something," Kutsik said. "Why did you choose to drive to Strelna from Moscow last night? It is very unusual for someone in your position, especially after such an exhausting few days in Paris. Why not fly in comfort and be picked up from the airport by a limousine?"

"I needed some time to think," Shevchenko said. "After my ordeal in Lefortovo and the Paris success, I wanted to be clear in my mind about strategy for my directorate. I have a few changes in senior personnel that I am considering making, and I like to ponder these things. A long drive with some classical music is perfect for that."

"And you came directly here, did you?" Kutsik asked, stroking his chin and fixing Shevchenko with a pair of black eyes.

Bozhe, he can't know.

"Apart from a couple of stops for coffee, yes."

And so it went on. There was another ten minutes of questioning about her movements, her thinking, her decisions. She fended off all the questions, at least for now. They had no proof, thanks to her disabling the tracker beacon hidden behind her exhaust system before departing Moscow, and they weren't going to mention that, for obvious reasons. Most of the questions came from Kutsik. Ivanov sat and listened in silence.

"I think we have taken this as far as we can—for the time being," Kruglov said eventually, to Shevchenko's relief. "We need to decide what we do about Operation Pandora now. Do we continue?"

"We must," Ivanov said, making his first contribution. "The last thing I want is for any of those secretaries of state to be in a position to tell how we engineered all this or name names. We do not want our processes, our secrets, our methods to be exposed to scrutiny. Otherwise they will shut all the trapdoors we have managed to open."

"So in that case we will instruct Georgi Tkachev to carry on?" Kruglov asked.

"Yes. That is the correct decision," the president said. "Tell him to continue."

Kruglov nodded. "Of course, Mr. President."

Putin rose to his feet. "That is enough for now. We will reconvene here after breakfast at nine o'clock. I will see you all then."

On the way out of the Marble Hall, Shevchenko found herself walking just ahead of Kutsik.

"Congratulations, Major General," he hissed from behind, a distinct undercurrent in his tone. "You handled that well."

She turned.

He's such a smiling viper.

"Thank you. You are so kind," Shevchenko said.

"Yes. But make no mistake. You are still being watched, despite Paris."

CHAPTER THIRTY-SEVEN

Saturday, April 25, 2015
Chokoloskee Island, Everglades National Park

The feel of his fingers trailing through the warm waters as his pedal kayak slipped away from the postage-stamp-sized beach outside his vacation house always had the same effect on Mike Costello. The stresses of his life instantly melted away, and all he had to think about was navigating and fishing.

He pushed a little harder on the pedals, and the kayak, his favorite Hobie Outback, responded. His intention was to head about a half mile south, following the route of the Chokoloskee Pass, and then a little east to where a few mangrove trees were growing on a line of oyster beds.

The tide was up, and he knew that nearby there were holes where water would now be flowing over the oyster bars, allowing the big trout, the reds, and snook to move in and hunt for morsels they couldn't normally get to when the water was lower. That would be a good opportunity to get them on the hook.

His hand moved reactively from the water to the pair of six-foot fishing rods placed on the kayak behind him, together with a landing net. At his feet was a small box with his favorite five lures, two of them gold paddle tails for catching snook, and a small bucket of live shrimp.

The Outback was an ideal kayak for fishing. Thirteen feet long and very stable, it was more maneuverable through the tight bends of the mangrove-lined channels common in this part of the Florida Everglades than his sixteen-foot two-man canoe. The pedal system also allowed him to move while keeping his hands free for fishing or taking photographs.

Twenty minutes later, using live shrimp for bait, he had reeled in a slam, which was the local fishermen's term for catching the big three. First came a large red, which he kept for dinner, followed by a snook and a trout, both of which he threw back.

Costello had first come to Chokoloskee Island forty-four years ago, at the age of fourteen, after his parents had bought the same two-story, three-bedroom vacation home he was still using, along with its garden, small pool, and private beach. At that time, the relatively new causeway connecting the island to Everglades City was still a novelty. Houses were few, and property was far cheaper.

To Costello, fishing here was the best kind of therapy. It remained reasonably peaceful, and the island only had about four hundred permanent residents. It gave him thinking time, something that was always in very short supply in his job as secretary of state for Florida.

Now into his sixth year in the role after a previous stint as a state senator, he could almost carry out the functions required of him blindfolded. But there had lately been huge complications that he certainly would not have envisaged in 2009, when he walked into the white R.A. Gray Building in Tallahassee for the first time.

He had cursed himself repeatedly for getting into this bind.

The proposition that came to him in 2011 was to earn more than a million dollars over the next few years in return for doing something that wasn't technically illegal, even though it did involve pushing the boundaries right to the limit.

He felt he couldn't say no. At a time when his marriage— later dissolved—was already in a difficult phase and he and his wife, Annabelle, had young twin girls to take care of, it had seemed like an answer to his problems.

All he had to do was push every lever he could to purge names from the state voters roll and to choose his methods carefully so that those purged were most likely to be Democratic voters.

He didn't attempt to do it all at once, of course, as that would have been too obvious. But very quickly, the numbers became significant.

From 2008 to 2010, the median purge rate in Florida had been only 0.2 percent of the total. Costello managed to get that up to 3.6 percent from 2012 to 2014 by concentrating on purging those who were on a list of noncitizens. The criteria for inclusion on the purge list was in many cases quite shaky, and there had been objections from civic groups and court challenges along the way. Other tactics involved making it harder for felons to have their voting rights reinstated after serving their sentences, and by restricting voter registration drives.

It had all helped to cull the rolls.

As he thought back to it all, a sudden cloud of depression descended over him, and he stopped pedaling for a few moments and looked up to the blue sky above.

Costello sighed, then resumed pedaling as he pondered.

Now he was heading west into some of the tiny islands

and mangrove islets forming the Ten Thousand Islands complex that separated mainland Florida from the Gulf of Mexico. Normally he would stop here and do some more fishing. It was almost impossible to cast a line and not get a bite, so plentiful were the fish in this area. However, today he decided to simply paddle and think. He would work his way through the usual channels and then head back home for a burger and a beer at JT's Island Grill, a gaudily painted blue shack that was a ten-minute walk up the island from his house.

To his left, on a muddy bank, two six-foot alligators lay motionless, their mouths partly open. There were many of them in this area. They looked sleepy, but the potential threat they represented seemed a very appropriate metaphor for the situation he was now in. He was swimming in dangerous waters, that was for sure.

It was obvious to him why he had been approached. Florida was a well-known swing state that had voted for President Ferguson in 2012 by a narrow one-percentage-point margin: 50 percent versus 49 percent. The aim was to turn the tide back in the opposite direction, in favor of the Republicans, who seemed certain to nominate the governor of Maryland, Nicholas McAllister, in the forthcoming election.

Even a few votes in either direction could make a big difference in the outcome.

The approach had come from someone he had known for a long time. Not much detail was given initially about the plan or its financial backers on grounds of security, and initially, Costello was told it was a political initiative. Although not overtly political himself, his tendencies were more toward the right of center than the left, and particularly coupled with the financial inducement, it seemed to make sense in some ways.

However, more information emerged as the money piled up in the numbered bank account he had set up in the Cayman Islands.

It had been revealed that the entire scheme was being driven by the Russians and was designed to tilt the odds toward a political party whose policies, for the time being at least, happened to be more aligned with the Kremlin's interests.

Costello had no doubt now that if the Democrats and the Republicans happened to change their stance on certain issues in the future, the Russians too would change tack.

The specter of Russian involvement had been the first thing that gave him pause. He had wanted to pull out at that point, but on the heels of one revelation came another. He couldn't get out of this mess even if he wanted to.

The second development, more recent and much more alarming, had been the discovery that one of his colleagues had stupidly decided to demand triple the payment for the entire group and had claimed that they would all reveal details of the scheme in the media if that demand wasn't met.

Inevitably, this backfired. It appeared that the Russians had taken this threat badly, because the individual involved had been killed while attending a conference in the United Kingdom.

Another had followed almost immediately. And to Costello's mounting horror, a third member of their group, the Georgia secretary of state, Chuck Driscoll, had been gunned down in cold blood along with his wife shortly thereafter.

It seemed to Costello that the Russians, having broadly gotten what they wanted from the people on their payroll, were balking at the foolish demands made and were now disposing of them one by one.

At that point Costello had booked a week's vacation and had driven his Ford F-150 pickup the 450 miles south down the coastal highway, past Tampa and Fort Myers, then along Interstate 75 to Chokoloskee. He figured that a week holed up by himself at his favorite happy place would give him a chance to think through his next move. Plus, it would be safer.

The truth was, he didn't have a clue what to do next. He could go to his boss, the state governor, and come clean about what had been happening. But that would likely put him straight behind bars. And although he would then be out of reach of any Russian assassin, it wasn't an attractive option.

Alternatively, he could flee the country, just disappear, and live off the money in his Cayman Islands account. At the moment, that seemed like the favorite option. It was simply how to accomplish that without leaving a trail that he needed to figure out.

One thing he was certain of: he was out of his league right now. Amending the criteria for voter rolls was one thing. The threat of being targeted by some Russian contract killer was quite another.

Costello pedaled his way clear of the final narrow channel through the mangroves and headed northeast across a short stretch of clear water back toward Chokoloskee. There was only half a mile to go now.

Why did I do it?

But even as he asked himself the question, he knew the answer.

He hadn't had a choice.

CHAPTER THIRTY-EIGHT

Saturday, April 25, 2015
Chokoloskee Island, Everglades National Park

Whoever had supplied the SVR's license plate maker in Houston with the requisite three sets of numbers had done a good job, Georgi Tkachev reflected as he finished his pizza at JT's Island Grill and washed it down with the remains of his orange juice.

He had twice changed the plates on his gray BMW R1200RT touring bike, and he had been through numerous traffic cameras, all of which he assumed had license plate recognition software. But at no point had the sirens and the blue lights come anywhere near him.

All the plate numbers were for similar motorcycles owned by other people and therefore didn't trigger red flags in the system. And that was what those guys were paid their three thousand bucks for. Also, they knew that if they screwed up once, they wouldn't be around for long to do it again.

He walked to the till, doing his best to minimize his limp,

and used cash to pay his $7.90 check with a 20 percent tip. He then headed across the covered porch and down a rickety set of wooden steps to his BMW, which was parked out of sight behind palm trees and two trailers stacked high with kayaks in the rough gravel parking lot to the left of the building.

The temperature was into the low eighties, but Tkachev found his lightweight leather jacket remained reasonably comfortable when riding the bike. It also served a purpose in that it enabled him to carry his Makarov unobtrusively.

He had now been in the United States for ten days. The Malta passport he was carrying, which gave his occupation as electrical engineer, had functioned flawlessly on his arrival at Houston from Monterrey in northern Mexico, where he had ostensibly been working on a power generation project.

Malta appeared to be the passport currently in favor with the SVR's forgery team at Yasenevo, partly because it offered travel to the United States and many other countries without the need for a visa and partly because it made it possible to live in the European Union and move money around internally without any questions. A lot of oligarchs appeared to be thinking along similar lines, judging by the numbers who were paying the $1.1 million required to buy a Maltese passport. The SVR didn't need to do that, of course.

Tkachev sat on his motorcycle for a few moments, thinking through his plan. After making his way to Florida from Atlanta following the Driscoll job, it had been easy enough to track down Mike Costello to his vacation house.

Like many people with ordinary military backgrounds, Costello appeared to have learned little about countersurveillance techniques. A quick hack into his Facebook page by the team in Yasenevo had yielded the address on Chokoloskee Island, and a call to his secretary at the Department of State building in Tallahassee had confirmed that that was where he had gone. It was all Tkachev needed.

He decided his best bet was to approach the house as if he were a tourist, of which there were many milling around, and pretend to be simply taking photographs across the water south of the island.

As he had arrived he saw Costello, a tall man with a full head of neatly groomed black-and-gray hair, wearing a green T-shirt and long blue swimming shorts, in the act of placing his fishing gear into his kayak. He launched the boat and headed off in a southerly direction. There were a couple of other people standing nearby, so Tkachev couldn't do anything at that time.

It had crossed his mind momentarily to rent a kayak and give chase. But Costello was probably more highly skilled on the water than he was, and also likely knew the maze of islands, channels, and mangrove islets much better. He had therefore ridden to Everglades City, explored for an hour, then returned to JT's, where he had settled down for lunch. There were no CCTV cameras either outside or inside, so he felt safe enough.

Maybe Costello was back now. He would go and check.

The street outside the house, a neat blue-painted two-story villa with a white tin roof, was deserted, so Tkachev pulled up beneath a tree and removed his helmet. He had hardly been there for five minutes when out on the water he spotted someone in a kayak heading in his direction from a group of islands half a mile away. Very soon, he could see it was Costello.

Tkachev pretended to check his phone for a few minutes, allowing Costello to draw near. Then, as Costello approached the beach, Tkachev walked to the water's edge and took a few photographs across the bay with his phone camera.

Costello, who he knew was in his late fifties, beached the

kayak about ten meters away, hopped out, and dragged it a short distance up the sand.

"It's really beautiful here," Tkachev said in his accented English.

Costello turned and looked up. "Yes, certainly is. Are you getting some decent photos?"

"Really good. By the way, are you Mike Costello?" He just wanted to be 100 percent certain.

"Yes, that's me. Why?"

Tkachev calmly unzipped his jacket pocket, swiftly removed the Makarov and its attached silencer, and turned off the safety in one fluid motion.

He heard a gasp of surprise from Costello, but before the Florida secretary of state could say anything, let alone shout for help, Tkachev unleashed two quick shots, the first into the left side of his chest, the second into his forehead.

Thwack, thwack.

Costello fell backward, neatly spread-eagled across the seat of his kayak, bleeding heavily into the boat, which was where Tkachev left him. Blood and flesh were splattered across the sand behind his body from the exit wounds.

Tkachev walked back to his BMW, donned his helmet, started the engine, and rode off.

* * *

Saturday, April 25, 2015
Langley

Vic threw the folder across his office desk to Jayne. "Take a look. All three of them were graduates of West Point in 1986. Very academic men. Maybe explains how they became secretaries of state. All three served in Iraq and Afghanistan at

about the same time. These are from my CID buddy, Dave
Payne. Just outline profiles, but it gives you an idea."

Jayne, still feeling exhausted from the all-night exfil operation out of Russia and the overnight CIA secure flight back
to Washington, picked up the file. Despite the urgency, she
had been clinging to a vague hope that Vic and Veltman
might take Saturday off work to do something normal, like a
day trip with their families, thus allowing her to head back to
Portland to see Joe.

Realistically, that wasn't going to happen. These guys were
driven, but with the White House breathing down their
necks and other secretaries to find before they were targeted,
it was hardly surprising.

When she called Vic after their Gulfstream IV landed at
Camp Peary, the CIA base 110 miles south of Washington,
she was told that Veltman wanted her to accompany
Vasilenko immediately for a debrief at a CIA safe house. The
property, in Georgetown, near the university, was the same
one where they had debriefed Shevchenko after her defection
the previous year.

The debriefing covered much the same material that the
Russian had disclosed earlier, except in even more detail.
They wanted to double-check his story and look for inconsis-
tencies.

There had been so many cases of double agents supplying
misinformation over the years that nothing anyone told the
Agency could be taken for granted, especially by a defecting
Russian agent, although Vasilenko was slightly different in
that he had already supplied valuable information to the
Agency and appeared to be genuine.

He had now been left at the safe house, supervised by two
of Vic's team, watching TV news and being fed cookies and
coffee.

Meanwhile, Vic, Veltman, and Jayne had decamped back to Langley for further discussions in private.

"Did they serve in the same regiment or even the same unit?" she asked as she opened the file Vic had given her.

"Same units at some stages of their careers, yes," Vic said.

Jayne removed a single sheet of paper. "Is this it?"

"Yes, so far."

The typewritten sheet listed the names of the three secretaries of state who had died, together with their dates of birth and a brief summary of their curriculum vitae.

All had joined the United States Military Academy at West Point, about fifty miles north of New York City, in 1982 at the age of eighteen and had graduated in 1986. They had then gone on to have careers in the army lasting about twenty years, all of them specializing in administrative, finance, and human resources roles rather than battlefield combat, but all did at least two tours of duty in Afghanistan and Iraq. The sheet listed their respective regiments and units but did not give any details of precisely what their roles were.

After leaving the army, they had taken on a range of employment, including civilian managerial positions. They had then secured secretary of state jobs in different parts of the country.

"These guys were all managers, not soldiers at the sharp end," Jayne said. "It all looks very coordinated, though, the way they moved into these secretary of state roles."

"Yes. But I guess they were all well qualified for that work," Vic said. "They were good at administration jobs. Organizers, planners, back-office type people."

"You wouldn't have gotten along with them," Veltman said, throwing Vic a sideways glance and then catching Jayne's eye.

Vic snorted. "I don't mind admitting my strength is in

operations, not managing. We're not here to push pens around."

Jayne knew that one of Vic's biggest challenges in moving up to the seventh floor at Langley had been to refine and improve his management techniques. Always an operational hotshot, he had never particularly enjoyed management, to the frustration of the Agency's human resources director, who was always nagging him to take various courses to improve his people skills. Vic usually replied saying he didn't have time as he was too busy trying to keep Russia, China, North Korea, and al-Qaeda under some sort of control.

Jayne put the file back on the desk. "I'd like to know a lot more about the links between them in the army. It's not going to be a coincidence their backgrounds were so interwoven and they've all ended up being killed by the Russians. I need to give Simone another call about it—I haven't had time yet."

"I agree," Vic said. "It's not enough. Really, this should be an FBI investigation, and Shepard is on it, but I feel responsibility here, and so I've already asked Payne to dig deeper. He said that he had mentioned the three names to one of his senior colleagues, and Curtis Steyn rang some sort of a bell with him. But they are having problems locating the files they need. He's going to get back to me tomorrow, hopefully, as soon as—"

But Vic was interrupted by a knock at the door.

Vic's secretary, Helen, put her head around it, her long red hair swirling around the door frame. "I thought you would want to know. There's a TV news flash. The Florida secretary of state has been found shot dead in the Everglades at his vacation home. Sounds like it's all gone a bit crazy down there."

Jayne and Vic shot to their feet almost simultaneously.

"My God," Vic said. "The president's going to have us on toast."

CHAPTER THIRTY-NINE

Sunday, April 26, 2015
Washington, DC

The phone rang twice before Simone Steyn answered it.

"Hello, is that Jayne?"

"Yes, hi, Simone, I've been trying to reach you, given what's been happening. I thought we should have a chat."

"Oh, I'm glad you called. How are you doing?"

"I'm all right but very busy trying to get to the bottom of everything. I've got some new information that I need your help with, actually."

"That sounds promising. Of course. What have you got?" Her voice sounded much more upbeat than when they had spoken last.

"Well, I can tell you—"

"Yes, yes, I'm coming."

"I'm sorry?" Jayne asked.

"Oh, I wasn't talking to you, Jayne. It was my attorney. He's waiting on me here. I'm afraid I'm going to have to call you back. The FBI wants to speak to me again, he's saying. They're on three times a day. And I have papers to handle with the attorney. I'm sorry, can I call you back a little later?"

Jayne exhaled in frustration and tipped her head back. After a couple of seconds she replied, "Yes, sure. Just give me a call as soon as you can. It's quite urgent, because we're trying to get to the bottom of what's been happening, as you can imagine."

"Yes, I will. Sorry again. Talk later. Bye." Simone ended the call.

Jayne, who was sitting on the edge of her bed in the spare room at Vic's redbrick house in the Palisades suburb of DC, where he and his wife, Eleanor, had invited her to stay, reflexively slammed her hand down onto the eiderdown.

This was more than irritating.

She wandered downstairs, where Vic was sitting at the kitchen table at his laptop, a pile of newspapers next to him. All the front-page headlines were focused on the secretary of state killings.

A small TV on the wall was showing *CBS This Morning*, which was in the middle of a bulletin from Chokoloskee Island. The reporter was standing with his back to a blue two-story house with a white tin roof and gesticulating with his hands to show where Costello had been found. The broadcast cut back to the anchor, who showed a map graphic demonstrating where the four murdered secretaries of state had been found.

"Pressure is mounting on the White House and the FBI to catch the killer who has carried out these murders," the anchor intoned. "The question that remains unanswered is how many other secretaries of state could find themselves under threat. We understand that the FBI is visiting the remaining forty-three secretaries of state to check whether they can help with the investigation or if they know anything that could lead to the arrest of the killer. So far they have obtained no leads, our sources say."

Vic reached for the TV remote control that lay next to him on the table and turned down the volume.

"They wouldn't get any leads, would they?" he asked. "If you'd been part of a scheme run by the Russians to rig the next presidential election, you're not going to admit it, even if you think you're in danger." He paused. "Costello was at West Point with the others too, by the way."

"I was assuming that might be the case," Jayne said.

Eleanor, an elegant woman with long dark hair, was tipping milk into two coffee mugs that were standing next to an espresso machine on the kitchen counter. Vic obviously didn't mind discussing classified information in front of her, Jayne noted.

"The news coverage is wall-to-wall this morning," Jayne said.

"Yes, and they don't even have the voter-roll-rigging part of the story yet," Vic said. "But that's only a matter of time, in my view. It would be better for the president to reveal it at his White House press conference, but he's hanging back. He thinks it could smack of him making political capital out of it, given that the Russians are trying to reduce his voter base."

"That's ridiculous," Jayne said. "Everyone can see this for what it is. It's about democracy, not about politics. Vasilenko said himself if the two parties' policies were differently angled, the Kremlin would have no hesitation in trying to take down the Republicans instead."

"Yes, we both know that. But Ferguson sees it differently, so far." Vic checked his watch. "I've been called in by Veltman for a Situation Room briefing with the president at noon. Just us two plus Bonfield and Shepard. You're not needed this time."

Jayne felt somewhat relieved. The whole experience of

attending a briefing with the president had been interesting but stressful. She felt happy to leave it to Vic and Veltman this time.

"I've been trying to speak to Simone," Jayne said. "She answered but then had to run. She had the FBI waiting for her."

Eleanor handed Vic a cup of coffee. "Would you like one too, Jayne?" she asked. "I'm guessing you probably would. Maybe some painkillers too?" She smiled.

Jayne nodded. "Yes, coffee would be great, thanks, Eleanor. You're right—I might need the painkillers at this rate." She sat down at the pine table opposite Vic and folded her arms.

"Listen," Jayne said. "If I can't get hold of Simone for a proper conversation about this, I was thinking it might be worth approaching some of the other wives of the secretaries who have been killed. Just to see what they know."

"Well, you won't get Eve Driscoll, obviously, so it's either Gareth Weber's wife or Mike Costello's."

"I found out Costello's is actually an ex-wife. Name of Annabelle. Still uses Costello for her surname, but they divorced some years ago. She might be more likely to talk, being an ex," Jayne said. "Maybe more willing to dish the dirt, if there is any."

"Or she might know less, if they've been separated for quite a long time."

"True. But my gut instinct says to try her first. Speaking face-to-face usually works best. I can head there while you're fending off the president."

Vic pursed his lips. "I'm quite happy to swap if you like."

"No, thanks."

"Where does Annabelle live?"

"She's in Boston now. I'll get a flight up there this afternoon."

Eleanor put a cup of coffee down in front of Jayne. "There you go."

"Thank you very much." Jayne picked it up and took a sip.

Vic studied Jayne for a moment. "Okay. Just be careful. Remember Tkachev's background. He seems to be navigating his way around the country without any problems so far. How he's doing that, I'm not sure. Perhaps our law enforcement brethren can answer that one."

He went back to his laptop.

* * *

Sunday, April 26, 2015
Boston

There were two large black Chevrolet Suburbans parked outside Annabelle Costello's address when Jayne, in a sedan rented from the airport, first approached the house. A man in sunglasses and wearing a black jacket was sitting on a low wall, smoking a cigarette. It was all something of a giveaway. The FBI, predictably enough, had doubtless been there for much of the day.

She immediately changed her plan and drove past without slowing down or staring. There was no way she could go anywhere near the house if the feds were inside. They certainly wouldn't appreciate Vic's interference with their investigation.

Jayne decided to wait twenty minutes, and then did another drive past the house, which looked as though it dated to the early twentieth century and was set on a narrow plot on Moreland Street in the Somerville area of Boston.

By then, one of the Suburbans had gone, as had the man

who had been smoking the cigarette, but the other vehicle was still there.

This could be a long wait.

Jayne headed to a coffee shop she had seen at the end of the street and settled in. She didn't mind waiting—she was used to that—but she just hoped that Annabelle wasn't being provided with a twenty-four-hour protection team. Otherwise her journey was wasted.

In fact, it took another two hours and three more times driving past before the other Suburban disappeared. Jayne parked a hundred yards farther down the street and walked past, using it as an opportunity to check carefully for any other signs of surveillance.

There were none. It was time to take a risk, although if the FBI had been at the house most of the day, Annabelle probably wouldn't welcome yet another visitor.

Jayne walked smartly up to the front door and knocked.

The door opened three inches, and Jayne, standing on the raised porch with its neat white-painted fencing, could only hear the deep-throated barking of some big dog on the other side.

Eventually, its owner quietened it down and opened the door of the three-story town house another inch.

"Hello?" The greeting was a question.

"Hi, I'm Jayne Robinson. I'm looking for Annabelle Costello."

The door opened farther still, and Jayne could see a plumpish woman with a mop of curly blond hair, holding the collar of a tall black standard poodle with equally curly hair. The barking had stopped.

"That's me. How can I help?"

Jayne had to stop herself from taking half a step back in astonishment. She immediately recognized the woman as the friend whom Simone had rushed from the café in Concord to meet following their get-together more than three weeks earlier. Simone had called her Anna, not Annabelle.

"Um, I was hoping you might be able to help," Jayne said, fighting to recover her poise and mentally process the connection between the two women. "It's about your ex-husband, Mike."

Annabelle frowned, her forehead creasing, and she clutched her head with her free left hand. "Who are you? What about him?"

"Well, I realize this might be a difficult time, and I'm guessing that the FBI or police will have been talking to you already today, but I'm also investigating the circumstances behind his death if you have time for a few questions."

"*Another* investigator? Where from?"

Jayne quickly calculated her options. It seemed best to be as honest as she could if she was going to persuade Annabelle to help her.

"I'm a private investigator," she said. "But I work with the intelligence services. You might have seen that a few secretaries of state have been targeted, not just Mike, and we're looking into that."

"CIA?"

Jayne nodded.

"You're a Brit, though, aren't you?"

Jayne nodded. "I work with British and US intelligence services."

Annabelle stared at her, blue eyes unblinking, visibly deciding what to do.

"I've just had the FBI here for the past several hours, going through everything. Don't you work with them? I thought the CIA don't do investigations here?"

"You're correct," Jayne said. "They don't. But this particular investigation has a strong international dimension." It was the best she could think of on the spur of the moment, and she immediately feared it wasn't going to have the desired effect.

"Do you have any identification?"

Jayne stepped forward, opened the small clutch bag she was carrying, and showed Annabelle her passport.

Annabelle immediately whipped out her phone and took a photograph of the passport. Jayne thought momentarily about stopping her but decided that would mark the end of any chance she had of getting her to talk, so she let her continue.

Then Annabelle took a step back and held the door. "You'd better come in. I don't have long, though, and I doubt I'm going to be much use to you."

Whatever the terms were of her divorce, Annabelle hadn't done too badly. Jayne guessed the property must have been worth at least half a million dollars, if not three-quarters of a million. And if her late ex-husband had a holiday house in the Everglades as well as a property in Tallahassee, there was clearly enough family wealth.

The house appeared to have been refurbished relatively recently. It was neatly decorated in a modern gray-and-white style with shiny new wooden flooring and recessed lighting. Annabelle led the way into a living room with two long maroon sofas and a selection of modern art prints on the walls. She indicated to Jayne to take a seat on a sofa and then sat at a right angle to her on the other. The dog lay down in the corner of the room.

"You have a nice house," Jayne said.

"Thank you. I moved up here from Tallahassee after the divorce. My parents live near here and help me with the children. They are at their house right now. Now, how can I help you?"

Annabelle folded her arms and scrutinized Jayne carefully.

Jayne explained that she was trying to work out the

connection between the four secretaries of state who had been murdered. "We know they were all at West Point and in the army together, and went to Iraq and Afghanistan. But beyond that we're trying to piece the puzzle together. Can you help with that?"

Annabelle leaned back on the sofa. "I don't think I can, not really."

"I know you've been questioned all day today, but it's important," Jayne said. "It's not just about the four murders of men who knew each other. We're worried that other lives could be at risk too. We're certain that the key to this lies in their previous connections."

Annabelle averted her eyes, tilted her head back, and sighed. "I really can't think of anything."

There was something in the sigh and the way she looked away that gave Jayne pause. Was Annabelle holding back?

"Are you sure? Did the FBI go through all this with you?" Jayne asked.

Annabelle appeared to be about to say something, then pursed her lips and wiped the back of her hand across her eyes. "I can't."

"I appreciate this is difficult, but there is going to eventually be a lot of scrutiny of what has happened. I know that if you're helpful, that won't go unrecognized."

There was a pause lasting more than ten seconds.

"This is really all about the voting rolls, isn't it?" Annabelle asked eventually. She eyed Jayne inquiringly.

Jayne felt a surge of adrenaline flow through her.

She knows.

"Yes, that's part of it," Jayne said, trying to keep a calm exterior. "What happened?"

"I don't know everything. Mike only told me a few bits and pieces. But this goes back quite a few years, to not long after he started in the secretary of state role. He was approached and a proposition was put to him. It was something I didn't entirely agree with."

"Who approached him?" Jayne asked.

"First it was one of the others—Curtis Steyn."

Jayne felt a jolt run through her. She decided to push Annabelle on how much, if anything, she knew of the Russian connection.

"So Curtis Steyn was the one who dealt with the Russians initially?" she asked.

"Yes."

Aha.

"And what was the proposition?" Jayne asked.

"I didn't get all the details, but basically it was to cull the voting rolls where possible to remove Democrats. In return, a large amount of money was paid. Now, Mike told me a little of this, but he never said how much money was involved, and I never raised it because it wasn't long before he discovered who was really running the scheme, and he said he didn't want to do it after that. He wished he wasn't involved. It became a difficult subject."

"Why did he do it, then, if he was against it?"

"Because he said he didn't have a choice," Annabelle said.

"Why not?"

Annabelle sighed. "I'm not sure. It was because of something that happened in the past. He wouldn't tell me what."

Now Jayne's radar was working overtime. This made sense. Had the Russians gotten something on Mike and the others? There were simply too many secretaries involved for it to be just about money.

"You think he was being blackmailed or something?" Jayne asked.

"Yes, something like that. To be honest, all this secrecy and underhandedness was one reason our relationship failed. I hated it. I felt I didn't really know him."

"I can understand that. Do you have any idea at all what the blackmail could have involved?"

Annabelle shook her head. "No, no idea."

Jayne paused for a moment. She seemed to be telling the truth.

Instead, Jayne decided to change tack and ask a question that had been bothering her. "So, what were you doing meeting Simone Steyn up in Concord three weeks ago?"

Annabelle colored a little. "I've known her for some time, just because our husbands knew each other. I just wanted to condole with her about Curtis, little knowing that the same thing would happen to Mike."

"And how did you find her? Did you discuss this whole situation, what we've been talking about?"

"I tried, a bit, but she didn't really seem to understand what I was saying or even want to engage with me about it. She was more interested in talking about how she would cope without Curtis. She seemed really distraught, to be honest—understandably so. So I didn't pursue it too much."

"We have four dead. Do you know how many people were involved in this voting roll scheme?"

"I heard it was six."

That tallied with what Vasilenko had said and gave Jayne some confidence about the veracity of what Annabelle was telling her.

"So you're saying there's another two secretaries of state out there who have also been doing this, stripping more people off their rolls than they should?" Jayne asked.

"Yes, I believe so."

"Who are the other two?"

"I don't know."

Jayne frowned, now feeling deeply frustrated. This was like walking against the wind.

"Were they all involved in this issue that happened in the

past that meant, like Mike, they couldn't say no to the proposition?" Jayne asked.

"I honestly don't know. But I do know that what happened was while they were in the army—I think in Iraq, but it might have been Afghanistan."

"So whatever happened there, I'm guessing it never became publicly known."

"Of course not."

"But the Russians did know about it?"

"It seems so. And that's been the problem all along."

It felt to Jayne that she had extracted all the useful information she could from Annabelle. Maybe she really didn't know the full story, as she claimed. After all, her marriage had been a difficult one. In any case, she could always return with more queries if she needed to.

But now she had a lead, even if it did raise yet another question. What exactly had these men done in Iraq or Afghanistan that enabled the Russians to blackmail them?

And who were the other two secretaries of state who had been involved? Hopefully the FBI were focused on that and concentrating on the swing states.

Then it came to her. Trying to squeeze confidential information out of the enormous military bureaucracy was always akin to navigating a maze. But one man who would know where and how to get it was sitting at his home in Portland right now.

Jayne thanked Annabelle for her help and made a note of her cell phone number and email, telling her she would be in touch if she needed any more information.

She headed back to her car and sat thinking for a short while. Then, instead of heading back to Boston Logan International Airport, she set the satnav to another destination.

Portland lay about 110 miles north up Interstate 95, and

the temptation to spend the night with Joe rather than fly back to the spare room in Vic's house, proved too much.

* * *

Sunday, April 26, 2015
Portland, Maine

"I'll tell you afterward, not before," Joe whispered in her ear, pointing up the stairs. His hands sank a little farther down her back and rested on the top of her buttocks.

Jayne giggled a little. "That's a deal, then. And you have to make dinner too. But if you don't deliver the goods, there'll be massive trouble. That's the only reason I drove up here, of course, so you'd better not let me down."

She leaned into Joe and kissed him again. They were both still standing in the hallway of Joe's house, next to a large framed mirror and a bench with cubby holes beneath it that were all crammed full of shoes and boots. She had taken him by surprise, turning up on his doorstep without calling ahead, and the unexpected visit seemed to have had the desired effect.

"I won't let you down, don't worry," Joe said. "Can't you tell?"

She had just explained briefly the supposed reason she had headed up the interstate to see him.

Joe pulled her tightly into him so she could feel his body heat, even through her sweater. She was always surprised how muscled he was for a man in his mid-fifties.

"What about your kids?" Jayne whispered. For some reason she always felt self-conscious about disappearing off into Joe's bedroom when Carrie and Peter were around during the daytime.

"Don't worry, they're locked in their rooms on their computers, chatting to their friends," he said. "They'll be ages. Anyway, they're way into their teens—they know."

Joe took her hand and pulled her toward the stairs.

Twenty minutes later, they were both lying side by side on Joe's now disheveled bed. She stretched across and placed her hand on his chest.

"I was worried about you over there," Joe said. "Mainly because of your track record. Makes me wonder what they might do if you were caught."

"That never happened, though," Jayne said. "I fended them off, even without your help."

"Usually you fend them off despite my help," Joe laughed. "What's it been like, working by yourself?"

"Different," Jayne said. It was true. In some ways, after more than three years working on operations with Joe, and prior to that being part of a big team at MI6, she had learned to rely to an extent on other people.

"How so?"

"I will be honest with you," Jayne said, "Despite being on a knife edge, I actually quite enjoyed it. It was definitely more of an adrenaline rush, being on my own. Nobody there to drag me out of a hole. But the people I worked with did a good job—Shevchenko, Vasilenko." She paused. "But we're not finished yet. The job's not done. I'll give you a proper report on how I feel about it when it is."

"Yes, I know. I've seen all the news coverage across TV and in the papers. Now, tell me exactly what you need from me."

Jayne explained in detail what she had learned, what was still required in terms of uncovering the links between the four men who had died, and the absolute urgency of identifying the other two secretaries of state who had been involved and whose lives might now be at risk.

"This should really be an FBI inquiry, you know that?" Joe said.

"I know. It *is* an FBI inquiry. They *are* working on it, so they say. But Vic and I are feeling an obligation to contribute."

"An obligation? You mean you think you can do a better job?"

Jayne shrugged. "You know what it's like. Vic's a competitive character, especially when it comes to the feds."

"Tell me about it." Joe gave a half grin. "You know what I would do?"

"Vic's already got a request in with someone he knows in CID, so don't suggest that. It needs to be another route."

"No, not CID. I think I'd initiate a discreet inquiry with the National Personnel Records Center down in Missouri. It's in St. Louis. They've got the military service files on all servicemen. Everything from their training, to their overseas postings, to their disciplinary record, their vacations, and much more. They might have what you need."

"Is that easy to do?"

"No. It would probably be difficult for anyone at the Agency to make a formal request for information. I mean, they've got no law enforcement jurisdiction in the US. So, the answer will be a straight no. Even if the FBI put a request in, the NPRC's wheels tend to turn at glacial speed."

"But?"

"But I have a good contact there, Len Hamblin, who's a military records expert, a kind of investigator. He's helped me with a number of war crimes inquiries over the years. I could submit an under-the-table request and say it's part of an inquiry I'm looking at. No questions asked. I'm sure he would get what you need quite quickly—I've also helped him out several times. It is possible, though, that they will ask for a letter of permission from a family member, a next of kin of the deceased veteran, before they let us see the actual documents."

Jayne's hand slipped a few inches farther down Joe's stomach muscles. She could feel the shape of his abs beneath her fingers.

"When we're finished here, I'll send an email to Annabelle Costello and ask for that permission, given that her deceased husband is involved. I know they were divorced, but her kids were his kids too. Hopefully that will work."

"You mean we're not finished here yet?" Joe had a glint in his eye.

"Maybe not."

Joe smiled. "An email from Annabelle might do the trick. I'll mention that to Len."

"How quickly could you call him?" Jayne asked.

"I'll give him a call first thing in the morning."

Jayne slipped her hand another couple of inches southward.

"And can you persuade him to get the job done tomorrow?" she pressed.

"He's normally pretty quick. I think he could do that, yes." Joe turned his head and grinned at Jayne.

"That's a good answer." She let her hand drift down farther until she found what she was looking for. "A very good answer."

She swung her right leg over Joe's thighs.

CHAPTER FORTY

Monday, April 27, 2015
Langley

In the end, Jayne's overnight stay in Portland proved more than worth the effort it took. Not only did she get to spend the night with Joe, but after flying back to DC the next morning, she found on arrival at Langley, just after half past eleven, that Joe's contact at the NPRC had already responded.

Joe forwarded an email from Len Hamblin containing a PDF copy of the military record for Mike Costello, which was facilitated by consent from Annabelle. Len had also included a similar record for Curtis Steyn, saying that he shouldn't be sending it without a consent but thought he would try and help out, given the gravity of the situation. There were no copies of the files for the other two deceased secretaries of state, but Len had helpfully copied and pasted a few relevant extracts from each of the files into the body of his email.

Jayne was unable to speak to Vic immediately, as he was locked in management meetings until lunchtime, but she grabbed a coffee and settled down in a small office farther down the corridor that Helen had procured for her. Then, she began to read.

The extracted segments told her all she needed to know. They confirmed all four men's service records, beginning in 1986 after they graduated from West Point, and the dates of their discharge, between 2005 and 2007.

The first attachment she read, a DD214 discharge notice for Costello, showed that he had left as a lieutenant colonel, and the box that listed his primary specialty stated that he had served in the Quartermaster Corps as a logistics expert, with particular expertise in petroleum supply.

The section headed Decorations and Medals contained a long list of awards, including an Afghanistan Campaign Medal with one service star, an Iraq Campaign Medal with one service star, a Global War on Terrorism Expeditionary Medal, a Kosovo Campaign Medal with one service star, and a whole host of others.

Costello had therefore been a senior army officer with a wealth of experience in a highly specialized logistics and procurement management role. Jayne knew from projects she had worked on in the UK at MI6 that organizing the supply of fuel to troops based in Afghanistan and Iraq had been a major logistical problem requiring the delivery and distribution of vast volumes of diesel and gasoline.

But in the section headed Character of Service, which indicated the terms of Costello's discharge from the military, a single word was typed: *General*.

That immediately rang an alarm bell with Jayne. She knew that anything other than an honorable discharge meant he had left under some sort of cloud.

Jayne scratched her head. This didn't look good. There

had most likely been some kind of disciplinary issue hanging over him when he left.

There seemed nothing untoward in the rest of the file, so she opened up the attachment for Steyn.

His record was very similar to Costello's, with an almost identical set of decorations and medals, and he had the same last major command listed and, interestingly, a similar Quartermaster Corps role. The record also noted his logistics and petroleum supply expertise. He had also been a lieutenant colonel.

Jayne immediately looked down to the Character of Service section, which also read "general."

This was too much of a coincidence.

Jayne immediately realized that if there was some disciplinary issue impacting the two men, then Vic's contact at the army CID, Dave Payne, might well have picked it up.

She knew that since Costello's death, Vic had contacted Payne again and added Costello's name to the other three he had on his list, but here was definitive proof that at least two of the men had red flags against their names.

Jayne finished her coffee and waited until she heard Vic greet Helen as he returned from his meeting. She then wandered along the corridor. His door was open, so she knocked and walked in.

Vic was sitting with his top button undone, his tie pulled down, and his feet up on his desk, looking pensive.

"What's happening, Vic? You're looking somewhat unhappy," Jayne said. The combined effect of the caffeine and the adrenaline rush from the files she had just read were giving her something of a buzz.

"The White House is gunning for me," Vic said, slumping back in his chair, forearm clutched to his forehead. "They want solutions. We're going to have to resolve this. I'm thinking of having another chat with Vasilenko to see if he's got any more ideas."

"Where is he?"

"We've moved him to an apartment near the American University. He's safe enough. It's only a fifteen-minute drive from here."

"You can hold fire on Vasilenko. I've made progress," Jayne said. "Seems there was some kind of issue involving both Steyn and Costello before they left the army in 2005. I've just been reading their DD214s in the files I've got from St. Louis."

Vic lowered his arm and removed his feet from the desk. "Really? What issue?"

"It doesn't say. But they both had general discharges. It needs checking out."

"Not honorable?" Vic sat upright.

"No."

"Shit. All right. I'll give Dave Payne a call and get him to hurry up." He pointed toward his office sofa against the far wall. "Take a seat."

Vic reached for his phone and tapped away. Jayne sat and listened as he explained to Payne what she had uncovered from the NPRC files.

"There's obviously something there, Dave. And we're under huge pressure. Can you—" Vic stopped speaking and held his phone out in midair.

"He's checking something now," Vic said to Jayne. "He had most of the detail pulled together but hadn't quite finished it. He says give him a few minutes."

Jayne could hear the faint, tinny sound of music playing down the line as Vic remained on hold for the next few minutes.

Then, finally, came the sound of Payne's voice as he came back on line. This time, Vic switched the call over to loudspeaker mode so Jayne could hear.

"What have you got?" Vic asked.

"You're right about the general discharges. There was an issue over both men," Payne said, his voice sounding distorted and synthesized. "They were being investigated by CID before they left. It was a big one—get this. It involved five million dollars' worth of fuel theft in Afghanistan."

"Five *million?*" Vic asked, his voice taking on a note of incredulity.

An electric shock went up Jayne's spine. She leaned forward in her seat, chin cupped in her hands, listening intently to the conversation.

"Yes. Overall, we estimate around fifteen million dollars of fuel was stolen by US military personnel since the start of the war in Afghanistan. You know, the usual type of corruption. Fuel was sold to locals instead of being delivered to units— that was the main scam. We were looking at this back in 2005, and as part of the wider investigation we were building a strong case against these two guys, Steyn and Costello, who we think accounted for about five million of the fifteen."

"Bloody hell," Jayne muttered out loud. She caught Vic's eye and raised both eyebrows.

This is dynamite.

"What were they doing?" Vic asked.

"There was a big fuel base on the Afghanistan-Pakistan border, near Jalalabad. Fuel used to arrive in those jingle trucks, as we called them. Brightly decorated fuel tankers, with ornaments attached by the local drivers. They were contracted to the base."

"Yes, I know what you mean," Vic said. "I remember those trucks well. What was going on?"

"The fuel was then distributed from the fuel base to other surrounding military bases, about thirty of them. Some of those bases were using two million gallons a week. Thing was, a lot of it was going missing before reaching the military bases. It was being sold off for cash. We worked out it was these guys who were masterminding it. They were Quartermaster Corps logistics experts who were responsible for the fuel supplies coming in and going out."

"So what happened?" Vic asked, his forehead creased. "Why didn't this come out?"

"Well, we thought we had them nailed—but then it all went to shit."

"Why?" Vic asked.

"Because a big file with all the evidence went missing from our office at Kandahar. The investigation was screwed, even though we knew it was spot-on. The file was definitely stolen."

"By whom?" Vic asked.

The Russians, Jayne thought immediately.

"We don't know," Payne said. "Could have been the men we were investigating, could have been someone else. We never found out."

"The Russians," Jayne muttered just loudly enough for Vic to hear but not Payne. "That's how they did the blackmail."

Vic caught her comment and nodded.

Now she understood. The Russians had the CID case file and sat on it, waiting for an opportunity. A few years later, as Steyn and Costello's careers took off, they struck. If that fuel scam had come to light and been proved, they would have gone straight to prison for a long time.

The Russians had the file and therefore had Steyn and Costello backed into a corner, Jayne thought, her mind now working furiously.

It was a typical Russian operation.

The acquisition of blackmail material.

The long game.

The patient wait.

And then the opportunity seized.

Jayne just wasn't clear on how all the other secretaries fit into the picture. Was it a similar situation for them too, she wondered?

"Couldn't you rebuild the evidence?" Vic asked Payne, jolting Jane out of her thoughts.

"No. Very difficult," Payne said. "It would have taken a very long time. We had all the original documents—the invoices, sale documents, and so on. There were no copies made as far as we could see. And by that stage, those men had left the army. All we could do was leave a note on the file saying an investigation had taken place and had been put on ice. All I've got is a few notes summarizing what the case was and the names of those we were investigating."

"And apart from these two men, were any others on the list?"

"Yes, a few others. People who were linked to those two who we thought were helping them on the periphery, even if they weren't the main perpetrators. We were eyeing them up as possible witnesses or informers."

Would that have been enough for blackmail? Jayne wondered.

"Which others?" Vic asked. He grabbed a pad and pen and sat poised ready to write.

"Two are the other names you gave me, Gareth Weber and Charles Driscoll—the guys who are dead. And then there's another two as well, Jeffrey Thomson and Gregory Chappleton. They were all senior commissioned army officers based in Afghanistan at that time and were known associates of Costello and Steyn."

Vic repeated the Thomson and Chappleton names to make sure he had them written down correctly.

Jayne tapped the names into a fresh notes page on her phone and then began to check them on Google.

"Were all of them given general discharges instead of honorable?" Vic asked.

"I believe only Steyn and Costello," Payne said. "We didn't have enough evidence on the others at the time to justify it."

"Do you have any other information?" Vic asked.

"That's all I have for now. I'll let you know if I see anything else that's of interest."

"That's great," Vic said. "Many thanks for your help. I owe you a steak dinner somewhere next time you're in DC."

Payne grunted. "No problem. A beer will do. Talk later."

Jayne tapped away on her phone as Vic ended the call. He stood up and placed his hands on his hips, a hint of a grin on his face.

"So there's definitely six of them," Vic said as he paced toward the window. "Two left alive. Now we need to trace Thomson and Chappleton. In fact, Chappleton rings a big bell. I know him from somewhere."

Jayne looked up from her screen. "He should ring a bell. He's the secretary of state for this state—he's Virginia's election chief. And Thomson's secretary of state for North Carolina."

"Ah, yes. Of course," Vic said. "Think I saw Chappleton doing a TV interview a few weeks ago."

He reached for his phone again. "I'm going to call Iain Shepard. The FBI are going to have to trace these guys, quickly. We've done most of their job for them by getting the names. They can do the rest and get some protection thrown around them—before Tkachev gets to them too."

CHAPTER FORTY-ONE

Tuesday, April 28, 2015
Langley

By lunchtime, despite a frantic wave of activity by Shepard's FBI teams, assisted by local police in both Raleigh, the North Carolina state capital, and Richmond, the Virginia capital, there had been no trace of either Thomson or Chappleton, to everyone's mounting concern.

Neither man had turned up for work on Monday or Tuesday at their respective government offices. Their homes were locked up and deserted, and their families were also nowhere to be seen. Their bosses, the state governors, and colleagues were as bemused about their whereabouts as the FBI. Even Thomson's personal assistant had no idea. They were still trying to track down Chappleton's assistant, Tina Coy, who had also disappeared.

"Looks like either they've run together or Tkachev's buried their bodies," Vic said to Jayne.

She had to agree. Since the shooting of Mike Costello on

Saturday, the story had been the lead item on almost every national news bulletin and had led most newspapers.

There were quotes from various other secretaries of state in some publications, leaving no doubt as to the level of fear among their community. Some had requested police protection. Many of them knew each other quite well from annual conferences and from frequent benchmarking and information sharing. As a group, they were shocked, grieving, and shaken.

Although there had been no announcement about the link to voting roll purges, many observers had drawn their own conclusions. Given that elections were a key responsibility of the secretaries of state, the news outlets had wondered about a connection, even if there was no concrete evidence. So, the entire issue of election manipulation had gone to the top of the political agenda, and a steady stream of politicians, analysts, and commentators on Capitol Hill were having their fairly forceful say on national media. Some of them, aware of previous speculation about Russian interference in the United States via social media, were suggesting that it might be the work of the Kremlin.

Vic and Veltman spent most of the day on phone calls and conference calls with FBI headquarters at the J. Edgar Hoover Building, a few blocks away from the White House, with which they were also in constant contact.

Jayne felt a little like a spare part, being unable to contribute much to the maelstrom of activity that was ongoing, and spent most of the afternoon in the small office down the corridor from Vic's on the seventh floor, trying to think of a way forward.

She left a voice-mail message for Simone, who eventually called back just after four o'clock.

"Jayne, I'm sorry I've been a little elusive," Simone said. "It's been a difficult time, and I've not really felt like speaking to anyone, despite the floods of calls I've been getting. We had Curtis's funeral on Friday."

"I'm glad you've called," Jayne said. "That must have been traumatic, the funeral. I'm sorry I wasn't there." She felt somewhat snubbed that there had been no invitation from Simone, although getting there would have been impossible given she had been en route home from Helsinki.

"We kept it small, a family funeral. I didn't want any fuss or media attention."

"Of course, that was wise," Jayne said.

"How are you doing, Jayne? Can I help?"

"You might be able to. We're in a real bind here, trying to locate two other secretaries whom we believe were linked to Curtis, apart from the others who have been killed. I was hoping you could help." She gave Simone their names.

There was a slight pause. "Curtis knew them, yes. What do you want to know?"

Jayne explained that she had discovered that Curtis had been the subject of a CID investigation in Afghanistan, to which Costello and the other secretaries of state had been linked. They believed that it was this that allowed them to be blackmailed into a larger scheme. "Do you know anything about that?"

"The Afghanistan business? I thought that was forgotten," Simone said. "He mentioned it a couple of times years ago but said it wasn't going anywhere and told me not to worry."

"It wasn't forgotten, just put on hold. But only because evidence disappeared from a CID office in Afghanistan."

"Ah, I see. He never told me that bit."

Jayne remained silent for a second. Was her friend being truthful with her? She wasn't sure.

"Ah. What about the more recent entanglements? The voting rolls?" Jayne said, trying to fish.

"Jayne, I . . . Curtis didn't really discuss his business much.

I never pushed it. He gave us a wonderful life, so I didn't ask too many questions."

Come on. But she decided not to push Simone right now. That could wait. What she needed was more urgent.

"I see. Well, do you have any idea where these other two secretaries might be?" Jayne asked. "Did they have any old haunts where they met, anything like that?"

There was another few seconds of silence. "Not really."

"You can't think of anything, anywhere?"

"The only thing I can think of is that several years ago, Curtis and I went with all of the others you have mentioned and their wives for a weekend away. Gregory Chappleton's father, or might have been his grandfather, had a holiday shack, a log cabin, in the Blue Ridge Mountains."

"Where?" Jayne's voice rose a little in pitch, despite her trying to keep it even and relaxed.

"Near Swift Run Gap, in the Shenandoah park. It's a rough place, up in the hills. Must be more than a hundred miles out of DC, as I recall."

"You think they might be there?"

"Look, I've really no idea. You asked me if there were any places and that's what sprang to mind."

"All right. Got the address?"

"I don't know if I have. This was a long time ago. Just a minute."

Jayne heard a clicking and tapping sound, presumably as Simone went through the contacts files on her phone.

"It's not in my phone," Simone said. "I'll just look in my old address book. It's in the drawer." There was a squeak and a clunk, followed by another long pause and the sound of pages being turned.

Jayne eventually heard a slight exclamation down the line. "Ah, I think this is it."

Then Simone gave an address. "That's it. That's all I have."

"Phone number for the house?" Jayne asked as she wrote down the address.

"I don't have one. And I recall that cell phone coverage was awful. It's right up in the hills. Middle of nowhere."

"Noted," Jayne said. "Did the FBI ask about this?"

It seemed obvious this was the first time Simone had told anyone about the place, but Jayne wanted to make sure. She would have to pass on this information to them.

"I've had several calls from them but haven't got back to them yet."

"Don't you think you should do?"

"Yes, I should. I've . . . been in a bad place, Jayne."

"I'm sure you have. It's awful."

Was Simone being sincere about this? Was grief clouding her judgment? Was she hiding information about Curtis, or did she have some kind of idealized view of him, particularly now that he was gone? Jayne wasn't sure.

"Simone, can I just ask something. How did you all come to be together at Chappleton's place? Any special occasion?"

Now her mind was whirring. Had this been when the entire plot was hatched?

"I don't think so," Simone said. "Curtis just received an invitation, so we went. It was an informal couple of days. A bit of walking, eating, wine drinking. You know how it is. The men did their thing, the girls did too."

"Is that how you know Annabelle Costello?"

"Yes. We've met a few times since then."

Jayne paused. Something had just struck her.

"When we met in that café in Concord a few weeks ago, you talked quite a lot about Curtis's shareholding in US Defense Systems and their link to Ukraine. I thought then it seemed irrelevant to his death—I mean, having shares in a company isn't usually grounds for having someone killed. And it seems very irrelevant now. Why did you mention that at the time?"

Her suspicion was that it was some kind of red herring, although she didn't want to directly accuse Simone just yet. What *was* going on with her friend?

Simone seemed slightly surprised at the comment, judging by the short silence. "I thought it was relevant when we met. I mean, the company is involved in Ukraine. The FBI were very focused on it."

"Yes, I know that, and the FBI is still focused on it, but as far as I know they haven't come up with anything of substance."

"I suppose that's true," Simone said.

There seemed little more of use Jayne could get from Simone right now, and the clock was ticking. "Thanks, Simone. I'll keep in touch. And take care of yourself. You've been through a lot."

Jayne said goodbye and hung up. Then she walked to Vic's office to relay the details of her conversation with her old friend.

"I think we should get down to this shack at Swift Run Gap and check it out," Jayne said when she had finished. "They might both be there. They don't seem to be anywhere else on the planet right now."

"They might," Vic said. "But I'm thinking we should get the Feebs and the cops to take care of this, given the legalities and the obvious potential danger."

Jayne winced inwardly. She had known he would say that. Her instinct was to finish the job she had started, and to hell with the protocols. That had always been her problem—her inability or lack of desire to delegate responsibility and take her hands off the controls when she should. She felt an almost gravitational pull, heard a voice in her head, that said she should finish what she'd begun.

But she knew that what Vic was saying made sense from a professional point of view.

"I agree," Jayne said. She assumed that Vic would pick up the phone and call Shepard immediately. When he didn't move to do that, she raised an eyebrow.

"That's my official position," Vic said. "My unofficial one stems from my concern that these guys might know something that we don't want broadcast at an FBI press conference, or even something we don't want FBI agents to know at all. I'm thinking about the Kremlin dimension and the sensitivities. I mean, how was this thing set up in the first place, and who did it—both in Moscow and over here? Is there an SVR agent, maybe an illegal, still at work inside the US whom we don't know about, who is coordinating all this? That's the big question."

"True," Jayne nodded. She could entirely see his point of view. "I know you, as deputy director of the CIA, are meant to follow the rules, but . . ." She let her voice fade away. She had a gut feeling that Vic was correct—there might be something major at stake.

Vic inclined his head from side to side in what Jayne interpreted as some kind of tacit agreement with what she'd said.

"I suppose that you, as a deniable freelance operator with no accountability to anyone, as a foreign national, don't have to follow such rules?"

Jayne shrugged. "I wasn't going to suggest anything. I was rather going to ask you, unofficially, if you might have a Walther PPK .32 and a couple of spare magazines in your weapons locker that I could borrow, just for general protection, not anything specific. And if you don't happen to have a pool car you can put at my disposal, I will rent one."

There came an almost imperceptibly faint trace of an upward curve at the edge of Vic's mouth.

"If you take anything from my weapons locker, we'll need to notify the Feebs where you're going. Just in case. And I think there are spare cars available. Ask Helen to fix it."

"Yes, they need to know either way," Jayne said. "I can do the notifying from the car, once I'm en route. I've got Shepard's number."

Vic shrugged and turned back to his laptop screen, muttering something under his breath that Jayne didn't quite hear.

* * *

Tuesday, April 28, 2015
Richmond, Virginia

The girl was tough, Tkachev had to grant her that. In her thirties and a US Army reserve staff sergeant, she had a fit, hard body that under other circumstances he would have liked to get his hands on in a different kind of way.

But right now, he had other priorities.

Yet again, he poked the sharp steak knife into the left side of Tina Coy's neck, less than half an inch from her throbbing carotid artery.

"I will ask you again," he said in his heavily accented English, his face only a short distance away from hers. "Where is your boss?"

Coy, who had now been lashed to the bed in her small apartment for several hours with only a few sips of water for nourishment, shook her head and said nothing.

"He must have told you where he was going. I know he

did. He has a big job. He would not dare go away without giving you a way of contacting him."

Why was this girl being so stubborn? Tkachev felt a grudging respect for her somewhere deep inside him.

He jabbed the knife deeper this time, and another trickle of blood ran down the side of her neck onto the pillow, which was already heavily stained red with the leakage from several other puncture marks he had made on the right and left side of her neck, near to her major arteries.

A series of internet searches, a few phone calls, and a request for the technical department at Yasenevo to hack into the Virginia motor vehicle registration system had given Tkachev the address he needed for Coy, who was Gregory Chappleton's personal assistant. He quickly established that she lived alone.

He had waited near the apartment building until Coy returned home from a twenty-minute run, and then, as she unlocked the communal door, he had approached from behind, slipping on a black ski mask as he did so.

Wisely, she had not done anything stupid, like scream for help. She seemed to have sensed that he wasn't bluffing.

Gregory Chappleton's phone remained switched off, and had been since Sunday afternoon. As the body count of Chappleton's colleagues had mounted, Tkachev had expected that might happen. He had also expected that Chappleton and the other one, Thomson, might run for it. Sure enough, it seemed they had.

But his backup plan had not yet produced the detail he needed.

He moved the knife away from Coy's throat and, noticing her eyes were closed, suddenly darted it into her open mouth before she could react. The tip pierced her tongue and again blood began to run.

"If you don't talk, I'm going to cut out your tongue. That's what we do, where I come from," Tkachev said. He began to saw at the side of her tongue, causing a significant cut and drawing a lot more blood, which trickled steadily to the back of her throat.

"Ugg, umm," Coy uttered. Her tongue flicked involuntarily upward, causing more blood to flow.

Tkachev removed the knife. "You want to tell me something?"

Coy coughed several times, quite forcibly. Some of the blood had gone down into her lungs, Tkachev could tell.

She could talk, or she could drown in it for all he cared.

When she stopped, he asked again. "Do you want to tell me, or shall I continue cutting?"

She winced in pain, coughed again, causing a spray of blood to splatter over her white T-shirt, and nodded. "I will tell you," she whispered.

CHAPTER FORTY-TWO

Tuesday, April 28, 2015
  Swift Run Gap, Virginia

The shack, as Simone had called it, was definitely something more than just a log cabin. As she rounded the corner, Jayne peered at it through the windshield of the Honda Civic sedan she had borrowed from the motor vehicle pool at Langley.

The house stood on the hillside at the top of a steeply sloping fifty-yard gravel driveway on a plot that must have amounted to several acres. A stream ran down the side of the property, which was backed by thick trees.

The structure was made of logs, true, but it consisted of two stories with an adjoining flat-roofed garage and a long covered porch that ran across the full width of the property. The plot was bordered by a white rail fence. In short, Jayne wouldn't ever have described it as a shack.

But Simone had been correct that the property was in the middle of nowhere. The house was on a poorly maintained road heading a mile or so north from Route 33, which climbed over the Blue Ridge Mountains from Stanardsville to Harrisonburg. Jayne had once, years earlier, walked the Appalachian Trail that ran a short distance to the east.

There was no sign of movement and no cars parked outside the property, but that didn't mean anything. Jayne pushed on the accelerator and drove on up the road past the driveway to the house, around another corner, and out of sight.

After she had gone another half a mile, she stopped and pulled the maroon Honda onto an area of gravel at the side of the road. There she waited, watching and checking for any indication that she was being followed. There was nothing. She started the car, turned around, and drove back the way she had come.

About three or four hundred yards before she reached the driveway to the house, she found another track off to the right where it appeared that some preliminary excavation work had been done, perhaps in preparation for another house construction project. She nosed the Honda up the track until she found a spot behind some trees where she could park unseen from the road.

She calculated that she could walk the rest of the way through the woods above the property and approach from the rear, which put her in a better position to scope out the situation.

Jayne glanced at the clock on the dashboard. It had taken her two and a half hours to drive from Langley. She switched off the engine and stuffed the Walther that she had procured from Vic's weapons locker into her belt and the two spare magazines into her pocket. She checked her phone, but it was precisely as Simone had warned her—there was no signal.

As discussed with Vic, she had called Iain Shepard from her car and briefed him on what she had discovered and where she was going. He had sounded a little irritated that the CIA had moved first but promised he would get FBI agents mobilized and there as quickly as possible. Jayne clearly had beaten them to it, but that had been the intention. She needed to see if Chappleton and Thomson had the information Vic needed before they were in FBI hands.

Jayne made her way through the trees, most of which were now in leaf, providing additional cover. Very soon, she found herself a hundred yards away from Chappleton's property. There she stopped behind a clump of rhododendrons and watched. There was still no sign that anyone was inside. Her guess was that if Tkachev had found the place, he wouldn't stay there for any longer than he had to. It would be a quick hit and out, in similar style to the other kills. She decided the odds were that he hadn't paid a visit.

Eventually she continued through the bushes and circled around the property. It had a long covered porch in the back similar to the one in front and a long white cylindrical propane tank on a concrete stand several yards away from the rear doors.

Jayne walked back to the front of the property and up a short flight of steps to the raised porch, then made her way past three old-fashioned wooden rocking chairs to the door.

She was about to knock when she heard a slight crunch of gravel from the left side of the house. With one hand on her Walther, she flattened herself into an alcove near the door.

There came a deep male voice. "Hello, is there anyone there?"

Jayne eased her head forward fractionally until she could see around the edge of the alcove. A man dressed in a smart check shirt and slacks stood at the bottom of the steps, his hands on his hips. She recognized him from the photographs she had seen. This was Chappleton.

Jayne stepped out. "Hello, I was looking for Gregory

Chappleton," Jayne said. "Curtis Steyn's widow, Simone, gave me this address."

"And you are?"

"Jayne Robinson. I'm working for the US government," she said, keeping it vague, but at the same time wanting to assure him that she wasn't a threat. "We're very concerned about you and a friend of yours, Jeffrey Thomson."

Chappleton, who had neatly coiffured gray hair and a broad pair of shoulders, but whose face looked somewhat gray and drawn, made his way up the steps and approached her.

"Simone sent you?" He sounded skeptical.

"Yes. She's actually an old friend of mine from the UK."

"You're a Brit too, judging by the accent."

"Indeed."

"So why are you telling me you work for the US government, then?" he asked.

"I'm a contractor." She pulled her CIA green badge from her jacket pocket and flashed it at him.

The man looked her up and down through craggy eyes. "CIA?"

"Like I said, contractor."

He scrutinized her carefully for a couple of seconds. "I'm Gregory, you're correct. I guess I don't need to ask why you're here."

"Probably not. The secretary of state shootings are something I'm fully occupied with. We didn't want you and Jeffrey to join the list of casualties. We discovered it's possible you might be on the list of the man we believe is carrying out the killings."

Chappleton pressed his lips together. "That may be true. Jeffrey's inside. We were just discussing our options. You're lucky to find us. We were planning to leave soon—whoever's been killing our colleagues seems good at finding people. You'd better come in."

He turned and checked behind him, looking down the hill toward the road. Then he took a key from his pocket, unlocked the front door, and held it open for Jayne to pass through. He then relocked it and led her along a wood-paneled hallway littered with camping gear, including a tent, a portable stove, and a couple of small gas canisters. Obviously the men were indeed about to disappear.

They came to a large open-plan kitchen and dining room, also wood paneled, that spanned the rear of the house. The porch was visible through French doors and picture windows. Two doors, both open, led off the kitchen to a pantry and a utility room with a washing machine and a drier that was whirring away noisily.

There, sitting at a dining table, was another man whom Chappleton introduced as Jeffrey Thomson. Shorter, much plumper, and largely bald, he was refilling a gold cigarette lighter from a large bottle of fluid. Chappleton explained to him who Jayne was, and she again showed her green ID badge.

Thomson put the bottle and lighter down, then rose and shook hands, scrutinizing Jayne through black-rimmed glasses. He also looked as though he hadn't been sleeping.

"Take a seat," he said as he picked up the lighter and lit a cigarette.

Jayne was about to say there was no time to sit and chat but realized she needed to at least explain herself and get the bare bones of their story too. She sat at the far end of the table nearest the wall, while Chappleton first went to turn off the noisy drier then sat to her left, next to Thomson.

"Listen, both of you," Jayne said. "We don't have much time. I believe you're both in some danger, as you've doubtless realized. But I do need to get to the bottom of what's going on. There's no point in you lying to me. We know a fair amount from the inquiries we have undertaken, but there are things I still need to ascertain regarding security issues that are in the national interest. Are you willing to help me?"

Chappleton placed his phone and door key on the table, picked up a coffeepot, and refilled his and Thomson's cups. "You like one?" he asked Jayne.

She shook her head, now feeling impatient. "No. Do you realize the situation you're in?"

"We do realize," Chappleton said. "But this was the only safe place we could think of to run to. Our families have gone into hiding too. They're all staying with relatives. We needed to separate."

"I know. The FBI have been trying to trace you. We need to get you out of here. And I need the details of what's been going on. I know this all stems from you aggressively purging your state voting rolls."

The two men looked at each other.

"We've done nothing outside the law," Chappleton said.

"I'm sure you haven't. I guess the Department of Justice and the courts will decide that. Voters groups might have a say in it, as well as those who have been disenfranchised."

Chappleton shrugged.

"I won't get into that detail now," Jayne said. "Just tell me what you've been doing. You don't need to bullshit. I know about the Afghanistan fuel scam and the CID file that the Russians obtained. What did the Russians blackmail you to do to the voter rolls?"

When they remained silent, Jayne continued. "This is a national security issue—if you cooperate, that will help you. Everyone up to and including the White House is watching this closely. Make no mistake, if you try and withhold information, you'll get hit by a sledgehammer. The FBI are on their way here now, so you can either talk to me or talk to them. Or you can talk to a judge."

Chappleton exhaled and placed his hands behind his head. "Shit," he said, looking at the ceiling.

"Come on."

"All right, all right." He glanced at Thomson. "I told you this is where we'd end up."

Thomson said nothing, but Jayne noticed he was clutching the edge of the table so tightly his knuckles were showing white.

"I'm waiting," Jayne said.

Chappleton fidgeted a little in his chair and folded his arms. "To clarify, the Russians didn't blackmail us. Not directly, anyway. They had Curtis and Mike on the hook first via the CID file—the one they stole from the Kandahar office. They approached Curtis soon after he had started his job in New Hampshire, and Mike was already in his role. And then Curtis persuaded us."

She eyeballed Chappleton. "But I don't see how that impacted you two. Or Gareth Weber and Chuck Driscoll. None of you were on the official inquiry."

Chappleton exhaled and stared at the ceiling for a few moments. Then he looked back at Jayne.

"We would have been eventually. And our names were in that file, and that's enough."

"You mean you were involved in it?" Jayne asked.

"Up to a point, yes," Chappleton said. "Not as much as those two. They organized it, and we helped on occasions later in return for appropriate payments. We didn't know the extent of it, but our hands weren't clean. We were all too close to one another for that."

"I see."

Choose your friends wisely, Jayne thought.

"So you felt you had to do it?" Jayne asked.

"Curtis told us we had to do it," Chappleton said. "Otherwise the Russians would name and shame us all publicly over the fuel scam. It would have been career ending. We could have gone to prison, I guess, if they discovered our exact roles."

"All right. Tell me about the voter roll purges."

Chappleton closed his eyes momentarily before answering.

"Gareth was recruited by Curtis early on. That made three of them. Then the rest of us were recruited by Curtis and Mike at the annual conference, the National Association of Secretaries of State annual get-together, in February 2013 in DC. The Russians wanted more swing states involved."

"And Virginia is a swing state?"

"Only three percentage points between the parties at the last election, yes," Chappleton said. He turned to his friend. "What was North Carolina, Jeffrey?"

"Two percentage points," Thomson said. "Doesn't take much to change that."

Jayne folded her arms.

On such margins democracy hangs.

"And how many voters were culled?" she asked.

"Millions. I don't know exactly right now."

"There's another thing I don't understand," Jayne said. "How did you all end up working as secretaries of state? And then how have you all been rigging your voting rolls? It looks a little too neat and extremely well coordinated from the start. Was it really all initiated by the Russians? Or was it the other way around?"

Thomson was shaking his head. "No. I know what you're thinking. We didn't come up with the idea. It wasn't coordinated by us at all, and the Russians did blackmail us. That's the truth. It just happened that we were all looking for a similar type of public administration work, where we could use our army experience after our discharges."

"You were all close, then?"

"We were," Chappleton said. "We'd been together since West Point. Curtis got a secretary of state's job first, and I think that got Mike interested, and he secured one. Those two then encouraged the rest of us—said it was a piece of cake. Well paid, similar or better money than the army, depending on rank, and easier. Which it has been, compared with working in Iraq and Afghanistan. So we all went for the roles when they came up, helped each other get through it. We advised each other on the process, gave practice interviews, all that kind of thing. Having had a senior military position was a massive help. The recruiters and the state governors all liked that, and so did the voters."

It crossed Jayne's mind that voters certainly wouldn't like their more recent activities, but she said nothing. Now that the two men were talking it would be better to simply keep the flow going.

"So what did you manage to do for the Russians?" she asked.

Chappleton folded his arms and looked at her. "We were told to get as many Democrats off the voting rolls as we could —to go all out. We used various methods, but the more we culled, the more money came in."

"How much money was on offer?"

"Millions of dollars, all put together."

The Kremlin must have really wanted this.

"Right, so if you've been so successful, why are you all being targeted now? That's what I don't get," Jayne said.

Chappleton exhaled and exchanged glances with Thomson. "Curtis told me he was going to meet his SVR contact at some out of the way place to negotiate a much higher fee for all of us in return for even more voters being taken off the rolls. Gareth agreed he should do it, but most of us didn't. And of course, he met some hired hitman, who's now targeting all of us."

Ah, greed, then.

"And that's why he was in Pevensey outside a pub?" Jayne asked. "An obscure meeting place, for sure."

"It seems so."

"How much more money was he demanding?"

"About triple, I think. But I'm not sure how——"

In the same instant, the kitchen window exploded with a loud bang, and Thomson was catapulted halfway across the kitchen, where his body slammed into a large iron stove.

As if in slow motion, bits of broken glass, flesh, and trails of blood splattered over the floor and table, some of it hitting Jayne in the face.

She reacted instantly.

"Get down!" Jayne screamed, as she threw herself on the floor. "Get down!"

Less than a second later, there came another loud gunshot from outside and another explosion as more glass was blown inward.

Jayne crawled as fast as she could past Thomson's body, which had a large hole in the chest, over fragments of shattered glass that covered the floor, and behind the granite-topped kitchen counter, which she figured would give her the best protection. She realized that they were being targeted by heavy rounds, probably .50 caliber, from a sniper rifle.

She glanced across to the other side of the table, where Chappleton was also on the floor. However, he had gotten there by falling backward off his chair and was moaning. She couldn't see a gunshot injury, but he wasn't moving.

"Get over here," Jayne shouted. "Gregory. Can you hear me? Move!"

No response. But almost immediately there was yet another loud gunshot and the fridge door next to Chappleton's head was torn apart.

Jayne felt wetness down the side of her neck. She put her hand to it, then looked at her hand. It was covered in blood.

* * *

Tuesday, April 28, 2015
Swift Run Gap, Virginia

"*Dermo*," Tkachev swore. He squinted through the telescopic sight attached to the Dragunov sniper rifle but could no longer see the second man, Chappleton. He must have either reacted much faster than Tkachev expected or had fallen off his chair in fright when the first round slammed into his friend.

Normally, he would have expected the element of surprise and shock to have rooted Chappleton to the spot for at least a couple of seconds.

Either way, in the brief moment between firing the first shot, realigning his telescopic sight, and loosing off the second, the American somehow moved, with the result that the shot had missed. He had fired a third, his line of fire as low as possible, just fractionally above the level of the window frame, but that had been a waste of a round, and he knew he had only hit a refrigerator.

Now what?

He would have to go and finish off Chappleton at closer quarters with a pistol, something he had hoped to avoid. He couldn't possibly walk away leaving him alive. This was his final chance.

Tkachev lowered his body behind the fallen tree in the woods fifty or so meters to the rear of the house, where he had taken cover. The tree had provided a very useful rest for the gun, and the downward slope toward the house had given him a good angle in through the kitchen window. He had had Thomson, sitting there with his cigarette and coffee, right in the middle of his sights. No chance of missing.

He quickly pressed the release latch on the side of the Dragunov, removed the magazine, and checked that there was no cartridge remaining in the chamber. Then he stuffed the magazine in his pocket and pushed the rifle behind some weeds growing right at the base of the fallen tree, as far out of sight as possible.

Tkachev decided to leave the rifle and pick it up on the way back, before returning to the Ford pickup he had parked half a mile farther down the hill toward the intersection with Route 33. He had swapped the motorcycle for the pickup after leaving Florida following the Chokoloskee Island shooting, figuring that even with another change of plates, police would be looking for a big BMW touring bike. He'd had it too long.

Normally, Tkachev preferred a different sniper rifle, the VSS Vintorez, which was far quieter to operate with its integrated silencer and subsonic 9x39mm SP5 cartridges. But the SVR's man in Houston, from whom he had obtained the rifle and the Makarov pistol, only had the Dragunov.

Out of long-practiced habit, Tkachev checked the Makarov to make sure it contained a fresh magazine. He grasped the pistol in his right hand, scrambled to his feet, and made his way cautiously across the grass toward the house.

There had been no visible sign of anyone else on the property, at least as far as he could see through the scope, and he guessed that Chappleton was probably still disoriented.

But one thing had slightly concerned him. While Thomson was seated at the table, he had seen him turn his head to his right, away from Chappleton, a couple of times, as if he were speaking to someone else.

Was there another person in the house? He would have to be wary, just in case.

CHAPTER FORTY-THREE

Tuesday, April 28, 2015
  Swift Run Gap, Virginia

Finally, Chappleton appeared to regain his faculties. He raised his head from the floor and looked over at Jayne.

"Come this way, crawl," she urged him. "Can you do that? We need to get out of this kitchen."

In the space between them lay the gory, bloodied mess that was once Jeffrey Thomson, pressed up against the stove, his head bent almost at ninety degrees to his neck and surrounded by a pool of blood, bits of flesh, and broken glass.

She turned her head away, feeling bile rising in her throat.

"Quickly," Jayne said. "He must know he missed you. He'll come for us again." She took her Walther from her belt, flicked off the safety, and racked the slide.

Jayne's gut instinct was that a sniper of Tkachev's skill would have known the exact outcome of each round that he fired. She was also certain that he would not want to leave

Swift Run Gap without having dispatched the last of the six secretaries of state who had been on the Kremlin's payroll.

Although Chappleton had said that the killings began after Steyn demanded more money from the Kremlin, Jayne wondered whether it hadn't always been the Russians' plan to kill all of them once the majority of the work to affect the election was completed. It made sense that they wouldn't want anyone left alive to give firsthand evidence, whether it be in court or to the media, of what they had plotted to do to the US electoral system and how they had engineered it.

Where the hell is the FBI when you need them most? Jayne thought.

Chappleton rolled onto his side and groaned loudly, clearly in some pain. Then he completed the turn onto his front, raised himself, and began slowly to crawl toward Jayne's position behind the counter.

"Slammed my head on the floor," he said. "Feels bad." He turned his head to one side and added a stream of vomit to the mess on the floor.

Jayne grabbed a towel from a rail next to the counter and threw it to Chappleton. "And use it to sweep that glass out of your way, else it will shred your hands and knees," she said.

Chappleton wiped his mouth and then did as instructed, clearing a path to crawl through.

Finally, he joined Jayne behind the counter. She pointed toward the hallway. "Let's go. Stay on the floor."

It was only when they reached the hallway and Jayne closed the kitchen door behind them that she felt safe to stand.

A few seconds later they heard a noise coming from the kitchen. Someone was trying the handle of the back door leading from the covered porch. Then came two muffled gunshots, each of which caused the door to rattle.

This was definitely Tkachev. And he was shooting through the lock.

Jayne glanced around. "Out through the front door?" she asked.

Chappleton put his hand in his pocket. "Shit, it's locked. And I've left the key in the kitchen."

There came a bang from the kitchen. It sounded as though the back door had slammed against the wall. Tkachev was in.

Jayne cursed. "Upstairs then?" It seemed a better option than ducking into a ground-floor reception room.

Chappleton nodded and made for the nearby staircase, Jayne right behind him.

As they reached the top, Jayne quickly surveyed the upstairs landing, which was in a U-shape with bedroom and bathroom doors leading off it. The only cover was at the far end behind a solid-looking oak chest on legs that raised it a few inches above the floor. That might be the best option.

"You have a gun?" she asked.

"In the bedroom."

"Get it."

Chappleton headed through a door at the far end of the landing while Jayne followed him. But instead of entering the room, she lay prone on the floor behind the chest and got herself into a decent firing position, resting on her elbows. She found from that position she could see beneath it to the top of the stairs and would have a chance of taking out Tkachev if he tried to come up.

A few seconds later she heard Chappleton behind her. She turned her head, put her finger to her lips, and signaled for him to also flatten himself to the floor behind her.

Downstairs, they could hear noises as Tkachev opened and closed doors leading off the kitchen. Finally there was a louder noise as he reached the door to the hallway and opened it.

Then came several seconds of silence that set Jayne's nervous system alight. She could picture Tkachev standing in the doorway downstairs, just a few yards from the bottom of the staircase, working out his next move.

"You can come downstairs," came his voice in heavily accented but clear English. "Throw any guns you have down first, then walk down, with your hands in the air. I am not going to shoot. If you do not, I will burn this place down."

Another several seconds of silence. Jayne again turned her head and put her finger to her lips. There was no point in giving themselves away. Better to keep him guessing too.

Again came the sound of footsteps, then a swishing, splashing sound. Within seconds, the unmistakable smell of lighter fuel reached Jayne's nose.

She swore to herself. He must have grabbed the bottle that Thomson used to refill his lighter. Surely the stupid bastard wasn't really going to set fire to the place, not with that propane tank standing a few yards away?

It wasn't possible to get down the stairs without becoming a sitting duck target for Tkachev, and they couldn't hit him with a gun. They were going to have to think their way out of this.

"I'm going to give you thirty seconds," Tkachev called. "If you're not down here by then, I set light to this staircase."

Jayne didn't move.

There was a prolonged silence that seemed to last far longer than half a minute.

Eventually, from downstairs there came the distinctive sound of a lighter being clicked, followed a second later by the *whoof* of petroleum fluid catching light.

My God.

Jayne rose to her haunches.

Now what?

The entire building was made of wood.

She turned to Chappleton and leaned over to whisper in his ear. "Window? Out over porch roof?"

Chappleton nodded. "Yes. Only option."

Already there was a strong smell of burning.

He turned and crawled back into the bedroom, Jayne now close behind. After she entered, she turned and shut the door, knowing that would help slow the progress of the fire.

Chappleton lifted up a sash window and peered out. Jayne moved across to join him, her gun in hand. The bedroom faced out to the front of the property, looking down the hill and over the valley. Two feet below the open window was the gently sloping corrugated tin roof of the porch.

This definitely looked like the best bet in terms of an exit.

"Have you got your phone?" Jayne asked. "Mine has no signal. We need to call the police."

Chappleton shook his head. "It has a signal, but I left it in the kitchen."

Jayne battled to contain a wave of anger that she felt beginning to surge through her. *Stay calm.*

"All right, let's get out of here," Jayne said.

She sat on the window ledge, swung her legs over, and stepped out onto the tin roof, which felt solid enough thanks to the wooden beams beneath but made a metallic, drumlike noise beneath her feet, even though she was trying to tread as quietly as possible. This wasn't good, but there was no way of avoiding it.

Chappleton followed, his feet generating even more noise than Jayne's.

The two of them moved as gingerly as possible to the edge of the porch roof and looked over. To Jayne, the best bet seemed to be to grab a supporting pillar and swing down.

She was about to shove her gun back into her belt and do

exactly that when from below came a click and a squeak as the front door of the property opened. Jayne froze. Tkachev must have realized what was happening. Either that or he had decided not to remain in the burning house.

Maybe she could work that to her advantage.

Their best chance was to somehow get Tkachev out in the open where she could get a shot at him. But how?

From inside the house came a loud bang, followed by another, as if something had exploded. Jayne guessed that the fire had just enveloped the camping gas canisters she had seen in the hallway. She glanced over her shoulder. A thin wisp of smoke was emerging from the bedroom window they were standing next to, the one they had just come out of.

They were running out of time.

She signaled to Chappleton to move right up against the house wall and away from the center of the porch roof. He complied.

"You're finished, Tkachev," Jayne said loudly. "The FBI and police are on their way. You will be behind bars soon."

"That is something you are wrong about," came Tkachev's voice. "Very wrong."

From his voice, she now at least had a bead on where Tkachev was standing beneath her, which she estimated was about twelve, maybe fifteen feet to her right. She lifted her Walther and fired three successive shots down through the tin roof at the spot she thought was correct.

That elicited a stream of curses in Russian, but within seconds a burst of gunfire came back the other way; she counted four rounds. Jayne had anticipated that and had flattened herself against the wall next to Chappleton so the rounds fizzed through the roof and harmlessly away.

However, they had left jagged holes in the corrugated tin, through which it was now possible to get a glimpse down onto the porch floor below.

Jayne peered into the bedroom window, an idea germinating in her mind. How bad was the fire in there? The closed bedroom door should be helping to hold it back for the moment. It was difficult to tell, but now Tkachev was outside, maybe she could surprise him from inside.

She sat on the window ledge and swung her legs back inside. There was a fair amount of smoke seeping in from beneath the bedroom door, but she decided to go take a look at the stairwell. She took a deep breath, opened the door, and moved quickly to the top of the stairs and looked down. The smoke was fairly thick and billowing upward, but it wasn't completely dense, and the flames appeared to be concentrated just to the right of the base of the stairs. She felt it might be a risk worth taking.

Jayne returned to the window and murmured in Chappleton's ear. "Take some shots at him through the roof, distract him. I'm going downstairs. I'll try and hit him through a window from behind."

Chappleton turned his head and responded in a similarly low tone. "That's very risky. The place could go up."

Jayne knew he was correct, and smoke inhalation was an even greater problem. But if they stayed where they were, in the absence of the Feebs turning up, they faced the serious likelihood of being shot by Tkachev from below if they failed to shoot him first.

"I'm going to risk it," Jayne said.

"Be careful."

"Wait, is the front room across the hallway unlocked?" She recalled the door had been shut, which might be a good thing in that it would limit the amount of smoke in that room.

Chappleton nodded. "Yes, unlocked. It's an office. There's a window that looks onto the porch. Be careful."

She knew both the gas canisters she'd seen in the hallway had already exploded. Were there more?

"You only had two gas canisters?"

"Yes."

Good. She held her Walther in her right hand and with her left took a handkerchief from her pocket and held it across her lower face. Then she took a deep breath and headed back as quickly as she could across the bedroom and around the landing and began descending the stairs.

Behind her she heard two shots as Chappleton opened fire. There was a raucous, almost primeval roar from outside. Had Tkachev been hit? They were immediately followed by two other shots, which she assumed was Tkachev returning fire.

At the base of the stairs, the smoke was thick, and Jayne could see the two lowest steps and the banister there were alight. There was a loud crackling noise coming from the burning wood. However, the main blaze appeared to be concentrated farther to the right along the hallway, around the door of the closet under the stairs. That was where the gas canisters and other camping gear had been.

Nevertheless, the fire overall was not as extensive as she had feared.

But her lungs were bursting. She needed oxygen, and she had to make an instant decision whether to go back or run down and through the flames at the bottom and try to reach the office across the hallway, from where she might just get a bead on Tkachev.

Right then came another volley of shots from outside. Jayne used them as cover to clatter down the stairs and jump over the flames licking the bottom two steps. She landed intact, hoping Tkachev wouldn't hear her. She moved across the hall through smoke that was now quite thick, opened the door of the office, and slipped inside. She shut the door behind, flattened herself to the floor where there was less smoke, and gulped in oxygen through her handkerchief.

She felt an overwhelming urge to cough, but knew she mustn't make any noise. This had to be quick. Ahead of her was the office sash window, which was closed.

From outside came three more gunshots that she could tell were coming from above. That was Chappleton again. And as before, they were followed by two more rounds from Tkachev that were coming from just left of the office window. That meant he was positioned right in front of the door.

Jayne knew what she had to do—get to the right of the window so she had an angle through the glass pane where she could see the Russian.

She rose to her knees and crawled past an ancient oak desk and chair toward the window, which had long curtains that touched the floor. To her right, two low shelves were filled with silver trophies, all for fishing. The upper shelves contained books.

Then, suddenly, she could see Tkachev a few yards away on the other side of the glass.

Jayne raised her gun and aimed carefully.

But as she did so, the urge to cough became irresistible. She tried to quell it but instead she let out a stifled, strangled noise that the Russian must have heard.

He spun around, raising his gun just as Jayne pulled the trigger of the Walther.

The window glass exploded and Jayne ducked her head, keeping her eyes fixed on Tkachev. But in the same instant, she felt a round whistle very close to her head and a clanging sound from behind her as it smashed into the fishing trophies, some of which fell to the floor.

She saw Tkachev recoil a little, and knew she had hit him somewhere on the upper body. In the same instant, she pulled her trigger again and then again, getting the impression that the first shot had missed and the second one had hit.

Through the smashed window, she heard Tkachev yell and stumble backward, dropping his pistol in the process.

Got the bastard.

Jayne rose to her feet, coughed violently, and moved toward the window. She urgently needed to get out of the smoke. She gasped, desperate for air, and could feel a growing irritation in her nose and throat.

She was about to lift the window and climb outside when she spotted Tkachev, now on the floor, trying to scramble to his knees. His gun was lying only a yard away.

She didn't think. She just took aim at Tkachev's upper body through the broken window and fired. The round hit home somewhere near his chest or shoulder, and he keeled back yet again.

Jayne immediately raised the sash window and climbed out onto the porch, now coughing uncontrollably and gasping as oxygen finally reached her lungs.

Unbelievably, the Russian was still trying to get to his knees, even as bloodstains spread across his shirt from his shoulder and chest.

Is this guy indestructible?

Jayne moved smartly across the wooden porch floor and grabbed Tkachev's pistol. Then she stood back and pointed her gun at him.

"Don't move," Jayne said. "Put your hands above your head."

CHAPTER FORTY-FOUR

Tuesday, April 28, 2015
  Swift Run Gap, Virginia

Jayne and Chappleton, who scrambled down unhurt from the porch roof, held Tkachev at gunpoint for what seemed like an interminable ten minutes as they waited for the feds to arrive.

While Jayne covered the Russian with her pistol, Chappleton searched him and removed his phone, wallet, and car keys. Tkachev screamed loudly as Chappleton grabbed him under the armpits and dragged him thirty yards clear of the house, putting all of them out of danger in case the propane tank at the back exploded.

As Chappleton released Tkachev, the Russian passed out, and he lay still on the ground, the effects of blood loss and pain from his gunshot wounds finally proving too much.

Chappleton, distraught at the prospect of his family vacation cabin being destroyed, then ran to the rear of the house and turned off the propane tank to try and minimize the risk of an explosion to the house itself. He also managed to get in through the rear door to retrieve his phone from the kitchen, which had not yet been impacted by the fire.

He returned to the front and used the phone to call 911, explaining to the operator that paramedics would be needed to treat multiple gunshot wounds.

But the FBI, who arrived six strong in two cars, beat all of them to it. By that stage, the house was well ablaze, and smoke was pouring from both upstairs and downstairs windows.

When the paramedics turned up, one of them set to work to stabilize Tkachev, while the other went to the rear of the property to confirm Jayne's view that Thomson was dead.

Jayne stood, arms folded, and watched as the paramedic gave Tkachev oxygen, put him on a drip, and staunched the bleeding from his wounds. The Russian slowly regained consciousness, at which point two FBI special agents carried out a formal arrest process.

Another FBI agent approached Jayne and asked for a brief account of what had happened, which she gave.

Two fire engines and a tanker from Elkton Volunteer Fire Company arrived next. Their crews rapidly unloaded their gear, ran their hoses to the front and rear of the log cabin, and began to pump large volumes of water into the building.

Jayne and Chappleton moved down the gravel driveway, a little away from the action, to allow the emergency services and FBI to do their work.

She gave Vic a quick call, using Chappleton's phone, and outlined what had happened, holding back from giving all the detail since the line was not secure. She promised to call back as soon as she was in an area where she could get a signal on her own phone and handed the phone back to Chappleton.

They stood there in silence for a few moments, watching the chaotic scene in front of them.

"I guess the feds will be driving me home when they've finished with Tkachev," Chappleton said eventually.

Jayne looked at him. "They'll be driving you, yes, but I doubt the first destination will be home. They'll have a lot of questions you'll need to answer, that's for sure. I don't know where you'll end up."

"Behind bars, probably," Chappleton said.

Jayne shrugged. "Yes, probably. Simone said that she came here once. You had a weekend here with all six of you and your wives. That's how I found you here. Just as well I did, for your sake, if somewhat late for your colleagues."

Chappleton closed his eyes momentarily, looking a little embarrassed. "Yes, we did all come here, a few years ago now."

"What was that for?"

"Oh, it was when we were finalizing things," he said, averting his gaze from Jayne.

Jayne removed her phone from her pocket and for Chappleton's benefit pretended to check it for a signal but actually turned on her voice recorder.

"Finalizing things?" Jayne asked. "You mean the plans for voting roll purges?"

"To be honest, yes, among other things. Remember, we all knew each other from way back. We were friends. It was a social gathering."

Jayne nodded. The paramedics were carefully maneuvering Tkachev onto an aluminum stretcher, where they secured him with safety straps before they lifted him slowly into the ambulance.

"There are two things I'm still unsure of," Jayne said. "How the voting roll idea came about in the first place, and who instigated it." She could tell that Chappleton, who looked somewhat shell-shocked, was now likely to tell her anything she asked and decided to press home the advantage to get a recording of what he had already admitted to her.

"I told you, it started with Curtis and Mike, and then Curtis persuaded the rest of us."

"Yes, I know that," Jayne said. "The Russians blackmailed you all over the Afghanistan fuel scam. But what I'm talking about is who instigated it for the Russians? Was it someone in the United States, or did they somehow run it from Moscow?"

"Oh. Someone in the US."

"Russian or American?" Jayne asked.

"Russian."

"Really? Do you know who?"

"A man who I think was based at the Russian embassy in DC. He was there for a year or two, then he returned to Moscow." Chappleton scratched his head. "He actually came to this house that weekend. He was here for an hour, telling us what was required and answering questions."

"He came *here*?" Jayne asked. "So, he met all of you?"

"Yes. I remember him saying it had been difficult to shake off his surveillance in DC. Anyway, he was obviously operating under instructions from Moscow, because I remember we had questions that required answers, and he had to go back to his boss to get them."

A thought exploded inside Jayne's head. *Simone met the Russian agent who had been the ringmaster behind all this. She knew absolutely everything all along.*

"How did they pay you?" Jayne asked.

"Straight into a numbered bank account in dollars. We had individual ones."

"Where?"

"Mine was George Town, Cayman Islands, and so was Mike's. I think Curtis's was in Zürich, and so was Jeffrey's. Not sure about the others."

An FBI officer approached. "We're going to take the Russian to the hospital in Harrisonburg," he said as he drew near, jerking his thumb in the direction of Tkachev behind him. "It's going to be a toss-up whether he survives, frankly. Two of us will accompany him with the paramedics in the ambulance and will remain with him in the hospital. I'm guessing we could be guarding him for some time if he pulls through." He turned to Jayne. "We'll need a detailed statement from you. Can I get your contact details?"

Jayne gave him her phone numbers, email address, and street address in Portland.

The agent then looked at Chappleton. "I'm afraid we'll need to take you for further questioning. Go and join my colleagues over there, please. They will give you a ride once they are done here."

There was no missing the look on Chappleton's face. He knew the game was up.

As the agent walked away, Chappleton and Jayne began to follow him back up the slope toward the house. The volume of smoke coming from the house was sharply reduced; the fire crews were obviously making progress.

Jayne decided now was the time to have one more push at Chappleton, who was clearly resigned to his fate.

"That Russian at the embassy who coordinated everything, who came here to meet you all," she said. "Do you have his name?"

Chappleton stopped and turned to Jayne.

"His name was Vasilenko. Pavel Vasilenko."

* * *

Tuesday, April 28, 2015
Swift Run Gap, Virginia

.   .   .

Jayne was desperate to make two calls. First to Vic, to give him the news she had learned about Vasilenko, who had clearly worked on the operation with the secretaries of state while doing his stint at the *rezidentura* in Washington and had lied about it.

Second, she needed to speak to Simone. She was finding it difficult to accept that her old friend had been so incredibly deceitful about what she knew.

But she first had to answer a few more questions from the FBI agents. The feds then put Chappleton in a car and drove him away, his face now pale, for a more detailed grilling at the J. Edgar Hoover Building. Jayne watched him go, glad she wasn't in his shoes, then walked up the hill to retrieve her car.

She had to drive back to Route 33 before she got a phone signal and was able to use a secure connection.

Her mind kept going back to the exfil boat journey out of Russia and Vasilenko's version of how the secretaries of state had been recruited.

They somehow got a grip on some of the secretaries of state . . . How they got control of them is something I am not certain of. They did not tell me every little detail . . . That is what Ivanov has done— his people have blackmailed and bribed these secretaries of state to remove voters from their rolls.

The deceit was astounding. *Ivanov's people?* She wished she could punch Vasilenko.

As soon as Vic answered her call, she got straight to the point. "Vic, you're not going to believe who I've discovered was running the show in DC for the Russians when this voting roll thing was being set up."

"Try me."

"Pavel Vasilenko."

There was a sharp intake of breath on the other end of the line.

"Holy crap."

"Exactly," Jayne said.

Jayne summarized what she had been told by Gregory Chappleton about Vasilenko's role in setting up the operation.

"Underhanded bastard," Vic muttered.

"Indeed. And he even met all six of the secretaries of state here in Swift Run Gap—including their wives, and therefore including my friend Simone. Either of them could have told us who the others were. We might have been able to save Costello and Thomson in time if they'd given us the names."

"This complicates things," Vic said. "Especially as I've got some unfortunate news for you too. Vasilenko has gone missing from our apartment. Went off radar at lunchtime. We've been scouring the city for him, but his phone's switched off. I don't like it."

"You don't think Moscow has got to him?" Jayne asked. It was the obvious question. There was no doubt an attempt at retribution would be made on Vasilenko at some point for having defected to the West.

"No, they wouldn't do it that quickly. They always wait months, if not years."

"What are you going to do?" Jayne asked. "You can't do a U-turn on him, can you?"

Vic grunted. "I'd like to, believe me. But let's be honest about this. The recruitment of those secretaries was a few years ago. Last year he gave us the information that enabled us to catch and recruit Shevchenko. Now he's given us the detail that has enabled us to bust this voting roll scam open. That's a big give. He takes a huge risk and defects. I'm not surprised he didn't want to tell us he had helped set up the scam in the first place. Would you?"

Jayne stayed silent for a moment. Vic had a point.

Vasilenko probably *wouldn't* want to admit it, unless forced to, given that he was now working in the open with the CIA. When the recruitment of the six secretaries took place, the situation was very different—he was an SVR officer and was just doing his job, to be fair. But on the other hand, his failure to declare his true role now had cost at least one secretary of state's life, if not two.

This was a classic example of how her trade could never be cast in black and white—there were always gray areas, and it was in that territory that the casualties of conflict were most often found. It was the most depressing aspect of her job.

"I don't know if I would," Jayne said. "Until you come face-to-face with the devil, you don't know if you're going to be able to stare him down and do the right thing or not. I'd like to think I'd have given the names, but I don't know. I would have felt seriously embarrassed at the very least to admit I'd orchestrated the whole scheme in the first place."

"Precisely. Well, either way, he's now done what we specifically told him not to do—get out of range," Vic said. "There's something going on."

"Financial?"

"No idea. We put half a million in his account this morning and gave him the paperwork. He gets a generous pension too, which kicks in immediately."

Jayne was stunned. "I'm clearly in the wrong business. Why pay him so soon? His feet have hardly touched US soil."

"Because frankly, the information he has already given is worth that. He's got no home. I know he's separated from his wife, but nonetheless, he's left what family he does have behind. We need to get him set up here as quickly as possible."

"The money's in a US account?"

"Yes."

"And he's got access?" Jayne asked.

"Yes. As I said, we gave him the paperwork."

Jayne remained silent for a short while, thinking. "Just a hunch, Vic, but have you checked the airports, flights out of DC?"

"We have that on our list, yes."

"Yes, but have you done it?"

"I'll check on our guys now," Vic said. "In the meantime, can you get yourself back to DC? The president is asking for an urgent briefing with us this evening. You'll need to be there with me, Veltman, and the feds. Sorry about that—I know it's not what you want after the day you've had."

"You can say that again. Okay, I'll be there. I'm heading back now."

"Thanks Jayne. You've done a great job. I'm sure that the Feds wouldn't have been able to get all that key information out of Chappleton and Thomson. Think we played it right, despite all the politicking it's probably going to cause. I have a feeling Bonfield and Shepard will have my feet to the fire over this one if they can."

"Don't worry about it. You might have more of an issue with Vasilenko. I mean, what the hell? The president will go ballistic. Although frankly, after seeing him put a bullet through those guys in the cupboard at the Strelna cottage, nothing would surprise me about him."

"We'll find him. We'll have him by the time you're back here."

"I hope so."

Jayne ended the call and quickly called Joe to let him know she was all right and was headed back to DC. She promised to update him on everything as soon as she could. Then she checked her messages.

There was one from Nicklin-Donovan, asking for an update and a call, as he had seen a briefing note outlining what had happened. That would have to wait for a while.

Instead, she dialed Simone's number. But the call went straight to voice mail.

CHAPTER FORTY-FIVE

Tuesday, April 28, 2015
Langley

When Jayne arrived outside Vic's office on the seventh floor in the CIA's Original Headquarters Building, she was somewhat surprised to see Vasilenko sitting on the sofa beneath Vic's row of red-and-green digital clocks that told him the time of day in five key time zones. Moscow, appropriately, she thought, was showing two minutes to midnight. It did indeed feel like a watershed moment.

She stood outside the office with Vic's secretary, Helen, and watched Vic and Vasilenko through the open blind over the window.

A few seconds later Vic came out, closing the door behind him. Judging by his slightly reddened face, they had been having an animated discussion.

"You can come in, Jayne," Vic said. "I've just heard from the feds. Shepard called immediately after he got a call from his guys at the hospital in Harrisonburg."

Jayne knew what was coming. "Tkachev?"

"Gone. Died in ICU."

A surge of relief passed through Jayne. The thought of having been responsible for someone's death was anathema to her, but in this case, it was very different. If it hadn't been him, it would have been her and Chappleton in the mortuary alongside all the others.

"The feds will need to speak to you further about him, of course," Vic said. "But don't worry. It'll be a formality." He nodded and smiled at Jayne.

"Thanks," Jayne said. "And I see you've located the defector." She indicated toward Vic's office. "Where was he?"

"Yes. Your instinct was correct. He was at the airport."

"What? He was actually flying off somewhere?" she asked.

"No. He was in a bar, drinking champagne."

Jayne felt slightly bemused. "Why would he go to Dulles to do that?"

"He wasn't drinking by himself. He was with someone."

"Who?"

"Your friend Simone."

Jayne took a step backward.

Simone was running?

"Where was she going?" Jayne asked.

"Is going. She'll be in the air by now. It's Zürich."

Jayne raised her eyebrows. "Zürich?" There would be only one reason Simone was heading to Zürich.

"Yes."

"To get her late husband's million dollars, I assume?"

"I think so."

Jayne shook her head, feeling slightly stunned. "Sometimes you think you know your friends. But I guess you never really do."

Vic shrugged. "We'll have to check if there's any way we can freeze the money or something, but I don't know. It was her husband's money, based on what he did, not her. And funded from Moscow."

Jayne nodded. "It's appalling. It's immoral. She can't be allowed to just keep the bloody money, surely? I'm astonished she wants to. And why was Vasilenko meeting her?"

"You can ask him yourself." Vic beckoned her into the office and closed the door behind them.

Vasilenko stood and offered his hand. "I'm sorry to cause you trouble," he said. "Simone and I were only acquaintances, but kept in touch a little. And I needed to apologize to her for what happened to Curtis. I never envisaged that happening when the whole arrangement began, of course."

Jayne ignored his proffered hand. "You've cost five secretaries of state their lives," she said. "And the life of one of their wives. And those of the men in Strelna, not to mention a CIA officer in Moscow. You've caused massive chaos—that's what you've done."

"It was several years ago when I recruited those men, and I—"

"Blackmailed them. Not recruited them," Jayne said.

"As I said, when I recruited them, I was just doing my job at the time," Vasilenko said. "I was told to recruit them, and that's what I did. I had my orders. You can't say the CIA or your MI6 operate any differently."

"I'll argue that point with you," Vic said.

Vasilenko folded his arms defiantly. "I have since, quite obviously, changed my mind about my allegiances. And I have to say, if Steyn hadn't demanded more money and threatened to derail the election process . . ." His voice trailed off.

"He'd still be alive?" Jayne asked.

"I think so. I don't know."

"And then the presidential election would have been built on a fraud."

Vasilenko said nothing.

"Why didn't you tell us everything as soon as we got out of Russia, when we asked you specifically if this had begun while you were in DC?" Jayne asked. "At least then we could maybe have saved a couple of those secretaries. Costello and Thomson."

Vasilenko stared at the floor. "I thought I would face a very angry reaction if I told you what I'd done. I didn't know what would happen. Whether you'd send me straight back to Russia. Put me in jail. I do realize I was wrong about it. I made a bad decision and I can only apologize."

"That's not going to bring back those men," Jayne said, her voice rising. Her stomach felt tied in knots, and she was struggling to contain herself.

Vic sat on the edge of his desk facing Vasilenko. "I'm debating whether to claw back that half million I put in your account this morning," he said.

Jayne looked at him. Was he joking? She decided not.

Vasilenko wasn't taking it as a joke either.

"Well, just remember what I've given up," the Russian said as he sat down again on the sofa. "And what I've given you. If I hadn't done what I did, Shevchenko would still be spying against you, not for you. Remember, I can put her out of action with a quick call or message, if I choose to do so. If Moscow found out, she would be thrown into the gulag in an instant. And also remember your election would be rigged. So be careful. I think I've earned that half million and the pension."

Jayne sat down on a chair opposite Vasilenko and stared at the Russian. "Don't even think about doing anything with Shevchenko," she said. "Don't you think she's been through enough? Five days in Lefortovo would finish off most people."

Vasilenko shook his head. "I don't intend to. Of course I don't. I'm just reminding you. Look, I will try and make it up to you in the future. I have said I'll work for you, and I intend to do that as best I can. What else can I say?"

Neither Vic nor Jayne replied.

Once again the thought ran through Jayne's head, as it often did, that the game she was in was a messy business. Yet more gray areas. Vasilenko had given a lot of invaluable information, but she still found herself disliking him quite intensely. He left a bad taste in the mouth and was infuriating to deal with.

And what of her friendship with Simone?

She knew that things could never be the same again between them. Their friendship was probably finished.

The trust had gone, despite the close bonds that had tied them together.

Jayne's mind went back once again to the night Simone had saved her life in that alley.

How could the same woman now have done *this*? Times had changed. Simone had changed.

It didn't make sense.

* * *

Tuesday, April 28, 2015
Washington, DC

The atmosphere in the basement of the West Wing was even more fevered than Jayne remembered it from her last visit almost four weeks earlier. There were people running everywhere, frantically carrying files and electronic equipment to unknown destinations.

She switched her cell phone off and pushed it into the lead-lined security box in the reception area outside the Situation Room before following Vic, Arthur Veltman, Iain

Shepard, and Robert Bonfield into the main conference room.

Two men were sitting on the far side of the long wooden table. One was Charles Deacon, and the other she recognized from TV and newspaper images as the attorney general, Brian Parker, a fresh-faced, bespectacled man with slightly spiky gray-blond hair that made him look younger than he actually was. Some of the tabloids had dubbed him Brains Parker.

Veltman introduced Jayne to Parker, who stood and offered a perfunctory handshake, then immediately sat again. He seemed preoccupied with the file in front of him, which he kept opening and closing.

Three minutes later, President Ferguson swept in, accompanied by someone whom Jayne also recognized from the media as his new national security advisor, Phil Anstee, a tall man with slightly lank, dark hair who had the air of a senior policeman. He had replaced Francis Wade the previous September.

"So the election casino has been loaded against us," Ferguson said without any attempt at greeting those present. "How are we going to fix it?"

He plopped a thick file in front of his chair at the head of the table, sat down, and looked around expectantly. Anstee walked behind him and sat next to Parker.

Nobody spoke.

"Brian, what do you suggest?" the president asked, looking directly at his attorney general. "We need to move quickly. We can't have a perception that our democracy is being undermined by the Kremlin. I know it's going to look like I'm trying to tilt the playing field back in my favor, but to hell with that. There's a bigger issue at stake here."

Parker nodded. "Yes, Mr. President. I agree. Our analysis is that if the number of people removed from voting rolls stayed off, it would undoubtedly be enough to tilt the vote against you in those states. They're all swing states. So that in turn would lose you the election."

"Proves my point," Ferguson said. "So what, then?"

"I suggest that first, we announce we're ordering these six states to go through their voter rolls with a fine-tooth comb and ensure that anyone who has been removed unjustifiably be immediately reinstated. We've got to restore confidence."

There were a few murmurs of assent around the table.

The president leaned forward, folding his arms on the table. "Yes, agreed. That will be a start. But what are you going to do to stop this from happening again? And to make sure other secretaries of state haven't been equally corrupted by some other paymaster, whether foreign or domestic? I want to be able to look the nation in the eye and say that every eligible American will have the right to vote. That can't happen now. I had a message from an Ohio senator this morning complaining that the state government starts the deletion process if someone misses voting in just one federal election. That's a bullshit kind of policy."

"My officials are already working up proposals, sir," Parker said. "We'll get them to you as quickly as we can. Just for a start, we're proposing an awareness campaign to get every voter to check online that they are properly registered, and if they're not, to tell them what to do about it. But there will be a lot more to it than that."

"Good," the president said. He fixed Bonfield with a stare. "Robert, what's happening with the one surviving secretary out of the six? What's his name? Chappleton?"

"We'll work with Brian on this, sir," Bonfield said, with a wave toward Parker. "It'll be public corruption charges most likely. Don't worry, he'll go behind bars. We're deciding whether to pursue his wife, who knew about this, like all of them, but did nothing. Might be difficult, though, because they weren't actively involved."

Ferguson nodded. "Fair enough. I'd like to be able to announce the charges against Chappleton quickly, though, so get moving with that. The other five have paid their penalty. Speaking of which, where's the Russian assassin?"

"He's dead, sir," Bonfield said. "Died in the intensive care unit earlier today."

"Good," Ferguson said, his face inscrutable.

The president paused for a second and looked Jayne in the eye. He smiled for the first time. "Now, I'd like to congratulate you, Jayne, for the work you've done for us again."

"Thank you, sir."

"I don't like the Brits taking the glory, and believe me you won't as far as the public is concerned. But in the privacy of this room, I'm telling you you've done well. It's clear to me that we're under a sustained attack on several fronts. As long as you keep delivering, we'll keep using you—make a note of that, Arthur."

"Noted, Mr. President," Veltman said. "And you're right. She did a particularly good job in Russia at a time when our chief of station and his team couldn't because of the heavy surveillance we're under." Veltman gave a polite nod in Jayne's direction, who accepted it with one in return.

"Do you believe this Russian scheme was part of Operation Pandora?" Ferguson asked, his attention still on Veltman.

"We believe so," Veltman said. "Although I don't like referring to that label publicly. It could create a feeling of paranoia out there, sir."

"I'm aware of that," the president said. "I'm being careful not to use the term in public. Don't want headlines with *Pandora* in them. Which brings me to another related question. Are you getting cooperation from our other main asset in Russia now? I hope so, given the amount of money we're presumably paying for it."

Jayne turned to Veltman, whose face visibly tightened.

The president hadn't used Shevchenko's real name or code name, but she knew Veltman and Vic didn't like any reference being made outside the seventh floor to the Agency's highest-value asset in Moscow. That included the Situation Room when people they didn't know well, like Parker and Anstee, were present. It was a security risk.

"We're getting good cooperation," Veltman said tersely. "A good relationship with Jayne."

"Where does the asset think the next threat will come from?" Ferguson asked.

Jayne saw Veltman was struggling to contain himself.

"We'll get a download as soon as we can," Veltman said, his lips now pressed firmly together. "We'll keep you informed. There's a high-level conference at presidential level that's been going on near St. Petersburg. The asset is there. We hope to hear more soon about their strategic plans."

"Right. Good. I think we're done for now," the president said. Then he looked at Jayne. "That guy of yours, Joe Johnson."

Jayne was slightly taken aback. "What about him, sir?"

"Has he made an honest woman of you yet?"

She smiled. "Why? Are you wanting to make me a US citizen?"

"Maybe. I've heard worse ideas."

"But then Vic and Arthur couldn't play the plausible deniability card, could they? The old line that no US citizen would ever get involved in anything like that?"

"Good point," Ferguson said. "A very good point."

He gave a thin smile, gathered up his papers, and made his way toward the door.

CHAPTER FORTY-SIX

Wednesday, April 29, 2015
  Moscow

To Shevchenko's relief, the US strategy conference at Konstantinovsky Palace was brought to a premature close by confirmation that the latest phase in Operation Pandora, to fiddle the voting rolls in six swing states, had been uncovered and that Georgi Tkachev had died in an abortive attempt to finish the final element of the job he had been sent to do.

Much of it had seemed inevitable following the defection of Pavel Vasilenko, but nevertheless, the pale face of Igor Ivanov as he relayed the news coming from the *rezidentura* in Washington, DC, to those sitting around the conference table, and the stony stare of the president told their own story.

The men around the table now appeared, at least at first glance, to accept Shevchenko's claims to have had Vasilenko under suspicion for some time. In that context, there was even a degree of embarrassment over her incarceration and interrogation at Lefortovo, and implied criticism of Sidorenko. However, Shevchenko had never received anything that approached an apology for her ordeal, and nobody mentioned it directly. Whether Sidorenko would be penalized or not remained unclear. She doubted it.

There had also been some initial criticism of the FSB director, Nikolai Sheymov, and his counterintelligence chief, Leonid Pugachov, for not moving faster, but this had faded after Sheymov gave a convincing account of how close the British agent Robinson had come to being caught due to Pugachov's efforts.

Instead, Sheymov firmly laid the blame for Robinson's and Vasilenko's escape at the doors of the deceased palace security director, Pyotr Timoshenko, and Gavriil Nikitin, and Ivanov and his colleagues had accepted that. Nobody dared to mention the elephant in the room—the issue of escort girls visiting the site at night without proper security checks—least of all in Ivanov's presence.

Putin announced that the conference would end immediately and would reconvene in a few weeks' time once further proposals for Pandora had been worked up in more detail.

The truth was that the strain of sitting around the circular conference table with men who she was intent on betraying at every possible opportunity, from the president downward, had proved a real challenge for Shevchenko. Unusually, she had found herself waking very early in her executive cottage, at three or four in the morning, and struggling to go back to sleep again.

That was despite the guarded congratulations, and even the odd slap on the back, following her triumph in uncovering the SVR mole in Paris who had been leaking secrets to the French.

Now, finally back in her fifth-floor apartment across the street from Petrovsky Park, following a long drive back down the M10, she poured herself a large glass of Jack Daniels, for which she had acquired a taste during her time in the US, and sank into her sofa.

There had been plenty of time during the journey home to ruminate on the contents of the conference. Despite the early finish, she now had a large amount of material that she would need to condense into a series of SRAC messages for dispatch to the CIA's receiver in the park, less than a hundred meters from where she was sitting. More detail could then be given once she managed to meet Jayne Robinson again, although it now seemed highly unlikely that the arranged meeting between them at site BUZZARD on June 20 could possibly take place. It seemed inconceivable that Jayne could be sent back into Russia for some time, and Shevchenko needed to keep her head well down.

There was one particular item from the conference that stood out.

"If we cannot undermine their election from beneath," Ivanov had said, following news that the voting rolls operation had been blown, "we will destroy it from above."

The president had liked that comment.

It had been Ivanov's response to a proposal by Kutsik to carry out an operation in the run-up to the next US presidential election, potentially attacking both the United States and the United Kingdom in one hit.

What the proposal did not contain was any detail on exactly how that attack would be carried out. Those details were being kept strictly confidential, even from the leadership team.

But even the concept was something that Shevchenko knew would send a shiver up the spine of Washington—and London.

She reached for her SRAC transmitter and switched it on.

EPILOGUE

Wednesday, April 29, 2015
Portland, Maine

Scotch on the rocks had always been Ken Robinson's favorite drink. Jayne had childhood memories of her father coming home from shifts as a detective with Nottinghamshire police, prior to his move to London, and pouring himself a generous measure over ice that he had broken with an ice pick originally bought in Prague.

When her parents separated and her father went to the capital, he took his whiskey collection with him, and his ice bucket and pick. She had seen the space in the drinks cupboard where his bottles had once stood as somehow symbolic of his absence.

So when Joe brought a bottle of his favorite Ardbeg single malt and a bucket of ice onto the covered porch at the rear of his house on Parsons Road, she decided she would have a glass too—for posterity and for memories. Her father usually bought cheaper brands, but every Christmas he treated himself to an Ardbeg, and he kept at least some of it for special occasions until the following Christmas, when he would buy a new bottle.

She took a sip and savored the smoky, sweet taste.

"That was your dad's favorite, wasn't it? Ardbeg?" Joe asked.

"You've got a good memory." She vaguely recalled telling Joe many years ago that her father loved Ardbeg. "How did you remember that?"

Joe shrugged. "It stuck in my mind. Probably because I also like it."

That was something she loved about Joe. He had a mind that retained things that were important to her, and he seemed to bring them up at the most appropriate moments. A typical historian.

"I missed that whiskey bottle in the cupboard when he left," Jayne said. "Always an Ardbeg there. Weird, really. I sometimes wish he had never moved to London, that they had never split up. But he saw that job as his calling, his destiny, and he knew he was doing important work."

"It must have been a tough time when he passed away."

"Yes, it was. I miss him so much, even now. That voice on the phone. The memory is what keeps me going, to be honest."

She paused, another vision of the tragedy outside the Voykovskaya metro station running through her mind. "It makes me wonder how Yvonne Broad's family feels right now."

They sat in silence for a few minutes.

"I've given up trying to understand many things about life and death," Joe said, eventually. He glanced across at her. "And what will you do about Simone? About your friendship, I mean?"

She shook her head. "I can't even process it. What was

she doing? What *is* she doing? She was obviously a party to what was going on, and now it seems she's gone to Zürich to collect the Russian money. I find it hard to reconcile with the friend I knew. Maybe one day I'll sit down with her and get to the bottom of it."

"Greed?"

"Maybe. Easy money. It can change people. Well, now she's lost her husband to it. I wonder if she still thinks it was worth it. I'm not sure what to think about her anymore. It sometimes seems you never really know anyone. Like marbles touching in a jar. Tiny points of contact but the center is never touched. Maybe it's impossible to really know someone properly."

"I know what you mean."

Jayne leaned back in her chair. "On a more upbeat note, guess what the president asked me yesterday?"

"No idea. Tell me."

"He asked if you were going to make an honest woman of me."

Joe burst out laughing. "You're joking. He didn't really say that, did he?"

"He did. And I pointed out that if you did, then Vic and Arthur wouldn't be able to claim deniability any longer, because I'd be on the fast track to becoming a US citizen. I don't think he'd thought that through properly."

That triggered another smile from Joe.

"So, tell me, are you going to make a habit of these solo operations?" he asked before taking a sip from his own whisky glass.

"You worried?"

"Possibly."

"Why? About me, or about you?"

"Ha! I'm always worried about you," Joe said. He leaned over and kissed her on the forehead. "And I couldn't cope without your help, even if you seem to do fine without me. So don't think of abandoning me to my own devices."

"Well, I've actually enjoyed working by myself more than I thought I would. Maybe it's the feminist in me that comes out. Maybe it's just that I'm quite an independent person— you know that."

"Yes, I know that. But there's a difference between being independent and actually enjoying working by yourself in a hostile environment, like you've just been doing."

"True. I know it's a bit risky. Maybe it's the adrenaline rush that gets me."

"Dangerous stuff, adrenaline. Addictive. Should come with a health warning."

Jayne took another sip of the Ardbeg. "What about your work? Do you feel like you're ready to reenter the fray?"

There were a couple of seconds of silence as Joe considered the question. "Yes, I'm getting there. If an interesting case came up, I'd probably go for it. People keep sending me proposals, and I'm reading through them. Don't worry—I'll let you know. We'll see."

"How are Carrie and Peter doing?" Jayne asked. She had seen neither of them since arriving back from DC that afternoon, as they were both out with friends.

"They both asked, separately, if you were okay last week," Joe said. "I think they consider you part of the furniture here now."

"I doubt it. I probably just have novelty value. Family foreigner. A bit like the dog over there," Jayne said, pointing to Cocoa, Joe's chocolate Labrador, who was lying on a mat in the corner of the porch.

Joe laughed. "No, I don't think so."

Jayne's phone vibrated twice in her pocket. She took it out and tapped on the screen. Both were secure messages for which she needed to enter her private key before reading.

The first was from Nicklin-Donovan, who, she realized to her dismay, she still hadn't called. She had better do that before drinking any more Ardbeg, otherwise he wouldn't get much sense out of her.

The second made her sit upright. It was from Ed Grewall in Moscow and had been sent to both Vic and Jayne.

SRAC received from VULTURE. Msg reads as follows: Congratulations on secretary of state operation. Am all good here. Do not get complacent. Operation Pandora rolls on. More detail to follow when available. END.

Jayne swore out loud.

"What is it?" Joe asked.

"Take a look." She passed the phone over to him.

"Holy shit. They never let up."

"No. They don't. Looks like more is coming my way fast. I need another drink."

Jayne downed the remains of her whiskey in one gulp and held out her glass to Joe for a refill.

* * *

THE NEXT BOOK:
Book 2 in the **Jayne Robinson** series

The Dark Shah

If you enjoyed **The Kremlin's Vote**, you'll probably like the next thriller I am writing—book 2 in this new **Jayne Robinson** series, entitled **The Dark Shah**. It is scheduled to be published later in 2021, depending on progress, and is available to pre-order in Kindle format on Amazon. Unfortunately Amazon does not allow pre-orders for paperbacks. If you make a pre-order the book will be automatically delivered to your reading device as soon as it is published. You will only be charged on delivery.

To pre-order just go to the Amazon website and type "Andrew Turpin The Dark Shah" in the search box. You'll see it.

I should mention here that if you like **paperbacks**, you can buy copies of all of my books at my own website shop. I can deliver to anywhere in the US and UK, although not currently other countries. That may change in future. You will find generous discounts if you are buying multiple books or series bundles, which makes them significantly cheaper than using Amazon. Buying this way also means I do not have to give Amazon their usual large portion of the sale price. Go to:

https://www.andrewturpin.com/shop/

To give you a flavor of *The Dark Shah*, here's the blurb:

A deadly provocation of the US . . . A drone attack on the Secretary of State near Tel Aviv. An Iranian nuclear chief, gunned down in Vienna. And a hitman with intelligence officer Jayne Robinson in his crosshairs.

Former Secret Intelligence Service spy Robinson is sent by the CIA to find out who left the Secretary of State fighting for his life in Israel and why.

She quickly discovers that the Israeli intelligence service, the Mossad, has the same agenda. But can she trust them?

Jayne finds she needs all her skills and know-how if she is to avoid the same fate as her much-loved father, who was blown up more than twenty years earlier in a mystery attack by pro-Iranian Hezbollah terrorists in London.

But who carried out that bombing—and who is on Jayne's tail now?

The Dark Shah, book number two in the new **Jayne Robinson series**, is a gripping modern spy thriller with unexpected twists that will be difficult to put down.

* * *

ANDREW'S READERS GROUP

If you enjoyed this book, I would like to keep in touch. This is not always easy, as I usually only publish a couple of books a year and there are many authors and books out there. So the best way is for you to be on my Readers Group email list. I can then send you updates on the next book, plus occasional special offers. There's no spam and you can unsubscribe at any time.

If you would like to join my Readers Group and receive the email updates, I will send you, **FREE**, the ebook version of another thriller, *The Afghan*, which forms a prequel to both the **Jayne Robinson** series and my **Joe Johnson** series and normally sells at $4.99/£3.99 (paperback $11.99/£9.99).

The Afghan is set in 1988 when Jayne was with Britain's Secret Intelligence Service and Joe Johnson was with the CIA —both of them based in Pakistan and Afghanistan. Most of the action takes place in Afghanistan, then occupied by the Soviet Union, and in Washington, DC. Some of the characters and story lines that emerge in my other books have their roots in this period. I think you will enjoy it!

The Afghan can be downloaded **FREE** from the following link:

https://bookhip.com/RJGFPAW

If you only like reading paperbacks you can still sign up for the email list at that link to get news of my books and forthcoming releases. Just ignore the email that arrives with the ebook attached. A paperback version of **The Afghan** and all my books is for sale at my website, where you will find large discounts on bundles of my books. I can currently ship to the US and UK:

https://www.andrewturpin.com/shop/

If you liked this Jayne Robinson book, you will probably also enjoy the Joe Johnson series, if you haven't read them yet. In order, they are as follows:

Prequel: *The Afghan*
1. ***The Last Nazi***
2. ***The Old Bridge***
3. ***Bandit Country***
4. ***Stalin's Final Sting***
5. ***The Nazi's Son***
6. ***The Black Sea***

To find all the books on my author page on Amazon just type "Andrew Turpin" in the search box at the top of the Amazon page — you can't miss the books!

* * *

IF YOU ENJOYED THIS BOOK PLEASE WRITE A REVIEW

As an independently published author, through my own imprint The Write Direction Publishing, I find that honest reviews of my books are the most powerful way for me to bring them to the attention of other potential readers.

As you'll appreciate, unlike the big international publishers, I can't take out full-page advertisements in the newspapers.

So I am committed to producing books of the best quality I can in order to attract a loyal group of readers who are happy to recommend my work to others.

Therefore, if you enjoyed reading this novel, then I would very much appreciate it if you would spend five minutes and leave a review—which can be as short as you like—preferably on the page or website where you bought it.

You can find the book on the Amazon website by going to the Amazon website and typing "Andrew Turpin The Kremlin's Vote" in the search box.

Once you have clicked on the page, scroll down to "Customer Reviews," then click on "Leave a Review."

Reviews are also a great encouragement to me to write more!

Many thanks.

THANKS AND ACKNOWLEDGEMENTS

Thank you to everyone who reads my books. You are the reason I began to write in the first place, and I hope I can provide you with entertainment and interest for a long time into the future.

Every time I get an encouraging email from a reader, or a positive comment on my Facebook page, or a nice review on Amazon, it spurs me on to press ahead with my research and writing for the next book. So keep them coming!

Specifically with regard to *The Kremlin's Vote*, there are several people who have helped me during the long process of research, writing, and editing.

I have two editors who consistently provide helpful advice, food for thought, great ideas, and constructive criticism, and between them have enabled me to considerably improve the initial draft. Katrina Diaz Arnold, owner of Refine Editing, again gave me a lot of valuable feedback at the structural and line levels, and Jon Ford, as ever, helped me to maintain the authenticity of the story in many areas through his great eye for detail. I would like to thank both of them—the responsibility for any remaining mistakes lies solely with me.

As always, my brother, Adrian Turpin, was a very helpful reader of my early drafts and highlighted areas where I need to improve. I also had very valuable input from Martin Scales, Richard Miller, and fellow author Valeriya Salt. The small but dedicated team in my Advance Readers Group went through the final version prior to proofreading and also highlighted a number of issues that required changes and improvements—a big thank-you to them all.

I would also like to thank the team at Damonza for what I think is a great cover design.

AUTHOR'S NOTE

As is always the case, I need to stress that this book is a work of fiction—it is designed purely for the reader's entertainment. The backdrop, as in most of my books, does include real-world events and themes, but the characters and the plot are all either from my imagination or used in a fictional sense. You should not read anything more into them.

However, I do take a keen interest in current affairs and news, and so my ideas are often drawn from what I read and hear in newspapers and on television and radio. I like to make my books relevant.

In the case of *The Kremlin's Vote*, the inspiration came from a long-running saga of attempted and actual interference in democratic elections and referendums by certain countries. These include the likes of Russia, China, and Iran, who are trying to shape the global political playing field to their own advantage and have targeted countries including the United States, the United Kingdom, and others within the European Union.

The focus of this interference has been partly on hacking of computer systems and disinformation and the use of social media to tilt voters' opinions in one direction or another. Many examples of this type of strategy and tactics were detailed in the March 2019 Mueller Report into Russian interference in the 2016 US presidential election, which made fascinating reading. Links to this report and others can be found in the following Research and Bibliography section.

However, there is another deeper issue which in some ways is more concerning, and that revolves around the right to vote, a cornerstone of all democracies.

I have a certain admiration for those who, over the centuries, have fought for the right to put their cross on the ballot paper in presidential, parliamentary, congressional, state, local council, and indeed any other form of election.

In some cases, the battle for such voting rights has resulted in campaigners giving their lives for the cause.

And it is only in relatively recent history that universal suffrage—the right to vote for all men and women—has been established. In the United States this was not fully implemented for all until the Civil Rights Act of 1964 and the Voting Rights Act of 1965. In the United Kingdom, the Equal Franchise Act was passed in 1928, granting women the right to vote on the same basis as men.

In Australia universal suffrage was only fully implemented in 1967, in Switzerland it was 1971, and in South Africa 1994. In Saudi Arabia, women were only given the right to vote in 2015 (although that has very limited significance given that Saudi Arabia is in practice a monarchy and there have been only seven elections in more than eighty years).

With all this in mind, it set me thinking when I saw that in the United States, despite universal suffrage, voter turnout remains low—54 percent in the 2012 presidential election and 59 percent in 2016, for example. In the United Kingdom, turnout in 2010 was only a little higher at 65 percent and in 2015 66 percent.

Why was that?

There have been many theories and many studies carried out into this phenomenon, and it is clear that the biggest issues have been ease of access to voting stations and systems and ease of registration to vote.

But it was a series of reports by the New York-based Brennan Center for Justice https://www.brennancenter.org/ which campaigns for voter rights, that caught my eye and went some way toward explaining what was happening in the US at least.

I have gone into more detail about the reports and information I used in the following Research and Bibliography section, so please check that out if you would like some inspiration for further reading.

Finally, on a lighter note, I should mention that the one thing that keeps me going through all the long months of research, writing, and editing before I can publish each book is coffee. I do enjoy a good latte—it is essential brain fuel!

So when I was invited to join **Buy Me A Coffee**—a website you might have heard of that allows supporters to give the providers of their favorite goods and services a cup or two—I thought it sounded like a good idea.

Therefore, if you enjoy my books and would like to buy me a latte, I would be extremely grateful. You will definitely be playing an essential part in the production of the next book!

You will find my online coffee shop at:

https://www.buymeacoffee.com/andrewturpin

Many thanks.
Andrew

RESEARCH AND BIBLIOGRAPHY

As has been the case with all of my books, I have done a large amount of research while compiling *The Kremlin's Vote*— spanning numerous books, articles, reports, and websites. I thought it might be useful for those of you who are interested in delving further into the topics I've touched on to include a few references and links as a starting point.

There are far too many to include all of them, so what follows is necessarily a short selection.

In the author's note, I mentioned that the Brennan Center for Justice, based in New York City, provided some inspiration, particularly through their reports into voting rights. The organization campaigns to improve democracy and highlights improvements in policy and the legal framework that are required to achieve this.

Their 2018 report, entitled **Purges: A Growing Threat to the Right to Vote**, found that from 2014 to 2016, US states removed almost 16 million voters from the rolls. That meant that almost four million more names were purged from 2014 to 2016 than from 2006 to 2008, an increase in numbers of voters removed of 33 percent, far outstripping growth in total voters registered of 18 per cent and population growth of 6 percent.

To read the report, go to: https://www.brennancenter.org/our-work/research-reports/purges-growing-threat-right-vote

A previous report in 2008 had equally disturbing conclusions: https://www.brennancenter.org/our-work/research-reports/voter-purges

The Economist carried a good article about the Brennan Center's 2018 report in its issue on August 11, 2018, which you can find at: https://www.economist.com/united-states/2018/08/09/many-states-are-purging-voters-from-the-rolls

The reasons for this large increase in purges lay chiefly in the processes by which election officials—usually the secretaries of state—removed supposedly ineligible names from voter registration lists. Clearly, it is a good thing for voter rolls to be kept up to date, which does require removal of ineligible names. But the Brennan Center found that too many of the purges were done incorrectly—and some of them illegally, for example in Florida, New York, North Carolina and Virginia.

The overall effect of the purges has been the disenfranchisement of many legitimate voters, often too close to the election for the errors to be rectified.

This, combined with the theme of Russian interference on both sides of the Atlantic, gave me the germ of an idea for the plot for this first thriller in my new Jayne Robinson series. She has a long history of confrontations with Russia, and I thought this would be an ideal start.

The Mueller report into Russian interference in the 2016 US presidential election, published in March 2019, can be found here: https://www.justice.gov/storage/report.pdf

There is also a very informative report published by the Senate foreign relations committee in January 2018 which is worth reading and covers Russian influence in both the US and Europe. It can be found here: https://www.foreign.senate.gov/imo/media/doc/FinalRR.pdf

In the UK, a Parliamentary Intelligence and Security Committee report into Russian interference was published in July 2020. It covered, among other topics, attempts to manipulate the outcome of the 2016 referendum on the UK's membership of the European Union, which as we all know, resulted in a "leave" vote. The report can be found here: https://docs.google.com/a/independent.gov.uk/viewer?a=v&pid=sites&

srcid=aW5kZXBlbmRlbnQuZ292LnVrfGlzY3xneDo1Y2Rh
MGEyN2Y3NjMoOWFl

I know many readers like to check out the places I have featured in my books and for the most part, I try to make use of real locations—buildings, streets, and businesses.

Pevensey Castle, which is about four miles east of Eastbourne on the Sussex coast in the UK, does exist—as it has done since the third century AD—and is open to visitors. Check out: https://www.english-heritage.org.uk/visit/places/pevensey-castle/

Several years ago, I had a lot of enjoyment playing cricket at the ground behind the castle which also features in the book.

The Royal Oak and Castle pub is an ideal location for refreshments after visiting Pevensey Castle and the last time I was there, they sold a fine pint of Harvey's Sussex Bitter. I apologize to the landlord for locating such a gruesome shooting outside his pub. See: http://royaloakandcastle.co.uk/

From the pub, the Old Mint House, a Grade II listed building, is clearly visible across the street. To best of my knowledge, this is no longer an antiques shop, although it appears to have been in the past.

See: https://www.eastbourneherald.co.uk/news/house-gruesome-past-goes-under-hammer-1039575

And: https://historicengland.org.uk/listing/the-list/list-entry/1284471

In Moscow, Lefortovo Prison is one of the most notorious institutions of its kind and has a well-deserved reputation for violence and torture. During Josef Stalin's Great Terror, many political prisoners who were taken there never came out again. There is a good background article in Time magazine at: https://time.com/5493599/paul-whelan-russia-lefortovo-prison/

The Konstantinovsky Palace at Strelna, west of St. Petersburg, is indeed an official residence of the Russian president Vladimir Putin and is open to visitors. It is a magnificent complex and well worth arranging a trip. See: https://www. konstantinpalace.ru/

The palace was reconstructed and restored between 2000 and 2003 at huge cost following the president's decision to make it his official residence. A fascinating report into this reconstruction project can be found at: https://www. geocasehistoriesjournal.org/pub/article/view/IJGCH_1_3_4

Moscow takes great pride in its metro stations, many of which are architectural gems. Voykovskaya station, on the Zamoskvoretskaya Line, which features in The Kremlin's Vote, is probably not the best example of its type, but its location suited my plot. If you want to find out more about the metro service, go to: https://en.wikipedia.org/wiki/ Moscow_Metro, where you will find many excellent photos of various stations.

To the best of my knowledge, there has never been an assassination outside the Carter Center, in Atlanta, Georgia, and certainly never one involving the secretary of state. I apologize to Jimmy Carter and his staff for locating the demise of Chuck Driscoll at their building, which is without doubt well worth visiting. I know the center does an excellent job in terms of raising awareness of human rights violations globally and in assisting with conflict prevention and resolution. See: https://www.cartercenter.org/

Chokoloskee Island, in the Everglades National Park in Florida, seems to me an ideal place to get away and chill out. Maybe I should take my laptop and write the next book there. As far as I know, no Russian assassin has ever targeted a Florida secretary of state there, so you should be safe, although be careful of the alligators. For more information, try: https://www.florida-everglades.com/chokol/home.htm

I have set a couple of the scenes in this book inside the

Situation Room in the White House. For those who are interested in what the Situation Room is like, I would recommend the following video on YouTube, produced in 2009 when Obama was still president: https://www.youtube.com/watch?v=T7ch13ZuMu8

If you would like to read more about the evolution of Russia following the breakup of the Soviet Union in 1991, there is a wide choice of books available. However, I would recommend an excellent account by one of the *Financial Times'* journalists, Arkady Ostrovsky, titled The Invention of Russia.

Ostrovsky describes how Russia, which appeared to revel in its newfound freedom in the first years after the breakup, ended up in a kind of autocracy once again at the hands of Vladimir Putin and his *siloviki*. The book includes some detail on how Putin sought to influence the 2016 US presidential election. It can be found in most bookshops.

For a further account of how Russia sought to try and influence the 2016 US election, I would recommend an article by a former CIA officer, John Sipher, in *The Atlantic*. It can be found here: https://www.theatlantic.com/ideas/archive/2018/08/convergence-is-worse-than-collusion/567368/

The above gives you at least a flavor of some of the sources and locations I have used in this book. I hope it is helpful—I am quite willing to exchange emails if readers have questions about any others not mentioned here.

ABOUT THE AUTHOR AND CONTACT DETAILS

I have always had a love of writing and a passion for reading good thrillers. But despite having a long-standing dream of writing my own novels, it took me more than five decades to finally get around to completing the first.

The Kremlin's Vote is the first in the **Jayne Robinson** series of thrillers and follows on from my **Joe Johnson** series (currently comprising six books plus a prequel), which pulls together some of my other interests, particularly history, world news, and travel.

I studied history at Loughborough University and worked for many years as a business and financial journalist before becoming a corporate and financial communications adviser with several large energy companies, specializing in media relations. I am now a full-time writer.

Originally I came from Grantham, Lincolnshire, and I now live with my family in St. Albans, Hertfordshire, UK.

You can connect with me via these routes:

E-mail: andrew@andrewturpin.com

Website: www.andrewturpin.com.

Facebook: @AndrewTurpinAuthor

Facebook Readers Group: https://www.facebook.com/groups/1202837536552219

Twitter: @AndrewTurpin

Instagram: @andrewturpin.author

Please also follow me on Bookbub and Amazon!

https://www.bookbub.com/authors/andrew-turpin

https://www.amazon.com/Andrew-Turpin/e/B074V87WWL/

Do get in touch with your comments and views on the books, or anything else for that matter. I enjoy hearing from readers and promise to reply.

Made in the USA
Coppell, TX
08 September 2021

61987442R10267